# DESPERATE MEASURES

## VOLUME 2

# DESPERATE MEASURES

## VOLUME 2

### SAMUEL VOYLES

Emmons House Publishing
Since 1981

ISBN: 979-8-9856321-4-9

Published in the United States of America.

Emmons House Publishing LLC

Corydon, Indiana 47112

emmonshousepublishing@gmail.com

Cover designed by Pixelstudio

To my mother

for having to deal with me throughout

the entire writing process.

# PART 1

# CHAPTER 1
## JE SUIS DE TOUT CŒUR AVEC VOUS

Julianna Burke had lived in Suite 160 at the Maple Valley Apartments for the past three years. During her time living in the apartment building, she always managed to keep to herself. Sometimes she would exchange pleasantries with other occupants, waving to them or just smiling in acknowledgment.

However, on this particular February day, she noticed something peculiar about the room next door to hers. Julie, as her friends called her, had heard strange noises that she hadn't before. Her curiosity had always gotten her in trouble, so she had tried to be cautious about exploring these sounds. But eventually, she couldn't stand these annoyances anymore.

Julie opened the door to her apartment and gazed down the hallway toward Suite 162. The door opened, and a man stepped out. He had brown hair and appeared to be in his mid-twenties.

"Excuse me," Julie said, stepping out of her apartment. "Would you, by chance, be more mindful of the racket next door? It's really becoming a nuisance."

The man looked her way, locking eyes with hers.

"Yeah?" he responded. "And why don't you just mind your own business."

He closed the door behind him and walked past Julie down the hallway. His response stunned her, but before she could come up with some comeback, he had already made it to the elevator, the door closing behind him.

She hmphed and proceeded to approach the door to his apartment. It seemed like it was quiet, but Julie continued to have a bad feeling about it. *There is no way that he was the only one making that racket.* She thought, looking down at the doorknob. *There's got to be someone else in there.*

Julie knocked on the door, but there was no response. "Hello?" she called out. "Is there anyone in there?"

She waited for some reply, yet there was still none. Finally, Julie sighed and turned back toward her apartment, feeling defeated. As she opened the door to her suite, she heard a crashing sound coming from next door. She released the doorknob and rushed back to the entrance of Suite 162. "Hello? Is somebody in there?"

Once again, there was no response, but Julie was determined to get into the apartment. She grabbed ahold of the doorknob and twisted it, opening the unlocked door.

Inside the apartment, Julie saw nothing but an average living room devoid of anyone. She looked around before finding the light switch, flipping it to provide light to the room. "Anyone here?" she called out as she stepped further inside.

As she turned around to head out, she noticed a hallway leading to a room with a closed door. Julie paused to consider whether she should explore what was behind it. Then, with some hesitation, she proceeded down the hallway. With each step, it felt as if it were getting darker.

Finally, she reached the door, stopping for a moment to take a deep breath. She knocked on the door and said, "Hello? Is there anyone in there?"

Julie's stomach felt as if it were filled with butterflies. She hadn't been this anxious over something in a long time, but she knew she needed to check behind the door. Something kept telling her to do so.

Finally, she opened the door and looked into the dark room. She found the light switch and flicked it on, illuminating the room. In the middle of the room sat a young woman tied to a chair. A lamp had been knocked to the ground beside her, answering Julie's question about the noise.

"Oh my God!" Julie cried out as she ran to the woman, pulling the gag from her mouth, allowing her to breathe. The woman looked exhausted as she caught her breath. Then, tears began to pool from her eyes.

Julie looked over the woman's face closely when she realized that sitting tied to the chair was Miranda Klimmings, who had just been reported missing earlier that morning.

"Oh my God!" Julie said again. "You . . . you're Miranda Klimmings! You've been next to me all along!"

Julie continued to pry off the ropes, tethering Miranda to the chair. Miranda couldn't help but turn her attention to the wall to her right, looking over all the images of herself covering it. As she examined it, she finally knew that she would be free.

* * *

*"I know it will be hard, but we must act as if nothing happened. Because if our family's influence is to survive, then we must remain strong."*

Peter's words rang throughout Vicki's head as she stood in front of the floor mirror in her bedroom. She looked back at the reflection, examining the person she saw. She didn't even recognize who she had become and what she had let her husband do three months ago.

Vicki turned to head out of her room, pausing when she stepped through the door to look back into her bedroom. Everything seemed so distant from her like nothing mattered anymore. Finally, she closed the door and proceeded to head over to the stairs, but before she descended down, she stopped as her gaze caught the attention of the door across the landing from her bedroom. It was Gabby's room. Vicki took a deep breath and sighed before heading down the stairs.

She rounded the bottom and made her way into the living room when it caught her eye. The large family portrait hanging behind the bar had since become burdensome for Vicki to look at, and every time she entered the living room, her eyes always stumbled upon it.

The smiling faces displayed across everyone's faces had since become the false display of cheerfulness that had vanished from the family. Delilah, who was in the picture, would soon become separated from the family, as the divorce between herself and Ben would become finalized later that day in court. Of course, Vicki had no plans to attend the hearing. She left Ben, Delilah, and their lawyers to handle the divorce proceedings.

But the most daunting part of the Klimmings family portrait was the image of Gabby. Each time Vicki crossed the picture, she always felt as if Gabby was staring deep into her soul, constantly haunting her and reminding her of the atrocious thing her family had done following her death.

"Mrs. Klimmings?"

Vicki jolted around from the portrait, seeing Denise standing in the archway to the entry hall.

"Is there something I can get you?" Denise asked her.

"No," Vicki said as she tried to flash a fake smile before taking a few steps toward Denise. "I'm fine, Denise. Thank you."

"It's always my pleasure, Mrs. Klimmings. Feel free to call for me if you need anything."

Vicki opened her mouth in anticipation to say something, but she couldn't bring herself to speak as Denise left the living room. So instead, Vicki sat there alone. She turned her attention to the empty fireplace listening for anything in the house but found nothing. No noise. All remained silent, allowing Vicki's thoughts to continue building inside her mind.

\* \* \*

Inside the Oval Office, Peter sat behind the *Resolute* desk mulling over paperwork. He shuffled them around, barely glancing at the latter documents, and proceeded to look up at Henry and Constance, who were standing in front of the desk.

"You sure these are the latest poll numbers?" he asked them as he set the papers off to the side.

"Yes, sir," Henry said. "They were conducted just over the weekend."

"I have a hard time believing that I am polling barely ahead of a potential Republican challenger. Hell, just a few months ago, you had me polling numerous points behind the opposition."

"Yes," Constance added. "However, after the slight de-escalation between the United States and China, Americans are beginning to see that you possibly could be beneficial for any future encounters with the Chinese."

"*Constance*," Peter said. "I more than doubled the amount of American troops at the Basa Air Base in the Philippines. All that did was cause the Chinese to pull back the ships they had congregating in the South China Sea and proceed to slap us with heavy tariffs. I wouldn't necessarily say that things have de-escalated between us."

"Well, Mr. President," Henry said as he sat in a chair in front of the desk. "The American people feel that what you did was right, and honestly, that's all that matters, isn't it?"

"I guess." Peter stood from his chair and turned to the window behind his desk. He looked out on the White House lawn, admiring the beauty of the grounds on a warming day in May.

"What do you mean by that?" Constance asked, taking the seat next to Henry. "Peter, isn't reelection what you're wanting?"

Peter turned back to face Constance and Henry. "What I want is to be remembered. I don't want to just be a president who's been in office for four or eight years. I want to be someone talked about and looked up to, like George Washington, Abraham Lincoln, and FDR."

"You could always be remembered like some of our more recent Republican presidents," Constance quipped before chuckling. Peter turned his attention to her and gave her a look.

"No. I don't want to be remembered like *him*. You know what I'm meaning."

Henry scooted forward a few centimeters in his chair before adding, "Mr. President, I think the vice president is onto something, though. It could be much worse for you. I mean, you've made it over halfway through your first term without any real big scandals to affect you politically." He turned to Constance. "I'd call that a win, eh?"

She smiled back at him. "I agree with Henry. Other than the hostage situation with your daughter last October, you haven't really had anything too troubling, Peter. I would say you've had a pretty smooth presidency so far."

"I guess so," Peter said as he sat back down in his chair. "The hostage situation and Gabby's eighteenth birthday were probably the only things to have really come up, weren't they?"

"That, and some people might add in your son's divorce," Henry added.

"Yes, but that *really* doesn't affect me, does it?"

"Perhaps we could add in Miranda's kidnapping too?"

"Maybe," Peter said. "But like I mentioned earlier, that wasn't necessarily something that affected the public's perception of me, was it?"

"No," Henry said. "If anything, that may have helped you, Mr. President."

The trio collectively laughed amongst themselves before Constance asked, "So, how is Gabby? Shouldn't she be coming home soon?"

"Actually, she's opted to stay at the school for some extra summer sessions," Peter lied. "I don't understand why, though. It's her last summer before college, anyway."

"Where did she go again?" Henry asked.

"St. Mary's in the Alps," Peter said. "It's that prestigious all-girls school."

"Yeah," Henry said, nodding his head. "I know what you're talking about."

"She loves it, though," Peter added before sighing. "I really do believe that choosing to go to this school was one of the best decisions she's made."

Peter turned his attention back to the papers, trying not to think

8

about Gabby and the lie he facilitated to cover up her unexpected death on that February night. Instead, he flipped through the papers, pretending to be looking for something.

"Is everything alright, Peter?" Constance asked, looking concerned.

He looked up from the papers at the vice president. "Yes, everything is fine. I was trying to find something, that's all." He smiled and adjusted the papers, tapping them on the desk to even out the stack.

"Well," Henry said. "If we have nothing else, then we best get going."

"Yes," Constance added, reluctant to take her attention off Peter. "We better get going."

The three exchanged their goodbyes before Peter led them to the door. Once the door latched behind Constance and Henry, Peter turned to face the *Resolute* desk and let out a deep sigh.

"Get it together, Peter," he said to himself as he adjusted his suit jacket. "You knew you'd have to make these tough decisions to stay in power. And right now, all that matters is keeping that."

\* \* \*

"All rise."

Everyone in the courtroom rose from their seats as the judge entered it. As he sat down and told the people to take their seats, he examined all those in the courtroom. To his right sat Delilah Applegate Klimmings and the family attorney, Winston Brown. Robert Green, the well-known member of the Klimmings family's clan of attorneys, was seated to the judge's left. He looked past the two tables before him and into the members viewing the court session. He promptly spotted the entire Applegate family sitting amongst the courtroom members.

The judge grunted and cleared his throat before speaking. "After some deliberation, I've finally reached a decision regarding the dissolution of marriage between the parties of Benjamin Peter Klimmings and Delilah Applegate Klimmings. If no one in the courtroom has any objections, I shall begin."

Delilah glanced at Winston and took a deep gulp before whispering,

"I'm nervous."

"It'll be okay, Delilah," Winston reassured her. "I think you're going to come out of this okay."

Delilah opened her mouth to respond to her lawyer, but the judge proceeded. "There were two major concerns brought to my attention that both parties had difficulty agreeing on, so I shall begin with the matter of division of assets."

The judge flipped through a stack of papers that lay on the bench. "First off, we have the townhouse owned by Mr. and Mrs. Klimmings. After further consideration, I have decided that I will award the home to Mr. Klimmings. Next, we have the title of ownership of a parcel of land purchased by the couple, which I have decided to award to Mrs. Klimmings."

Delilah glanced over to Winston, who slightly shrugged his shoulders, signifying that they didn't get what they wanted but accepted the judge's ruling.

"Then we have the accumulation of assets by both parties throughout the duration of the marriage. Mr. and Mrs. Klimmings have been married for four years now, which means that the two have managed to acquire a diverse set of assets. These range anywhere from stocks, to materials, to money and so on." The judge swallowed, allowing saliva to coat his mouth before finishing speaking. "I hereby declare that Mr. and Mrs. Klimmings will split their assets down the middle, equally sharing one-half of their assets."

"Your honor . . ." Robert Green stood up from his seat at the table next to Delilah and Winston. "May I ask how we will go about separating assets between the two families?"

"The court will appoint an auditor, Mr. Gates," the judge spoke. "And once a full audit has been conducted and assets separated, the court will equally take payment from both parties to compensate the auditor."

Robert retook his seat, and the judge proceeded on. "Finally, we have the issue of custody of the child shared between Mr. and Mrs. Klimmings. After further review and investigation into Mr. Klimmings' current situation . . ." The judge directed his attention to Robert, who remained silent, offering no explanation as to why Ben wasn't present at the divorce hearing. Then, the judge swallowed and continued. "I feel that sole custody should reside with Mrs. Klimmings, with visitation with Mr. Klimmings occurring every other weekend."

Delilah turned to Winston, who was smiling with victory. "We won, Delilah," he whispered to her. "You get Katherine."

"Mrs. Klimmings," the judge said, addressing Delilah. "Please stand."

Delilah rose from her seat. "Yes, your honor?"

"Have you and Mr. Klimmings sought out every attempt possible to resolve your marriage difficulties before deeming it irreparable?"

"Yes, your honor," Delilah responded.

"Thank you. Please be seated." The judge turned to Robert. "Mr. Green, with your client not in attendance today, I must ask you instead. Do you believe that your client and Mrs. Klimmings have sought out every attempt possible to resolve their marriage difficulties before they deemed it irreparable?"

"Yes, your honor," Robert said.

"Fine," the judge said, leaning back in his chair. "I guess I see no reason then to deny the dissolution of marriage. So therefore, I hereby grant the divorce between Mr. Benjamin Peter Klimmings and Mrs. Delilah Applegate Klimmings." He leaned forward. "Am I right in reading that Mrs. Klimmings requested reverting her legal name back to her maiden name?"

"Yes, your honor," Winston said, standing from his seat.

"I'll grant it."

The people of the courtroom stood as the judge exited behind the bench, and Delilah turned around, seeing her parents and Ryan in attendance. She made her way to them and threw her arms around Jeremy, hugging him tightly. Tears had begun flowing from her eyes, and she clung to her dad.

"It'll be okay, Delilah," Jeremy comforted her as he patted her back. "It's over now."

"I just can't believe it," Delilah cried. "My marriage has ended."

Cathie put her arm around her daughter, also trying to console her.

"It's time for a new beginning, Delilah. A fresh start."

As her parents continued to provide comfort to Delilah, Winston approached the family. Ryan, standing alongside them, extended his hand and shook Winston's. "Thank you for representing my sister."

"It's no problem," Winston said. "I've been your family's attorney for many years."

"Well, we appreciate it."

Winston turned toward Delilah, seeing how she was being comforted. "I was going to speak with her about this," he said, turning back to Ryan. "But I plan to reach out to her once the auditor has completed the audit."

"Thank you," Ryan said again. "I can relay that message to her later."

"Thank you. Now, I'm going back to the office and working on a few things."

"Of course."

Winston stepped away, leaving the Applegate family to themselves in the courtroom, each comforting Delilah in their own way.

\* \* \*

It was well after eleven o'clock as Vicki made her way upstairs. She stopped at the landing and took inventory of the bedroom doors. Miranda's was closed, as it had been for most of the three months since her disappearance and kidnapping by her ex-boyfriend, Jason. Vicki approached the door but paused before opening it. She knew Miranda needed the time alone, as she was still processing the traumatic experience. But Vicki wanted to be a comfort for her.

Then, she turned and headed over toward Ben's door. It was slightly ajar, so she gently pushed it open, seeing him lying passed out on his bed. It took no time for Vicki to notice the bottle of whiskey sitting on the bedside table, and sadness once again filled her. Her son had regressed so much the past three months after finally getting a grasp on his problems.

She closed the door and headed over to her bedroom. Before

opening the door, she turned toward Gabby's room. She sighed and entered her bedroom, closing the door tightly behind her.

Vicki sat on the side of the bed and took off her shoes. A late frost was expected, so she could hear the fireplace crackling. Then, she went to the walk-in closet to change into her pajamas. While changing, she heard the bedroom door open and close.

"Vicki?"

She stepped out of the closet, dressed in her nightwear. Peter was setting his briefcase by the door and untying his yellow tie. "What?"

"I was just checking to see if you were in here," Peter replied as he pulled his tie out from under his collar. "How was your day?"

"It was fine," Vicki said. She made her way over to the bed and climbed under the covers. "How was yours?"

"It was better than what I had expected it to be," Peter said as he walked into the closet. "Constance and Mr. Gates visited with polling numbers. I'm polling ahead of any Republican challenger right now. They believe I can win next year."

Vicki sighed and glared at Peter, disappointed with what he said to her. "So you're still running for reelection then?"

"Of course," Peter said as he stepped out of the closet in his pajamas. "We're planning on announcing my candidacy for reelection next week. I'd love it if the family attended."

"You'd love it if the family would attend . . ." Vicki started. "Are you kidding me, Peter?!"

"What? I thought we were all in this together?"

"You thought we were in this together?" Vicki flung the sheets off herself and stepped out of bed. "Are you kidding me? What the hell is wrong with you, Peter?!"

Peter stood in the bedroom aghast. "What the hell are you talking about, Vicki?"

"What am I talking about?" Vicki continued. "Our daughter killed herself, Peter. Benjamin found her dead in her room. Has that not affected you at all?" Tears began running down Vicki's face.

"Of course, it's affected me, Vicki," Peter said. "But we have to move on."

"Move on?!" Vicki shouted. "How *dare* you suggest we move on? You didn't even let it bother you!"

"You think it doesn't bother me?" Peter asked before turning around and pressing against his temples with his right hand. Then, he turned back to face Vicki. "Our little girl was found dead, Vicki! Of course, it bothered me! I was saddened a great deal by it!"

"YOU NEVER LET IT BOTHER YOU!" Vicki shouted at Peter as she cried. "YOU DIDN'T EVEN GIVE IT A CHANCE TO! YOU JUST TOOK HER OUT TO THE CEMETARY AND BURIED HER . . . WITH NO HEADSTONE . . . NO MARKER . . . NOTH-ING!"

"You damn well know why I had to do it!" Peter yelled back at Vicki. "We *had* to protect the family!"

"DID WE?! DID WE?!" Vicki screamed. "LOOK AT YOUR CHILDREN, PETER! BENJAMIN IS BACK TO DRINKING ALL THE TIME, AND MIRANDA WILL NEVER COME OUT OF HER ROOM!"

"*MIRANDA!*" Peter was furious now. "I HAD NOTHING TO DO WITH MIRANDA!"

Vicki wiped the tears from her eyes. "Maybe if you weren't the president, then maybe she wouldn't have been . . ." Vicki stopped her sentence, but it was too late. Peter had already inferred what she was about to say.

"Are you assuming that if I weren't the president, then maybe our daughter wouldn't have been kidnapped?"

Vicki remained silent.

"Somebody better call the damn pope because obviously Saint Vicki hasn't been recognized by the Catholic Church yet!"

"You don't have to be an ass about it, Peter," Vicki said. "I slipped up. I'm sorry."

"Don't lie," he snapped back. "It's all my fault, isn't it? That's what you believe."

"BECAUSE YOU HAD GABRIELLA BURIED IN THE CEM-ETARY OUT BACK!!"

"I ALREADY TOLD YOU THAT I HAD TO DO IT TO

PROTECT OUR FAMILY!!"

"PROTECT *US*?! YOU DID IT TO PROTECT YOUR CAREER!"

"MY CAREER HAS PROVIDED FOR THIS FAMILY! YOU, MIRANDA, BEN, AND GABRIELLA ALL BENEFITTED FROM MY GODDAMN CAREER!!!"

"AND YET GABBY'S DEAD BECAUSE OF IT!"

The room fell silent, allowing the two to stew on the tense exchange they had just had. Then, Peter went to the bedroom door and opened it. He stepped through the threshold and turned back to Vicki. "I'm sleeping downstairs tonight."

She didn't respond, and he slammed the door shut, leaving Vicki alone in the bedroom.

\* \* \*

"Can you believe all the crap that's gone down in this place?" Delilah asked Clark, who was sitting across from her at Finley's restaurant.

Clark laughed before taking a sip of his Scotch. "I try not to think of it . . . and my behavior."

Delilah smiled. "Honestly, I feel like that night set things in motion."

"You think so?"

"Yes," Delilah said. "I literally ran out of the restaurant and left everyone at the table wondering where the hell I went."

Clark chuckled. "You should have seen the looks on their faces when you left. They didn't know what to do." He took a sip of his Scotch. "And all Ben could do was drink."

The smile fell from Delilah's face, and Clark noticed, causing him to feel a little guilty.

"I'm sorry," he apologized. "I shouldn't have said that."

Delilah remained silent for a moment before she finally spoke. "I think if I could change how things happened, I wouldn't have run out."

"Why?"

"Clark," she began. "Ben started drinking heavily after the anniversary dinner. I am the reason why he has a problem."

Clark reached out, taking Delilah's hands in his. "Do you really believe that Ben wouldn't have started drinking if you had chosen to stay in the restaurant?" He locked eyes with hers. "Delilah, he was drinking before the dinner, anyways."

Delilah looked down at the place setting and then back into Clark's eyes. She saw the worry and concern in the way he looked at her. Yet, he did love her and would do anything to make her happy.

She smiled and rubbed her thumb against his hand. "I love you, Clark."

"And I love you too, Delilah."

They leaned across the table and kissed.

\* \* \*

Miranda stood in her bathroom, looking down at the pregnancy test box in her hands. Inside, she felt immense worry and stress but couldn't share this with anyone. A tear formed in each of her eyes as she looked at the box.

She took a deep breath and set the box on the counter, using her hands to wipe the tears.

"Not today," she said to herself. "I can't do this today."

She stepped out of the bathroom and into her bedroom, looking at the baby blue décor throughout the room. Miranda took a few deep breaths and composed herself. Then, she made her way out of her room and to the landing at the top of the stairs.

Across the way was Ben's bedroom door, which stood ajar. Miranda sighed and went over to it, pushing it open and peering in. Ben sat up on the bed. "Delilah?! Iz dah chu?!"

"No, Ben," Miranda said, taking a step in. "It's me, Miranda."

Ben gagged. "Get duh hell away from me."

Miranda opened her mouth to say something but stopped herself. She figured it wouldn't do any good to say anything to Ben while he was drunk, so she decided to step out of his bedroom and head downstairs.

She rounded the corner and stepped into the living room. The house was so quiet. Miranda couldn't even hear where Denise was. She took the remote to the TV and turned it on. It was already on the Channel 8 News, which was airing a special report. Jeff Craig was speaking about President Klimmings, who was about to make a formal announcement regarding his reelection campaign.

Miranda sat on the sofa as the coverage cut to Peter, who was standing at a podium in front of a large naval aircraft carrier lined with a dozen American flags. To his right stood Constance and her husband, James. To Peter's left stood Henry Gates. On the front of the podium was a blue sign that read, "Klimmings" in great big, bold letters, along with an "Upholding the American Dream" positioned below.

Finally, Peter began speaking, "My fellow Americans, over the course of the past two years, we have come together to accomplish so much. In my administration, we have helped boost the American economy by creating jobs and raising wages for so many workers."

The large crowd in front of Peter clapped and cheered. He smiled and then continued, "Along with revitalizing the economy, we have pushed back against China and the corrupt ways of President Wu and his regime."

Once again, the crowd erupted in cheers. Peter turned to Constance, who smiled back at him and nodded. A smile grew on his face, and he turned back to the podium, facing the crowd.

"And with that," he continued. "I am announcing my reelection campaign. There is so much more we need to accomplish, and I would be honored to have your vote!"

Cheers and applause spread throughout the crowd. Peter looked over to Constance, who was clapping along with the people, and then over to Henry, who had a giant smile on his face. Then, he heard the crowd beginning to cheer, "Four more years! Four more years!"

* * *

Peter's announcement played on the TV during the morning news.

"Along with revitalizing the economy, we have pushed back against China and the corrupt ways of President Wu and his regime," Peter said.

17

"Hmmm."

President Wu turned off the TV and tossed the remote onto his desk. He examined the dark red walls, accented with gold trim and golden dragons.

"Regime?" President Wu said to himself. "Well, if it's a regime you want, then it's a regime you'll get."

He stood up from his desk and turned toward the window overlooking Beijing behind him.

"You might think it's over, Peter Klimmings . . . but it's not. You've taken advantage of your position and criticized my country for far too long. But that changes today. If you think you've seen everything we can do, Peter, you've not seen anything yet."

# Chapter 2
## Portrait of a Family

Rebecca White watched closely as the commentators discussed and analyzed Peter Klimmings' reelection announcement when her secretary stepped into her office. She tore her attention away from the TV screen and directed it toward her secretary. "Yes?"

"Speaker White," Rebecca's secretary began. "I have your final speech ready for you to review. Would you like me to print it or email it to you?"

"Print it," Rebecca said. "I absolutely hate reading things from a screen."

"Are you sure? What if some of the environmental people get wind of it?"

Rebecca leaned forward. "Well, then let's just make sure they don't find out about my chronic printing habits."

She leaned back in her chair and ran her hands through her hair, turning her attention back to the TV. The commentators had poll numbers displayed on the screen, and they were discussing potential matchups between Peter and certain members of the Republican Party.

Rebecca's name finally appeared on the screen, representing a matchup between her and the president.

"If the election was held today," one of the commentators said. "President Klimmings would definitely outperform Speaker White in the Electoral College."

Rebecca sighed and turned back to her secretary, who was still in the doorway.

"How did this happen?" she asked her. "A couple of months ago, I was the favorite . . . I was going to win." She turned back to the TV and gestured to it with her right arm. "Now look at this. What the hell happened?"

"Speaker White," her secretary said as she sat across Rebecca's desk. "You're still the favorite to win the Republican nomination."

"But I'm not the favorite to win overall!"

Her secretary sighed. "Yes, but remember this . . . a lot can still happen between now and next November. Don't count yourself out just yet."

* * *

Miranda sat on the sofa in the living room. The TV was turned on, but she remained absent from whatever was playing on it. The only thing that occupied her mind was the continual reminder of the pregnancy test lying upstairs on her bathroom counter. Not only was it constantly filling her mind, but it managed to invade all subsequent thoughts.

"Miss Miranda?"

Miranda broke her gaze and turned toward the archway to the entry hall. Denise was standing in it, with a woman next to her. "Yes, Denise?" Miranda said as she looked the woman over. She felt she recognized her but couldn't figure out who she was.

"Miss Miranda," Denise repeated before continuing. "Julie Burke is here to see you. She said that you know her."

Before she spoke, Miranda realized where she had recognized this woman. "You," she said. "You're . . . you're the one who rescued me."

Julie smiled slightly. "Yes, I am."

20

Denise glanced at Julie and then back to Miranda. "I'll leave you two be."

"Thank you, Denise," Miranda said as she rose from the sofa, extending her arm to offer a seat to Julie. "Why don't you have a seat?"

Julie thanked her and sat on the opposite end of the sofa. Miranda made her way over to the bar. "May I get you something to drink?"

"Just a water, please," Julie quietly said as she looked around the immaculate living room. "This is such a lovely place, Mrs. Klimmings."

"Please," Miranda said as she turned from the bar. "Call me Miranda." She turned back to open a bottle of water. "We're definitely far from using our last names."

Julie remained quiet as she heard the water pour into a glass, cracking the ice it ran over.

"Are you sure you only want water?"

"Yes. It's early in the afternoon. I don't drink this early."

"Sometimes I need a drink to hold me over to the evening, you know?"

Julie chuckled as Miranda bent down and pulled out a bottle of white wine from the wine fridge below the bar. She grabbed the electric bottle opener from the bar and put it on top of the bottle. As she prepared to press the button to pull out the cork, she paused and remembered staring at the pregnancy test in her bathroom. Her mind returned to the test, which sat on the counter. She felt the tears begin to pool in her eyes as she laid her hand on her stomach, feeling a connection between herself and a potential fetus that might be residing in her.

"Miranda?"

She snapped out of it and turned back toward Julie, standing from the sofa. "Is everything alright, Miranda?"

"Yes," she said as she set the bottle on the bar. "Everything is fine."

Julie looked concerned still. "Are you sure?"

"Yes," Miranda said as she put the wine on the bar. "I just decided that I didn't want to have a glass of wine right now." She took the glass of water she had poured for Julie and handed it to her. "Here you go, Julie."

Julie took the glass and slowly sat back down on the sofa. "Are you sure you're okay, Miranda? You got a little quiet over there earlier."

Miranda took her seat on the sofa. "Yes, I am." Miranda looked around the room, taking in a deep breath. "There's just something that's been on my mind."

\* \* \*

Vicki sat alone in her office, staring blankly at the wall across from her desk. Her mind raced back and forth, considering everything she had done. *Was it me? Is it all my fault?*

She looked down toward her desk. Her eyes gazed over the family pictures sitting near the corners. She paused when she ran across Gabby in one of the family photos. Vicki studied the photo looking at the smiling faces of each member of the Klimmings family. She looked at Delilah, standing next to Ben. She reminisced on their marriage and its explosive ending. The toxicity between the two escalated each other's weaknesses: Delilah's infidelity and Ben's drinking habits.

Then, she looked back at Gabby and her smiling face. *How could we have not known? Why didn't we pay more attention to her?*

Vicki recalled her last conversation with Gabby before they found her. She tried to think about what she had said that might have set her off the edge.

*Vicki tapped on Gabby's door. "Gabriella," she said. "I know you're in there."*

*She paused for a moment, waiting to hear a response. There was nothing but silence that came from her bedroom. "Gabriella . . . open up!"*

*Finally, the door cracked open, and Vicki could see a hazel eye peering back at her. "What do you want?"*

*"Let me in," Vicki said to Gabby. "We've got to talk."*

*Gabby opened the door for Vicki to step inside. She made her way back to her bed and plopped onto it. "If you're going to try to talk to me about what Dad asked, then you can go ahead and leave."*

*Vicki sighed as she moved Gabby's desk chair closer to her bed.*

*"Gabriella," she began as she sat down. "You are free to do as you please, honey."*

*Gabby looked up from her pillow. "What?"*

*"You heard me. Your dad isn't going to keep you from being yourself. You understand that, right?"*

*Gabby sat up. "What do you mean?"*

*"I understand he doesn't want you to publicly come out until closer to the election, and I understand his reasons for that. However, he isn't going to inhibit you from finally being open with yourself and those whom you love around you."*

*"Are you telling me to ignore what Dad asked of me?"*

*Vicki sighed again. "Gabriella, I am telling you to do what you feel is best." She stood from the chair and made her way over to the door. She stopped and turned back to Gabby. "Gabriella, this is your life. It is what you make it out to be. You get to make these decisions for yourself."*

*Gabby smiled. "Thank you, Mom."*

*"I love you."*

* * *

Behind the *Resolute* desk, Peter sat scrolling through his tablet. In front of him sat Constance, who looked concerned. "What is it?"

"Those sons of bitches," Peter said as he tossed the device down. "They've implemented tariffs, Constance! Wu strikes again!"

"What?! Constance exclaimed. "I thought we were done with him."

"We're never done with the Chinese!" Peter stood from his seat and walked to the minibar to his right. He took a bottle of Kentucky bourbon and poured himself a glass. Then, he turned back to Constance and asked, "Would you like one?"

"Peter," she said. "It's before noon."

"So," Peter said as he put the cap back on the bottle and set it down on the minibar. He went back to his seat and took a sip. "It's five o'clock somewhere!"

Constance leaned forward, adjusting the back of her jacket. "So, what do you suppose we do?"

Peter took another drink of his bourbon before setting it back down on the desk with a thump. "We're gonna slap tariffs on them too!"

"Okay," Constance said. "And what about the American people? How are you going to explain the increase in prices for the products we import from China?"

"Oh, Constance," Peter sighed. "I'll just explain it in a way where it sounds like it's all for the good of the country."

Constance rolled her eyes. "I don't know how you think of this crap, but it's worked for you so far." She stood up from her seat. "Would you like me to call the commerce secretary and inform her of your intentions?"

"Yes," Peter said as he rose from his seat. "And I need to call the secretary of defense."

"Okay." Constance turned to head out of the Oval Office. She stopped at the door and turned back to Peter. "I'll let you know how my conversation goes with the secretary."

"Thank you, Constance."

The door closed behind Constance before Peter took the phone off the receiver and dialed the number the reach the secretary of defense. He heard the ringing sound on the other line a few times before the secretary picked up.

"Eric," Peter said as he spun his chair around to look outside. "We need to speak."

\* \* \*

"U.S. officials have confirmed that the reports of tariffs imposed by the Chinese government are accurate. These tariffs, which haven't been seen since the trade war between the United States and China during the Trump Administration, target agricultural products the highest, placing a much larger burden on farmers across America. The Klimmings Administration has yet to comment on a plan to deal with the increased tariffs between the two countries, but we expect a press briefing from the White House later today."

Cathie muted the TV and set the remote down. "Jeremy!" she called out. "Get in here!"

A few seconds passed before Jeremy made his way into the living room of the Applegate Homestead. "What?"

"Explain this." Cathie pointed toward the TV, showing Jeremy the headline about the increased tariffs on the country.

Jeremy examined the TV with a puzzled look. "Wh-what the hell? What's this?"

"Do you have anything to do with this?"

Jeremy looked back at Cathie. "What makes you think that I would have anything to do with this?"

"Well, I recall Peter mentioning something at Thanksgiving about how you planned to take down the Klimmings' with President Wu. Then, I've also walked in on you talking to him over the phone. You lied to me and told me you were speaking to someone from the company."

Jeremy sighed. "Okay," he confessed. "I lied to you when I was on the phone with him, but that was whenever China flew those planes by that base in the Philippines, and tensions were high."

"And *you* had something to do with that?!"

"No, Cathie. I didn't. In fact, I had told him to tone it down."

Cathie remained silent.

"I haven't spoken to him since."

Cathie glanced back to the TV before turning back to her husband. "Then maybe you should reach out to him and tell him to calm down."

Jeremy opened his mouth to respond to her but was cut off by Delilah, who had just entered the living room.

"What's going on?" she asked as she looked at the TV.

"The Chinese have implemented tariffs against the United States," Cathie said. "Your dad swears he's had nothing to do with it."

"Because I don't!" Jeremy snapped back. "I promise you that we haven't been in communication for a few months."

"China's always been a thorn in the Klimmings' side," Delilah added. "Peter would always gripe about them anytime the family would be over."

Before anyone else could comment, Delilah's phone began ringing. She made her way over to the coffee table where it lay, picked it up, and examined the screen. "Winston is calling," she said to her parents.

"Well, answer it," Jeremy said. "See what he wants to say."

Delilah accepted the call and put the phone to her ear. "Hello."

"Delilah," Winston said on the other line. "I have got some news for you."

She looked at her parents and stepped out of the room and into the kitchen. "What's going on?"

"Delilah, as the auditor was creating a list of assets shared between you and Ben during your marriage, we came across something interesting."

"And?"

"Were you aware that Ben purchased a significant portion of Klimmings Incorporated stock in January?"

Delilah stood in the kitchen, puzzled. "I wasn't, but what would this have to do with me?"

"Delilah, he made this purchase back in January. You and he were still married at the time . . ."

"Which makes me entitled to half of it . . ." Delilah interrupted.

"Exactly," Winston said. "Delilah, it appears that you are going to be coming out of this marriage with something pretty significant."

"Wait," Delilah said. "How is this going to affect me? The Klimmings family is privatizing Klimmings Incorporated and pulling it from Wall Street. My stocks will be worthless."

"Not entirely," Winston said. "They have to pay every stockholder for their stocks whenever they privatize the company."

"So how much would that be?"

"I don't exactly have a number pinpointed, but Delilah, it's going to be somewhere up in the tens of millions."

"Oh my God," Delilah sighed. "That's going to hurt them."

"But Delilah," Winston added. "It's yours. You deserve it."

Delilah sighed, considering all that had gone on between her and Ben throughout their marriage. "Do me a favor, Winston."

"Sure, what is it?"

"Don't tell my dad about this."

* * *

Inside the President's Bar and Grill were Ryan and Clark. They were sitting in a booth in the back corner of the restaurant. Both had beers in front of them, but the conversation between the two would hardly be pleasant.

"What are your intentions with my sister?" Ryan asked Clark.

"What do you mean?" Clark responded, puzzled, before taking a sip of his beer.

"I think you know exactly what I mean," Ryan said. "It's not every day when a twenty-two-year-old waiter decides to start dating a very wealthy woman, ultimately destroying her marriage in the process."

Clark sat, not knowing what to say.

"Although, I'm not mad about that last part," Ryan continued. "Her marriage to that Klimmings piece of garbage needed to end."

"Ryan, I don't understand where you're coming from here. If you're concerned that I'm with your sister for her money, then you're sadly mistaken."

"Then why the hell else are you with her?"

"Truthfully," Clark said. "I met her a while back during a dark time in her life. It was a time in both our lives when we needed each other . . . and we found one another." He paused for a moment to take a swig of his beer. "After that, we hit it off and started seeing each other."

Ryan sighed. "Look . . . I don't know if you're telling the truth or not, but if you are, be careful."

"What do you mean?"

"Clark, you're in the big leagues with Delilah. Even though she's divorced now, the Klimmings family still holds a lot of money and power. They can take you down anytime they want."

"But they wouldn't, would they?"

Ryan leaned toward Clark. "I don't think Ben will, but his father might. Clark, you hooked up with the daughter-in-law of the president of the United States. Do you honestly not see any repercussions coming from all of that? The man is batshit crazy."

Clark swallowed hard before gulping his beer. "So what do I do then?"

"Lay low," Ryan suggested. "Don't be seen out in public with Delilah too often. It'll cause people to . . . notice." Ryan took another sip of his beer. "But don't neglect seeing her either. If there's something you need to know about my sister, it's that she has a hard time with loyalty."

"What?"

"Clark, do you think that you were the first side boyfriend that that woman has ever had? Yes, you may have been during her marriage to Ben, but when she was in high school, everyone knew that if they wanted to, they could hook up with Delilah." Ryan took another sip. "In fact, rumors went around that she had a neon sign on her bedroom door that said 'Open for Business.'"

Ryan chuckled to himself before sipping his beer again.

"Did she really?" Clark asked in bewilderment.

"Hell no," Ryan exclaimed. "Those were just rumors. But really, though, watch yourself, Clark. If she ain't happy, she'll find someone who'll make her."

\* \* \*

Thunder rumbled, and lightning lit up the Klimmings Mansion as Miranda made her way into the living room, where Vicki sat on the sofa watching the evening news. Like most news channels had throughout the day, Channel 8 News was reporting on the new tariffs implemented by China and providing insights into how they would affect the U.S. economy. Miranda took a seat in the chair to Vicki's left and split her attention between the TV and her mom.

"How was your day?" Miranda asked Vicki, who continued to be glued to the TV.

"Oh," Vicki began without taking her eyes off the news. "It was okay. We've almost finished the company's privatization. It'll be soon when I need to call a family meeting regarding voting shares." She finally turned her attention to Miranda. "I really need your brother to be sober if I am to justify granting him any shares."

"What do you mean by that?"

"You know how your father is and how he feels about Benjamin's involvement in Klimmings Incorporated. In fact, he says it's his fault we have to privatize the company in the first place."

"He isn't wrong, though, is he?"

Vicki sighed. "I guess it's Benjamin's fault, but I'm not going to tell him that. He's been through so much."

Suddenly, Vicki felt herself taken back to that night. First, she stood in the family plot, peering into the open grave. Then, she heard the words coming from Peter's mouth. *"We must act as if nothing happened."*

"Mom?"

Vicki's attention snapped back to Miranda, looking at her puzzled. "Is there something going on between you and Dad?"

Vicki sighed. "It's just been a little stressful lately, that's it."

"Ever since Gabby left for St. Mary's, I've noticed a tension between the two of you. Maybe it's time we go visit her."

Vicki stood from the sofa. "Well, that's not going to happen anytime soon," she said, feeling a lump grow in her throat.

"Where is Dad anyways?" Miranda asked, trying to change the subject away from Gabby. "It's not like him to be out this late."

"Your father told me he was working late tonight," Vicki said. "He may stay the night at the White House. Now, if you'll excuse me, I'm going to go find Denise."

Vicki proceeded to leave the living room, making Miranda the only person in the room. She got up and rounded the archway to head up the stairs. When she reached the landing at the top, she noticed Ben's door was open. Hesitating for a minute, Miranda stepped over and peered inside.

Ben was fast asleep on his bed, lying on the covers.

"Ben, how I wish you would get better," Miranda sighed. "I need you right now."

She spotted the bottle of bourbon sitting next to him on his bedside table, and Miranda snatched it and left his room without thinking twice. She headed across the landing to her door and stepped inside her room, latching the door behind her. A flash of lightning lit up her room before she turned to head into her bathroom. She approached her sink, popped the top off the bourbon, and poured it down the drain.

"There," she said to herself. "This should help."

After the last drop left the neck of the bottle, Miranda set it down on the counter beside the sink. That's when her eyes caught it. The pregnancy test was still there.

Miranda could feel a lump growing in her throat as she glared at the test. She knew it would give her the dreaded answer to her question, but she kept considering whether she wanted to know that answer.

Finally, she snatched the test and took it out of the package.

"There's only one way we're going to find out," she said before turning and closing the door behind her.

* * *

The Beast traveled down a rural road as the rain continued to pour outside. To the front and back of the Beast were the usual police cars that made up the typical presidential motorcade. However, their police lights were off, concealing the motorcade as it traveled down the road.

Inside the Beast sat Peter Klimmings and Eric Bird, the secretary of defense. "Are you sure you got this set up?" Peter asked him.

"Yes, Mr. President," Eric said. "They will be there whenever we arrive."

"They best be," Peter said as he took a sip of the glass of Kentucky bourbon he had in his hand. "I sure as hell am not risking everything for them *not* to be there."

Eric took a deep breath. "Mr. President, are you sure you want to do this?"

Peter considered his question for a moment, and before he could respond to Eric, the partition between the back and the front of the vehicle opened. Don, who was sitting in the passenger seat, said, "We're here, Mr. President."

The Beast came to a halt in front of an abandoned barn. The front doors to it opened, and the driver and Don stepped out. They felt the cold May rain hit their skin. Don took an umbrella from the door pocket and opened the back door so Peter could step out.

"Thank you," Peter said as he took the umbrella out of Don's hand and opened it. He looked around and saw no houses nearby. The only structure around them was the rundown abandoned barn in front of them.

"Are they in there?" Peter said to Eric, who was behind him.

"Yes, sir," he said. "We can go in together."

"Yes," Peter said. He looked at the Secret Service agents around him. "We'll go in alone."

"Sir!" Don exclaimed. "It could be dangerous."

"Don, if anything happens, you'll be right outside, so you can come in quickly."

Don sighed and turned to the rest of the Secret Service agents around them. "They'll go in alone."

"Thank you!" Peter said with a grin. "Eric, come on!"

The two approached the side door of the barn and stepped inside. While the inside remained primarily dry, the occasional water drip fell from the ceiling. A few lanterns illuminated the interior, showing the small group of five young Chinese men sitting in the middle of the barn.

"Hello, President Klimmings," the group's senior member said. He appeared to be in his late twenties or early thirties and had a smile planted on his face.

"Kang Tu!" Peter said as he approached the man without his hand extended for a handshake. "I'm so glad to meet you finally!"

"Same goes for us," Kang said. "The Grand Rebellion has prayed for this day for so long. Finally, we can say that we have the American government on our side!"

"Unfortunately," Eric stepped in. "You can't. Our meeting must remain a secret."

"What do you mean?" asked one of the other rebels.

"Exactly, Shao," Kang said. "Why wouldn't we be able to inform the others in our group that we have your support?"

"Because we aren't officially meeting," Peter said. "Listen, boys. We are offering our support here. All we ask is that our involvement remains a secret. We cannot be found out."

"And how are you planning to offer your support?" Shao asked.

"Well," Peter said. "We will supply you with whatever you need. Guns, ammo, whatever you need to make President Wu's life hell."

"Are you being serious?" Kang asked.

"Yes," Peter said. "President Wu has been a thorn in my ass for way too long, and it's about time that his reign in China come to an end."

"What do you want us to do?" Shao asked him.

Peter glanced over to Eric, who stood there silently. Then, he turned his attention back to Kang, Shao, and the rest of the members of the Grand Rebellion. "I need you to overthrow him, and we will support you by whatever means necessary." Peter stepped forward. "My administration supports you all, but we must remain in the dark."

"So you want to be a silent partner then?"

"Yes," Peter answered. "If I am to be reelected, then we must get rid of Wu by whatever means necessary."

# CHAPTER 3
## MAY THE CUP RUNNETH OVER

Two pink lines. That's all it took to give Miranda Klimmings the answer she anxiously worried about. With dread, she held the pregnancy test in her palms, unable to sort through the plethora of thoughts that conglomerated inside her head. *How can this be? Why is this happening? I don't want this.*

Finally, Miranda was able to set the test on the countertop. She stepped out of the bathroom, still in disbelief. No matter how hard she tried, the horrors of her kidnapping continued to haunt her, reminding her of being trapped by Jason.

She made her way over to her bed and sat down. As she continued to process what she learned, Miranda began to consider how she would tell her family.

* * *

On the thirtieth floor of Klimmings Tower, Vicki sat watching the city come alive. She always found peace watching the city crews make their way up and down streets, clearing any tree leaves, twigs, and other debris after the previous night's storm. While she stood looking out the window, a buzz came across the telephone on her desk. Vicki turned and pressed a button. "Yes, Pam?"

"Mrs. Klimmings," Pam said over the speaker. "Your daughter-in-law is here to see you."

Vicki stood there confused. "Who?"

"I'm sorry," Pam apologized. "I'm not used to it yet, but Delilah Applegate is here to see you."

"*Really?*" Vicki said, intrigued. "Send her in."

Vicki went around to the front of her desk, making her way to the door. Just before reaching it, Pam opened it and directed Delilah inside.

"Hello, Delilah," Vicki said with a faint smile. "What do I owe the pleasure?"

"I need to talk to you about something," Delilah said to Vicki, glancing back at Pam, who was still in the doorway.

Vicki looked over to Pam. "I'll let you know if I need anything."

"Alright," said Pam as she closed the door. Vicki directed Delilah to a seat in front of her desk before heading behind it and sitting in her chair.

"So what is going on?" Vicki asked. "Last time we were in the same room together, you had completely cut ties with my family. I wouldn't see why we would need to speak about anything."

Delilah smiled in acknowledgment. "To be honest, Vicki," Delilah began. "I wouldn't have thought so either. At least, until I received a phone call from my lawyer yesterday."

"Okay? And what did he have to say?"

Delilah grew more uncomfortable as she tried to formulate a way to tell Vicki about her revelation. "Well, you know how our attorneys are conducting an audit over the assets owned by Ben and myself?"

"Yes."

"Well, they found something that I'm entitled to . . . as a result of our divorce."

"And?"

"It seems that before our divorce, Ben purchased a large amount of

Klimmings Incorporated stock. Stocks that he ultimately would use to help pass the resolution to privatize the company."

Vicki fell silent, waiting to hear what Delilah had to say.

"According to my lawyer, I am supposed to be granted fifty percent of the stocks he purchased."

"There's no way," Vicki said. "Benjamin purchased those with his own money."

Delilah cleared her throat. "The money was used from our joint bank account. Vicki, these stocks were acquired through our money."

"But," Vicki said, trying to come up with some excuse to convince Delilah that she wasn't entitled to the stocks but kept falling short. "You're not going to sue us for moving on with the privatization without your approval, are you?"

Delilah sighed. "No," she said. "I'm not suing you all. In fact, to tell you the truth, I don't even want the stocks. However, my attorney said that I'm supposed to get them, and you all were supposed to buy my stocks out during the privatization process."

"Oh my God," Vicki sighed as she planted her face into her palms. "My financial team is going to kill me."

"But I have another proposal," Delilah said. "One that wouldn't get you in trouble with your financial department."

Vicki popped her head up, intrigued by what Delilah had just mentioned. "What would that be?"

"Allow Ben to keep my share of his stocks. I understand that you plan to award voting shares to the majority stockholders, right?"

"Yes," Vicki said. "That would end up being myself, Miranda, Benjamin, Charlotte, and I guess now you."

"*Charlotte?!*" Delilah exclaimed. "When did she ever own stock in the company?"

"Whenever we did that big buyout. She purchased a small amount, so I figured I ought to award her *some* voting shares whenever the privatization becomes finalized in a couple of weeks."

"Oh," Delilah said, shrugging her shoulders. "Anyway, I want you to let Ben keep my shares. In fact, don't even tell him that I own half of his stock right now."

"Why?"

Delilah sighed. "Vicki, if I'm being honest, it just doesn't feel right with all that I've done to him. He deserves to be cut free of me."

Vicki didn't have a response. Instead, she just fell silent and turned her attention to her desk. Finally, after a few seconds of silence filled the room, she said, "Delilah, I don't hold you responsible for what happened between you and Benjamin. The downward spiral that occurred in your marriage wasn't either one of your faults." She looked back at Delilah. "I think that too many outward forces caused tension between you two, and as a result, you did what you did, and Benjamin turned to alcohol."

Delilah let a smile flash across her face. "Thank you, Vicki. That's so kind of you to say."

"I mean it, Delilah. Even with the divorce, I still feel that you and Benjamin are right for each other."

Delilah slightly nodded her head. She didn't know whether to disagree with Vicki or agree with her. Since her divorce, that question had come up in her thoughts a few times. *Were Ben and I really meant for each other?*

"Well," Delilah finally said. "I best get going. I have a lunch date to make later."

Vicki stood from her seat. "Well, thanks for dropping by," she said as she led Delilah to the door. "And thanks for informing me of your discovery."

"Yes," Delilah said as she stopped in the doorway. "And if you don't mind, let's keep this between us two. I haven't told anyone else about it yet, because I don't want it to get out."

Vicki smiled. "I can definitely understand why. Thank you, Delilah."

"Thank you, Vicki."

Vicki smiled as she closed the door, leaving her the only one in her office. She let out a deep sigh as she headed back to her desk and plopped down in her chair. She spun herself around so that she could continue watching the crews cleaning the streets. However, it wasn't long before she swung back around and opened the top drawer on the left-hand side of her desk. Unfortunately, her eyes went right to the un-opened package of cigarettes lying there.

She sighed as she took the pack out of her drawer and examined them. Then, finally, she opened the package and pulled one out, placing it inside her mouth. *Oh, how I've longed for one of these.*

Vicki took a lighter out of another drawer and lit the cigarette in her mouth. She inhaled the sweet taste of the tobacco and breathed out the smoke in a therapeutic way. Then, she placed the package and lighter back into the drawer and closed it before returning to face the window and resume watching the happenings on the below streets.

\* \* \*

"I'm so sorry if I woke you, Mr. Benjamin. I was just checking in to see how you were."

Ben's eyes drifted to the doorway to his bedroom, where he saw Denise standing with her hands on her cheeks.

"I can give you some privacy, sir," she said as she began to close the door.

"Wait," Ben struggled to get out. "Don't leave."

Denise paused, with her head cocked. "Yes, Mr. Benjamin? Is there something you need?"

Ben forced himself to sit up in his bed. His body felt so stiff and ached. "What the hell happened?"

Denise stepped forward. "Sir, you've been indulging yourself in quite a bit of alcohol. In fact, I don't remember seeing you step foot outside of your room in a few days."

"Damn," Ben said as he tried to orient himself in his bedroom. "Have I really been in here for a few days?"

"Yes, sir. I wish I could tell you differently, but . . . I'm sorry, sir . . . I shouldn't be saying all this."

Denise turned to try to leave but was stopped by Ben. "Denise, you're fine. You're just telling me the truth."

Denise held her head down, avoiding making eye contact with Ben, who was trying to get himself out of bed.

"This damn headache," he said to himself. "Gah!" Ben laid his head back on his pillow and stared at the ceiling. "Denise, I do need something."

"Yes?"

"Would you please grab me some painkillers? This headache is quite the beast."

"Sure."

Denise closed the door behind her, leaving Ben alone in his room. He turned his attention to the bedside table and noticed that the bottle of bourbon he had placed there was missing. *Strange. I don't remember drinking that.*

As Ben tried to search through his thoughts, he realized that the worst had begun to happen: he was starting to blackout and lose track of things he'd done. *Oh my God. How have I let myself get to this point?*

\* \* \*

The news coverage had shifted its focus entirely after Rebecca White released her announcement video as a candidate for president of the United States. As Miranda sat, taking in the news and trying to keep her mind away from the result of the pregnancy test taken the previous night, she heard the front door to the house open, and her aunt, Charlotte, stepped into the living room through the archway to the entry hall. She stopped next to the sofa and sighed loudly.

Miranda looked at her curiously and asked, "Did you just come in through the front door?"

Charlotte gave Miranda a look. "Yes," she said. "I just walked in. I don't want to have to deal with your servant. My house workers still haven't been able to get those coffee stains out of my dress from the time she dumped it all over me!"

Miranda sighed. "Aunt Charlotte, I hardly believe that Denise intentionally spilled your coffee on you on purpose."

Charlotte sat down on the sofa next to Miranda. "Miranda," she sighed. "Why must you be so naïve? That woman hates me."

She flipped her hair and adjusted her skirt, trying to get more comfortable on the sofa. Miranda considered how to respond to her aunt but figured it wasn't worth it. Internally, she knew she had much more significant issues than her aunt's outlandish conspiracies regarding the Klimmings family's housework.

However, the silence was too much for Charlotte, as she redirected her attention to Miranda, asking, "Where's your mother?"

Miranda turned back to Charlotte. "Aunt Charlotte, it's the middle of the day. She's in her office at Klimmings Tower."

"Hmmm," Charlotte sighed. "You think she'd be upset if I stopped by?"

"I don't think she would."

Charlotte stood up. "Great! I'm going to head over there then!" She went through the archway and into the entry hall but stopped short of the door and turned back to Miranda. "Text her for me and let her know I'm on my way."

"Will do, Aunt Charlotte."

She smiled at Miranda and then made her way out of the front door. Miranda shook her head slightly and then looked back at the TV, where Rebecca White was being interviewed.

"Jeff," Rebecca said on the TV. "I just feel that America needs a change. For two years, this country has been held hostage by the Klimmings Administration, and if the midterms are any indication of how Americans feel toward the president, then we know that they aren't happy with how he's running things."

Miranda watched in disbelief. "Speaker White," the news anchor said. "What do you feel that the president has been doing that makes Americans feel this way?"

"It's simple, Jeff," Rebecca responded. "President Klimmings is ruining our country. His reckless behavior last year with China and the issue over the Basa Air Base wasn't handled very well at all. In his recent reelection announcement, he managed to further anger China by referring to the Chinese government as a regime!"

"Did he really?"

Miranda turned her gaze to the archway next to the TV and fireplace where Ben was standing. "Yes, he did," she said to her brother.

Ben shook his head, came over to the chair to Miranda's left, and sat down. Silence fell between the two, allowing only Rebecca White's rants on TV to echo throughout the room. Finally, Miranda used the remote to turn off the TV before tossing it onto the sofa. Then, Ben said, "I guess I missed a lot, haven't I?"

Miranda remained quiet, not knowing how to respond to Ben's question. She hadn't considered all the time he had spent drunk or hungover in his bedroom for the past three months. Instead, she had just been focused on herself, dwelling on her own problems and continuously remaining miserable with the memories of her kidnapping and subsequent pregnancy.

Her unplanned pregnancy.

Her unwanted pregnancy.

Her pregnancy that no one else knew about.

The pregnancy that she wanted to remain a secret.

Finally, Miranda spoke up, "You've missed some stuff. You do know that Gabby is in Switzerland, right?"

"*Really?*"

"Yeah, she decided that she wanted to go there and finish out her senior year. Apparently, the drama between her, Dana, and Michelle continued to escalate and stuff."

"Hmmm." Ben contemplated everything Miranda had stated. He felt as if he had forgotten something but couldn't pinpoint exactly what it was. "That's interesting," he said. "The last time I saw Gabby . . ."

*When was the last time I saw Gabby?*

He tried to think about it but kept coming up short. *Why can't I remember this?*

Then it hit him. It confirmed what he had feared. His repetitive drinking habits were taking their toll on his memory, cutting away at events he had experienced and rendering them obsolete.

"I'm going to be honest," Ben said. "I can't remember the last time I saw Gabby."

"You don't?"

"No, I don't" Ben pressed his fingers against his temples. "I have a problem, Miranda."

"No, you don't, Ben. You've just been hit with some difficult times, that's all."

"Miranda," Ben said. "I have a drinking problem. I think it's time that I face that and finally admit that I need to get some help."

* * *

"I'm Rebecca White, and I'm running for president!"

Peter watched in disgust as the news coverage continued to focus on Rebecca White's campaign announcement.

"That bitch is at it again!" Peter declared as he turned to Henry, standing beside him in the West Wing dining room. Henry glanced at Peter and then at the TV hanging above the fireplace.

"Mr. President," he said. "This can be good for us. It's taking the attention away from those absurd Chinese tariffs enacted earlier this week."

"True," Peter said as he sat in one of the dining table chairs. "But we've got some things to take care of before her campaign begins in full swing."

Henry looked at Peter, confused. "What do you mean by that?"

"Mr. Gates, in order to maintain this government, we've had to do some things that some people might find . . . unethical."

Henry nodded his head. "Oh, I understand now. This would be like the U.K. Tax Deal you've negotiated with the British Prime Minister, right?"

"Yes," Peter said. "But that bitch already knows about that. We've got to get rid of some of the things that would bring unnecessary attention to us." Peter paused for a moment and looked back at the TV showing clips from Rebecca White's campaign announcement video. "Mr. Gates, I need you to direct the West Wing to start shredding documents that would paint us in a bad light."

Henry looked at Peter in disbelief. "Are you serious, Mr. President?"

"I am, Mr. Gates. We have to get rid of this crap."

"Do you understand how bad this will make us look if this gets out?"

Peter turned back toward Henry, who was looking very concerned. Then, in as serious of a look as he could display, Peter looked him in the eye and said, "Then don't let it get out."

\* \* \*

"Dammit, Wu!" Jeremy said into his cell phone while he paced in his study in the Applegate Homestead. "Why would you implement these tariffs?"

"It's simple, Jeremy," President Wu responded. "Peter continues to speak out against me and my country."

"What? Is this because he called your government a regime? Wu, he's running for president! What do you expect him to do? Praise your leadership?"

"I expect that he remembers the strength of China. What you saw earlier this year was only a small piece of the might of the Chinese people."

Jeremy stood speechless. "Wu, what the hell are you planning to do?"

"You'll see, Jeremy . . . you'll see."

The phone call ended, leaving Jeremy standing in disbelief. He took the phone away from his ear and looked around the room, considering all the implications that could come from whatever President Wu was planning.

\* \* \*

Charlotte barged into Vicki's office, startling her at her desk. Pam was right behind her, trying to get her to stop.

"Why is it so difficult to see anyone around here?" Charlotte asked as she made her way into the room.

"I'm so sorry, Mrs. Klimmings," Pam said. "I tried to get her to stop, but she wouldn't listen."

Vicki sighed. "Sounds like my sister." She looked at Pam. "Thank you, Pam."

She offered Charlotte a seat while Pam exited the room, closing the door behind her. "Is she like this with everyone?" Charlotte asked as she fluffed her blond hair.

"Well," Vicki said as she sat back down in her chair. "Usually, people let her notify me before they just storm into my office."

"Hmm," Charlotte sighed. "Well, she just needs to take it a little easy next time."

Vicki rolled her eyes and shook her head. Before she responded to what Charlotte had said, she realized that her ashtray containing her cigarette butt was visible on her desk. Nonchalantly, she shifted some papers to hide them and turned her attention back to Charlotte.

"So, Charlotte, what do I owe this visit from you?"

"Well," she started. "I came over to your house, and you weren't there. Miranda said I'd find you here."

"Yeah," Vicki said. "I'm here pretty much every day."

"That's why I wanted to see you," Charlotte continued. "I haven't seen you nearly as much since I moved into my own home. You never call me or anything. What's going on?"

Vicki sat silent, considering how to respond to Charlotte. Internally, Vicki wanted to tell her that she wasn't feeling up to seeing anyone. She hadn't since Gabby's death in February; however, Charlotte knew nothing about that night. If she were to tell her, it would lead to Charlotte's suspicion and create further questioning for her.

"I've just been busy," Vicki sighed. "You know we've been transitioning the company back to being privately owned by the family, right?"

"Yes, I am," Charlotte said. "Which makes me want to remind you that I owned a portion of the stock whenever we voted for the change."

"I remember, Charlotte. In fact, I just had a conversation earlier today about you owning a portion of the stock."

"*Really?* With who?"

"I don't recall," Vicki lied. "We were talking about voting shares and all that crap." Before continuing, Vicki decided it would be best to change the subject. "Why did you come to visit anyways?"

"I told you," Charlotte said. "I wanted to see you. It's been months since we've last spoken. We need to go do something together."

"Well, what do you have in mind?"

"We could go visit Gabby in Switzerland! I know she's probably lonely and could use a visit by family. I also miss her a lot too. She's my favorite niece."

Charlotte smiled as she looked at Vicki for an answer, but she only saw a blank look on her face.

Vicki sighed. "I wish we could," she said. "But St. Mary's doesn't allow visitors."

"Come on!" Charlotte insisted. "You're the freakin' first lady of the United States! They ought to let you spend *some* time with her."

"They won't," Vicki responded, trying to keep the conversation regarding Gabby as minimal as possible.

"Have you tried?" Charlotte asked. "Give them a call right now and talk to them."

"I said they won't let me see her!" Vicki shouted at Charlotte, who slightly leaned back in her chair, astonished at Vicki's sudden frustration toward her. Vicki took a deep breath and recollected herself. "It's been a little rough these past couple of months, Charlotte."

"I can tell," Charlotte said as she fluffed her hair before standing up from her seat. "Well, think about it, then. And let's get lunch sometime."

"Definitely," Vicki replied. "We will."

"I'll see you then," Charlotte said as she opened the door. "Think about it."

Charlotte closed the door behind her, leaving Vicki alone in her office. Immediately, she planted her face into her hands and sobbed.

\* \* \*

Inside a room filled with grey walls and illuminated by fluorescent lights, Ben Klimmings sat in a circle with a group of people. One by one, the members of the group spoke to one another, talking about their weeks and how they managed to resist any temptation they might have encountered.

Finally, it was Ben's turn to speak. Before he said anything, the person leading the group introduced him, "If you haven't noticed yet, we have a new member with us today. Ben, feel free to introduce yourself."

Ben smiled back at the group leader and said, "Thank you." He paused for a moment and took a deep breath. "My name is Ben Klimmings, and I have a drinking problem."

# Chapter 4

## The Shareholders Meeting

Peter listened carefully to what Secretary Eric Bird was saying in the Cabinet Room. He was addressing the entire Cabinet, informing them about the new military drills China was conducting in the South China Sea.

"Mr. President," Eric said as he scanned across the rest of the Cabinet members before stopping at Peter. "The Chinese military has once again been flying close to the Basa Air Base in the Philippines, prompting emergency action at the base."

Eric looked back over the Cabinet members, examining the expression displayed on their faces.

"Secretary Bird," a woman wearing a purple pantsuit said. "How close exactly have they been flying to the Basa Air Base?"

"Right now," Eric continued. "We've recorded flights close to fifty miles away from the base. We've also noticed an increase of Chinese battleships and aircraft carriers in the sea as well."

The woman scratched the back of her head before speaking again. "I'm sure the president shares the same concerns as me, Secretary Bird.

We don't want to repeat the crisis that occurred in the South China Sea earlier this year."

"No, we don't, Janet," Peter said, looking particularly concerned. "But ever since the start of this administration, China has been the one pain in the ass I've been unable to get rid of."

"So, what would you say we do?" Janet asked Peter.

Peter waited a moment before responding to Janet. "Well, it's clear that China didn't receive the message the last time we had an altercation with them . . ." He paused a moment, weighing options in his mind. "Eric, contact the Changi Naval Base in Singapore. Inform them that we will be moving an aircraft carrier to the port." Peter stood from the table, prompting the rest of the Cabinet members to rise as well. "Hopefully, that'll calm President Wu's ass down."

He turned and made his way out of the Cabinet Room, passing Martha's desk and making his way into the Oval Office. Henry followed behind him quickly.

"Mr. President," he called out. "Are you sure deploying an aircraft carrier to the region will help calm tensions with China?"

"Nope," Peter said as he plopped into the chair behind the *Resolute* desk. "But I am certain that it'll send the message to China to cut this shit out."

Henry sat down in a chair in front of the desk. "You think the secretary of state is concerned about this?"

"Of course she is!" Peter exclaimed. "We all should be." He leaned forward toward Henry and lowered his voice to a whisper. "If we don't respond to this properly, it could jeopardize my chances at winning a second term."

"True," Henry said. "We've really got to think this one out."

Peter opened his mouth to respond but was cut off by the door to the Oval Office flinging open and Constance barging in.

"Peter," she called out. "Why the hell are you deploying an aircraft carrier to the South China Sea?! Won't that just escalate tensions more?!"

Peter rose from his seat. "Technically, Singapore is not in the South China Sea . . ."

"Well, it's still going to cross through the sea! What ship are you planning to send anyway?"

"Constance, Constance, Constance . . ." Peter said. "Why don't you take a deep breath and come over to the mansion tonight? We can meet in my office there and go over everything."

Constance looked at Peter, confused. "Why can't we just speak about it here?"

"Because I haven't had everything hammered out yet." Peter sat back down in his chair. "Trust me, Constance. I'll fill you all in tonight."

\* \* \*

The oak doors to the board room at Klimmings Incorporated opened, and Vicki made her way in. Seated at the table were Miranda, Ben, Charlotte, and Robert Green. As the door shut behind her, Vicki took her seat at the head of the conference table.

"Thank you all for joining us today," Vicki began. "I invited our attorney, Robert, here today as we begin to hand out voting shares following the privatization of the company."

"Thank you for having me here, Mrs. Klimmings," Robert said, smiling and then looking at the other members seated at the table.

"Before I hand the floor over to him," Vicki added. "Let me be clear about what these voting shares mean. With the absence of a board, you all will be serving in a sense as its replacement. Once you receive your voting shares, you will have the authority to vote in and out company leadership. The percentage granted to you today serves as a representation of your voice in company decisions." Vicki looked over at everyone at the table. "Does anyone have any questions?"

Miranda shook her head, and Ben looked back at her and Charlotte. Once no one had any questions, Vicki continued, "Alright, then I'll turn the floor over to Robert then."

She turned to Robert, who was opening a binder and beginning to flip through some pages. After he made his way through a couple of pages, he stopped and looked back at the rest of the people at the table.

"I'm going to skip a lot of the formalities to try to keep our meeting quick and simple," he began. "So I'm going to start with handing out the voting shares." He scanned over everyone's faces, looking for any objection, and then continued. "Keep in mind that each of your shares will reflect the portion of stock you owned before the company's privatization. So, with that, I plan to begin with the most significant amount of shares which will go to Vicki Klimmings. She will receive thirty-five percent of the voting shares.

"Following Vicki, each with thirty shares apiece, will be Miranda and Benjamin Klimmings. Then, finally, the last five shares will be handed to Charlotte."

"*Five?!*" Charlotte exclaimed. "Why do I only get *five*?!"

"Charlotte," Vicki began. "You owned the least amount of stock."

"I know that, but . . . I'd have thought I'd have gotten at least ten."

Charlotte held her head down to sulk in her own pity. As she did that, Miranda sat up in her seat and said, "Mom, what about Gabby's shares?"

Vicki froze. *How could I have forgotten about that? Miranda gave Gabriella a significant portion of stock before her death! How am I going to explain this?!*

"Vicki," Robert said, breaking her away from her thoughts. "You didn't mention Gabriella's stocks, nor did I find anything about it."

As she finalized her explanation, Vicki sighed. "Because it was never made official. Miranda gave Gabriella fifteen percent of the stock at Christmas last year, but she never had it notarized before the privatization took effect. In fact, Miranda used her stock to retain me as CEO of the company. She also used it to make herself chair of the board."

"I needed to do that to save the company, though," Miranda piped up. Then, she turned her attention to Robert. "Is this final? Can we grant some of my shares to Gabriella?"

Robert hesitated for a brief second. "Well, it is final. However, if you want to sign over some of your shares to your sister, then you're more than welcome to do that at any moment you'd like. They're your shares."

"Then I want to gift ten of my shares to Gabby."

"Miranda," Vicki sighed. "Are you sure you want to do this?"

"Yes," Miranda said. "Gabby deserves these shares." She ran her hand through her hair. "Now, can we like call her or something?"

"Oh no!" Charlotte exclaimed. "Don't mention that to your mom! I did that last week, and she flipped her lid on me!"

"When did this happen?" Ben asked, reminding everyone that he was still in the room.

"Oh, it was last week," Charlotte began as she leaned into the table. "I came over because I wanted to see your mom, but she wasn't there, so I talked to Miranda some. That's whenever Miranda told me that your mom was here, so I quickly left that house because who knows when that crazy lady you've got working for you would come around and spill another coffee on me again. I got in my car and drove all the way across town . . . hit about every red light too. Then, when I finally arrived at Klimmings Skyscraper – or whatever you all call it – I rode the elevator all the way to the thirtieth floor, got off, and made my way into your mom's office. Her crazy assistant also followed me in, screaming at me to wait until she called your mom, but I wasn't having it. That's when I finally got to speak with your mom, and I suggested going to see your sister in Sweden or wherever she is. And that's . . . when she flipped out."

The conference room fell silent as Charlotte leaned back from the table and fluffed her brown hair. Finally, Ben spoke, "Aunt Charlotte, do you even know where you are right now?"

"Of course!" she said. "I'm in Klimmings Skyscraper!"

Vicki rolled her eyes and turned toward Robert. "This is why I insisted that she only get five voting shares." Then, she turned back to Miranda. "Miranda, if you want to gift ten of your shares to Gabriella, go ahead. However, St. Mary's has a strict no-contact policy, so we cannot talk to your sister until she comes home."

It pained Vicki to lie to her family, but she remained the only person in the room who knew about Gabby's unfortunate death and subsequent cover-up.

"Well," Robert sighed. "One last piece of business is that Mrs. Klimmings now ceases to be the company's chief executive officer, which means that you all now need to conduct your first vote as shareholders and elect someone to serve as president of Klimmings Incorporated."

"Well, that should be easy then," Ben said, holding his hand toward Vicki. "Mom is obviously the only candidate for the job."

"So, do you vote your thirty shares for Mrs. Klimmings then?"

"Yes, I do," Ben said as he leaned back in his chair.

"And I'll vote my twenty shares for my mom as well," Miranda said. "Gabby can decide how she wants to vote her ten whenever she returns."

Robert nodded his head. "Since she isn't present at the meeting, her shares will remain noted as an abstention." Then he turned to Vicki. "Mrs. Klimmings, how do you vote your thirty-five shares?"

"Well," she said. "I do enjoy working for the company, so I vote my shares to instate myself as president of the company."

Robert recorded Vicki's vote and then turned toward Charlotte, who remained particularly quiet throughout the entire voting process. "Mrs. Lee, how about your five shares?"

The rest of the eyes at the table directed their attention to Charlotte as she began to sit up.

"What difference does it make how I vote my shares?" she asked. "Vicki already has eighty-five votes in her favor, so it doesn't matter how I vote; she'll still end up as president."

"True," Robert nodded. "But for the record, do you want to cast a vote?"

Vicki looked at Charlotte, intrigued. Finally, Charlotte said, "Just cast my shares in my sister's favor."

"Alright," Robert said as he recorded Charlotte's vote. "With ninety votes and ten votes to abstain, Mrs. Klimmings, you are officially the president of Klimmings Incorporated."

* * *

She knew she should be getting ready for her dinner date with Clark, but Delilah found herself sitting in the nursery, watching Katherine sleep in her crib. As she watched her daughter sleep, she mulled through the thoughts that kept coming in and out of her head. Most pertained to Clark and what she saw their relationship becoming. However, she found herself allowing images of Ben to make their way into her head. At first, she dismissed them, but after a while, more thoughts started about Ben.

She recalled their first wedding located in the countryside in Virginia. Delilah remembered the day like it had been yesterday.

*"You look gorgeous," Cathie told Delilah as she looked her over in her wedding dress. Delilah's dress contained an elegant rhinestone design that outlined the top of her dress, going down the sides and curling upward. There was no train because her dress mimicked a ballgown dress.*

*"I don't know," Delilah sighed. "I thought the bottom part would be bigger . . ."*

*"Bigger?!" Cathie exclaimed. "Your father, brother, and myself could all fit under that! I think it's big enough!"*

*Delilah smiled back at her mom. "Is it normal for me to feel nervous?"*

*Cathie sat on the sofa by the door, inviting Delilah to sit beside her. "I can remember when your father and I got married," she began after Delilah sat down. "It was a small ceremony with some family and a few friends." Cathie looked over at Delilah. "He had just started Applegate Technology and had accumulated a massive amount of debt, so we couldn't afford a lot."*

*Delilah looked at her mom in disbelief. "You mean to tell me that you and Dad faced money problems at one time?"*

*"Yes, we did. We definitely faced some hardships."*

*"Wow!"*

*"But," Cathie continued. "I kinda liked it that way. We spent so much time together and would just enjoy one another's company."*

*Delilah smiled at her mom and opened her mouth to say something but was interrupted by the door opening and Vicki entering.*

*"Peter is driving me crazy out there!" she exclaimed as she latched*

*the door behind her. Then she looked at Delilah, seated on the sofa, and took in her gorgeous dress. "You look so beautiful."*

*Vicki stepped over and hugged her.*

*"What's Peter doing out there?" Cathie asked as Vicki and Delilah released from their hug.*

*"Oh, you know," Vicki said. "He and Jeremy are looking for anything they can to argue over."*

*"What are they arguing about?" Cathie asked.*

*"When I left, Peter was complaining about the shade of white on the wedding cake frosting," Vicki replied. "Jeremy swears up and down that it is a pearl shade of white, but Peter won't budge away from cotton." Vicki rolled her eyes as she let out a deep sigh.*

*"I'd have thought that Peter announcing his candidacy for president would have stopped the ongoing feud between the two," Delilah said.*

*"One would think . . ." Vicki sighed. "I'm convinced they'll always be at each other's throats . . ." She looked at Cathie. ". . . even if Peter is elected president."*

*"That's what I'm worried about," Cathie said. Then she looked over at Delilah and said, "But let's not think about all that right now. This is your day, Delilah!"*

*"Yes, it is," Vicki said. "Just ignore what your dad and my husband are doing today. They're going to try to make it all about themselves anyway."*

Delilah continued reminiscing about her wedding day. She thought about walking down the aisle to Ben standing at the end. She recalled her vows and remembered the reception afterward when Ryan threw a beer at Peter and ended up being ejected from the event.

Finally, Delilah took out her cell phone and chose Clark's name in her contacts. She put the phone to her ear and waited for him to answer.

"Hey, baby! I can't wait for our date tonight."

"About that," Delilah began. "I'm not feeling the greatest tonight. I think I may have picked something up."

"Oh no!" Clark responded. "Do you need me to get you

something?"

"No, no. I just think I need some rest. That's it."

"Well, try to start feeling better, honey."

"I will, Clark. Thanks for understanding."

She ended the call and set the phone on the table beside her. Then, she resumed watching Katherine sleep in her crib, thinking about what could have been.

* * *

Denise opened the door to see Constance standing outside. "Hello, Madam Vice President."

"Thank you," Constance said as she stepped inside. "Where is Peter?"

"He hasn't come home yet," Denise said to her. "Would you like something to eat? Drink?"

"Yes," Constance said. "I'd love a cup of coffee."

"I'll get it for you, ma'am. If you want, you can wait for him in the living room or in the sitting room."

"Thank you. I'll be in the living room."

Constance turned through the left archway and took a seat on the sofa in the living room. She took in the scenery of the room when Miranda stepped in through the archway on the other side of the room.

"Oh," Miranda said, startled. "I'm sorry. No one had told me that you'd be over."

"Your father invited me over. I'm waiting on him to get here," Constance said before offering Miranda a seat beside her on the sofa. "Come sit, Miranda."

Miranda made her way across the room and sat down next to Constance. "I haven't heard much about you lately," Constance said to her. "How have you been?"

"Since the kidnapping?"

"Well, I mean . . . in general. How are things?"

"They've been fine," Miranda said softly.

"That doesn't sound very convincing," Constance admitted,

sensing that something was one Miranda's mind. "Seriously, Miranda. You can talk to me."

Miranda looked Constance in the eyes, considering whether to tell her about her secret. She hadn't told anyone about it, and the idea of dealing with her pregnancy alone was killing her.

"There is something I've been keeping to myself," Miranda whispered, looking around for anyone. "I haven't told anyone about this yet, so you can't tell Dad."

"I promise, Miranda. What is it?"

Once again, Miranda looked around to make sure they were alone. "Constance, I'm pregnant."

Constance's eyes widened. "Oh," she responded, pausing before continuing. "Is it his?"

"Yes . . ."

"Oh, Miranda," Constance sighed. "I'm so sorry." She leaned in to give her a hug. "What are you going to do?"

Miranda sighed. "I've been weighing all of my options."

"Abortion?"

"Yes," Miranda admitted. "I've looked into it, and it's legal here in Maryland."

"You know I've had three abortions myself, right?"

"What?" Miranda said, stunned. "I had no idea!"

"I don't normally share that out," Constance said. "But the first was when I was seventeen, the second was when I was twenty-four, and the third time was when I was running for the House seat in 2018."

"If you don't mind me asking," Miranda responded. "Why?"

"Well, I wasn't ready at seventeen and twenty-four. I was really wanting to focus on my career at that time, and a baby would've just complicated everything. It was sort of the same in 2018, but James and I had already decided that we didn't want children. So that's what led me to have the abortion then."

Miranda remained silent in self-reflection. *Is this really something I want to do? Do I want this baby or not?*

To add some additional comfort to Miranda, Constance said, "Sometimes you have to take desperate measures when it comes to situations that'll change your life forever." She leaned forward and took hold of her hand, looking her directly in the eyes. "Do what you feel is best for you."

Before Miranda could respond, the front door opened, and Peter stepped into the entry hall of the Klimmings Mansion. He turned the corner through the archway into the living room. "Well, I'm sorry if I interrupted something," he said as he took off his jacket. "I was caught up at the White House, and then there was a protest in front of it that the Secret Service had to push back so that I could leave . . . it was a damn nightmare!"

"Well, what kind of nightmare do you think it'll be whenever China learns that you're sending an aircraft carrier over into their seas?" Constance asked.

"What?!" Miranda exclaimed. "Why are we doing that?!"

Peter put out his right hand, trying to diffuse the situation. "It'll be *fine*. We're not sending the carrier to China. We're going to Singapore to reinforce our presence in the area." He turned back to Constance. "Constance, let's go talk in my office."

She rose from the sofa and began to follow Peter out of the living room, but she stopped midway through the archway and turned back to Miranda, who was still seated.

"Miranda," she said. "Remember, I'm here for you."

Miranda smiled back at Constance before she continued to follow Peter down the entry hall, through the family room, and down another small hallway leading to the library. Halfway down the hallway, Peter opened a door on the left and led Constance into his office.

The office looked like a scaled-down version of the Oval Office. The room retained a circular shape with a brown desk planted in front of floor-to-ceiling windows with navy drapes decorating their top and sides. Two cream-colored sofas in front of the desk, with a navy rug beneath them.

Constance looked around the room, taking in its resemblance to Peter's office at the White House. "Am I trippin', or is this just like the Oval?"

"It is," Peter said as he closed the door behind them. "I had always appreciated the look of the Oval Office since before I had ever considered running for president. So when I had this house built, I consulted with the architect to model my office here after the president's."

"Wow," Constance let out as she took a seat on one of the cream-colored sofas.

"It's a shame it doesn't get used much anymore," Peter said, sitting across from the vice president. "When I was the president of Klimmings Incorporated, I operated out of this office most of the time. Working at Klimmings Tower was always a pain in the ass as people would come in and out all the time, never leaving me alone."

The room fell silent for a moment before Peter continued. "It's a shame that I couldn't continue to use this as my office. It'd save me from a lot of the shit I have to go through at the White House."

Constance wasn't having any of it, as she didn't even try to conceal her eye roll. "Peter," she began. "You invited me over here to describe your scheme with China." She crossed her legs after adjusting herself on the sofa. "So what is it? What are we doing?"

"Constance," Peter sighed. "One of the biggest things about being president is that you have to learn to be patient. Patience is key for any plan to be set in motion."

"Peter . . . what the hell does that mean?"

"It means, Constance, that we have a plan to handle China."

She listened closely, waiting for an answer. However, Peter stood from the sofa and proceeded to make his way behind the desk, peering out of the window toward the back patio and pool. He pulled one of the navy drapes back to get a better look at the illuminated back part of the mansion.

"What's the plan?!" Constance asked, frustrated.

Peter turned back to Constance, who was glaring at him, anticipating his response.

"Have you ever heard of the Grand Rebellion?"

Constance looked lost as she ran her hand through her hair. "No."

"They're a rebel group based in China. Their intent is to initiate a rebel movement in the country that would result in Wu's resignation." Peter made his way to the front of the desk and then leaned onto it, partially sitting on the desk. "They aim to be peaceful and swift, Constance. And we plan to distract President Wu so that he doesn't realize what's going on in his own country."

Constance was in disbelief. "You mean to tell me that we are meddling with a foreign government?"

"No, no, no," Peter lied. "We aren't in any type of communication with them at all. U.S. Intelligence was made aware of the group, and myself and Secretary Bird made the decision that we needed to step up our presence in the region so that this rebel group could have a chance."

Peter moved to the sofa across from Constance, leaning closer to her. "Just think, Constance. Could you imagine the fall of the last great communist government? Imagine the publicity and popularity it would attract us! Think about how we would be remembered in American history!"

Constance remained looking at Peter. "But why? Your approval ratings were high enough already. You have been predicted to be reelected next year. Why must we take down the Chinese government at this time?"

Peter remained quiet, thinking about how to respond to Constance without unveiling his plan to aid the Grand Rebellion in their quest to overthrow the Chinese government.

"Is that it then?" Constance asked. "Nothing else?"

Peter sighed. "I guess so."

"Well," Constance said as she stood up. "I'm going to head out then." She made her way over to the door. "I'll see you tomorrow."

"See you tomorrow, Constance," Peter responded. "Let me walk you out."

He followed Constance out of his office and closed the door behind him.

* * *

She stepped out of the car to the roar of protestors. Ahead of her, she saw the signs saying, "Let your baby live!" and "Roe was overturned for a reason!" As Miranda proceeded to step forward, she turned around to Constance, who had just stepped out of the car.

"You alright?" she asked Miranda as she adjusted her jacket. "We can always get back into the car."

Miranda looked around at more of the signs as she took in the chants of the protestors outside the facility.

"Yeah," she said to Constance. "Let's get this over with."

Constance proceeded to lead Miranda to the entrance of the facility. As they moved along, flanked by Secret Service agents, Miranda kept getting drawn to the roars of the people protesting. Finally, she stopped in her tracks as her eyes stopped on an older woman standing amongst the crowd.

Intrigued, she moved closer to the woman, noticing her ragged clothes and gray straggly, long hair. When she reached the woman, Miranda just stopped and looked at her. The woman slowly licked her lips as she raised her head to meet Miranda's eyes. As the two locked eyes with each other, the woman mumbled something, but Miranda couldn't determine what it was.

"Excuse me?" Miranda said. "What was that?"

The old woman motioned for Miranda to lean in closer. As she did, the woman once again licked her lips and cleared her throat before saying, "God will hate you for this."

Miranda flung herself up in her bed. She was breathing heavily and felt sweaty.

"It was just a dream," she whispered to herself as she caught her breath. Then, she grabbed her phone, lying on the right bedside table, and looked at the time. It was only shortly after eleven, so Miranda unlocked her phone, scrolled through her contacts, and chose Constance's name before putting the phone to her ear.

"Constance," Miranda said after she answered. "I can't do it. I can't end this baby's life."

* * *

Peter opened his bedroom door, noticing Vicki lying in bed with the TV on. He stepped inside the room and closed the door behind him.

"Busy day?" Vicki asked from the bed.

Peter took off his shoes and looked up at Vicki. "You wouldn't imagine." He made his way across the room and into the closet. "How did your day go?"

Vicki waited before responding, mulling over potential replies in her mind. However, as soon as Peter stepped back into the bedroom, her entire mood shifted, and the overall feeling in the bedroom became very tense.

"It was fine," Vicki said as she directed her attention back to the TV. The news anchors had begun speaking about the events of the day at Klimmings Incorporated.

"Klimmings Incorporated has released the names of the company's voting shareholders after fully privatizing a few weeks ago. During a closed-door meeting, Vicki Klimmings was granted thirty-five voting shares, the most of any of the rest of the shareholders. Miranda and Ben Klimmings were granted thirty shares each, and Charlotte Lee, the sister of Vicki Klimmings, was granted five shares. In a stunning move, Miranda Klimmings signed over ten of her own shares to her younger sister, Gabby Klimmings, who remains studying abroad."

"What did she do?"

Vicki turned her attention to her right to see Peter standing in the doorway of the closet. His pajama bottoms were on, but he was still fluffing out a shirt.

"Well," Vicki began. "The meeting went a little off the rails today."

"Off the rails?" Peter asked. "Vicki, why would you let Miranda sign over ten of her own shares to Gabby? You know she can't do that!"

Vicki sighed. "Don't you think I know that?! But what was I supposed to do? Was I supposed to tell her right there that her sister is dead, and you decided to secretly bury her out back? Peter, one of our family lawyers was in the room!"

"You could've come up with something," Peter said as he put his shirt on.

"I'm tired of lying about this, Peter. Don't you know the emotional toll this is having on me?"

"Oh my God, Vicki! You act like you're the only one who's been affected by this! It tore me up that we had to do this to our daughter . . . my favorite! It's affected me, and it's affected you." Peter extended his right arm to the side, pointing at the closet's back wall. "And it's damn well affected Ben. So why in the hell would you allow him to have thirty shares?!"

"Because Delilah had requested that I give her shares to Benjamin!"

"What?! *Her* shares?!"

Vicki swallowed hard. "After Benjamin and Delilah's assets were separated, Delilah was awarded half of Benjamin's stake in Klimmings Incorporated. Because we hadn't purchased her stocks from her, Delilah would then be entitled to voting shares in the company."

"Then why the hell didn't you just buy them from her?"

"She visited me in my office and requested that I just give Benjamin her voting shares."

Peter couldn't hide the confusion on his face. "Ben's just going to squander his voting shares away anyways. You've seen how much he's been drinking lately."

"He's enrolled himself in a recovery program, Peter! Of course, you'd know this if you ever came home and had dinner with the family!"

"I am trying to run a county, Vicki! Sometimes I have to work late!"

"You can always leave early."

Peter opened his mouth to snap back at Vicki, but his attention was snatched by the TV when a breaking news graphic flashed across the screen.

"We have some developing news coming out of the South China Sea. Channel 8 News has received reports that the Chinese military has performed some type of blockage on an American aircraft carrier in the region. In addition, we have unconfirmed reports that at least five Chinese naval ships have surrounded the carrier, prompting it to stop in the middle of the sea. Earlier today, the president issued the order for the aircraft carrier to be moved to the Changi Naval Base in Singapore in an attempt to de-escalate the growing tensions between the United States and China. So far, there has been no comment on the matter from the White House."

# CHAPTER 5
## CRISIS IN THE SOUTH CHINA SEA

"And we continue to bring you breaking news coverage of the events occurring in the South China Sea. For those just joining, we received reports that the Chinese Navy has formed a blockade on a United States aircraft carrier on its journey to the Changi Naval Base in Singapore. So far, there has been no comment from the White House or from the U.S. Navy."

Cathie stood up from the sofa in the living room at the Applegate Homestead and made her way down the hall, leaving Ryan in the room to watch the news coverage on his own. She was irritated as she passed the staircase and took a right down another small hallway. Then, she turned to the first door on her right and opened it without knocking. Jeremy sat behind a desk with a laptop open. The room was dimly lit, with most of the light coming from the desk lamp beside Jeremy's laptop. He looked up from behind his reading glasses and set the papers he was mulling through onto the computer.

"What?" he asked in curiosity. Cathie generally didn't barge into his office without at least knocking first, so Jeremy knew that something was up.

"Come look at this," Cathie said quickly. She stepped out of the room and headed back to the living room. Jeremy placed his glasses on the desk and promptly followed her.

Once in the living room, Jeremy immediately knew why Cathie had called him into the living room. He looked at the news coverage in shock.

"They did not," he gasped.

"Oh, they did!" Cathie responded as she sat down on the sofa. "I thought you had spoken to them and got them to leave us alone."

"I couldn't get him to understand, Cathie. He wasn't having anything." Jeremy took a seat in his chair to Vicki's right. "That damn Wu was insistent on me waiting to see what he was going to do."

Cathie remained silent.

"What did he say he was going to do?" Ryan asked.

"He didn't."

\* \* \*

People were scrambling around the West Wing, coming in and out of rooms. Some were holding stacks of papers, and others were just quickly hurrying down the halls. The sounds of phones ringing echoed up and down the corridor.

Inside the Oval Office, Peter was seated in a chair in front of the fireplace, examining paperwork handed to him. He was wearing sweatpants and a t-shirt, which he had quickly thrown on before leaving the Klimmings Mansion. Ahead of him, Constance and Henry were seated on the sofa to his left and Eric and Janet were on the sofa to his right.

"Mr. President," Eric interrupted. "We've been able to confirm that it was the *Biden* that the Chinese have performed the blockade on."

"The USS *Biden*?" Peter asked.

"Yes," Eric continued. "We were able to make contact with the carrier's captain, who informed us that the Chinese haven't made any efforts to make any demands from them. Their ships are just stationed in a way where we can't move."

"Have they considered contacting the Chinese at all?" Constance asked. "Perhaps they're just waiting to see what we'll do."

"I'll tell you what we need to do," Peter said as he took the papers away from his attention. "We *should* be shooting some rockets at those sons of bitches. But *someone* won't let me do that." Peter glared over to Eric, who had already explained to Peter the implications that would come with initiating a conflict with the Chinese.

"Mr. President," Henry spoke up. "Now is not the time to let our emotions and anger drive our decisions. This is a very volatile situation, and the wrong move could trigger something terrible."

"Does it look like I'm concerned about that?" Peter asked. "We've got our sailors stranded in the South China Sea. I just can't sit here and do nothing!"

"Peter," Constance chimed in. "Have you considered calling President Wu?"

"Not yet." Peter turned around to the door behind him. "MARTHA!"

Within a few seconds, the door opened, and Martha stepped into the room. "Yes, Mr. President?"

"I need to speak with President Wu. Get him on the phone for me."

Martha nodded her head and proceeded out of the room, letting the door close behind her. Peter turned over to Janet. "You've been very quiet."

"I'm just taking it all in, Mr. President," she said. "This is a tense situation. We must calculate our moves. The last thing we need right now is another Cuban Missile Crisis."

"I will nuke the hell out of them before they do any stupid shit like that," Peter snipped before heading over to the minibar to the right of the *Resolute* desk. He grabbed the decanter of Scotch and poured himself a glass full as he continued. "The damn Chinese have been a pain in my ass for too damn long. Someone's gotta take care of them. It might as well be me."

Henry leaned close to Constance and whispered, "Do you really think he needs to be speaking with President Wu right now?"

"I was just thinking that," Constance whispered back. "The best we can hope for is that he doesn't answer."

Peter headed back for his seat and took a sip of his Scotch. "What is taking her so long?" He looked over at the door. "MARTHA!"

The five on the sofas listened for a response, but nothing came. "MARTHA!"

Finally, the door opened, and Martha stepped in. "Sir," she said. "We cannot reach President Wu. We aren't getting any response from them."

"Are you kidding me?!" Peter shouted. "That son of a bitch does this shit, and we get nothing back from him!"

"Mr. President," Henry interrupted, hoping to stop another outburst from Peter. "Can I speak with you in the study?"

Peter remained silent before responding, considering what Henry wanted to speak with him about. "Sure."

The two men made their way through the door opposite the minibar. Then, they began making their way down a narrow hall and into the next room on the left. There was a small desk in the room with bookcases lining the walls. Henry took a seat in one of the chairs in front of the desk as Peter sat behind it, setting his Scotch down.

"What did you want to speak about, Mr. Gates?"

"Go home," Henry said. Peter looked shocked as he hadn't expected this to be something Henry would tell him to do. "Go home. Go to bed. It'll all be here tomorrow, Peter."

Peter took a quick sip of his Scotch. "Mr. Gates," he began. "I'm the president of the United States. I cannot just leave in the middle of a crisis and go to my house in Silver Spring. We have an aircraft carrier full of men out there surrounded by the Chinese."

"And they'll still be there in the morning. If the Chinese had wanted to attack them, they already would've."

"But how am I going to look if I just leave to go to bed?"

"You're not the first to sleep as president, Peter. Heck, Reagan took naps daily when he was in office."

"But Reagan was a Republican . . ."

"So what?" Henry exclaimed. "Just go home, get some rest, and deal with this tomorrow, Peter. It'll all be here when you return."

Peter looked at his Scotch and then back at Henry. "I guess you're right, Mr. Gates."

"That's why you hired me, isn't it?"

The two men laughed for a moment before Peter took another quick sip of his Scotch and placed it on the desk. "I guess I'll be getting ready then."

Henry smiled as Peter left him alone in the study. Then, as the door closed, Henry's display of joy fell from his face as he processed all the events that had just played out before him.

"Oh, Peter," Henry sighed. "This isn't good."

* * *

Denise opened the front door to the Klimmings Mansion, revealing Charlotte, who was positioned on the front landing outside in the overcast morning.

"Ugh," Charlotte groaned. "*You . . .*"

Denise inconspicuously rolled her eyes before stepping aside to allow Charlotte inside.

"They in the dining room?" Charlotte asked as she passed Denise.

"Yes, Miss Lee," Denise said. "They've just begun eating their breakfast."

Charlotte stopped in her tracks. "Such a good girl . . . finally calling me by my last name."

"I only refer to our guests by what they'd prefer to go by," Denise said. "I don't get to call them what I'd want."

Charlotte cocked her head to the side and stepped forward. "Really . . . and what would you call me?"

Denise smiled. "I value my job too much to say."

As she opened her mouth to respond to Denise's quick comment, Ben stepped out from the stairwell and into the entry hall.

"Aunt Charlotte?" he said, trying to figure out who was speaking to Denise.

"Benjamin!" Charlotte exclaimed as she approached him to give him a hug. "So good to see you!"

"Thanks," he said as Charlotte released him from her hug. "We're eating breakfast right now. Why don't you join us?"

A smile flashed across Charlotte's face. "That's what your help said, but she held me up by making snarky remarks."

Ben peered around Charlotte at Denise, who stood wide-eyed, demonstrating her dwindling patience with Charlotte.

"C'mon," he said, motioning for Charlotte to follow him into the dining room. They turned through the archway into the dining room, where Vicki and Miranda were seated. As always, Vicki sat at the head of the table, directly in front of the archway. Miranda was sitting on Vicki's right on the opposite end of the table. Charlotte took a seat in the chair directly to the right of Vicki, and Ben made his way to the seat across from Miranda.

"What do we owe this pleasure of having you here?" Vicki asked Charlotte before taking a sip of her morning coffee.

Charlotte seemed surprised by Vicki's directness. "Well," she said. "I came by to see what the hell was going on?"

Vicki looked confused.

"What is your husband doing, Vicki?" Charlotte asked. "My divorce attorney is trapped in Taiwan because they won't allow any flights in or out because of this damn debacle occurring in the ocean over there." Charlotte ran her hand through her hair. "Can't Peter just have them move that boat out of there and make everyone happy?"

"It's not that simple," Ben said before Vicki could respond. "China has been an issue for at least the past decade. Dad is just showing them that we won't back down."

"Well," Charlotte scoffed. "He's really throwing a wrench in my attempt to divorce George."

"How long have you two been trying to divorce, anyway?" Miranda asked.

"Too long."

"Charlotte," Vicki finally chimed in. "What good do you think this is going to do? Peter has been out all night trying to deal with this. I believe he came home around four this morning or so. He's in bed right now, and then he'll be back at the White House for the rest of the day."

"In bed?!"

Charlotte jumped up from her seat and made her way to the archway, aiming to go upstairs to wake Peter. However, before she could leave the dining room, Ben grabbed her arm, stopping her.

"Aunt Charlotte," he said to her. "You can't wake him."

She looked into Ben's eyes. Then, she sighed and went back to her seat.

"I think it's just ridiculous how he's let this blow up so much," Charlotte continued. "He had all that handled. Now, it's all over the news."

"He's been going through a lot," Ben said. "We've all been, Charlotte. Cut the man a break."

"And where the hell is Gabby?" Charlotte questioned, tossing her arms into the air and looking around her. "It's nearly the end of June, and we haven't heard anything from her." Charlotte turned to Miranda. "I swear, I'm about to get on a plane and visit her at St. Ruth's or wherever she is."

Charlotte leaned closer to Miranda, attempting a whisper but was still loud enough that the entire table heard. "What country is she in again? Italy?"

Vicki opened her mouth to respond, but she was cut off by a voice behind her.

"Gabby has chosen to stay the summer at St. Mary's and has spoken with me about traveling across Europe over the next six months."

Peter had entered the dining room and was now making his way to his seat in front of the fireplace.

"Does that answer your question, Charlotte?" he asked as he sat down.

"For now," Charlotte scoffed before reaching for a coffee mug. She looked down and noticed that there was nothing set in front of her at the table. Then, without hesitation, she looked around for Denise. "Where's your servant at?"

The side door behind Charlotte opened, and Denise made her way into the dining room, pushing a cart full of coffee, milk, and orange juice.

"I'm right here, you bitch," Denise said as she stopped the cart.

The different members of the Klimmings family each had their own responses: Miranda covered her mouth with her right hand, Peter tried to contain his silent laughter, Ben's eyes widened in shock, and Vicki planted her face into her palms.

However, Charlotte's reaction was more turbulent than the others. She lurched from her seat to the cart, facing Denise down. "What the hell did you call me?"

"Well, you asked what I wanted to call you . . . I just gave you my answer."

Charlotte gasped. "You no good, piece of trash. No wonder why nobody wants you. The only thing you *can* do is serve people . . ." Charlotte leaned in toward Denise. ". . . because you're worthless."

Charlotte grabbed the pitcher of orange juice and splashed it onto Denise before storming out of the dining room. Vicki and Miranda jumped up to check on Denise as the echo of the front door slamming filled the entry hall and spread into the dining room.

"Oh my God, Denise," Vicki said as she took a napkin to Denise's face. "Are you okay?"

"I'm fine," Denise said, orange juice dripping from her onto the hardwood floor. "Just let me head down to my quarters, and I can change, Mrs. Klimmings."

Vicki continued to pat Denise's face before letting her leave the room. The two Klimmings women stood by the cart, examining the mess of orange juice that was covering the floor.

"Just look at this mess," Vicki said to Miranda. "How dare Charlotte react in such a violent manner!"

"Well, she's *your* sister," Peter chimed in. Vicki whipped her head around to face her husband, glaring at him.

Miranda quickly noticed the tense exchange between her parents and immediately intervened. "Mom, why don't you go sit back down."

"Why?" Vicki asked, breaking her gaze with Peter.

"Because there's something I've been needing to tell you."

Vicki looked at Miranda, concerned, but Miranda motioned for Vicki to sit back down. Finally, she returned to her seat and gave

Miranda her attention.

"What's going on, Miranda?" Ben asked, intrigued.

"Just listen," she said as she sat back down in the chair Charlotte had been in. This wasn't exactly how she had planned to tell everyone, but she figured now was better than any other. "Before you all chime in with questions and comments, please just let me finish speaking."

"Okay," Peter said, completely ignoring what Miranda had just requested from her family. "What is it?"

Miranda took a deep breath and began to tell her family about her pregnancy. She mentioned how she had gone almost three months suppressing the idea that she was carrying Jason's baby, even going as far as to mention her struggle with the concept of terminating her pregnancy. Throughout her entire monologue, the members of the Klimmings family sat in silence, listening and taking in every word that she had to say.

\* \* \*

Constance made her way into the Oval Office after lunch. She had managed to steer clear of the president and the continued chaos within the White House; however, she felt that at some point, she needed to make herself present during this crisis.

"Madam Vice President," Henry said as Constance entered the room. "Come take a seat with us. You'll want to be a part of this conversation."

She looked at the cream sofas and noticed Peter sitting with his back to her. Henry was standing, facing her, where he had stood up to welcome her into the room.

"Please," Peter said, turning to her. "Join us."

Constance made her way over to the sofas and sat next to Peter, crossing her legs as she made herself comfortable.

"Madam Vice President," Henry began. "I was just speaking with the president about how the Japanese prime minister organized a summit for next week, should the U.S. decide to take part in it."

"Do what?" Constance said, confused. "When did all of this

happen?"

"Ma'am," Henry continued. "Things have been happening very quickly. Prime Minister Yamashita has already spoken with President Wu, who has agreed to participate in the summit."

"Where would this be located?"

"London," Peter added before turning to Henry. "I'm going. Please tell Prime Minister Yamashita that I'll be at the summit next week."

"Are you sure?" Constance asked. "Do I need to come with you?"

"No," Peter said as he stood from the sofa and made his way over to the bar to the left of the *Resolute* desk. "I need you here, Constance. I don't trust the Chinese, even if we are in another country. Apparently, they've already infiltrated Iceland's perception of us."

Constance sat confused. "I don't understand. What does Iceland have to do with all this?"

"Oh, you haven't heard," Peter said, turning back to Constance. "Iceland has called on the Arctic Council to suspend all U.S. shipments through the Arctic." Peter returned to making himself a drink. "They've called us reckless and irresponsible, and they hold us completely responsible for the escalation in tensions with the Chinese."

\* \* \*

Delilah led Ben into the nursery, where he laid a sleeping Katherine down in her crib. He ran his hand through her growing, soft dark hair before turning back toward Delilah, who motioned for him to lead the way out of the room. Ben broke the silence as the two made their way down the hall. "It's amazing at how quickly she is growing."

"I know," Delilah said. "It just seems like yesterday when she was born."

"Seems like so much has changed in these past six months," Ben said, stopping in the hall.

"What do you mean?"

Ben turned his attention to Delilah. "Miranda told us yesterday morning that she is pregnant."

"That's wonderful!" Delilah said without considering who fathered

Miranda's baby.

"Well," Ben continued and proceeded to make his way down the hallway with Delilah following. "Her ex is the father. You remember that she was kidnapped, right?"

Delilah remained quiet, trying to think of something to say, but Ben continued on.

"She said that it must've happened sometime before the kidnapping. She even spoke with us about how she had considered having an abortion and keeping it all to herself."

"Damn," Delilah let out. "I'm sure that's rough." They made their way into the living room, where the TV was on. "I don't even know what to say about all of that."

"Me neither," Ben said before looking around. "Where's your family at?"

"Oh, Dad and Ryan stayed late at the office, and I think Mom is somewhere shopping or eating with friends. It's just me here tonight."

"Do you normally just leave the TV on?"

Delilah looked back at Ben. "You've met my father, right?" she asked sarcastically, allowing for a chuckle between the two.

"I can just imagine him sitting here getting all mad at the TV when he sees my father on there."

"I swear he turns it on just to make himself angry."

"Do you remember right after we got married, when my dad was running for president, and he decided to pay for all of those ads attacking him?"

"Oh, yes," Delilah smiled. "He decided to be cheap about it, and they all ended up having that spelling error in them."

Ben laughed. "I don't think you were there, but you should've seen my dad's reaction when he noticed it."

"Dad was furious," Delilah said. "I'm pretty sure I remember Mom making him sleep in a different room until he had cooled down afterward."

The two sighed after they continued to laugh. They probably would have gone on reminiscing longer had the TV not caught Ben's attention.

"The crisis in the South China Sea has continued into its third day," a female news anchor said. "This continues after the Chinese Navy performed a blockade against the U.S. Naval aircraft carrier, the USS *Joseph R. Biden Jr.* While President Klimmings hasn't spoken publicly about the increased tensions between China and the U.S., his press secretary stated that the United States was deploying the USS *Doris Miller* to the region to provide support if tensions continue to rise between the two countries."

"This is just horrible," Delilah let out. She turned to Ben. "Do you think that this will become worse?"

"I can't see it getting any worse," Ben said. "If I know my dad, he's probably got something planned to fix it."

"Earlier today, the Japanese prime minister, Akio Yamashita, announced the formation of a summit between the President Klimmings and President Wu of China set for next week in London. Prime Minister Yamashita expressed optimism for a swift end to the escalation in tensions between the two superpowers," the news anchor continued. "Meanwhile, House Speaker Rebecca White and candidate for the Republican nomination for president introduced the formation of yet another investigative committee focusing on President Klimmings, making it the fourth one to do so."

The news coverage cut to an interview with Rebecca White outside the House Chamber. "I believe it is imperative that we begin looking into the president's conduct," Rebecca said on the TV. "As each day continues in this man's presidency, we learn more and more how dangerous he is. I believe that it should be every American's highest priority to determine just how we can prevent him from leading us even further down the path to a dangerous outcome."

# CHAPTER 6
## THE SUMMIT

Aboard Air Force One, Miranda made her way to a seat next to Julie, who was invested in a book. She sighed after sitting down, which prompted Julie to take her attention away from her book.

"How is he?" Julie asked as she placed a bookmark in her book and set it on the table beside her.

"I don't know," Miranda said as she placed her arms on the armrests beside her. "The door to his office was closed, and the Secret Service agents wouldn't let me in to speak to him."

"His own daughter?" Julie asked. "If anyone would have been able to see him, I would've thought it'd been you."

"Well, one would think."

Miranda peered down the hallway on the plane, and Julie decided to change the subject. "So, how are you feeling? Do you need me to get you anything?"

"I'm fine," Miranda said. "The baby has been fine so far. I just think getting used to being pregnant is going to take longer than I had thought it would."

Julie adjusted herself in her seat. "If you don't mind me asking, what does it feel like? Do you feel any different?"

"Not really," Miranda said. "Just feels like my normal self."

Miranda continued to look down the hall, trying to see if there was any activity near Peter's office.

"Do you want it?"

Miranda turned her attention to Julie, processing the question she was just asked.

"What?"

"Do you want it?" Julie asked again. "It's a pretty simple question."

Trying to decide how to respond to the question, Miranda looked back down the hall, hoping that something would happen to prevent her from answering Julie. Finally, Miranda let out, "Of course I want it. What kind of question is that?"

Julie sighed. "I only asked that because I know who the father is." Miranda's attention continued to be drawn away from Julie, but she continued. "Miranda, have you considered talking to someone or getting some help? Not everyone chooses to carry the baby of their ex who kidnapped them."

"I'm fine, Julie," Miranda quickly added. "I don't need to speak with anyone about anything."

Once again, Julie sighed. "Okay," she said as she picked up her book and continued reading. Miranda continued to look for activity down the hall but failed to see anything going on. Inside Peter's office, another story was going on.

"What do you mean?" Peter said on the phone. "I need you to make sure any evidence that we met with the Grand Rebellion disappears." He waited for a second and then continued. "Do you understand, Eric? No evidence."

"Yes, sir," Eric replied on the phone. "I will make sure to get into the Secret Service logs and wipe clean everything that indicates we've been in contact with them."

"And don't forget to clear the phone records too. I've spoken with Kang Tu a few times, and I don't need that bitch to find out about that."

Eric remained quiet for a moment as he made a note of what he needed to do. Then, he added, "She's really serious about taking you down, isn't she?"

"Of course she is!" Peter exclaimed. "She's always been!" He turned to look out the window as the plane began its descent into London. "I gotta go, Eric. You make sure to take care of this!"

Without allowing Eric to respond, Peter slapped the phone back onto the receiver and stood up from his seat, making his way over to the window to take in the sights of London. As he looked out and saw landmarks like the Tower Bridge, the Palace of Westminster, and the Shard, a knock was heard on his door. As Peter turned around, the door opened, and Henry stepped into the room.

"Mr. President," he said. "I just wanted to let you know that we are completing our final descent to Heathrow."

"Thank you, Mr. Gates," Peter said as he sat back down in his chair.

Henry smiled and stepped out of the room, leaving Peter alone to ponder his thoughts and prepare for his summit with President Wu.

\* \* \*

"Yes?" Vicki said to Pam, who had just entered her office.

"Mrs. Klimmings," Pam said as she closed the door behind her. "I need to speak with you about something."

Seeing how nervous Pam seemed, Vicki offered a chair to her secretary. Pam took a seat in front of Vicki's desk and adjusted her top.

"What is it you need to speak with me about?" Vicki asked Pam.

Pam swallowed hard and took a deep breath. "Mrs. Klimmings," she began. "You know how I've been seeing someone for the past year?"

"Yes?"

"Well, it's been going great lately."

"Okay."

"And he asked me to marry him."

Vicki remained quiet, anticipating what Pam would tell her next.

"And," Pam continued. "I said, 'Yes!'" Pam held up her left hand, showing off an engagement ring.

Vicki's face lit up with a smile. "That's amazing, Pam!"

"Thank you," Pam said before clearing her throat. "There's just one downside to all of this . . ."

"Yes?"

"He has taken a job in Fairbanks."

"*Fairbanks?!*"

"Yeah," Pam said. "I'm not too thrilled about dealing with the cold weather, but I really love him, Mrs. Klimmings." Pam sighed. "I couldn't see myself staying here when he moves to Alaska."

Vicki looked Pam in the eyes. "I'm assuming this is your notice, then?"

Pan swallowed hard. "Yes, ma'am."

Vicki slowly shook her head. "Well, I can't lie and say that I'm not upset, Pam. However, I am thrilled for you to begin your life with your husband."

"Thanks, Mrs. Klimmings," Pam said. She stood up and began to make her way over to the door but stopped and turned around before opening it. "Ma'am, I can stay on until you find a replacement. We aren't moving until the end of July."

"Thank you, Pam," Vicki said, remaining seated at her desk. "I'll be sure to post the position soon. I definitely want to make sure you have some time off before leaving to visit friends and family."

Pam smiled once again and exited Vicki's office, leaving her alone. Vicki took a deep breath, let it out, and leaned back in her chair. Then, after pressing her fingers against her temples, she leaned back forward and opened her right desk drawer to take out a pack of cigarettes. She took one out of the package, put it in her mouth, and lit it.

\* \* \*

Peter made his way into the Palace of Westminster, where he approached the United Kingdom's prime minister and the Japanese prime minister, Akio Yamashita, who were both waiting for him in Westminster Hall.

He first shook the United Kingdom prime minister's hand and thanked him for allowing him to visit the palace. Then, Peter turned his attention to Prime Minister Yamashita, smiled, and shook his hand.

"Thank you, Mr. President," Prime Minister Yamashita began. "Thank you for accepting my invite to this crucial summit between you and President Wu."

The smile fell from Peter's face as he turned and began to look serious. "Well, I wasn't given much choice," Peter said. "If that bastard wouldn't have started this shit, then perhaps we wouldn't have had to go through all of this."

Prime Minister Yamashita was taken aback by Peter's use of language. He swallowed hard, licked his lips to wet them, and continued.

"President Klimmings," the Japanese prime minister said. "I do ask that you try to keep an open mind in this exchange. The fate of the world depends on this summit."

It wasn't until this moment that Peter considered the summit's gravity between himself and President Wu. His attention faded from Prime Minister Yamashita and turned down Westminster Hall, observing the massive room in front of him. He sighed and then turned back to the prime minister.

"Are you going to be mediating this?"

"Yes, sir."

"Good," Peter said as he adjusted his jacket. "We're probably going to need it." He turned back to Don, who had followed him into the hall. "Don, just wait out here until after this is over."

"Are you sure, Mr. President?"

"I am."

Peter turned back to Prime Minister Yamashita, who motioned him to enter the Grand Committee Room. He followed the prime minister's motion and made his way into the room, where he found President Wu already seated at a long table. Peter looked around the room and noticed a lot of Chinese and American flags decorating the chamber. Then, he turned his attention back to President Wu, who stood up and extended his right hand.

"President Klimmings," he said with a menacing smile. "It is so good to see you again."

\* \* \*

Denise made her way out of the living room, leaving Ben alone. He was on the phone with Delilah.

"Are you sure you want to allow her to spend the weekend with me?" Ben asked Delilah. "After all, it's your weekend, Delilah."

"I'm sure of it," Delilah said on the phone. "The more I've thought about it, the more I've begun to realize how unfair that judge's custody ruling was."

Ben sighed and then looked up at the TV. A special report had taken over the channel, and news anchors were discussing the summit between President Klimmings and President Wu.

"King William has expressed his optimism for the summit between the United States and China during a visit with members of the British Army," one of the news anchors said. "With the closed-door meeting between the two leaders continuing on, fears have already been sparked by a multitude of NATO countries after President Klimmings and President Wu failed to perform a formal handshake in front of cameras. The White House has already spoken out, stating that the situation made it inappropriate for the two leaders to pose in front of cameras and that President Klimmings was more concerned with meeting the Chinese president and negotiating a way to end the crisis."

Ben turned away from the TV, going over to the family portrait on the wall above the bar. He looked over the photograph, which still hadn't been updated since his divorce in May.

"Well," he continued. "If you're okay with it, then I guess I'll see you this weekend."

"That would be perfect," Delilah said.

"See you then."

Ben ended the call and set his phone on the bar. He turned back to the TV, where coverage was continuing.

"Amidst all of this, North Korean leader, Kim Jong Un, has conducted another testing of a ballistic missile into the Pacific Ocean," another anchor said. "The UN strongly condemned the testing by the country, but more sanctions are not expected to be placed on the nation anytime soon, as the world's attention remains focused on the tensions between the U.S. and China."

Ben turned back toward the bar, where his eye caught the bottle of Kentucky bourbon sitting directly in the middle. Immediately, his eyes widened, and everything else around him seemed to matter no longer.

*"Benjamin . . ."*

He lightly bit down on his lip as he contemplated what to do. He could hear the bottle calling out to him as if it knew how badly he was craving a drink.

*"Benjamin . . ."*

Finally, he placed his hand on the neck of the bottle and picked it up. Carefully, he examined the label, feeling the liquid slosh around inside. Then, he set the bottle back onto the bar and called out, "Denise!"

Within a few seconds, Denise came through the archway to the entry hall. "Yes?"

"When you get a chance, can you lock up all of the alcohol on the bar?" Ben asked.

"But Mr. Benjamin," Denise said. "Mr. Klimmings loves his night-caps. Don't you think that he will be furious when he learns that the alcohol is gone?"

"Denise, I need you to do this for me. He won't be here for a few more days, and I have to have this temptation removed."

Denise smiled. "Okay, Mr. Benjamin. I can do that."

Ben began to exit the living room through the archway to the stairs but stopped as he put his left leg onto the first step.

"If it helps," he said. "Tell him where the alcohol is whenever he gets home."

* * *

Vicki waved her hands in the air, trying to disperse any smell of second-hand smoke in her office. She quickly set the butt of her cigarette into the ashtray on her desk, which already had two others from the day in it. Then, she pulled some papers over it, concealing it from view. As she stood up, the door opened, and Charlotte stepped into her office.

"What took so long?" Charlotte asked. "I was out there waiting forever!"

"I was busy with something," Vicki told her sister. "What brings you here?"

"Well," Charlotte said as she sat across from Vicki's desk. "I came by to see how you were doing with Peter gone." Charlotte looked down at Vicki's messy desk. "But I see here that you're keeping yourself busy."

Vicki looked down at the mess on her desk and then sat down in her chair. "I guess you can say that I have," Vicki said. She pressed her fingers against her temples and then continued. "Pam resigned today."

"The secretary?" Charlotte asked. "There's a whole crisis going on involving your husband, and the secretary resigning is what is on your mind?!"

"I like Pam," Vicki said. "She'll be difficult to replace."

Charlotte sighed. "Well, if you need someone reliable, just hire me."

Vicki's eyes widened. "Are you serious?"

"Yes. I need something to do. After all, my divorce lawyer is still stuck in Taiwan, thanks to your husband."

"I'm sure that's what's on his mind right now as he speaks with the Chinese president."

"I sure hope so," Charlotte said as she crossed her legs. "But that's not a bad idea, though."

"What is?"

"Me becoming your secretary."

"So you were actually serious about that then?"

"Of course," Charlotte exclaimed. "I wouldn't have to stop by your house and deal with that dreadful bitch anymore. I could just see you here."

Vicki cocked her head. "That dreadful bitch's name is Denise," she said. "You and her need to learn to get along."

"As long as she knows her place," Charlotte said before standing from her seat. "I'm gonna head out and get something for lunch. Do you want to go with?"

Vicki sat for a moment, considering Charlotte's offer. "Are you buying?"

Charlotte sighed. "I guess so."

"Then I'm in!"

Vicki jumped up from her seat and grabbed her bag. She made her way over to the door with Charlotte behind her and opened it, allowing her sister to step through the threshold first. Then, she closed the door behind her and said, "Pam, I'm going to be out for lunch."

Then, Vicki turned toward Pam's desk and noticed a young woman standing next to it.

"Mrs. Klimmings," Pam said. "This woman claims to know you."

Vicki looked at the woman and began to recognize who she was. "Michelle?"

"Mrs. Klimmings," Michelle said quietly to her. "I was wondering if you could talk to me for a moment."

*Gabriella's friend . . .* Vicki's mind was taken back to that night. She remembered everything that had happened in Gabby's room and the family plot. She remembered Don shoveling dirt into the grave he had dug to conceal Gabby's body. Scoop after scoop, Gabby was buried like a dog. There was no funeral. No words of remembrance were spoken. The only thing mentioned was how they were doing this to protect the family's legacy . . . Peter's legacy.

*Peter . . .*

When Michelle spoke again, Vicki's eyes were wide, "Mrs. Klimmings?"

She turned her attention back to Michelle, allowing her face to move back into its resting position. "What is it?" Vicki asked her, coming off slightly ruder than she had intended. "What do you want to talk about?"

"Ma'am," Michelle began. "I've tried texting Gabby, calling her, and messaging her through Instagram. I haven't heard anything back from her."

"Oh no," Charlotte interjected. "Don't talk to her about Gabby.

82

She's a touchy subject with my sister!"

Vicki glared at Charlotte and then cleared her throat. "Gabriella's at St. Mary's in the Swiss Alps. She's not allowed visitors, so I don't think she has her phone on her very much. And even when she does, I don't think the cell reception is very great there."

"But I don't understand, ma'am," Michelle continued. "Back in February, she had an incident with Dana at school, and then we never heard from her again. She just disappeared to this place in Europe."

Charlotte turned toward Vicki, waiting to hear her answer to Michelle. Instead, Vicki sighed and said, "I don't know what to tell you. Have you considered writing her?"

*Why did I mention that? Gabriella isn't at St. Mary's. She's dead.* Vicki's mind raced with thoughts, trying to figure out how to take back what she had just suggested to Michelle.

"I hadn't," Michelle said. "But that's a good idea. Do you have the address?"

"Not with me," Vicki said. "I may have it somewhere at home."

"If you find it, can you send it to me?"

Vicki sighed again. "I guess I can."

"Thank you!" Michelle smiled at Vicki, who reluctantly returned the gesture and then made her way down the hall to the elevator.

Charlotte turned back to Vicki. "What the hell was that all about?"

"I don't want to talk about it," Vicki said. "She and Dana were so awful to my Gabriella. Did I ever mention about how they outed her earlier this year?"

"*They did?!*" Charlotte exclaimed. She flung her purse to Vicki. "Hell, let me see if I can catch her so I can kick her little ass."

"No. Don't do that." Vicki stopped her sister from pursuing Michelle. "Let's just go to lunch, Charlotte. Then, we can head back to the mansion and relax."

\* \* \*

The door to the lobby of Klimmings Tower opened, and Michelle stepped outside. She put the phone to her ear and started talking.

"Dana, I met with Gabby's mom, and she wasn't any help. Something is up with that family. They're hiding something about Gabby, and I don't like it. Call me back as soon as you get this."

* * *

Miranda and Julie stepped off the red double-decker bus and onto the sidewalk of Piccadilly Circus. "Thank you," Julie called out to the bus driver before he took off. Then, she turned back to Miranda, who was looking toward the Shaftesbury Memorial Fountain. Tourists were seated around the fountain, resting from their travels of the day.

"It's interesting how simple things can be for people," Miranda said, not caring whether Julie heard. "Sometimes I wish my life were as simple as theirs."

Julie cocked her head to the side, taking in what Miranda had said.

"Miranda," Julie said. "Your life can be whatever you want it to be. You do know that, right?"

Miranda turned back to Julie. "I know," she said. "But sometimes with Dad being the president . . . it makes things difficult, you know."

"Well, my dad never was the president, so I wouldn't know."

The two chuckled as they began walking down the sidewalk, taking in all the shops and illuminated screens covering buildings in the area.

"This is like Times Square," Miranda said. "Scaled down a little, but still the same."

"I've never been to New York," Julie confessed. "It's on my bucket list, though."

Miranda whipped her head around to Julie. "Oh, we got to go! You will love it."

Julie smiled as the two continued walking. "After your baby is born, let's plan it."

Miranda stopped on the sidewalk and placed her hand on her stomach. She was still too early to show, but she still could feel changes inside her body.

"Julie," she said to her friend as people passed by, ignoring the two as they stood on the sidewalk. "Am I an awful person for considering an abortion?"

Julie struggled to keep her mouth from dropping open. "Are you?"

"Not anymore," Miranda said. "But earlier, before I had told any-one, I was considering getting one. I even spoke with the vice president about it."

"And what did she say?" Julie asked.

"Oh, she told me that she had had three of her own," Miranda said. "She was rather calm about it all too."

"God," Julie swore. "Don't let anyone else know about that! Could you imagine the scandal?!"

"I know . . ."

The two began walking down the sidewalk again but only got a few steps in before Julie's attention was taken to one of the giant screens that curved around one of the buildings. Miranda turned toward the screen and saw the logo of BBC News with its red background.

"This is a BBC News Special Bulletin," said a male news anchor seated alone. In the background, viewers could see some of the workers in the newsroom. "The BBC News has just received word that negotiations between U.S. President Klimmings and China's President Wu have deteriorated during their summit at the Palace of Westmin-ster."

A gasp amongst the people in Piccadilly Circus was heard as Miranda looked around at people's reactions. Immediately, she could feel their fear as the BBC News anchor continued on.

"President Wu was seen leaving the Palace of Westminster earlier." The video cut to a clip of the Chinese president leaving the palace in his motorcade. Flashes from the cameras reflected off his procession as it passed, turning down Bridge Street, passing the Elizabeth Tower, and then making its way across Westminster Bridge. "President Klimmings of the United States is holding a press conference right now. Let's tune in to hear what the president has to say."

The video cut to one of Peter in front of a podium with the pres-idential seal on it.

"Mr. President," called out one of the reporters. "How can you describe the summit with President Wu?"

"Well," Peter began. "All I can say right now is that we won't be meeting again until China decides how a negotiation with the United States actually works."

Camera flashes began lighting up the frame as photographers took pictures. Peter continued on.

"For right now, the USS *Joseph R. Biden Jr.* will remain in the South China Sea, along with the USS *Doris Miller*, which I had sent there last week to provide support. When I return to the U.S., I plan to conduct a meeting with my entire cabinet, as well as our top military generals, where we will be discussing issues of national security and actions we can take to further implement pressure on China.

"In the meantime, I strongly urge all Americans in China to book a flight home now. It is no longer safe to be there, and my administration will do everything in its power to ensure a safe arrival back to the mainland. In addition, I have spoken with the Japanese prime minister following the deterioration of communication between President Wu and myself, and he has agreed to help aid in evacuating our nation's citizens.

"As for the remainder of Americans at home or in one of our allied nations, please do not worry. Your government and its leadership are doing all they can to ensure peace at this time. But should those efforts fail, remember that I am prepared to use the full power of the American military to defend this country, its Constitution, and the people it protects."

# CHAPTER 7
## MISCOMMUNICATION

Chants were heard from the crowd as Peter waved to them. Barricades lined with Secret Service members contained the unruly crowd protesting the president. However, that didn't seem to bother Peter in the slightest, as he continued waving at them and smiling while Don opened the door to the Beast.

"Mr. President," Don said with a sense of urgency. "It is imperative that we get you in the Beast and on your way back to Air Force One."

"Why are you in such a hurry?" Peter asked as he waved back to the crowd, ignoring their protests. He called out to them. "You'll all soon be thanking me for taking such a strong stance against President Wu!"

Peter turned back to Miranda and Julie, who anxiously awaited him to get into the car.

"Dad," Miranda said nervously. "Maybe we should go ahead and get into the car?"

"Miranda," Peter said calmly. "It'll be okay. I've done these types of events all the time . . ."

Before he could finish speaking, Peter heard three loud gunshots followed by an immediate scream of panic from the crowd as they began to disperse. He turned to catch what was going on but was yanked into the car by Don. Then, another member of the Secret Service abruptly shoved Miranda and Julie in after him as they began to hear more gunshots erupt. Then, the door was slammed shut, and the tires squealed as the Beast took off, fleeing the scene.

* * *

Charlotte pulled her car over to the side of the road in front of Klimmings Tower and put it into park. "What is all of this?"

She motioned for Vicki, seated beside her, to look at the ensuing crowd in front of the skyscraper. Vicki looked puzzled as she saw the group of people and then looked back at Charlotte.

"Why are they here?" Vicki asked. "The building closed to the public a couple of hours ago."

"I don't know," Charlotte said. "I didn't hear anything about what happened today when we went shopping after lunch."

Charlotte leaned forward and used her car's touchscreen to turn up the volume for the radio.

"We once again want to update you on the dramatic turn of events that occurred at today's summit between the United States and China today," said the radio DJ. Charlotte leaned back in her seat and glanced over to Vicki, who was listening intently. "We have received word that President Klimmings has survived an assassination attempt as he was readying to depart from London. Sources say that he and his daughter were pushed into the presidential limousine before being rushed away from the scene. The only person sustaining any minor injuries was a member of the president's top Secret Service detail, who was able to be treated aboard Air Force One."

Charlotte noticed the look on Vicki's face and turned the radio off as the DJ mentioned that the president was en route back to the United States.

"Take me home, Charlotte," Vicki said to her.

"What about your car?"

"Just take me home."

Charlotte could see the irritation on Vicki's face, so she took the car out of park and drove off.

\* \* \*

"Are you sure?" Delilah asked Ben over the phone. "I told you earlier that I was fine with you having Katherine this weekend."

"Delilah," Ben said. "There's no way I can get over there to get her." He looked out the window of the sitting room. Along the road was a growing crowd of protesters who had convened there following the communication breakdown between Peter and President Wu. "It's a complete madhouse out there."

"I hate this," Delilah said. "What happened anyways?"

"I don't know," Ben sighed. "But it's getting bad. How are your parents doing?"

"Well, Dad has been making phone calls like crazy. Applegate Technology has a building in Beijing, so you can imagine how concerned he is."

"I can imagine," Ben said as he heard the front door to the house open.

"Benjamin!"

He stepped out of the sitting room, looking down the hallway toward the entry hall, where he saw his mother standing. "Have you heard from your father?" she asked him.

"No," Ben replied. "I haven't heard anything."

"Great," Vicki let out. Then, she stormed off down the entry hall before Ben could say anything else.

"Delilah," Ben said on the phone again. "I'm going to have to get off of here. It's not going to be good in the Klimmings household."

\* \* \*

Hours had passed before Peter and Miranda finally arrived back at the

Klimmings Mansion, making it after one in the morning when they came through the front door.

"I'm going to bed," Miranda said as she left her suitcase in the entry hall. "I can deal with that in the morning."

"Are you sure?" Peter asked her. "Denise can get it if you want."

"Dad, it's early in the morning. I'm not going to have Denise get out of bed to take care of my luggage."

"You're right," Peter said. "Everyone is probably asleep anyways."

"Not everyone."

Peter turned to the archway to the living room and found Vicki standing, waiting for him. The TV was on in the living room, but the volume had been muted, so no one could hear the news anchors talking.

"Vicki," Peter said. "I'm surprised to see you up."

"Well, you shouldn't be," she let out. "Peter, we need to talk."

"I'm going to bed now," Miranda said as she stepped away, trying to avoid the tension between her parents. "Goodnight!"

Vicki wished Miranda a good night's sleep. Then, she waited for Miranda to head upstairs before turning back to Peter. "What the hell went on over there?"

Peter sighed. "Well . . . nothing really."

"*Really?!* You call this nothing!" Vicki gestured to the TV. Peter turned to look at it and saw how the news coverage was showing images of protests that had broken out across the country, along with panic buying in some of the nation's largest cities. They also cut to the airports, which had been inundated with people seeking to flee from the United States.

"Peter, people are scared! This isn't a game anymore."

"I never said it was a game!"

"Really, Peter! You're playing with fire right now, and what is going to happen is that you're going to get burned."

Peter went to the bar to make himself a drink but found that all of the alcohol was missing. "Where's the liquor?"

"Dammit, Peter!" Vicki swore. "What the hell are you doing?"

"Vicki," he said, returning to his wife. "I have to make this stand against China. My reelection depends on it. I don't need people thinking that I am going to cave to a Communist regime."

"Peter," Vicki said, raising her voice. "How is this helping your reelection? You have pushed the country close to war! What are you going to do if China doesn't back down?"

"I'll stand firm. If that means engaging in a conflict, then we'll damn well be in one."

"Peter, they have nukes."

"And?" Peter replied. "So do we."

Vicki's eyes widened as she took a step back from Peter. "You're scaring me, Peter."

He sighed. "Vicki, don't be."

"How in God's name am I not supposed to be scared when all this shit is happening in the world right now?!"

"I have a plan!"

"What is it? Destroy everything?"

"No, no, no," Peter said. "Just trust me, and you'll see it." He stepped in closer to Vicki. "Just trust me, and everything will end up being okay."

\* \* \*

The weekend passed, and desperation among the American people grew. Police began wearing riot gear in anticipation of riots in cities across the country. Protests continued, panic buying worsened, and more Americans fled the country. As a result, Mexico closed border crossings to the United States, resulting in a dramatic reversal of illegal immigration as some Americans resorted to crossing the Rio Grande into Mexico, only for their border patrol to send them back.

As all of this continued, Peter sat in the Oval Office with the TV on. He was alone in the office and on the phone.

"Dammit, Kang," he said into the receiver. "How long is it going to take you and your Grand Rebellion to pressure Wu?"

"Mr. President," Kang responded. "We're trying the best we can. Protests have ramped up, but we still haven't gotten close enough for Wu to notice . . . or even care."

"Well, you best hurry the hell up," Peter stated. "I am putting everything I have on the line for you people. My political future depends on your success, and my country has gone to hell."

"I know," Kang said. "We're doing the best we can."

"Well, do better!"

Peter slammed the phone onto the receiver and looked back at the TV. The news had cut to Rebecca White, who was visibly furious.

"I struggle to understand what the president is trying to accomplish with this," she said on the TV. "He is endangering the lives of all Americans and is threatening the future of our country."

The door to the Oval Office opened. Martha stood holding the door as Henry, Constance, and Eric each made their way into the room.

"I just got off the phone with Don," Henry said as he approached the *Resolute* desk. "He expects to leave the hospital either today or tomorrow. Then, he'll spend the next few months at home to recuperate and fully recover."

"That's fantastic news, Mr. Gates," Peter said as he stood from his chair and stepped over to the bar. "I'd say that should call for a drink!"

"I would have to respectfully disagree, sir," Constance spoke up, sitting down in one of the chairs in front of the *Resolute* desk. Peter turned around with a decanter of bourbon in his hand.

"Excuse me?"

Constance crossed her legs and continued. "Sir, the shooter wasn't aiming at Don. They were aiming at you." Constance flipped her hair. "They did this because of the outcome of the summit between you and President Wu."

Peter set the decanter back onto the bar, which made a sharp thud.

"We learned that the man was from Ireland and had illegally brought that handgun into the United Kingdom," Peter clarified. "He was crazy."

"Yes," Constance agreed. "But he did it because he was scared." She gestured to the TV, which continued to show panicked Americans. "The same goes for those people, Peter. Look at them!"

Peter glanced over to the TV and took in what he saw.

"Peter, these people are scared out of their minds," she continued.

"They're resulting to rioting, looting, and some are even fleeing the country!"

"Constance," Peter sighed as he rounded his desk and sat back in the chair. "This will all blow over . . ."

"Blow over?!" Constance exclaimed. "What the hell do you think this is, Peter? A scandal?"

"I think what he's meaning is that as the days progress on, the people will begin to see things in a better light," Henry butted in, reminding the two that he and Eric were still in the room. "It's only been a week. Give them some more time, and they'll begin to see how this isn't as serious as everything believes it to be."

Constance sighed and then stood up from her seat. "I want you to address the nation," she said to Peter. "No ifs, ands, or buts. You *have* to speak with the people."

Peter refrained from rolling his eyes. *She's got to be kidding me, right?* He looked at Henry and then at Eric.

"It's actually not a bad idea," Eric said in agreement with the vice president. "Perhaps if you spoke to the people, you could stifle some of the abrasive actions they've been taking."

*Really? Him too?* Peter took a deep break and then spoke. "Fine. Constance, get with the press secretary and let her know that I plan to address the country this evening."

"So you're doing a primetime address then?" Constance asked.

"You want me to address the nation, then what better way than to do it when I would get the most views!"

"Alright."

Constance turned around and made her way out of the Oval Office, leaving the three men in the room. Peter turned his attention to Henry. "Why did you lie to the vice president?"

"I didn't," Henry said. "After a few more weeks, the tensions between us and China will die down. They always have."

"Mr. Gates," Peter began. "Have you not been following the news? Earlier today, I notified Janet that I want to clear out the embassy in China and that I plan to expel the Chinese from their embassy here."

"Why would you do that?!" Henry exclaimed. "Mr. President, do you know how much that will escalate things?"

"That's not all," Peter said before turning to Eric. "Eric, I need you to direct the United States Navy to move two nuclear submarines to our naval base in Guam."

"Oh my God," Henry let out. He looked utterly lost for words. "I thought you wanted to find a diplomatic solution to all of this?!"

"Mr. Gates," Peter calmly said to him. "Growing up, my father would always be the one to say, 'If you want something done, you just gotta do it yourself.' You hung around him a lot, so you definitely should remember hearing him say this."

"Yes," Henry said, nodding his head. "I recall."

"Well, I have taken it upon myself to take care of this whole situation. So I have upped the game for President Wu, and we'll see if that bastard continues to play or if now is the time that he decides to finally step back."

"This is a gamble," Eric said as Henry processed Peter's statement.

"Life is a gamble," Peter continued. "However, I must ensure that I am reelected next year. I cannot allow this creep to destroy everything I've worked so hard to build."

"Mr. President," Henry said. "President Wu hasn't shown any more interest in your company since the plan he formulated with Jeremy Applegate last year."

"I'm not talking about my company."

"Then," Eric interrupted. "What *are* you talking about?"

Peter looked up at Eric, then at Henry, and then back to Eric. "I'm talking about my country."

\* \* \*

"This is utterly ridiculous! Just look at what he's driving our country to do!"

Rebecca White sat at her desk in the speaker's office, pointing to the TV. Her secretary was in the room with her, who was just as glued to the news coverage as Rebecca.

"This is just awful."

"You think?!" Rebecca exclaimed. "I swear the more and more I think about that man, the more I just want to punch him in the face . . . just like he punched the Chinese president last year."

"But Madam Speaker," her secretary said. "You'd go to jail for assaulting the president!"

"It'd be worth it!" Rebecca glanced around the room and let out a grunt of frustration. "The thought of dealing with him for another year-and-a-half as president is absolutely repulsive!"

"But Madam Speaker," Rebecca's secretary spoke. "Aren't you investigating him on pretty much everything he's done?"

"Yes," Rebecca said. "But we can't do anything until we have substantial evidence that President Klimmings has committed an impeachable offense. When we find that – and I say when because it's only a matter of time before we find something – then we can proceed with formally acting against him." Rebecca sighed. "Until then, we're just wasting our time and using up news coverage with every investigation we've opened against him."

"Can't you use what he's doing to the country right now against him?"

"Yes and no. We definitely can spin this politically and remind the people that the president is impulsive and only thinks about himself. However, legally, we cannot do anything. He's actually doing what he can right now to handle this situation." Rebecca leaned in toward her secretary. "Between you and me, I heard that it was actually President Wu who called off the summit between him and Peter."

"Really?" her secretary said. "Do the people know this?"

"No!" Rebecca called out. "And they don't need to know this. I need them to be absolutely convinced right now that Peter knows nothing about how to run a country."

\* \* \*

Vicki sat on the cream sofa in the living room. She was on the phone with Charlotte, who was at the Klimmings Incorporated offices. In front of Vicki lay numerous papers indicating that she had been working from home.

"Charlotte," Vicki said. "Can you just do this for me? If I could come in, I would, but the Secret Service is being a real pain in the ass right now."

"Well, how is Peter getting to and from the house?" Charlotte asked.

"He's not. He's staying in the Executive Residence at the White House."

"Really?"

"Yes, Charlotte," Vicki said, becoming more irritated with her sister. "Just do what I asked, please."

Without hearing what Charlotte added, Vicki ended the call and tossed her cell phone onto the coffee table. She leaned back onto the sofa and pressed her fingers against her temples, letting out a long sigh. *I could really use a cigarette right now.*

"Stressed?"

Vicki turned toward the archway leading to the stairwell, where Ben was standing with a cup of coffee.

"Denise made some coffee," he said to Vicki as he came into the living room and sat in the chair to the left of his mother. "Would you like for me to get you some?"

"I need more than just coffee," Vicki said. After speaking, she realized that it was Ben who had all the alcohol moved from the bar in the living room. "Well, maybe I could use some coffee."

Ben set his mug on the coffee table and rose from his seat. As he made his way across the room, his attention was drawn to the TV, which was still covering the chaos across the country.

"Dad has really screwed this one up, hasn't he?"

Vicki looked up. "Yes, Benjamin. He has."

"Do you think he can recover from this at all?"

Vicki remained quiet, refraining from saying what she had wanted to. Ben sensed the hostility emanating from his mother, so he opted to change the subject.

"Have you heard from Gabby?"

Once again, Vicki remained quiet. *How much longer am I going to have to do this?*

"No," Vicki finally said. "Can you get me that cup of coffee, please?"

Ben stood still for a brief moment, considering whether to ask his mom how she was doing, but instead chose to continue making his way out of the room toward the kitchen. As he crossed the entry hall, Miranda rounded the corner from the stairwell.

"Where are you going?" Ben asked her, noticing that she was dressed to go out.

"I have my doctor's appointment," she said to him. "Baby's due for a check-up."

Vicki overheard the chatter and made her way out into the entry hall. "Are you sure leaving is a good idea?" she asked Miranda. "Have you seen the protesters out front?"

"I've heard them," Miranda said. "I had my window open this morning and could hear their chants from the road."

"So you know there's quite the crowd then?"

"Yes, but they're not protesting me," Miranda added. "They're protesting Dad . . . and he's not here." She stepped closer to her mom and placed her left hand on Vicki's shoulder. "I'll be fine, Mom. I can handle myself out there."

Miranda smiled at Vicki before stepping past her mother and going out the front door of the Klimmings Mansion. As the door closed, Ben turned to his mother.

"I'm sure she'll be fine, Mom," he said. "She did have a point about Dad, though. They're not here to protest her."

"I know," Vicki sighed. "But it still worries me . . ."

"Mom, Miranda is your oldest child," Ben began. "You've got to stop worrying about her. If there's anyone you should be concerned about, it would be Gabby. No one has heard from her for months."

Vicki looked up at Ben, staring at him. She considered whether he had remembered anything from the evening of Gabby's death. So she asked, "You don't remember anything from that night, do you?"

"What?" Ben looked at his mom, puzzled.

Vicki took in a deep breath, defeated, and then said, "Nothing."

2

She passed Ben and turned left to head up the stairwell, leaving Ben alone in the entry hall.

\* \* \*

"Dammit, Wu!" Jeremy cursed as he took his cell phone away from his ear. "Answer your phone from time to time!"

Jeremy locked his phone and tossed it across his office in the Applegate Homestead. He turned around in his chair and found Ryan standing in the doorway. Jeremy swallowed hard before speaking. "He's not answering my calls."

"Why would he?" Ryan asked as he closed the door to Jeremy's office.

"Ryan," Jeremy began. "Applegate Technology has quite a substantial division in China. Unfortunately, with this crap going on between President Wu and Peter, our business is beginning to suffer."

"Ah-ha!" Ryan said as he approached Jeremy at his desk. "So you aren't doing this because Mom had asked you to. You're doing this because it's hurting the company."

"No, I'm partly doing this because of her. The other part is to try to save everything we've built."

"Dad, why don't you just go over and speak with President Wu?"

"Ryan . . . who the hell is able to get on a plane and travel to China right now? Have you not seen the news?!"

"I have, but you also have the Applegate Jet."

"The Applegate Jet?!" Jeremy exclaimed. "How am I supposed to jump on a private jet, fly across the Pacific, and somehow not get stopped by our government or the Chinese? I would be shot down before I ever made it over the mainland."

Ryan remained quiet as he considered other options Jeremy could take. Finally, he smiled and chuckled to himself.

"What is it?" Jeremy asked. "What are you thinking?"

"Well," Ryan laughed. "You've been trying to destroy the Klimmings family for forever. So just let Peter continue doing what he is."

"What?!"

"Listen," Ryan continued. "You can continue to allow Peter to screw up this entire thing. Then, you can raise the prices of all of our products. And, when the pushback comes, blame it on the rising costs due to the increased tensions between us and China."

"So, blame it all on Peter," Jeremy said. His face lit up with a smile, and he perked up in his chair. "Ryan, that's an excellent idea!"

"Right?"

"But wait," Jeremy said again. "How am I going to deal with your mother when I've suddenly raised the prices and pushed the blame onto Peter?"

"Tell her like it is," Ryan said. "It's the rising costs of labor and supplies." He leaned onto Peter's desk. "You don't have to directly blame Peter, Dad. All you have to do is mention the escalation between the two countries."

"But wait a moment," Jeremy said. "If I'm thinking about this right, won't this also give us a boost in China too?"

Ryan smiled. "As long as you blame President Wu too."

\* \* \*

"How worried is she?" Miranda asked Ben on the phone. She sat behind the steering wheel of her blue car as she drove down the small highway that took her to the Klimmings Mansion.

"To be honest, Miranda," Ben said over her car's speakers. "Mom hasn't come downstairs since you left."

"What?" Miranda let out. "It's almost eight. I left a little after one!" Miranda looked ahead at the road and tried to think about what to say next. "She didn't even want to know where I've been since I left my appointment."

"Well, I figured everything was fine, and you ended up going shopping for some stuff."

Miranda chuckled. "You know me too well, Ben."

Ben laughed along with Miranda briefly and then cleared his throat before speaking again. "I got a question for you."

"Yes?"

"Do you think Mom has been acting weird lately?"

"Ben," Miranda said. "Both Mom *and* Dad have been weird lately."

"True," he said. "But Mom asked me something weird after you left."

"And that was . . ."

"Well, I mentioned that if she needed to be worried about anyone, then she should be worried about Gabby because no one has heard from her for a few months."

"True," Miranda interrupted.

"Anyways," Ben continued. "She looked at me and asked me if I had remembered anything from – and I'm repeating exactly what she said – that night."

Miranda fell silent, considering what Vicki could have meant by that. As she thought it over, she drove passed the Applegate Homestead and began to slow down as she approached the group of protesters gathered in front of the Klimmings Mansion.

"Ben," Miranda said. "I'm about home. Let's talk about this after I get through these protesters."

She reached forward and ended the call by pressing the button on her car's touch screen. Then, Miranda directed her attention back to the road as she started maneuvering through the protesters. She could hear their chants inside her car, and as she approached the driveway, Miranda sensed that perhaps Vicki was right. Maybe she shouldn't have gone out after all.

"Hey!" she heard one of the protesters yell out. Miranda looked to her left and saw a guy standing beside her car, pointing at it. "It's one of them!"

Before she could react, a mob of angry protesters surrounded Miranda's car. They began rocking it from side to side, calling out numerous obscenities and offensive slurs directed toward the entire Klimmings family.

As she panicked, Miranda braced her head behind the steering wheel, aiming to hit the brake. However, just as she had anticipated for her car's slow roll to stop, it jerked forward in an abrasive movement, flinging the people off, and sped past the Klimmings Mansion and away from the group of angry protesters. Finally, she looked up from behind her steering wheel, and she realized she was speeding toward oncoming traffic, which had been stopped already because of the protests.

Instinctively, she screamed and jolted the steering wheel to the right, flinging her car back into her lane. As she attempted to straighten the car back up, she overcorrected, spinning her blue car around and causing her left taillight to clip the stopped car in the other lane. This flung Miranda around, causing her car to flip into the ditch on the side of the road. With the abrupt impact into the earth, Miranda's car came to a stop just as the airbags deployed, which pummeled her before ultimately knocking her unconscious.

# CHAPTER 8
## GOD BLESS THE LITTLE CHILDREN

President Wu stood in his office, looking out the window at the city of Beijing. It was early in the morning in the city, and the sun still hadn't risen. However, as he looked upon the great city, he noticed a growing number of people lining the streets than usual. Concerned, he returned to his desk and took his phone off the receiver. He pressed a button and waited for someone to pick up on the other end.

"How is our censorship of that rebel group going?" President Wu asked the man who had picked up.

"President Wu," the man responded. "Unfortunately, despite our efforts to hide the Grand Rebellion's presence in our country, their influence has grown significantly over the past few weeks."

"Tell me about it," President Wu said as he went to the window to look back outside. "Because I'm looking outside my window right now, and I see people wandering the streets at such an early time in the morning."

"Well," the man began. "Hong Kong has already greatly accepted their influence."

"Figures," President Wu said. "Hong Kong always caves into whatever the big trend is. They've been a big pain in China's ass since the British transferred it to us almost forty years ago."

"But Hong Kong isn't the only place affected by the Grand Rebellion's influence . . ."

"What?"

"Well, there's been a growing movement on social media with millions of young people planning a mass protest. They've seen how the Americans have responded to the breakdown in talks, and we believe we are about to see something more like what they've seen over there."

President Wu thought over what the man had said. Finally, after thinking things over, the Chinese president said, "Cut the internet."

"What?"

"Cut the internet. They can't organize mass protests if they can't access the internet, so cut it."

The man on the other line hesitated before agreeing to the Chinese president's request. Then, President Wu placed the phone back on the receiver and resumed looking out the window at the city lights of Beijing. He took in everything he saw, and he mulled through his thoughts. *I am the president of this country. I am the ultimate power here, and no Grand Rebellion will ever push me out of my position of authority.*

\* \* \*

Peter took a seat behind the *Resolute* desk. He straightened his tie and adjusted his jacket while looking up at the camera in front of him. "How do I look?" he asked one of the cameramen.

"Perfect, Mr. President," he said back to Peter.

Peter smiled and looked down at his desk, where a binder was placed in front of him. Nothing else remained on the desk except for it, which prompted him to look over to Henry, who had come into the Oval Office.

"Keep the binder or not?" Peter asked his chief of staff.

"Keep it," Henry responded. "Just leave it closed."

Peter took in a deep breath. "Great, are we ready?"

"Whenever you are, Mr. President," the cameraman said.

"Now, Mr. President," Henry interjected. "Remember how important this is. Constance was onto something when she suggested it." He paused before continuing. "You know . . . before you decided to escalate tensions even further."

"Mr. Gates," Peter said firmly. "I had already told you why I had decided to do that. We have *got* to show China that we mean business."

Henry refrained from saying anything, trying to prevent Peter from announcing anything during his address that would further escalate tensions with China and the American people.

"Let's get this show on the road then," Peter said as he adjusted his jacket again.

The cameraman called out for quiet in the room and quickly repositioned the camera, properly framing Peter in the shot. Then, he started counting down, and when he finally reached the end, Peter began his address.

"My fellow Americans, tonight I want to speak with you about our nation's unprecedented response to the growing crisis between China and our country. Last week, I attended a summit with the Chinese president. During this meeting, I attempted to negotiate a peaceful outcome to this dramatic crisis in the South China Sea, following China's aggressive manner in performing a blockade against one of our country's aircraft carriers, the USS *Joseph R. Biden Jr.*

"Following the failed summit, I vowed to the American people that I would do whatever I needed to ensure the protection of our country and the people who reside within. To uphold this promise, I have consulted with top government officials and will be announcing some dramatic but necessary actions to protect the well-being of this great nation.

"Earlier today, I spoke with my secretary of state and made the decision to clear out the U.S. embassy located in Beijing. China has made it clear that they remain hostile to all Americans by refusing to continue negotiations with us. In addition, I have also made the order to expel every Chinese official from their embassy in Washington. Our nation is no place for the enemy to be in.

"In order to make these new measures work, I have also instructed the Federal Aviation Administration to ground all domestic and international flights in the United States, as well as close our airspace to every nation, except for Canada and Mexico, who have agreed to limit the number of flights into our airspace. I recognize that these new measures will have severe implications for all who live in the United States. Just know that these decisions were not made lightly.

"From the beginning of time, nations have always had their differences. Whether over territorial disputes, politically motivated, or driven by economic factors, negotiations have taken place, and solutions have become solidified. In this case, nothing was able to be crafted after China's inept ability to make compromises.

"It is also worth noting that their influence has also expanded outside their own borders. Before addressing you all tonight, I learned from our ambassador to the United Nations that the U.N. Security Council voted to impose sanctions on the United States over China's blockade. Because of our veto power, our ambassador joined with the United Kingdom to enact a veto that prevented any sanctions from being imposed on our great nation.

"As we progress through this crisis, I offer this passage from the book of Psalms that I feel will resonate with all Americans at this moment: 'I have set the Lord always before me: because he is at my right hand, I shall not be moved.'

"I pray for each and every one of you and hope that you find solace in those words. Thank you. God bless you, and God bless America. Goodnight."

Peter continued looking into the camera until the cameraman called the all-clear. Then he looked over to Henry, who seemed quite distraught over the address.

"You grounded all flights?!" Henry exclaimed. "Don't you think you should've even mentioned it to me before you decided to tell the whole damn world?!"

"I had figured you already knew," Peter said as he stood up from his seat. "I needed to make sure that America knows I plan to keep them safe from China."

"Well, you should've at least told them that you grounded all the flights so that we could better monitor America's airspace," Henry said. "At least, that's why you did it, right?"

"Of course," Peter said as he took off his suit jacket. He laid it on the desk chair as the door to the office opened, and Martha stepped into the room.

"Mr. President," she said, garnering his attention. "I just got off the phone with Walter Reed Army Medical Center."

"Yes?" Peter said, looking concerned.

"They informed me that they are anticipating the arrival of your daughter by ambulance," Martha continued. "They mentioned something about a bad wreck."

"Son of a bitch!" Peter swore. He turned around and snatched his jacket. Then, he turned to Henry. "Get my motorcade ready."

"I'll get Marine One ready for you, Mr. President," Henry said, disregarding Peter's request. He darted out of the room, leaving Peter with Martha and the cameraman.

"She's pregnant," Peter said to the two. "Dammit, she's pregnant!" He paced back and forth. "I gotta get there."

* * *

Ben turned away from the TV in the waiting room at the Walter Reed Army Medical Center. Peter's address to the nation was playing in real-time as he sat beside his mother, putting his arm around her.

"I'm sure Miranda is going to be okay," he said to Vicki.

"Why didn't she listen to me?" Vicki asked Ben, wiping tears from her eyes. "The doctor could've come to see her at the house."

Ben swallowed hard, not knowing what to say. He turned back to the TV, which was now on a group of news anchors discussing the president's address. The news banners on the lower third of the screen alternated between statements about the U.S. Embassy being closed, the FAA grounding all flights in the country, and that U.S. nuclear submarines had been moved to Guam. Finally, Ben turned back to his mom.

"She's going to be fine," Ben said to her. "Miranda is a fighter."

Vicki lifted her head as a doctor approached the two.

"Mrs. Klimmings," the doctor began. "We've stabilized your daughter. She came in with intense abdominal pain sustained from the accident, but she is awake now. You can go see her if you would like."

Vicki turned back to Ben, who motioned for her to go on without him. She hesitated for a moment and then proceeded to follow the doctor down the hall to Miranda's room.

The first thing she heard when she entered was the vital signs monitor beeping regularly in the room. Then, she noticed Miranda lying in the bed. She was conscious and turned to Vicki.

"Mom," she struggled to let out. Vicki could easily see that she was exhausted.

"Don't," Vicki said as she approached Miranda's bed. She sat in a chair on the opposite side and took Miranda's right hand. "Don't strain yourself, honey. Rest."

Miranda coughed, trying to clear her throat. "Mom, what happened?"

Vicki glanced up at the doctor, who was still standing in the doorway to the room. He nodded.

"Miranda, you were in an accident," Vicki began. "I don't know all of the details, but from my understanding, there were some protestors, and you tried to avoid hitting them."

Miranda sighed, looking around the room. She opened her mouth to say something but stopped short of it. Instead, Miranda crunched up in the hospital bed and let go of Vicki's hand to clutch her abdomen. She let out a cry as the doctor rushed over to her bed. Vicki rose from her chair in a panic.

"What's wrong?" she asked. "What's going on?"

A group of nurses and other doctors rushed into the room as Miranda cried out in pain, grasping her stomach. Vicki continued to question what was happening, panicking more and more with each cry from her daughter.

"Someone get her out of here!" the first doctor called out as he tried to check more of Miranda's vitals and pinpoint what was going on.

A nurse took Vicki by her right arm. "Come on, Mrs. Klimmings," the nurse said to her. "We need the room."

"No!" Vicki shouted, resisting the nurse. "I can't leave her!"

Another nurse joined in and took Vicki's left arm. "Mrs. Klimmings, we need the room."

"No! What is going on with her?!"

The nurses continued to try to remove Vicki from the room but failed to succeed in their efforts. Finally, the doctors pulled up the side rails to Miranda's bed and began to move her out of the room.

"She needs an emergency cesarean if we are to save her and the baby!" a doctor called out as they rushed Miranda down the hall toward one of the surgery rooms.

\* \* \*

Henry sat in his office, mulling through documents on his desk. A desk lamp was all that illuminated the room. In the corner, a TV was on with continuing coverage of the crisis between the United States and China. Outside his office, the West Wing remained quiet, just like it usually was after midnight.

As Henry continued to flip through the papers, his attention was taken away by something a news anchor said.

"An increasing amount of Russian troops have been seen increasing along the border near Vladivostok. This raises more concerns about how the Russians may take advantage of the increasing tensions between China and the U.S."

Henry set the papers down and took a sip of his coffee as he became more intrigued with the TV.

"So far," one of the news anchors continued. "There have been no comments made by the Russian president."

He looked back down at the papers and let out a deep sigh.

"Please, Peter," Henry said to himself. "Please don't let this be a part of your plan."

\* \* \*

Clark stepped inside the George and Jefferson Coffee Shop. He looked toward the bar and began scanning the tables before seeing Delilah seated. Her back was to him, and she was scrolling on her phone. He smiled before proceeding to make his way over to her.

"Hey," he said as he took the seat across from Delilah.

"Clark!" Delilah exclaimed as she set her phone down. "You scared me!"

He apologized, noticed her drink, and continued. "What did you get to drink?"

"Oh," Delilah began, picking up her drink. "I just got an iced coffee." She took a sip from her coffee. "It's the perfect drink to help cool down on this hot July day."

Clark let out a forced laugh. As he looked at Delilah and then back at her coffee, he began thinking about why he was meeting her here.

"So," Clark began before deciding to change the subject. "Did you hear about what happened to Miranda last night?"

"Oh my God," Delilah let out. "I did. It's so horrible! I'm so concerned for her and the baby!"

"I barely caught it on the news," Clark said. "So much of it has been consumed with what's happening in the Pacific."

"I know." Delilah took a sip of her coffee. "And you know all of this will blow over. I was married to Ben for four years, and I dealt with the president all the time! He'll get sidetracked with something else and then move on."

Clark shook his head slowly. "I don't know," he said. "It's all so concerning."

"Yes, it is," Delilah sighed. She took another sip of her coffee and then sat it back down on the table. She glanced around the room, trying to formulate something to discuss next with Clark. However, before she could come up with something, Clark decided to come out and ask her his own question.

"Delilah, why did you ask me here this morning?"

She looked up into Clark's eyes. She could see that he knew why she wanted to meet with him. All she needed to do now was to say it to him. But with every attempt she made, Delilah couldn't form the words.

Clark sighed. "This is it, isn't it?"

Remaining silent, Delilah slightly nodded her head. All that could be heard were the conversations of others that filled the coffee shop, along with the sounds of coffee grounds in the grinder. For an exchange that took only seconds, it felt like an eternity.

Finally, Delilah sighed and said, "I didn't want things to turn out this way, Clark."

He looked at her as she continued explaining herself.

"I had every intention of making this work with you, Clark," Delilah said. "I really did."

Clark tried to hide the disgust he had inside him, but the look he displayed told Delilah that he didn't understand her reasoning.

"I'm sorry," Delilah said.

"Are you?" Clark asked. "Are you, Delilah?"

"Yes."

"You led me on for over a year! You promised that you would leave your husband. You got pregnant and had his child, Delilah. Then, when you finally divorced . . . i-it's almost like you're done with me."

Delilah remained quiet at the table. She tried to come up with something to say but couldn't form the words with her lips.

"Don't waste your breath, Delilah," Clark interjected. He leaned forward slightly, trying to make better eye contact with Delilah. "Be honest with me, Delilah . . . you still love him, don't you?"

Delilah didn't say anything.

"Don't you?!"

Once again, she said nothing. Clark swallowed hard before standing up from the table and running his hand through his hair. He began to say something but refrained from adding any more to the conversation. Instead, he sighed deeply and then headed out of the coffee shop, leaving Delilah to herself.

\* \* \*

Jeremy stepped into the living room to see Cathie taking in the news from the TV. He glanced toward it to see that the report was covering the accident that Miranda Klimmings had been involved in. Immediately, Jeremy took a deep sigh.

"Have you seen this?" Cathie turned to him. She tossed the remote onto the coffee table and stepped toward her husband. "Do you see what you've caused?"

Jeremy stood shocked at what his wife had said. "*I've* caused?!"

"Yes," Cathie responded. "You caused this, Jeremy! If it hadn't been for your obsessive desire to spite the president, perhaps none of this would have happened!"

"Cathie," Jeremy began. "I had nothing to do with this. Peter did it on his own when he pissed off the Chinese president and then tried to outdo him. As a result, we have this crisis that's going on in the Pacific!"

Cathie didn't respond but instead turned back to the TV. Jeremy took in a deep breath before he added to his comment.

"Besides, why would I have deliberately done something to harm my business in China?"

Cathie turned back to Jeremy. "I don't understand you sometimes, Jeremy. Sometimes you act like you would do whatever it takes to get back at Peter and then other times . . ."

Jeremy waited for her to finish her comment. However, she didn't and instead turned back to the TV.

"Other times, I what?" Jeremy asked, stepping between Cathie and the TV.

She stared at her husband and took a sigh.

"I'm calling Vicki," Cathie said before turning and grabbing her phone from the end table behind her. As she passed by Jeremy, she said, "Don't bother me."

* * *

Charlotte searched file after file on her computer in the lobby of Klimmings Incorporated. She wasn't looking for anything, in particular, other than what may be hidden away on the company servers.

The office had been eerily quiet throughout the entire day. This wasn't a surprise to Charlotte as most of the country continued panicking because of the escalating crisis with China, and the Klimmings family was preoccupied with Miranda's condition in the hospital. Given that, Charlotte hadn't considered how incredibly dull it would be sitting at the receptionist's desk all day. She had received no visitors, seen no other employees, and hadn't even had to answer a single phone call for the entire time she had been in the office.

As she continued to mull through the files on the Klimmings Incorporated server, she heard the elevator open from behind her. She quickly minimized the window on the computer and turned to see a young woman whom she recognized coming into the lobby.

"Michelle?" Charlotte said as the woman stopped by her desk. "It is Michelle, right?"

"Yes," Michelle said, adjusting her hair slightly. "Is Mrs. Klimmings in here today?"

"No," Charlotte said as she stood from her seat. "She's at the hospital with her daughter."

Michelle sighed and looked disappointed. This reaction irritated Charlotte, who cleared her throat and continued speaking to Michelle.

"Speaking of her daughter . . . it came to my attention that you and your friend, Diane . . ."

"Dana," Michelle interrupted.

Charlotte glared at her before continuing. "Whatever . . . but you and *Dana* acted foolishly to my niece when you last saw her. In fact, I learned that you not only cut her out of your little group, but you also had the audacity to make a social media post labeling her as a lesbian."

Michelle hung her head in embarrassment, and Charlotte continued. She let her anger toward Michelle control the words she spoke.

"My older sister may have the capacity to forgive you, Michelle, but I, on the other hand, do not. How *dare* you insult my favorite niece and then proceed to parade in here asking for her whereabouts?!"

Michelle looked back up at Charlotte and wiped a tear from her eye.

"Ma'am," she said. "We just want to apologize to her. We were absolute assholes to her. And now that she's disappeared and we've graduated, we want to make amends – at least before we part ways and head to college."

Charlotte rolled her eyes. "Well," she began before pausing and thinking about what to say. "If you're so concerned about finding her, then why don't you just write to her?"

"That's why I'm here," Michelle replied. "After I stopped here last week, I was able to make contact with St. Mary's."

Charlotte perked up. "You did what?"

"I called the school Gabby is at," she said. "They answered, and I asked about Gabby."

"And what did they say?"

"Nothing. They wouldn't answer any of my questions. I literally got nowhere. And now, I have no other choice but to ask Mrs. Klimmings if she can take me to see her."

Charlotte let out a soft laugh. "Good luck with that. I've been trying to visit my niece for the past couple of months now, and every time I bring up the idea, Vicki shoots it down." She let out a deep sigh. "It's like . . ."

She stopped mid-sentence, forcing herself not to dive into deeper speculation. However, Michelle caught what she was about to say and continued the thought.

". . . she's hiding something?"

Charlotte looked back at Michelle.

"Ma'am," Michelle said. "You don't think she is, do you?"

"I don't know," Charlotte shook her head. "No. Vicki wouldn't hide Gabby away from all of us. It's not in her character."

"Are you sure?"

Charlotte remained silent, not knowing how to answer Michelle's question. She didn't want to agree with her, but the more she had been left in limbo regarding Gabby, the more she had begun her own speculation about what was going on.

"Look," Charlotte finally said. "I don't know what to tell you, girl. You're just going to have to ask Vicki whenever she is back in the office."

"Do you know when that will be?"

"No. I can't tell you anything about what is going on at the hospital with Miranda. I haven't been able to reach anyone about it."

Michelle sighed. "Well, I guess I'll be back sometime next week or so." She began to head back to the elevator but turned back to Charlotte again. "Thank you for your help. And I hope that Miranda is alright."

"Yeah, me too."

Michelle drew down the corners of her mouth and slightly nodded before turning back to the elevator and leaving Charlotte alone again in the lobby. She looked around and let out a deep sigh before sitting back down in her chair. She glanced over toward the empty office that used to be Ben's and then moved her gaze to Vicki's. She pondered over the many thoughts racing through her head and then got up and made her way over to the door. She opened it and stared into the dark office. The only light shining in the room was the bright sunlight barely showing through the drawn shades.

Charlotte stepped into the office and walked over to Vicki's desk before sitting in her chair. She looked over the items on the desk and then drew open Vicki's right top drawer. The first item she saw was a pack of cigarettes that had been opened. She picked them up and examined them. *Why does she have these in here? I thought she had stopped smoking before Miranda's birth.*

She placed them back in the drawer and quickly slammed it closed. In doing so, a picture frame fell over onto the desk, laying face down. Charlotte sighed in annoyance and then picked it up. She looked at the face of it and saw an image of the Klimmings children posing in front of a Christmas tree. All three of them appeared much younger, with Miranda and Ben clearly in their teens and Gabby as a young child. Charlotte recognized the background of the image as the living room in the Klimmings Mansion, so she knew that it had to be from a family Christmas from years past.

As she looked over the image, she thought back to what Michelle had alluded to. *Was Vicki hiding something about Gabby?*

She placed the picture frame back onto the top of the desk and then made her way out of the office and back to the receptionist's desk. She spun herself around in her chair so that she was facing her computer and promptly opened a new tab on the browser. She typed in the words: *St. Mary's.*

Charlotte looked over the search bar for a moment, questioning whether to continue looking into this. Then, she took a deep breath and pressed the "search" button.

\* \* \*

Peter sat alone in the waiting room at Walter Reed. Vicki had just stepped out with Ben after they finally convinced her to go for a brief walk and try to get some fresh air. He hadn't been alone for long before his phone rang. Peter took out his phone and looked at the screen before answering it. "Mr. Gates?"

"Mr. President," Henry began over the phone. "We need you back at the White House as soon as possible."

Peter's eyes widened, and his mouth dropped open a bit. "What the hell for?" He stood up from the seat he was in. "I am at the hospital right now waiting for my daughter to get out of the operating room."

"I understand, sir," Henry continued. "But a situation has started to arise within the last twenty-four hours. The National Security Council wants to call together an emergency meeting in the Situation Room."

"What is this emergency, Mr. Gates?" Peter asked. "Can you give me something to go by, or are you just going to leave me in the dark so that I'm like a duck swimming out onto a pond on opening day?"

Henry sighed over the phone. "Mr. President, we've received recent intel that the Russians are gathering troops near the Chinese border, similar to what they did with the invasion of Ukraine over ten years ago."

"And?"

"Mr. President, I'm concerned that if this isn't taken seriously, we could end up in a much more dire situation than what we're already in."

Peter paused for a moment, looking around the waiting room and out into the hall to see if anyone was listening in.

"Mr. Gates," he said. "Don't worry about any of it. I have it all under control."

"What does that mean, sir?"

"It means . . . I have it all under control. I'll fill you in more whenever I return to the White House. For now, keep everyone calm."

Peter waited for a response but hadn't received one quickly enough. He continued on.

"Mr. Gates . . . trust me on this one. It's all going to be fine."

He looked up and saw the surgeon approaching him. "I've got to go, Mr. Gates. I'll text you when I'll be arriving back."

He ended the call and placed his phone into the pocket on the inside of his suit jacket. Then, as he adjusted himself, Peter looked up to the surgeon, who had just made his way out of the operating room. He approached Peter in the hallway.

"Mr. President," the surgeon addressed him. "Your daughter made it out of surgery."

"How is she?"

* * *

Henry tossed his phone onto his desk, leaned back in his chair, and ran his hands through what little hair he had left.

"What did he say?" Constance asked him. She was sitting in front of his desk along with Secretary Eric Bird and Secretary Janet Steele.

"He blew it off," Henry let out. "I don't understand him anymore. He's acting like this whole thing is no big deal!"

"Perhaps it's his daughter right now," Janet tried to suggest. "She was just in a serious accident. I mean, the girl is pregnant."

"It's not just that," Henry continued. "He's been blowing off this crisis from the beginning. He keeps saying that he's got it all under control!"

"What if he does?" Constance asked. Henry turned his attention to her as the room fell silent. The growing quiet spoke volumes as each person glanced at the other. No words were spoken, yet each knew what they were thinking.

* * *

Miranda slowly opened her eyes, taking a couple of tries to open them fully. Still drowsy, she looked around the dim room. She only heard the heartbeat monitor continuously making the familiar beeping sound, telling the technicians that her heart rate was steady. As she continued to look around, she noticed her dad sitting beside her bed.

"Dad?" she said, trying to figure out whether he was real or not.

"Honey," Peter said, taking her hand. "It's okay."

Miranda looked confused. "What happened?"

"You were in an accident," Peter began. "The doctors . . . they did all they could do . . . you have to understand that."

"What?" Miranda asked, still confused. "What about my baby? How's my baby?"

Peter remained quiet as he placed his other hand on Miranda's. Then, he leaned forward and continued on. "They said that you had something called a traumatic uterine rupture caused by the airbags deploying from your accident. They hadn't noticed it when you first came in, but once you started hemorrhaging, the doctors had to act fast."

Miranda began to look distraught. "What about my baby, Dad? What happened to him?"

Peter swallowed and quietly cleared his throat. "We lost the baby." He looked Miranda in the eyes and lightly patted her hands. "But you . . . you're going to be okay, Miranda." He slightly squeezed her hand as a tear pooled up in his eye. "You're going to be okay."

# CHAPTER 9
## BABY BLUES AND TEARS

"Panic buying and mass hysteria have continued across the country for the better part of two weeks now, following President Klimmings' failed summit with the Chinese President in June. After a nontraditional Fourth of July, Americans are continuing to worry about the future of our country."

Henry gestured toward the TV in the Oval Office with his attention focused on Peter.

"Do you see what I mean?" Henry asked. "The country has gone to hell-in-a-handbasket."

Peter glanced at Henry and then back to the TV.

"Some promising news occurred this morning when China began to recall ships from the South China Sea and the Pacific to deal with growing unrest in the country caused by members of the Grand Rebellion who are seeking to oust President Wu and replace him with new leadership."

"See, Mr. Gates," Peter added. "I told you it was all under control."

"Mr. President," Henry exclaimed. "That doesn't account for the growing number of Russian troops near the Chinese border! We cannot just brush this off and pretend like nothing is happening over there."

"Mr. Gates," Peter said. "I've told you over and over again that it was all under control, yet you continue to doubt me in everything that I am saying."

"Because you're not listening to us!"

"I don't need to listen to you all! I know exactly what is going on!"

"No, you don't, sir!"

"Yes, I do, Mr. Gates!" Peter hesitated before finally saying, "It's me!"

Henry stopped for a moment. "What?"

Peter took a deep breath and ran his hand through his blond hair.

"Sit down, Mr. Gates," he said before he rounded the *Resolute* desk and led Henry to one of the cream-colored sofas before taking a seat across from him. "Let me talk to you about something."

\* \* \*

President Wu looked out the window in his office. Down on the streets, more and more people gathered in protest. He watched all the people march up and down the road. Some were holding signs, and others were just chanting loud enough that President Wu could hear some of their muffled sayings in his office.

"President Wu?"

He turned around and saw one of his advisors standing in the doorway to his office. "Yes?"

"President Wu," the advisor continued. "Unfortunately, our actions against the Grand Rebellion haven't had the effect we had wanted."

"Are you saying that our efforts have failed?" President Wu asked.

The advisor swallowed. "I am, sir."

The Chinese president nodded his head. "Thank you."

"Sir?"

President Wu looked back up at his advisor. "Yes?"

"I also regret to tell you that many in the Communist Party have started questioning their confidence in your ability to lead the country."

President Wu cocked his head slightly. "What?!"

"I'm sorry, sir," the advisor said again. "But some of them have begun calling for your resignation."

"This is ridiculous!" President Wu exclaimed, growing more furious. "No president has ever resigned over protests before!"

The advisor remained silent with his head hung until President Wu stopped talking.

"I'm sorry," he said to the Chinese president. "I'm just telling you the truth. I've served with you for many years, and I know that you'd want to know."

President Wu let out a deep sigh. "You're right. You were only doing your job." He turned back to look out the window at the growing number of people marching along the street.

"Do you need anything, sir?"

"No," President Wu said without turning back. "That's all."

The advisor opened his mouth to say something else but stopped short of it. Instead, he turned and stepped out of the office, leaving President Wu alone to continue his observations and mull over his options.

* * *

"So *you* were behind it all?"

"That's what I said," Peter responded to Henry, who was slightly shocked.

"You met with the Grand Rebellion *and* the Russians secretly?" Henry asked.

"Not the Russians," Peter clarified. "I only spoke with the Russian president over the phone. He seemed eager to rebuild relations with the United States."

"But you met with the Grand Rebellion," Henry said, shocked and somewhat lost for words. "How did you know that they weren't going to kill you whenever you had your meeting?"

"I didn't go there alone," Peter said. "I took Secretary Bird with me, along with my Secret Service detail." He paused for a moment. "That, and Kang Tu and Shao Cheng wouldn't have done anything to have jeopardized any shot they had at ousting President Wu. They hate him."

"But . . ." Henry continued. "Why did you continue to escalate things? Why did you ground all air travel and close the border and allow all those people to think that a war was coming?"

Peter sighed. "Mr. Gates, I had to convince the American people that this was real. I had to show them that I would do whatever I could to protect this country and its people."

"But, Mr. President, did you ever consider the implications that this would have?"

"Hell yeah, I did! Being reelected is the only thing that is important right now!" Peter leaned back and smiled. "Once this is over, I will have more than solidified my chances of reelection."

"Sir," Henry added. "Have you even checked any of the headlines recently?"

"Yes."

"All of them?"

"What the hell do you mean by all of them? I told you that I read the headlines!"

Henry pulled out his phone from his jacket pocket. He clicked on a couple of things before showing Peter the phone. Peter took it from Henry and looked closely at the screen. He scrolled through the headlines: "White Champions Polls Against Klimmings"; "Klimmings Conundrum: Crisis in China Kills Reelection Chances,"; and "Why a Second Peter Klimmings Term Would Destroy America." Peter scrolled through the feed and saw more headlines similar to what he had just read.

Peter looked up at Henry in shock. "How long have these been circulating?"

Henry cleared his throat. "They started shortly after the crisis in China began."

Peter looked back at the phone and then tossed it onto the coffee table between him and Henry. "Dammit!"

"Mr. President," Henry said, taking his phone from the table and looking it over. "We need to de-escalate all of this. We can't allow this to continue on."

"No, I can fix this!"

"Mr. President, this has gotten more out of hand than what you had anticipated. You can't let this keep going on."

"It will be fine, Mr. Gates! When the American people learn that I've begun a dialogue with the Russians and calmed tensions in that realm, the polls will fix themselves."

"No, they won't, Mr. President," Henry stated. "Nothing is going to fix itself until you fix this damn crisis!"

Peter's eyes widened, shocked by this response. He swallowed and calmly said, "I think it's time you step out of my office, Mr. Gates."

"I think so, too," Henry responded. He stood up from the sofa and headed to the door that would take him down the hall to his office. He opened it, paused, and then turned back to Peter.

"Mr. President . . . think about it all. The last thing I would want is for you to lose next year." He started to step out but stopped once again. "Your father wouldn't want your legacy to die because of this."

Before Peter could respond, Henry had already stepped out of the office, leaving him alone with his thoughts.

* * *

Charlotte sat behind the receptionist desk at Klimmings Incorporated with the contact information pulled up on her computer. She looked over the phone number one more time and then took her phone off the receiver and dialed the number. She rolled her eyes and sighed as she put the phone to her ear, expecting she wouldn't get through once again.

"Hello?"

Charlotte's eyes widened after hearing a woman with a distinct Swiss accent answer.

"Hello?" Charlotte responded. "Are you there?"

"Yes," the woman said. "Our phones have been down. A strong mountain clipper came through and knocked out our phone lines."

"That explains a lot, then," Charlotte said.

"Sorry, ma'am. We just got them fixed. Is there something I can help you with?"

"Yes," Charlotte began. "This is the number for St. Mary's in the Alps, right?"

"That's right," the woman said. "St. Mary's Academy for Young Women . . ."

"Great. I am calling to inquire about one of your students."

"Who would that be, ma'am? We have a lot of high-profile students at our school, so I can see if I can give you any answers you're looking for."

"Well," Charlotte continued. "I'm Charlotte Lee, sister-in-law to President Klimmings of the United States."

"Oh."

"I just wanted to inquire about his daughter, Gabby . . . I mean, Gabriella. She started there around February . . ."

"Ms. Lee," the woman interrupted. "I can't give you any information on the president's daughter, but I will add that St. Mary's does not accept any mid-year enrollments."

"What?"

"It's board policy that every student must begin at the start of the academic year."

"So there's no way that she could have started in February?"

"Ms. Lee," the woman repeated. "As I said earlier, it's board policy . . ."

"I know . . . I know . . ." Charlotte paused, mulling through her thoughts. "Can I speak with the head of the school?"

"The headmistress doesn't like to discuss students and academics over the phone, Ms. Lee."

"That's fine," Charlotte said. "Set up a meeting between herself and me. I'll fly over there if that's what it takes."

\* \* \*

The car ride home was silent. The radio remained off as Vicki drove down the small highway that would take her and Miranda to the Klimmings Mansion. She looked over at Miranda, who remained motionless and silent, looking out the window at all the passing scenery. Numerous times throughout the drive, Vicki opened her mouth to offer more comforting words to Miranda but failed to get anything out. She wrestled with whether remaining silent or trying to get Miranda to talk about her feelings would be the best way to go.

Instead, she decided to remain quiet. *Perhaps she's sorting through her feelings right now?* Vicki continued to think things over as she drove. As she looked ahead, she spotted a young woman standing beside the road. Vicki recognized her and her blond hair.

"Gabriella?"

Miranda took her attention away from the scenery and looked over at Vicki. She still didn't say a word, but it was enough for Vicki to glance back over at her.

"I thought I saw something," Vicki said. "Must be tired."

Miranda turned her attention back to the window, ignoring the entire exchange she had just had with her mother.

Once again, Vicki opened her mouth to say something else but stopped short of it, deciding that now was not the proper time to engage in any conversation with Miranda.

* * *

"Dana, I'm so glad you made it over!"

Michelle held the door open so that her friend, Dana, could enter her apartment.

"Well, I received text after text from you," Dana said as Michelle closed the door behind her. "I could only assume that someone died or something."

"That's the thing," Michelle said as she moved over to sit on her couch. "I think somebody did."

Dana looked confused as she took a seat in an old chair adjacent to the couch. She looked around the apartment, noticing how run-down it appeared. The wallpaper was peeling off the wall in some spots, and there were a few stains on the carpet.

"This all you could afford?" Dana asked her.

"Don't change the subject!" Michelle snapped back. "And for your information, this is only a temporary living spot for me. After my parents learned what we did to Gabby, they kicked my ass out of that house."

Dana shook her head. "That's a damn shame, then."

"That ordeal really screwed things up for us," Michelle continued. "It ruined relationships with our friends and family and put a huge strain on us."

"I know," Dana said. "Sometimes when I think back at some of the things we did . . ."

"I know," Michelle said before shifting the conversation back to where she had wanted it to go earlier. "Anyways, I need to talk to you about Gabby."

"Why her?"

"Dana, we single-handedly screwed up her life. And then, after February, she just disappeared."

"I do have to admit," Dana added. "That is pretty strange."

"It is," Michelle said. "And every time I try to talk to her mom about it . . ."

"You've what?"

"I've tried to talk with her family and . . ."

"Dammit, Michelle! I've told you that you need to leave them alone! They've got nothing to say to any of us. They haven't before, and they won't ever!"

"But that's the thing, Dana. I met with her aunt, who is starting to believe that the Klimmings family is hiding something about her."

"Seriously?!" Dana exclaimed. "What did she say?"

"She's said that she has questioned about Gabby a few times and hasn't gotten anywhere. The only thing we know about her is that she is at some school in Switzerland."

Dana raised an eyebrow. "Perhaps she doesn't want anything to do with us anymore, Michelle. We were extremely shitty to her. Do you blame her for wanting to get away from us and never wanting to see us again?"

Michelle remained quiet as Dana stood up from the chair she was in. "I'm going to head out, Michelle." She headed over to the door and opened it.

"I wouldn't screw around with that family, Michelle," Dana continued. "I highly doubt they're going to give you anything that'll get you any closer to Gabby."

Dana closed the door behind her, leaving Michelle alone in her apartment. She wiped a few tears from her eyes before heading over to the refrigerator and taking out a wine cooler. She popped off the cap and took a sip, calming herself.

* * *

"So, how is she doing?" Delilah asked Ben in Katherine's nursery. "Is there anything I can help with?"

"I think she's going to be fine," Ben said as he picked Katherine up from her crib. "It's just going to take some time."

Delilah nodded as the two headed out of the room and proceeded down the hall. As they continued, Ben asked, "So, how are things going with you?"

Promptly, she stopped in the hall and sighed. "They're going."

"What do you mean by that?"

"Well, I had been seeing someone, but that ended yesterday."

Ben looked confused. "Why?"

"I don't know," Delilah sighed. "There were just some conflicting things between us, and it didn't work out."

"Was this with Clark?"

Delilah remained quiet. She hung her head and then responded. "Yes."

Ben let out a soft laugh. "Isn't it ironic that the relationship that ended our marriage didn't last?"

Delilah smiled as she looked back at Ben. "I guess it is."

The two continued down the hallway as a muffled sound of thunder rustled through the house.

"You know our old townhouse was burned down, right?" Ben asked Delilah.

"What?!" she exclaimed. "When?!"

"A few days ago," Ben responded. "A group of protestors attacked it and set it on fire."

"Damn," Delilah said. "I liked that little house too."

"I know you did . . . but I wouldn't want to move back into it after I've been staying at the mansion."

"True. Since I've been home, I don't know that I would ever want to move back into something that small again."

Finally, the two made it to the living room and the front door. They noticed Ryan in the living room with the TV on.

"Is he planning to leave soon?" he asked.

"Yeah," Ben said. "I was just about to take Katherine home for the weekend."

"Well, it looks like you'll be here for a while," Ryan said, motioning to the TV. Delilah and Ben both turned their attention toward it.

"There's a big storm rolling in," he continued. "There could be some hail along with it." Ryan stepped closer to Ben. "I wouldn't want my niece to get hurt in it."

"Ryan!" Delilah interrupted. "Ben knows how to take care of his daughter!"

"It's fine . . . it's fine . . ." Ben said. "I handled your brother's smartass comments for four years. I think I can still put up with them today."

Ryan raised an eyebrow as if to come back with another comment, but Delilah interjected, preventing any further disputes between the two.

"Don't worry about him," Delilah said to Ben. "Let me take you to the den. I'll wait with you in there until after the storm."

\* \* \*

Denise opened the door just before the rain began to fall, allowing Vicki and Miranda to step inside without getting wet.

"Thank you, Denise," Vicki said as the house servant closed the door behind her. "It was beginning to look scary out there."

"I heard," Denise replied. "The thunder was rattling the entire house earlier."

Vicki stepped into the living room and went behind the sofa to peer out the window. "It's very dark out too. We haven't had a good storm like this for a while."

Denise followed her into the living room and then asked, "Where did Miss Miranda go?"

Vicki turned around just to catch a glimpse of Miranda heading up the stairs.

"She went up the stairs, Denise," Vicki said. "She's having a difficult time with all of this."

Vicki proceeded to make her way over to the bottom of the stairwell but stopped short of going up them.

"It's so sad," Denise added. "It's happened to someone so sweet and undeserving."

"I know . . ." Vicki said. "And I don't know how to help her with any of it."

* * *

Miranda made it to the landing at the top of the stairs. She looked at each of the doors before turning left to head into her room. She latched the door behind her and stood in her dark room. Lightning flashed, and thunder rumbled in the background as Miranda looked at the baby blue curtains that hung beside her windows. Then she stepped over to her bed and lifted the covers before crawling in.

She lay in the dark, under her bedsheets, listening to the rain patter on the roof above her.

* * *

Vicki looked down at her watch, which indicated that Charlotte was calling. She went back into the living room and over to her bag, which was sitting on the coffee table. She dug through it and pulled out her phone.

"Yes, Charlotte."

"Vicki," Charlotte said over the phone. "I hate to do this to you, but

I need to be out of the office for a few days."

"What?" Vicki responded. "I've been counting on you to be there while I've been out."

"I understand, but I need to deal with some things right now with George. He keeps stalling out this divorce."

Vicki sighed. "Fine, Charlotte," she said. "I'll figure something out."

"I really am sorry. I just hope that George finally agrees to make a deal with the lawyers."

"I understand," Vicki said. "Let me know how it goes."

"I will."

Vicki ended the call and looked at Denise. "My sister . . ."

"Mrs. Klimmings," Denise added. "I could say many things about that woman, but I value my job too much."

Vicki smiled as she sat her phone down on the coffee table.

"Is there anything you need right now, Mrs. Klimmings?"

"No, Denise. I'm fine."

"Well," Denise added. "If you need me, I'll be in the kitchen."

Denise stepped out of the room, turning down the entry hall and taking a right down the side hall. Vicki turned toward the bar and stepped over to it, looking at the family picture on the wall. It still hadn't been changed since Ben and Delilah's divorce, showcasing everyone in the Klimmings family. As Vicki looked over the image, her eyes stopped on Gabby. Suddenly she had been inundated with memories of her youngest. She recalled the first moment she held her and the first time she started school.

Vicki felt tears pooling in her eyes, so she turned away from the image and made her way over to the sofa. She sat down and adjusted her hair before she wiped her eyes with her hands. Then she fell over to her side and made herself comfortable on the sofa, listening to the rain outside and soft thunder in the distance.

* * *

Charlotte put her phone in her bag and looked over to the seat next to her on the airplane where Michelle was seated.

"Are you sure this is a good idea?" Michelle asked her as she buckled up her seatbelt.

"Yes, I am," Charlotte said. "It's been too long since we've heard anything about Gabby, and I want some answers."

* * *

Delilah stepped into the den after laying Katherine down, seeing Ben looking through his phone.

"Have you seen this?" he asked her as she sat in a chair next to him. "President Wu just stepped down."

"President who?"

"President Wu," Ben reiterated. "The Chinese president." He paused to see if Delilah was understanding yet. "The guy who's been the biggest pain in the ass to my father."

"I thought that was *my* dad," Delilah said before laughing.

Ben joined in with her. "True, true. But things have gotten pretty scary between my dad and President Wu." Ben locked his phone and set it on the armrest of the chair. "Perhaps this will be the end of this terrible ordeal."

"I hope so," Delilah said. She looked at Ben just as he turned to look back at her.

"Are you sure I can't head back over there?" Ben asked, trying to change the subject. "It doesn't sound that bad out."

"I think it's lightened up some," Delilah responded. "But I think that it wouldn't hurt to wait for a little longer."

"I guess," Ben said. "I just think taking Katherine home right now would help things with my mom."

Delilah nodded. "Yeah, I think that Katherine would help to ease some of the feelings over."

"Yeah." Ben fell silent, looking down toward the ground.

As silence fell between the two, Delilah felt herself wanting Ben. The attraction she felt for him was incomparable with any she had before.

"Ben," Delilah said, garnering his attention. "Why didn't you ask why my relationship with Clark ended?"

Ben looked up at Delilah. "Why?"

"I think you know the answer to that, Ben."

He looked Delilah in the eyes and smiled slightly. "You know . . . I never stopped loving you, Delilah."

"I know," she smiled back at him. "Neither did I."

Delilah leaned in closer to Ben, letting her lips connect with his. He placed his hands on the side of her face, holding her. As the two continued kissing, Delilah reached over to the lamp and flicked it off.

\* \* \*

Ding-dong!

Vicki opened her eyes. The rain outside had stopped, and she could tell that a few hours had passed since falling asleep on the sofa. She sat up and rubbed her face with her hands.

Ding-dong!

"Denise," she called out. "Would you get that?"

Vicki stood from the sofa and stretched her arms before letting out a big yawn.

Ding-dong!

She sighed and rolled her eyes. "Nevermind, Denise!" Vicki said. "I got it."

She made her way into the entry hall and over to the door. She took a deep breath to try to wake up even more. Then she took the doorknob and opened it.

Standing in the doorway was a familiar teenage girl with blond hair. She smiled as she saw Vicki, who looked utterly shocked.

"*Gabriella?!*"

# CHAPTER 10

## GABRIELLA

Vicki stood in the doorway in shock. She couldn't believe what she was seeing. Her eyes widened as she looked over her daughter.

"Gabriella?" Vicki asked. "Is that you?"

"In the flesh, Mother!" she said. "Now, are you going to let me in or not?"

Vicki looked confused but stepped aside so Gabby could step inside. "W-what . . . why . . . h-how?"

"Shhhh," Gabby said to her mother. "Don't ask questions. It'll take too long to explain to you."

Vicki still looked bewildered as she closed the door. She opened her mouth to say something else but was stopped whenever Denise turned the corner into the entry hall.

"Miss Gabriella!" Denise exclaimed when she saw Gabby. "I'm so glad to see you back home again!"

Gabby opened her arms to hug Denise. As the two embraced, Vicki stood off to the side, still in disbelief.

"Gabriella," she said. "Let's step into the living room."

"Are you going to ask about my stay at St. Mary's?" Gabby asked her, giving a stern look that showed she knew everything that had happened since she had left.

"Denise," Vicki said. "Could you excuse us for a moment?"

"Sure," Denise said. "Dinner is almost done. Would you like for me to go ahead and set the table?"

"Yes. We'll be in whenever Peter gets home."

Vicki turned back to Gabby and led her into the living room, where the two sat down on the sofa.

"Gabriella," Vicki began. "How did this happen? How are you here right now? We found you dead in your room. Your dad had you buried in the family plot. I saw you being placed into the ground. How can this be?"

Vicki began tearing up and started wiping her eyes with her hands. While she did this, Gabby took her right hand in hers.

"Mom," she said. "Dad had it arranged to where I was sent off somewhere between the time you and Ben went downstairs and when Dad and that Secret Service guy took my body outside."

"But that just sounds too crazy," Vicki said, wiping the rest of the tears from her face.

"Because it is too crazy," Gabby continued. "Dad had me taken to a place out in the middle of God-knows-where, and they did all these tests and stuff." She paused as she pushed her hair back behind her ears. "Basically, they saved my life."

Vicki coughed quietly. "So basically, you were alive this entire time?"

"Basically."

"And you heard all the news reports and such?"

"I heard some stuff," Gabby said. "Someone mentioned to me about the St. Mary's cover. Why the hell would you say that I was sent off to school in Switzerland?"

"*Language . . .*" Vicki said, correcting her. "And that was your father who came up with that crock of bull story."

Gabby rolled her eyes and shook her head. "Where is everyone, anyways?"

"Well," Vicki sighed. "Your father should be coming home anytime; Benjamin is picking Katherine up from the Applegates', and Miranda is upstairs."

"Upstairs?!" Gabby exclaimed as she jumped up from the sofa. "Why didn't you say anything sooner?"

She started past Vicki but was stopped by a tug on her shirt. She turned to see Vicki holding onto her.

"Gabriella," she said, looking deep into her eyes. "I need to tell you something about Miranda."

* * *

Miranda lay alone in her room. Because the thunderstorm had subsided, no light had shown inside her bedroom, leaving her in the dark with just her thoughts. She hadn't fallen asleep throughout the entirety of the time that she had been in her bed.

Then, the door cracked open, allowing the light from the landing to shine into the room. Miranda slowly turned toward the door, squinting her eyes as she tried to figure out who it was that was standing there.

Finally, the person in the doorway stepped into the room, and Miranda recognized who it was. "Gabby?"

"Miranda," Gabby said as she came over to her sister's bed. She sat down at the end and made eye contact with her sister. "I'm so sorry."

A few tears welled up in Miranda's eyes. "You're back from St. Mary's," she said as she tried to wipe her eyes with her bedsheet.

"I am," Gabby lied. "I just wish I had been here to help you with what happened."

"Gabby," Miranda sighed. "You wouldn't have caused it to come out any other way."

"I know . . . but I feel like I could've just been there to help you with some things."

Miranda shook her head. "No. You can't think that way, Gabby."

She looked Miranda in the eyes. "You know I love you, right?"

"Gabby," Miranda sighed. "I have always known that. We've

always had that sisterly connection."

"I've missed that," Gabby said. "I haven't had anyone to talk to about things for a while now."

"So," Miranda added. "Do you think you will be staying home for a while or heading back to St. Mary's?"

Gabby smiled. "I think I'll be here for a while."

* * *

Peter stepped into the entry hall, closing the door behind him. He took in a deep breath of relief and placed his suitcase down by the door. He took one step down the hall before Vicki turned the corner from the living room.

"About time you got home," Vicki said. She had an expression of fury that Peter had only witnessed a few times before.

"What the hell is going on?" Peter asked. "Why do you look so pissed off?"

"Come into the living room, Peter," Vicki said slyly. "We need to talk."

Curious, Peter followed Vicki into the living room. He took a seat in the first chair in the room. Vicki sat down on the sofa.

"What are you wanting to talk to me about?"

"Peter," Vicki began. "I don't know why you do some of the things you do . . ."

"Does this have to do with the whole China ordeal?" Peter asked.

"No, but I wish it had something to do with the China problem."

"Then what is it?"

Vicki took in a deep breath. "Would you like a drink?"

"What the hell, Vicki? Just tell me what you want to talk to me about."

"You want a drink with this," Vicki said as she got up and headed to the bar. "What'll it be . . . Scotch or bourbon?"

"For something that's this suspenseful," Peter said. "I guess I'm gonna need a Scotch."

Vicki took the decanter of Scotch and poured Peter a glass. Then, she turned around and made her way over to him, giving him the drink.

"Thank you," he said as he took a sip of the Scotch.

"Someone came by to visit today," Vicki said after sitting on the sofa.

"Really?" Peter said, surprised. "Who?"

"I think you know who it is."

"Vicki, would you just tell me who the hell it is? I've been busy all day."

"Well," Vicki began. "I just want you to understand what went through my head whenever I received a knock at the door and I saw Gabriella standing there."

Peter's eyes widened. "She came here?!"

"Oh, she's *still* here." Vicki crossed her legs on the sofa. "In fact, she's just upstairs right now."

Peter looked upward toward the ceiling. Then, he looked back at Vicki. "I suppose she told you everything then."

"Exactly," Vicki said. "Peter, why the hell didn't you ever decide to tell any of us? Why the bull story with St. Mary's in the Alps? Why fake the burial in the backyard?" Vicki leaned forward. "Peter, don't you understand the strain you have caused on our marriage?"

Peter nodded his head. "Vicki, I just thought that I was doing what was best for all of us here. I didn't know if the doctors would help Gabby at all. It was an experimental thing, and with my reelection campaign firing up, I couldn't have this sort of pressure placed on me to become public."

Vicki rolled her eyes. "But Peter . . . you could have told me. You could have told Miranda and Benjamin. Why don't you see that? We would have all supported you! So now, we have to figure out a way to tell the whole family about what you decided to do."

"No, we don't," said a voice from the opposite end of the room.

Vicki turned to see Gabby standing in the archway that led to the room with the stairwell. She had a slight smile on her face.

"What do you mean by that?" Vicki asked her.

"I mean, we don't have to say anything," Gabby said as she came in and sat down in the chair across from Peter. "Everyone already believes I was at St. Mary's. Why should we change the whole story and confuse them anymore?"

"She does have a point," Peter spoke up. "Everyone already thinks that she's been attending St. Mary's for the past six months."

"You're just agreeing with her because you don't want the other two to know about the cover-up you did," Vicki said.

"No," Peter responded. "I think it'll be too difficult to explain it all. After all, what do you think the other two are going to think when they find out I sent her off to be saved?"

Vicki glanced over toward Gabby.

"He has a point, Mom," she said. "Dad would look a lot better in their eyes."

Vicki sighed. She was disappointed about having to continue the lie she had been telling since that awful night in February. "Fine. We'll stick with the damn St. Mary's story."

"Great!" exclaimed Peter. "When's dinner? I'm starved!"

* * *

"Thank you for calling, Delilah," Miranda said. She stood outside the dining room in the entry hall. "I appreciate it."

"If you need to get out and get your mind off things, we can always go out for lunch," Delilah said over the phone. "I know we're no longer sisters-in-law, but that doesn't mean we can't be friends."

"Sure," Miranda said. "I think that would be great."

"Let's set a date," Delilah responded. "I don't want to keep you away from your family. Ben mentioned something about Gabby being home and a family dinner."

"Yeah, she came back earlier this afternoon."

"Tell her that I'm glad she's finally back."

"I will," Miranda said. "Goodbye."

"Bye."

Miranda ended the call with Delilah and set her phone on one of the buffets in the entry hall. Then, she turned around and headed back into the dining room.

"About damn time you got off that phone," Peter said from the head of the table in front of the fireplace. "I thought I was going to have to have Denise microwave the food."

Miranda rolled her eyes as she rounded the table to her seat to Peter's left. She looked across the table where Ben was seated with Katherine in a bassinet next to him, and at the other end of the table sat Vicki with Gabby to her left, leaving Miranda the only one on her side of the table.

"I'm sorry, guys," Miranda said. "Delilah called about the baby. She was offering her condolences."

"You sure she wasn't wanting anything out of it?" Ben asked as he checked on Katherine.

"I'm sure, Ben," Miranda said. "She was very genuine."

Miranda looked down toward Vicki and Gabby and rolled her eyes.

"Well, I'm glad to see that nothing has changed since I left," Gabby said before laughing.

"Nothing will ever change," Vicki responded, glaring down at Peter. She was still quite bitter about the entire ordeal that occurred with Gabby. *Why didn't he just tell me? It would've been so much easier in the long run.*

"Perhaps one day it will," Peter said as he looked down at Gabby. "Do you want to tell her what you talked to me about earlier?"

"Sure," Gabby said before turning toward her mother. "I was talking with Dad about the company today. He said that you've been running it on your own lately."

"Well, yes and no," Vicki said. "I've been the only one in the office lately, but everyone in this room has voting shares in the company. They have the ability to remove and vote in a new company president." She checked to make sure Gabby was following along. "In a way, the company still runs like it did whenever we had a board, but now, instead of board members, the company is run by people who hold voting shares."

"Dad said something about it," Gabby said. "He mentioned that I even have some shares in the company."

"You do," Miranda chimed in. "I signed over some of mine because I wanted to make sure you weren't cheated out of any shares of yours."

"Hell, everyone has a voting share in that place," Peter said. "Even your aunt, Charlotte, has one."

"Yeah," Vicki responded. "Let's not get into how she managed to do that."

"Speaking of," Ben said. "Where is she anyways? I would've thought that she would be here to see her favorite niece?"

Miranda fell silent at Ben's comment. She was saddened that Charlotte would openly say she had a favorite niece.

"That's because she's out dealing with her husband," Vicki said. "She called me earlier to tell me that she would be out of the office for a while."

"That's perfect, then," Gabby added. "Because I was talking with Dad about how I wanted to be an active part of the company."

"Really?" Vicki asked, taken aback. "You want to come to work with me?!"

"Well . . ." Gabby said. "It doesn't have to be in a leadership spot. I can fill in for Aunt Charlotte if that's okay."

Vicki looked over to Ben, ensuring it was okay with him. He nodded to her. Then, Vicki looked back at Gabby.

"Gabriella," she said. "If you're going to work at the company, you will be in leadership."

"No, no, no," Gabby replied. "I can work my way up."

"I insist," Vicki said. "You can even use Benjamin's old office. We'd just need to call together a shareholder's meeting to allow you to become part of the leadership team."

"Are you serious right now?" Gabby asked in disbelief.

"I am."

"Mom, I love you so much."

"I love you too, Gabriella. I'm so glad you're back home."

Gabby stood from her seat and held out her arms to embrace her mother. Vicki got up and wrapped her arms around her, holding her daughter tight.

\* \* \*

A rumble of thunder shook the room, causing Vicki to open her eyes. She looked at the white walls of the living room and sat up.

"Gabriella?" she called out, looking around the room. "Gabriella?"

She stood from the sofa and rushed into the entry hall, turning right toward the front door. She opened it and looked outside at the pouring rain. Vicki looked past the driveway toward the gazebo. Her eyes moved between the house and the road and then over to the left at the turn-around.

"Mrs. Klimmings?"

Vicki turned around to see Denise standing behind her. "Is there something I can help you with?"

"No," Vicki said. "I just thought I had heard something, that's all."

"If you need me, ma'am, I'll be in the kitchen."

Vicki nodded to her as she turned back down the side hall. Then, Vicki closed the front door, accepting that she had just woken from a dream she wished had been real.

# CHAPTER 11

## SWAN SONG

Peter entered the Oval Office with an enormous smile planted on his face. Already seated by the *Resolute* desk were Henry and Constance.

"If it hadn't been for that damn thunderstorm last night," Peter said as he rounded the desk, and the two seated in front rose from their chairs. "Then I would've invited you both over to the mansion, and we would have had one helluva party!"

"Mr. President," Constance said. "I wouldn't celebrate too much. Just because Wu has resigned as leader of the Communist country, doesn't mean that we're in the clear yet."

"I know, Constance," Peter responded, holding his hands up. "But I have a real good feeling about the new leadership that's about to take over." He glanced over to Henry, who gave him a look back. "Mr. Gates, have you heard anything about the potential new leadership in China?"

"I have not," he replied. "All we've gotten intel on is that the Grand Rebellion will be playing a large role in the selection of the new president; however, that doesn't necessarily indicate that the new leader won't already be a member of the Communist Party."

Peter rolled his eyes. "Well, I figured that, Mr. Gates. The damn commies have been running that country since forty-nine!"

"I just wanted to give you all of the details, sir," Henry said.

"So if I could suggest," Constance began. "I don't think it would be a good idea to recall any of the ships you sent out in the South China Sea."

"Thanks for the suggestion, Constance," Peter said. "I think that'd actually be a good idea." He looked over to Henry, who knew Peter was just saying this to appease the vice president. "Constance, would you call Secretary Bird and inform him of our decision to maintain our troops in the Pacific until such a time that we deem it necessary to withdraw them?"

"I will," she said as she started out of the room. "Is there anything else you need of me?"

"No, that's all. Thank you, Constance."

Constance nodded before opening the door and stepping out of the office.

Henry waited until the door closed before turning to Peter. "You got lucky, sir."

"See," Peter said. "I told you I had it all under control. My plan worked like a damn charm."

"Sure," Henry said. "But I must remind you that several people are still calling for your resignation."

"I know . . . I know . . . but once Kang Tu and Shao Cheng form a government, and I normalize relations with China, the people are going to come back over. Just wait . . . you'll see."

Henry shook his head. "Mr. President," he said. "I guess I do need to apologize to you."

"Why?"

"Because for a moment there, I doubted you. I started to think that you didn't have it in you to really pull this off."

Peter laughed and patted Henry's shoulder. "Oh, Mr. Gates. This isn't anything new. From the moment I founded Klimmings Incorporated in the nineties, I faced loads of doubters. Almost forty years later, where do you think those doubters are?"

Henry thought for a second. "I don't know . . . where?"

"Who gives a shit?" Peter said before laughing again. "The point I'm trying to make is that Klimmings Incorporated became something big. It catapulted my family into one of the richest in the country, and it allowed me to become the president of this great nation." Peter placed his other hand on Henry's shoulder, holding him where he could look into his eyes. "All those doubters shut their mouths after my success. They wanted in on all the deals and the profits, and I said, 'Hell no!' Nobody should ever bet against the Klimmings family."

* * *

Vicki studied the family portrait hanging above the bar. She looked over each member of the Klimmings family but consistently found herself looking at Gabby's image. *This was her last portrait. She's never going to be in one again.*

She pulled open one of the drawers to the cart and shoved items out of the way until she pulled out a pack of cigarettes. After opening the package, she pulled one out and lit it, inhaling tobacco fumes and temporarily calming herself. Then, she let out a deep sigh as she breathed the smoke out.

"Why'd you have to kill yourself?" Vicki said to the portrait. "You had everyone's support. Mine, your sister's, your brother's . . . even your father's." Vicki took another long draw from her cigarette. "Him and that damn reelection campaign. If that's the reason . . ."

Vicki felt a few tears in her eyes, so she turned around and stepped over to the TV. She turned it on, trying to take her mind off of things.

"The DOW Jones spiked seven hundred points today, following the announcement of President Wu's resignation as leader of China," said Jeff Craig, the news anchor. "Across the United States, reports of panic buying and looting are down; however, calls for President Klimmings' resignation continue from members of the Republican Party."

The news cut from the shot of Jeff in the studio to a video clip of a press conference from Rebecca White.

"I am still in a state of continued shock and dismay," she said in front of a group of reporters. "It has become increasingly obvious that President Klimmings has no idea what he is doing, and the fact of the matter is that he jeopardized the safety of every American during this completely avoidable ordeal."

Vicki turned off the TV as she drew another long drag of her cigarette. As she let the air flow from her lungs, she heard someone coming down the entry hall. She quickly darted to the bar and found a small tray where she could place her cigarette. As she turned around, Vicki spotted Denise turn the corner.

"Mrs. Klimmings," Denise said. "How are you doing today?"

Vicki sighed. "I'm doing okay, Denise," she said. "Have you seen Miranda at all today, or is she still upstairs in her room?"

"She spent most of this morning in her room, but she finally got up and went out back by the pool."

"So she's swimming?"

"No," Denise said. "She's outside, laying on one of the lounge chairs by the pool."

"Okay," Vicki said. "Has she said anything to you at all?"

"Very little. She mentioned something about someone named Julie coming over."

"Julie . . ." Vicki said, trying to remember who Julie was. "Oh, Julie! She's her friend who went with her on that trip to London."

"Mrs. Klimmings," Denise said. "I have a few things that I need to get to . . . would it be okay if I went off to do them?"

"As in leave?"

"No, ma'am," Denise said. "I need to vacuum the bedrooms and change some sheets. If I'm upstairs, would you let me know if Julie comes by so I can greet her and take her to Miss Miranda?"

Vicki smiled. "I got it, Denise. You just do what you need to do, and I can take care of Julie whenever she gets here."

"Thank you," Denise said as she started past Vicki and turned right to go through the archway.

"Denise," Vicki called out to her, stopping her from heading upstairs. "Have you seen Benjamin at all today?"

"No," Denise said. "I haven't seen Mr. Benjamin today."

Vicki looked downward, sorting through the plethora of thoughts that inundated her mind. "I hope he hasn't done anything he would regret."

\* \* \*

Ben stared up at the ceiling. He was lying in a bed he had been in before and had recognized the room he was in. However, he hadn't been here for a few years. As Ben thought things over, the last time he was in this room was before his marriage to Delilah.

"They're gone," Delilah said as she stepped into the room, closing the door behind her. She walked over to the bed and sat at the end. "My dad took forever to leave this morning. He was enraged by the Chinese president's resignation."

"I bet," Ben said as he sat up in the bed. He stretched his arms upward, allowing the sheets to fall just above his waist, revealing his bare chest. "Where are my clothes at?"

Delilah smiled. "I'm afraid they're scattered all over the floor here." She looked around on the floor, slid off the bed, and picked up a pair of boxer briefs. "Well, here's your underwear." She tossed the pair to him. He caught it and smiled back at Delilah.

"If you step out or turn around, I can put these back on," he said as he adjusted the article of clothing.

"*Benjamin*," Delilah sighed. "I was married to you for four years. So I know exactly what you're packing down there." She smiled and glanced downward. "That, and after what we did last night . . . you definitely don't have anything to hide."

Ben chuckled. "Yeah, that was good!"

Delilah lay across the bottom of the bed. "I missed that, Ben."

"Me too."

The two looked at each other for a moment before Ben decided to ask a question that had been running through his mind since he awoke. "So, what does this mean about us?"

"What does what mean about us?" Delilah asked.

"Like, was this a one-night thing, or are we planning to make this something bigger?" Ben asked.

"I don't know," Delilah responded. "What are you wanting it to be?"

Ben took a deep breath. "Delilah, I just don't want either of us to get hurt."

"Then let's not hurt each other," she said, crawling toward Ben. She reached up and locked her lips onto his.

"I'm not ready for a relationship just yet," he said to her after he could pry his lips from hers. "I don't want to rush into anything."

"That's okay," Delilah said. "I can be a friend with benefits."

Ben smiled. "What am I going to do with you?" He leaned forward and kissed her again. Then, he looked down at his watch.

"Crap!" he exclaimed. "I need to get home now!"

"Why?" Delilah asked, looking confused. "What happened?"

"I've only been sober for about two months now," he said, climbing out of bed and pulling on his boxer briefs. "Mom is going to think I've fallen off the wagon or something."

"You didn't tell her you were staying the night here?"

"No. Last she knew, I was coming over to pick up Katherine."

"Well, just tell her that you had to stay the night because of the storm. You can say you slept in the guest room downstairs."

"Perfect!" Ben exclaimed as he pulled up his pants and buttoned them. He snatched his shirt off the floor and headed over to the door. "I'm going to get Katherine and head out." He looked Delilah in the eyes and smiled. "Goodbye, Delilah."

"I'll see you soon," she said, crossing her legs.

Ben stepped out of the room and closed the door behind him. Delilah smiled great big and leaned back on the bed, giggling in glee.

* * *

Julie opened the sliding glass door to the back patio and pool at the Klimmings Mansion. She stepped outside and spotted an open umbrella directly at the bottom of the three steps leading from the patio to the pool area. Julie closed the door and went down the steps to the umbrella. As she crossed between it and the pool, she saw the lounge chair with Miranda lying in it.

"Lovely day for a swim, isn't it?" Julie said as she pulled one of the other lounge chairs closer and sat on the side to face Miranda. As Julie waited for a response, she looked over at Miranda carefully. She was wearing blue shorts with a white t-shirt and oversized black sunglasses on. She didn't bother to move but rather lay there and stare at the sky.

Julie took in a deep breath. "Miranda . . . you can't keep on like this." She looked at Miranda, seeing that she still looked disassociated from the entire conversation. "It's been over a week since the miscarriage, Miranda. At some point, you have got to move on."

Finally, Miranda turned toward Julie. "You just don't understand, Julie."

"What am I not understanding?" she asked. "Miranda, you were five months pregnant. You kept it a secret for as long as possible, for what?"

Miranda turned away from Julie, who was waiting for an answer. "Why didn't you tell anyone about the pregnancy sooner?"

"I don't want to talk about it, Julie."

"You're going to, Miranda." Julie adjusted herself slightly as she sat on the edge of the chair. "You have to face it, Miranda . . . Now, what happened when you were held in that apartment?"

Miranda pulled her shades off and tossed them to the side. She wiped her eyes with her hand. "He . . . he . . ."

"He raped you, didn't he?" Julie calmly asked. "That's how you got pregnant, isn't it?"

Miranda stumbled over her words, trying to answer Julie's question. Instead, she could only respond by nodding her head.

"Oh, Miranda," Julie said, taking her hand. "I'm so sorry."

"I-I-I . . . just didn't . . . know h-how to say . . . anything about it," Miranda managed to get out between sobs.

"And when you found out you were pregnant," Julie continued. "You didn't want it."

Tears streamed down Miranda's face. She tried to wipe her eyes again but got nowhere with it.

"And then when you finally accepted it, you had the miscarriage . . . and lost the baby."

"Don't call it that!" Miranda snapped.

"You've got to call it what it was, Miranda," Julie said. "It was *your* baby."

"It . . ."

"Say it, Miranda!"

She fell silent, only allowing her sobs to be heard.

"Say it."

"MY BABY!" Miranda shouted before jumping from the lounge chair and taking off alongside the pool. Julie leaped from her seat, chasing after Miranda, finally catching her at the opposite corner near the curved windows where Peter's office was located. She held Miranda in her arms as she broke down uncontrollably.

"Why did my baby have to die?!" Miranda cried out. "Why couldn't he have made it?!"

\* \* \*

"President Wu!" Peter exclaimed over the phone as he turned his chair around to look at the pictures on the table behind his desk. "What do I owe the pleasure of speaking to you?"

"Cut the pleasantries, Peter," President Wu snapped back over the phone. "You cost me everything!"

Peter sighed. "Oh, Wu . . . you should have known that from the moment you started conniving with Jeremy Applegate, you would end up kissing your leadership goodbye."

"I don't know how you did it," President Wu said. "How could you get away with conspiring with a terrorist organization? What do the American people think about all of that?"

"They don't know about it," Peter said. "They don't see the Grand Rebellion as a terrorist organization. Instead, they view them as a symbol of democracy in a state where a dictatorship is instituted."

"And your conversations with the Russians aren't contradicting to that?"

"They don't know about that either. After all, official conversations between the United States and Russia have been non-existent for over ten years now."

"And yet you come out of all of this as an unsung hero," President Wu said. "I promised myself that I would destroy you, Peter Klimmings, and yet, while I failed this time, there will come a day when I will have my revenge. What do you people say – you'll be caught with your hand in the cookie jar – and I will be there to make sure you face the biggest punishment that you can receive."

Peter turned his chair around, leaning onto the *Resolute* desk. "Now listen here, you son of a bitch. Had you never put a hand on my wife, none of this would have ever happened. You couldn't control your ego and sexist ways, and you just had to try to touch her." He took a deep breath before saying, "You deserve everything that you got . . . and I hope that Kang Tu, and Shao Cheng, and the rest of the Grand Rebellion have their way with you and you never see the light of day again."

President Wu fell quiet before letting out a light laugh. "We'll see about that, Peter . . . we'll see . . ."

The phone clicked before Peter could respond. He took it away from his ear and slapped it down on the receiver.

"MARTHA!!!" he shouted out.

Within a few seconds, the door to his right opened, and Martha stepped in. "Yes, sir?"

"Get me Secretary Bird," he said. "He and I need to discuss something."

\* \* \*

Powdery snow fell from the clouds as a black car approached a large brick building. Once it stopped, the back passenger-side door opened, and Charlotte stepped out. She had on a thick pink coat, which she tugged closer to herself as the cold air hit her. On the opposite side of the car, Michelle stepped out, shivering.

"Couldn't this place be any more out of the way?" Charlotte asked, turning to Michelle. "It's over an hour away from the nearest town. And why does it have to be on the side of this damn mountain!"

"Maybe this is why they chose this school?" Michelle mentioned as she rounded the back of the car. She looked up at the large brick building, which had the words "ST. MARY'S ACADEMY FOR YOUNG WOMEN" plastered across the face of it. She looked back over to Charlotte.

"You think we're going to find her in here?" Michelle asked.

"We better!" Charlotte said. "I didn't fly all the way over here to meet with the headmistress just to be told the same crap again!"

Charlotte approached the building's front door, which opened as she made it part of the way up the stairs. A woman, who appeared to be in her late sixties and had silver hair, stood inside the building holding the door open.

"Come on inside," she called out to Charlotte and Michelle. "It's freezing outside!"

The two hurried up the stairs and made it inside the school. The woman closed the door behind the two of them.

"You must be Charlotte," the woman said to her.

"And you must be the headmistress," Charlotte said to the woman as she shook her hand.

"Oh, please," the woman said. "Call me Ava . . . but if you must feel formal, then you may call me Headmistress Sallenbach."

"Thank you," Charlotte said before turning to Michelle. "This is my friend, Michelle."

"Hello, Michelle," Ava said, shaking Michelle's hand.

"I brought her along because she is just as curious about seeing Gabby as I am," Charlotte added. Ava let go of Michelle's hand, and her facial expression fell to a serious tone.

"You're going to want to come to my office," Ava said. "We have a lot that we need to discuss."

\* \* \*

*"Vicki," Peter said as he approached Vicki. "I need you to step away*

*from her. We're going to take care of everything."*

*"Where are we sending her?" Vicki asked her husband.*

*"Nowhere," Peter said. "I have some people preparing her final resting spot now."*

*Vicki's eyes widened. "We're burying her tonight?!"*

*"Yes, Vicki. It has to be this way."*

*Vicki looked back down at Gabby's lifeless body on her bed. She examined the gunshot wound to her chest and let her eyes look over her blond hair. "My baby . . ."*

"So," Peter said, pulling Vicki's attention back to the breakfast table. "Today will be the last I'm here for a few days."

"Where are you going?" Ben said, sitting in his seat next to Peter's.

"Well," Peter said. "After lunch, I'm joining a call with the captain of the *Biden* after they dock in Point Loma. Then, I plan to travel out to Iowa tomorrow to meet with some Democratic leaders in that state. Then, I'm holding my first rally."

"Do you really need to?" Ben asked. "Since you're running for reelection, don't you already have the nomination in the bag?"

"No. The governor of California announced a few days ago that he wants to challenge me for the Democratic nomination. I certainly feel that with my success in China that I am easily going to win the nomination . . . but you can't ever be too careful with these things."

Peter looked down the table at Vicki, who was sitting quietly. "Vicki, would you like to go with me?"

She looked up at Peter. "No. I've got some things that I need to get done here."

"Are you sure?" Peter asked again. "I'd love to have you come along."

"I told you," Vicki reiterated, sounding a little testy. "I'm busy."

Ben looked between the two of his parents. "How about I go see if Katherine is awake," he said. "I left her in the bassinet in my room."

"Why don't you go get her?" Peter suggested. "Maybe her presence in here will brighten up the mood a little."

Ben smiled and then took his napkin from his lap and set it on the table beside his plate of scrambled eggs and bacon. As he left the dining room and crossed the entry hall, Miranda slowly stepped into the dining room.

"Miranda!" Peter exclaimed, standing from his seat. "It's so good to see you this morning."

She looked over at her father and then back to the trays of food sitting on the breakfast bar along the dining room wall. She took a plate and began to scoop herself out some scrambled eggs. Then, she took some bacon and added it to her dish. Finally, she turned and walked over to her seat next to Peter.

"I haven't eaten in a couple of days," she said before taking a bite of her scrambled eggs.

"Well, I understand, Miranda," Peter said. "The past few weeks have been hell for you."

Vicki looked up at Peter, glaring at him.

"Julie stopped by yesterday," Miranda said. "She put a lot of things into perspective." She took a bite of her bacon. "I can't continue to stay holed up in my room. I have to get back to my life."

"Miranda," Vicki said, trying to be consoling. "Are you sure you're going to be okay? If we need to get you a therapist or anything . . ."

"Mom, I don't need a therapist. I am just fine."

Vicki set her fork on the table just as Ben came into the room with Katherine.

"Look who woke up," he said, holding Katherine.

Miranda looked at Ben and Katherine, considering what could have been with her own baby. A tear formed in her eye, but she quickly pulled her napkin up to wipe her eye.

"There's my girl," Peter said, stepping over to Ben and holding out his arms.

Ben handed Katherine over to Peter, who bounced her up and down softly and rocked her back and forth. Vicki watched closely and was taken back to the birth of Gabby. She recalled laying in the hospital bed, holding her for the first time. She remembered looking at her blue eyes.

It was her youngest daughter.

Gabby was her last pregnancy.

She remembered Peter holding her for the first time. She thought back to the joy displayed on his face whenever he looked at her – the thirteen hours of labor she spent to deliver her made it all worth it when she finally got to see her daughter and witnessed the look of pure happiness on Peter's face.

"Mom," Ben said, causing her to snap back to reality.

"Would you like to hold her?" Ben asked, determined to gain her attention.

Vicki looked over to Ben, confused. "Would you like to hold Katherine, Mom?"

She smiled a little. "Yes, Benjamin. I'd love to hold her."

* * *

Delilah sat at the island in the kitchen in the Applegate Homestead. She was eating a grapefruit and watching the sunrise from the window facing the Klimmings Mansion when Cathie walked in. She was still in her nightgown.

"Mom," Delilah said. "You didn't get dressed?"

"Not today," she said as she made her way to the coffee pot. "Since your dad is too cheap to hire house staff, I decided that I would act like every other middle-class family in this country." She poured herself a cup and took a sip, turning to face Delilah. "After all, he's not home right now because he's heading to China, so I am going to do as I please. I may even run around naked later."

"Oh my God, Mom," Delilah said as she tossed her fork onto the island and pushed the bowl of grapefruit away from her. "Why did you have to put that image in my head?"

"You started it," she said before taking another sip. "And I finished it."

Delilah shuddered and then pulled the bowl closer to her. She looked at the grapefruit, contemplating whether she wanted to eat any more of it.

"Speaking of images in heads," Cathie said as she set her coffee cup on the island. "I stumbled on something interesting a couple nights ago."

Delilah looked up at her mother. "What?"

"Well, I went to ask you a question, and whenever I got to your bedroom door, I heard some pretty peculiar noises coming from inside."

Cathie raised her eyebrows at Delilah, who tried to hide her embarrassment.

"It got me wondering . . ." Cathie continued. "Who could have been in your room with you . . . after all, Katherine was still in the nursery . . ." She slightly cocked her head and let a small gin appear on her face. "And Ben was supposed to have picked her up that night."

"It wasn't him," Delilah lied. Cathie examined Delilah's reactions and doubted what she was saying.

"And whenever I spoke to Ryan, he said that Ben was staying at the house until the storm was over."

"Fine," Delilah confessed, once again pushing the grapefruit away. "It was Ben. We slept together, okay?"

"Delilah, he was supposed to be waiting out the storm, not creating one with you."

"Oh . . . my God, Mom," Delilah let out. "Why must you put things like that?"

"It's true!" Cathie said. "You two were going at it for a long time."

"How long were you listening at the door?!"

"Long enough . . . I didn't even know Ben used some of those words in his vocabulary."

"Go away," Delilah ordered her mother. "Get out of this kitchen, now."

"It's *my* kitchen," Cathie said. "You leave."

"I'm still eating my breakfast."

"Then you're just going to have to deal with it then."

Delilah rolled her eyes and then went back to eating her grapefruit. As she took a bite, Cathie took a sip of her coffee and decided to shift the tone of the conversation to a more serious one.

"So," she said, setting her coffee cup back onto the island. "What is going on with you and Ben? Are you two back together, or are you two just friends with benefits?"

Delilah sighed. "I'm not sure. We've gotten really close lately, but when Ben left yesterday, he mentioned that he wanted things to be taken slowly."

"And how do you feel about that?"

"I'm not sure. One part of me was excited because I didn't want to call our marriage quits whenever we filed for divorce. However, I can also see Ben saying he wants to take it slow and then decide that he doesn't want it to go any further."

"True," Cathie said. "But do you see him doing that?"

"No," Delilah said as she moved her grapefruit around with her fork. "But I fear that all it can take is something big to cause him to run away."

"Like what?"

Delilah took in a deep breath. "A couple of months ago, following the divorce proceedings, Winston Brown called. He told me that I was entitled to half of Ben's assets."

"You got that," Cathie interrupted. "So how would that change Ben's mind? It's already been handled."

"Not entirely," Delilah continued. "I was also entitled to half of Ben's shares in Klimmings Incorporated."

"So that means . . ."

"I should have half of his voting shares in the company."

"Delilah," Cathie said. "Do you have any idea the percentage of voting shares you would have?"

"I never asked," she said. "I allowed Ben to keep them all."

"That would be like fifteen percent of the voting shares, Delilah," Cathie said. "He would flip!"

"Exactly. That's why I haven't told anyone about it except for Vicki."

Cathie's eyes widened. "Your father doesn't know about this, does he?"

"I just said that I hadn't told anyone."

"Whatever you do, don't tell him," Cathie suggested. "He would be all over those shares. Both he *and* Ryan would push to whatever means they could to influence any decisions with those shares."

"I know," Delilah sighed. "It would be literal hell if they ever found out about it."

Cathie nodded her head before taking another sip of her coffee. "Now that President Wu has stepped down in China, I don't know what your dad would do to get back at the Klimmings family."

* * *

Vicki made it to the landing at the top of the stairs. She started toward her bedroom door but stopped and found herself turned around to Gabby's room. She hadn't been in there since her death in February. Vicki looked over the door and then at the doorknob. She took a step toward it and paused as soon as she got to the door. She took a deep sigh and placed her hand on the door handle.

As Vicki turned the doorknob, her mind flooded with memories of times she spent going into Gabby's room to speak with her about whatever was going on at the time. There had been so many times that she had to talk with her about something that had happened at school, how she had acted when visitors were over at the house, and how she interacted with her siblings.

She looked into the bedroom at the yellow wallpaper. Her eyes moved down the walls toward the floor and then over to the bed. She examined the yellow comforter that lay over the top of it. At that moment, her mind was taken back to the scene where she saw Gabby lying in that bed.

*"What's wrong, Ben . . ."* Vicki *fell silent when she saw Gabby's lifeless body. "Oh my God!"*

*She came into the room and fell to her knees beside Gabby's bed. "No. No. No. No. No. This can't be happening," Vicki cried. "Peter, this can't be happening! She's our baby girl!"*

She sat down on the side of the bed and ran her hand over the comforter. As she continued, Denise came to the door. "Mrs. Klimmings?"

Vicki looked up at Denise. "Yes, Denise."

"I've finished your lunch. Would you like it in the dining room or outside?"

"I'll take it in the dining room. Will anyone be joining me?"

"Miss Miranda and Mr. Benjamin left a little bit ago," Denise said. "I'm going to set your plate in the dining room and then head out back to work on the pool. Apparently, the groundskeepers couldn't get all the leaves out of the pool from the storm a few days ago."

Vicki smiled. "Thank you, Denise."

Denise turned and went down the stairs, leaving Vicki alone in the bedroom. She sighed before standing from the bed, straightening up the comforter, and then heading out of the room, turning the light off as she left.

She descended the stairs and turned to the right, passing the guest bedrooms before crossing the entry hall to the dining room, where a plate with a turkey sandwich and some plain chips sat in her seat. Vicki approached her chair and stared at her plate. She took it and rounded the table to Peter's seat, where she sat the plate down. She pulled out the chair and sat down in her husband's seat.

This wasn't a view of the dining room she typically had. Usually, she was always facing the fireplace, but as she looked down the table, she saw the other side of the room. She saw through the archway into the entry hall. Vicki took a deep breath as her eyes moved toward her usual chair and then over to the right, where Gabby had always sat.

Family dinners, breakfasts, Thanksgivings, and Christmases filled Vicki's thoughts. She recalled all the times spent together as a family with herself, Peter, Miranda, Ben, and Gabby. There wouldn't be times like that ever again. Gabby was dead, and for the first time, it had finally hit Vicki.

There would be no more family dinners with Gabby.

There would be no more breakfasts with Gabby.

There would be no more Thanksgivings with Gabby.

And there would be no more Christmases with Gabby.

Her family would never be the same ever again.

Finally, after holding in her genuine emotions for the better part of five months, Vicki finally let it all out. Tears flowed from her eyes as if the dam holding it all in broke. She placed her hands on the edges of the table as she cried. Her wails echoed from the dining room into the entry hall and filled most of the lower level of the house.

For in this moment, Vicki had finally accepted that there would never be a chance that Gabby would ever come home, and her hopes of having a complete family again would never come to fruition.

* * *

Rebecca White's secretary stepped into the speaker's office with a few papers in her hands. "Speaker White," she said. "Here are some documents about some of the proposed bills that the House is considering."

"I just don't get it," Rebecca said, looking up from her computer and taking off her red reading glasses. "Why would he step down?"

"Who?" the woman asked.

"President Wu," Rebecca said. "For a moment, I thought that the president would finally have his judgment day, and the tables would finally turn against him. Now, it's like he's the hero of the day."

"Madam Speaker, I don't necessarily believe that he's going to fair very well from this."

Rebecca glared at the woman. "And why do you say that?"

"Well, the polls haven't bounced back, and he's already had one challenger for the Democratic nomination. Some people in his own party have even turned their backs on him."

Rebecca smiled. "But I need the entire country to turn their backs on him." She turned her chair around so that she could peer out the window at the National Mall. "Dammit, Sue. How did this come out in his favor?"

Sue shook her head. "I'm not sure, ma'am. Do you think that the president had something to do with the Grand Rebellion's rise in popularity in China?"

"That's the only explanation I can come up with," Rebecca said, turning back to Sue. "It's worked out too well in his favor for this to be coincidental."

"But how are you going to prove it?"

Rebecca nodded her head. "That's the only issue. Something has got to happen to cause someone to turn on him. Then . . . and only then will I be able to take him down and make him face the consequences he so deserves."

\* \* \*

Denise stood behind a tripod with a phone mounted in Peter's office at the Klimmings Mansion. In front of the tripod sat Vicki at the desk. Behind her, the sun was setting outside, creating a sky with deep reds and dark blues forming a majestic purple hue.

"You think this is good?" Denise asked Vicki.

"Yes," she said as she fluffed her hair some. "Now, Denise, remember, I want this to be live across my first lady account on Facebook. This is an announcement I only want to have to make once."

"I understand, Mrs. Klimmings," Denise said, looking back at the phone to ensure the camera was aligned well with Vicki.

"Denise, I want you to understand that you are going to hear me talk about some things that may sound distressing to you. In fact, it's going to be a surprise whenever you hear it. But I can only speak of it once. Do you understand?"

"Yes, ma'am," Denise said with a confused look on her face.

Vicki adjusted herself in the chair. She straightened up the light blue blazer she was wearing and the white button-up shirt she had on beneath it. "When you're ready, Denise."

Denise pressed some things on the phone screen, beginning the video, and then she nodded to Vicki to indicate that she was alive.

"Good evening," Vicki began. "I am addressing you all tonight with some news that has shaken the Klimmings family at its core, and I feel it is only fair of me to share this news with the American people before it hits the press. As most know, my daughter Gabriella Klimmings has been studying in Europe after some bullying issues ensued at the school she had been attending here in Washington. Throughout the past couple of months, communication with her has been limited."

Vicki paused for a moment to take a deep breath before continuing on. "Earlier today, we learned that our daughter, Gabriella, had taken her own life." She stopped again to wipe a tear away from her right eye and to take another breath in an effort to remain composed.

"With Gabriella's death comes a period of mourning that will captivate my family. I ask everyone to please allow my family to pay their respects to Gabriella in private without having to deal with the press and photographers that may hound us. As we privately lay Gabriella to rest, I only ask that we can do so as a family."

Vicki looked over at Denise, who had a look of shock on her face. Her mouth hung open as she took in the words that Vicki was saying. Then, Vicki turned her attention back to the phone.

"Thank you in advance for all those prayers offered to my family, and God bless you," Vicki said. Then, she looked at Denise and slightly nodded, telling Denise to stop the video.

She pressed the "stop" button on the phone and looked at Vicki. "I'm so sorry, Mrs. Klimmings."

"Don't," Vicki said as she stood from the chair and rounded the desk. "I don't want to talk about it anymore." She passed Denise and stepped out of the office. Then, she turned back to her and added, "I'm heading to the White House."

As Vicki went down the hall toward the family room, she considered all who had just viewed the video she had posted. There was Delilah, who had seen it at the Applegate Homestead with Cathie; Constance and her husband, James, who watched it at Number One Observatory Circle; Charlotte and Michelle, who came across the video on the plane ride back to the United States; Miranda, who heard the radio DJs speaking about it as she drove back to the Klimmings Mansion; Ben, who saw it on a TV at a store where he was shopping for Katherine; and Jeremy saw it displayed across Chinese news programming.

Everyone who wanted to see her address was able to see it, and the news of Gabriella Klimmings' death spread like wildfire across the country and the globe. Even Peter was watching the video in his office when Martha came in to interrupt a brief meeting between himself and

Secretary Bird. He clasped onto the phone intently as he took in every word Vicki spoke of, his heart dropping at times out of fear that she was about to spill the secret they had been keeping for so long.

"What the hell is she doing?!" Peter called out near the end of the video before looking at Eric and Martha's reactions. "Why couldn't she just let me make the damn announcement?!"

"Mr. President," Eric said somberly. "If you need to head home to be with your family, nobody will blame you."

"Exactly," Martha chimed in. "We can handle things here. The vice president can come in . . ."

"Shut the hell up!" Peter shouted. "I do not need to go home! I'm not going to let this get in the way of what I need to do!"

"But sir," Martha said. "She's your daughter . . ."

"I know," he said as he rounded the *Resolute* desk and fell into his seat. "I know . . ."

Peter looked down at the top of his desk, thinking about everything Vicki had said in the video. She had announced to the world that his youngest had died without changing the storyline he had created to cover it all up.

"I think it would be best if we both gave you some space, Mr. President," Eric said before turning to Martha.

She nodded to him, and they both turned to proceed out of the Oval Office, leaving Peter alone to his thoughts.

* * *

Vicki placed her black car in park as she stopped in front of the north façade of the White House. While she shut off the ignition, a butler opened her door and greeted her. She got out of the car and looked at him, saying, "I need you to get the bag out of the trunk."

As he did so, she looked up at the hanging lantern, illuminating the inside of the façade. Then, she heard the trunk shut, and the butler, carrying a luggage bag, led her to the front door of the White House, where it opened. She stepped inside the Entrance Hall and turned toward the butler.

"Are you here to see the president?" he asked her once he stepped inside.

"Yes," she said. "It's quite urgent."

The butler indicated for her to follow him, and he took her down the West Colonnade, where they entered through a door into Martha's office.

"Mrs. Klimmings," Martha said as she stood up from her desk. "I wasn't expecting you here tonight."

Vicki nodded, saying no words to her.

"I'm so sorry about your daughter, ma'am," Martha continued. "If there is anything that you need, please let me know."

The butler could tell Vicki was in no mood for pleasantries, so he stepped in. "Ma'am, she needs to see the president."

Martha's eyes widened. "I'll let him know you're here."

She turned and opened the door to the Oval Office, closing it slightly behind her. The butler looked at Vicki, who held a serious display on her face.

"I can take the bag in," Vicki said to him. "I need to speak with him alone."

Finally, Martha opened the door, holding it for Vicki. "He's ready to see you."

Vicki knelt slightly and picked up the bag, taking it with her as she passed Martha into the Oval Office. Peter was standing behind the *Resolute* desk with a glass of bourbon in his hand, and before Vicki proceeded any further into the room, she turned to Martha and said, "Thank you."

Martha took that as her queue to close the door, so she did, leaving Vicki and Peter alone in the Oval Office. She stared at her husband for a moment and then took the bag over to the coffee table between the two cream-colored sofas and set it on it.

"I thought you were heading to Iowa tonight."

"I was," Peter said before taking a sip of his bourbon. "But Secretary Bird couldn't meet with me until today, and then I was informed of a video you posted to Facebook." He looked her up and down. "Why the hell would you do that, Vicki?"

"I needed to finally get it out there," she responded. "Do you know how hard it is holding in those feelings for five months, Peter? It eats at your heart day after day after day!"

Peter set the glass onto the desk as he stepped over to his right. "You're acting like Gabby's death has only affected you, Vicki." He put his right hand into the air. "I'm her father too. Don't you think it hurts me to know that she killed herself in our home?" He took a step closer to the front corner of the desk. "Don't you think it pains me to know that we could've done things differently, and she would probably still be here with us?"

"*We* could have done things differently?!" Vicki shouted. "Peter, *you* could've done things differently! You are the reason she's dead!"

"*I* could've done things differently?!" Peter shouted back. "What the hell are you saying, Vicki?!"

She stepped closer to Peter, holding out her arm and pointing to him. "I'm saying it's your fault she's dead."

Peter became enraged. "MY FAULT?! WHAT THE HELL DO YOU MEAN MY FAULT?!" He turned away from her briefly to take a deep breath and then turned back. "You're acting as if I could have prevented her from shooting herself."

"YOU COULD HAVE!" Vicki shouted back. "When she came out to us right before she shot herself, you responded with an asinine favor for her to wait until you started your reelection campaign so that she would publicly come out and make you some hero of the gays!"

"Vicki, I wanted her to wait because I wanted her to know that she had the support of so many people."

"That's the biggest crock of bullshit I've heard so far, Peter. You wanted her to wait because you wanted the votes." She stepped in closer. "Admit it, Peter. You wanted to use our daughter for your benefit."

He took a deep sigh. "Fine, I'll admit it," he said. "I thought that her coming out would help me in the long run. I figured she could campaign with me, and while she helped me in the polls, I would help her to accept who she was more." Peter looked at Vicki as his mind raced with too many thoughts to count. "And as a result, she shot herself. So, in a desperate attempt to save my reelection chances, I impulsively acted to have her buried in the family plot alongside my father and mother."

Vicki glared at her husband as the fury burned inside her. "And how's that going for ya right now?"

"Well, I'm standing here with you right now, aren't I? I could very well be on a flight to Iowa so that I can meet with Democratic leadership in the morning . . ."

"I'm not asking about your reelection campaign," Vicki said calmly. "I'm . . ."

"Shouldn't you be?" Peter interrupted. "After all, that's what it seems like you came here for." Peter turned, took a deep breath, and then faced Vicki again. Vicki, I am facing a tough challenge from the California governor. If I don't start heading out . . ."

"I don't give a damn about your fucking campaign, Peter!" Vicki screamed. "I care about the damage you've done to this family! You've driven your son to be an alcoholic! You're solely responsible for the preventable miscarriage of one daughter!" Tears began streaming down Vicki's face. "And you're the bastard who is responsible for the suicide of your youngest daughter!"

Peter stood in silence while Vicki cried. She pulled out a tissue from her blazer and dabbed her eyes. "I told myself I wouldn't cry," she said as she dried her face.

"Vicki," Peter said as he stepped closer to her to console her.

"Don't touch me!" she shouted as she stepped away from him. "I can't stand to have your hands on me right now. I can't stand to even look at you!"

"Honey, let me try to make this up to you. When we get home . . ."

"You're not coming home, Peter," Vicki announced, stepping away from him. "I brought you a bag with some of your clothes for the next couple of days. Denise will pack up the rest and send it over to you."

Peter stood in shock. "But . . . how long?"

Vicki stood tall. "Permanently, Peter. We're separating. I don't want you at that house, and I don't want you near the rest of my family right now. Do you understand?"

"But . . . but . . . where the hell am I supposed to stay?"

"Try the second floor. Other presidents used it as their living quarters. You can too."

She turned around and headed over to the door. As she opened it, she turned back toward Peter and said, "Goodbye, Peter."

He stood there in complete astonishment as she closed the door and proceeded through Martha's office, down the West Colonnade, and back into the Executive Residence. As she started down the Cross Hall, she came upon a portrait of herself and Peter which had been taken during Peter's first year in office. They were posing in front of the mantel in the Oval Office.

"Ma'am," the butler said after finally catching up to her. "Is something wrong?"

"Yes," Vicki said, turning her head to him. "Take this down."

"Excuse me?"

"Take down this picture."

"What do you want me to do with it?"

"I don't care," Vicki said as she turned her attention back to the portrait. "Burn it. Trash it. I don't give a damn what you do with it."

She turned away and proceeded through the Entrance Hall and out to her car, leaving the butler stunned. Then, she got into her car, started it, and drove away.

* * *

Dana Gomez sat in her bed watching Vicki's announcement play on the evening news. She usually didn't watch the news before bed, but after seeing talk of the first lady's shocking announcement plastered across social media, she knew she needed to check it out.

As the news commentators discussed some of the ramifications of Vicki's announcement, Dana became consumed by her thoughts. She was taken back to the night Gabby died, recalling the dramatic exchange between the two.

*"Miss Gabriella," Denise called up the stairs as Dana waited beside her. "Your friend Dana is here."*

*"Dana?!" Gabby responded. "What the hell is she doing here?"*

"She said she wanted to talk to you and that it was urgent," Denise responded. "Do you want to see her?"

There was silence from up the stairwell for a few seconds before Gabby called down for her to send Dana up. Denise looked over to Dana and said, "If you need anything, I will be outside helping Ramón repair some of the concrete after one of the other workers damaged it trying to scrape ice off."

"Is there anyone else here in case we need something urgent?" Dana asked.

"No. Just me," Denise replied. "But I will be outside if you need me. She stepped away from Dana, leaving her alone at the bottom of the stairs. Then, Dana went up the stairs and turned to the right at the landing.

"What the hell do you want?" Gabby said, sitting on her bed. "Did you come back for another punch?"

"No," Dana said as she stepped into Gabby's room. "I came to apologize to you again for the douchey thing I did to you. I shouldn't have . . ."

"Shut the hell up," Gabby interrupted. "You just got your feelings hurt when I kicked your ass right there in that hallway at school." Gabby laughed. "You took my friends away from me, and I made your pride my bitch."

Gabby continued to laugh as Dana stood in her room, looking downward. She let Gabby get to her again. As she stood there, taking it all in, she remembered the Glock inside her coat.

Dana wasn't sure why she had initially brought the Glock. Perhaps she was afraid Gabby would come at her? Nonetheless, Dana had no intentions of actually using the weapon. However, as Gabby continued to laugh at her, she reached into her pocket and pulled out the gun. Then, she found herself looking it over, considering whether to use it or not.

"What the hell are you doing with that?!" Gabby exclaimed as she jumped off the side of her bed, standing in front of Dana. "What are you planning to do . . . shoot me?"

But Dana didn't pay any attention to what Gabby had said. Instead, *she just continued to look over the gun before raising it up and firing a shot into Gabby's chest.*

*Gabby blew backward, falling onto her bed. Then, she put her left hand on her wound and examined the dark red blood that covered it.*

*"You . . ." Gabby managed to get out as she looked at Dana. "You're . . . a real . . . bitch . . ."*

*Life left her, and Gabby's body lay motionless on her bed. Dana immediately dropped the gun in a panic and then turned to leave the room. She stopped halfway, turned around, and snatched the gun from the floor before she bolted down the stairs. She turned around the corner of the stairs, hurrying to get out of the house, but ran into Denise.*

*"Oh my goodness," Denise said, adjusting her work outfit. "I'm so sorry."*

*"It's fine," Dana said, holding the gun down to her side and out of sight of Denise. "I was just about to leave."*

*"What was that loud noise? Ramón and I could hear it from the back patio."*

*Dana's mind flooded with excuses. She couldn't tell Denise that she had just murdered Gabby. As she mulled through all the reasons she was able to manufacture, she decided that the best she could come up with was that Gabby had shoved something over in anger and that it was for the best that she leave now before she upset her any further. To her amazement, Denise believed it and headed back outside to help Ramón further.*

In her bedroom, Dana shook her head slowly from side to side. She knew all along that the St. Mary's story was fraudulent and that Michelle's constant pursuit of her would lead her nowhere. And from the announcement that Vicki Klimmings had made earlier, Dana's mind was put at ease because she knew that she was the only person to truly know what happened to Gabriella Marie Klimmings on the night she passed away.

# PART 2

# CHAPTER 12
## TWO THANKSGIVINGS

Vicki turned into the long driveway of the Klimmings Mansion. She sped up the driveway, turned right, and drove around the turnaround before stopping and shutting the car off. She took a deep breath before opening the door, rounding the front of the car, and proceeding up the stairs to the front door. She opened it and stepped inside the entry hall of the Klimmings Mansion. Miranda and Ben turned the corner from the living room as she shut the door behind her.

"Mom," Miranda began. "Why didn't you tell us?"

Vicki looked at both of her children. "Let's step into the living room," she said. "I need to talk to you two about something your father did."

\* \* \*

Four months passed by, and July changed into November. The leaves had turned on the trees, and cooler air had swept into the DC region. Miranda sat in her seat in the dining room, eating her breakfast and admiring the fall decorations Denise had laid out for the Thanksgiving celebration next week. She then looked at her plate of biscuits and gravy before taking another bite. As she chewed her food, Vicki came into the dining room dressed in her business attire.

"Denise outdid herself this morning," she said as she approached the breakfast bar. She took a plate and began scooping some biscuits and gravy onto it. Then, she turned and headed to the table, sitting in her seat. "Good morning, Miranda."

"Good morning, Mom," Miranda said before taking a bite of her breakfast.

"I have so many things to do at the office today," Vicki said as she placed her napkin onto her lap. "I have a meeting with some architects about our planned nuclear power plant along the Big Sandy River in West Virginia. Then, afterward, Denise is swinging by with the final menu for Thanksgiving next week."

Miranda nodded her head. "About Thanksgiving," she began. "Have you decided whether Dad would be spending it with us?"

Vicki placed her fork on the table and looked up at Miranda. "No. He will not be joining us. Has he asked you about it?"

"No. I haven't spoken to him since before you told us about what happened to Gabby."

Vicki took in a deep sigh. "I hope you understand why I had to kick him out."

"I get it," Miranda said. "But you two are still married, Mom. Have you seen some of the news reports lately? It's not fairing very well for him."

"If you want to spend Thanksgiving with him, then do so," Vicki said as she stood from her seat. "But I'm not going to have that man back in my house."

"Who?"

Vicki turned around, and Ben was standing in the archway to the dining room. She took a deep gulp and then grumbled, "Your father."

"Oh," Ben said as he passed by her and made his way to the breakfast bar to pour himself a cup of coffee. "Is this about the whole Gabby thing?"

"Yes," Miranda quipped. "I had asked Mom if Dad would be joining us for Thanksgiving, and what you walked in on was her response."

Ben took a sip of his coffee. "Well, you two are still married. You *could* come together for the holiday and celebrate what you are thankful for."

"No," Vicki said. "I already told Miranda once, and I'm not going to repeat it." She stormed past Ben and to the side door. "I'm going to work now. I'll see you two tonight." She opened the door and left the dining room.

Ben turned back to Miranda and shrugged.

"She still doesn't even want to see Dad," Miranda said. "I don't understand. They've been married for thirty-six years, Ben. How did it come to this?"

"That's easy," Ben said as he rounded the dining room table with his coffee and sat in his seat. "Dad had Gabby's death covered up, and he buried her in the family plot without giving her a proper burial."

Miranda glared at Ben. "I don't understand why he did that, either." She took a bite of her breakfast. "You found her, didn't you?

Ben sighed. "Apparently, but before you even start asking about it, I don't remember anything from it."

"How?"

"Miranda, do you not remember how I took to drinking earlier this year? I drank so much that I lost memories."

Miranda fell silent as she processed what Ben had told her. "So your drinking was really bad then?"

"Of course," he responded before taking another sip from his coffee. "I struggle with it every day still."

"I'm so sorry, Ben."

"Don't be. It was my fault, and I have to sort through it all."

Miranda nodded before taking another bite of her breakfast and pushing the plate away. "This might be petty of me, but you know what really makes me mad?"

Ben looked at his sister. "What?"

"The fact that Mom knew that Gabby was dead and still allowed me to give her ten of my voting shares."

Ben smiled. "I don't think that's petty. Have you asked her about it?"

"I can't, Ben," Miranda said. "Every time I bring it up, she changes the subject." Miranda took her coffee in her hands. "Ben, I think she just took my shares for herself."

Miranda proceeded to drink from her coffee.

"But why would she do that?"

"Aunt Charlotte," she said. "Mom hated that Aunt Charlotte managed to get five voting shares. And now that she controls forty-five percent of the voting shares, she can effectively cancel out anything Charlotte tries to do."

Ben looked over at Miranda. "But why would she want to do that?"

"Don't you understand?" Miranda asked her brother. "Those two have always been at each other's throats. They love each other, but they also can't stand one another."

Ben took in a deep breath, deciding to tell Miranda something that had been on his mind since the start of the conversation. "Miranda, I don't think I will be celebrating Thanksgiving here this year."

"Why not?"

"I texted Dad yesterday about Thanksgiving," Ben began. "And he asked me if I wanted to come over to the White House and have a Thanksgiving meal with him." He leaned forward some. "He asked me to invite you too."

Miranda lowered her head. "Ben, I love you, and I love our father . . . but I can't go over there if this is the way Mom still feels about him."

Ben's expression faded some on his face, but Miranda continued.

"Also, this is the first Thanksgiving for both of our parents without Gabby. Maybe it'll be good for you to be with him, and I stay at home with Mom?"

"That's true," Ben said before taking another sip of his coffee. "How do you think Mom will take the news?"

"Well," Miranda said. "I believe that she will take it about as bad as you would expect her to."

\* \* \*

"Good morning and a Happy Thanksgiving! Security is tight in New York City for the hundred-and-ninth running of the Macy's Thanksgiving Day Parade, marking the first big gathering in the United States following July's crisis between the U.S. and China. We'll talk with the NYPD's police commissioner about how security is being handled differently this year."

A graphic ran across the TV screen, transitioning from footage of police officers to Peter at the White House.

"Klimmings gone coo-koo? During the annual turkey pardoning, President Klimmings seemed to snap at reporters when asked about his marital issues."

"President Klimmings," said a reporter in the audience. "Can you make a statement about the relationship between you and your wife? Will you two be spending Thanksgiving together?"

"Listen here," Peter said as he came alongside the turkey he had just pardoned. "It's none of your damn business how things are going between my wife and me. That's between us, and there's not any room for you all to be sniffing into my business."

"This comes after Speaker White continued to make more calls for the president's resignation."

"I think it's time," Rebecca White said as the footage cut to her. "It's time for Peter Klimmings to step down and let Vice President Zeemer take over."

The TV shut off, and Peter tossed the remote onto the coffee table in the Oval Office. He turned to Henry, who was standing just behind him.

"What the hell is this, Mr. Gates?" he exclaimed. "That bitch honestly doesn't know when to stop!"

Henry sighed. "Mr. President," he said. "I think she's just concerned about your well-being."

"My well-being is damn fine, Mr. Gates!" Peter responded. "It's hers that needs to be evaluated!"

"Mr. President, sit down," Henry said as he sat on one of the cream sofas. Peter looked at him and then sat on the one across from him.

"Mr. President, you've been acting very strange over the last four months," Henry said. "You've had to endure the death of your daughter and then the separation of your wife not long after."

Peter rolled his eyes. "And?"

Henry took in a deep breath. "Mr. President, nobody will blame you if you need to take a break. Let the vice president take over for a few weeks while you mentally recharge."

"Mr. Gates," Peter started. "I have less than a year to convince the American people to re-elect me to a second term. If I take a few weeks off for my mental health, what will the American people think?"

"I would think that they would understand, sir."

"Sure, and then Rebecca White will be going on live TV saying that I'm a sissy and need to resign. It's always the same with that bitch."

"Sir, your behavior has become even more erratic over the last month. You've not been seen out much, and people are noticing. Your approval rating is half of what it was at this time last year."

Peter laughed. "Mr. Gates . . . over the last month, I decided that I wanted to write my memoir, *Freedom Ain't Free*. That's why people haven't seen me, but they'll soon understand it whenever it's published."

"Uhhh . . . I didn't think you could publish a book while you were in office."

"The hell if I care!" Peter said. "America needs this book."

Henry sighed. "Sir, it's Thanksgiving. What are you doing today? Why are we spending this morning in here? Don't you have some family members coming over?"

Peter fell silent. "My son is," he said. "Ben is coming by for lunch."

"Then why don't you go get ready for that," Henry said. "Treat today as your mental break."

Peter took in a deep breath and then let it out.

"I guess," he said as he stood up. "I'll be up on the second floor of the Executive Residence then if you're still here and need me." Peter stepped over to the door leading to the colonnade but stopped and turned to Henry. "Mr. Gates, if you're not doing anything, you can join us."

"Thank you, Mr. President," Henry said, standing from the sofa. "But I'm heading to my daughter's to celebrate with her and my grand-kids."

Peter smiled. "Good. I hope you enjoy your day."

"Thank you, sir. At my age, you have to cherish all the time you have with family. After all, you never know when it will be your last."

* * *

Vicki stepped into the kitchen, where Denise was hard at work putting together the Thanksgiving meal. Finally, she stepped over to the oven and opened it, peeking at the turkey.

"Oh, Denise," Vicki said as she closed the oven. "You look like you've outdone yourself once again this year!"

Denise smiled at Vicki. "Thank you, Mrs. Klimmings," she said. "Thanksgiving is one of my favorite holidays to prepare for."

"It's one of my favorites, too," Vicki said as she went over to the stovetop to stir the corn. "And I'm so glad the Applegates took my offer again this year to spend Thanksgiving with us."

Denise looked up from what she was doing with a confused look. "Ma'am, did I hear you correctly? Did you say that the Applegate family was coming over?"

"Yes," Vicki said. "I thought I had told you that they would be here."

"Wouldn't that be a little awkward with Mr. Benjamin? He and Delilah haven't even been divorced for a year yet."

"They'll be fine. Plus, Benjamin won't even be dining with us. He is spending his Thanksgiving at the White House."

Denise nodded her head. She wanted to ask about Peter but decided against it. There had been too many times that she had witnessed some type of argument ensue whenever Peter's name was brought up, so she didn't want to learn what Vicki's response would be this time.

"Well," Vicki said as she set the spoon to the side of the corn. "I'll leave you be."

She turned around and stepped out of the kitchen just as the doorbell rang. "I'll get it, Denise," Vicki called back to her in the kitchen. She proceeded a few steps down the side hall before turning left to the front door in the entry hall. She opened the door and saw the Applegate family standing on the other side.

"Vicki!" Cathie exclaimed as she went in for a hug. "It's so good to see you!"

"You too, Cathie!" Vicki said before releasing from the hug. "It's been too long!" She looked over at the other three Applegates standing with Cathie. "Jeremy, Ryan, and Delilah . . . it's so good to see you too!" She smiled as they exchanged their pleasantries back. However, it didn't take long before Vicki noticed that there was a member who was missing. "Where is Katherine?"

"Ben came by this morning and picked her up," Delilah said, stepping forward some. "Since I have her so much, I figured I would let Ben take her for Thanksgiving with his father."

"I suppose we won't be seeing him today?" Jeremy quipped.

"Jeremy!" Cathie exclaimed, elbowing him slightly in the side. "Not today!"

"Ouch!" Jeremy reacted as he glared at Cathie and held his side. "Are we just going to stand out here, or are we allowed inside?"

"Oh goodness," Vicki said, stepping to the side. "Please, come in. Come in!"

The three stepped inside the entry hall and took off their coats, hanging them on the coat rack beside the door.

"Please," Vicki said as she led them into the living room. "Take a seat in here. Denise is still cooking, and we just have to wait on Charlotte and Julie."

"Charlotte?!" Jeremy said. "Keep that woman away from the bird!"

"Will. You. Quit." Cathie jabbed her husband in the side with each word. "Be civil, honey!"

Ryan looked over at Vicki. "Sorry about my dad," he said to her. "He's been in a mood since the re-formation of the Chinese government. He's lost thousands . . ."

"Millions!" Jeremy interrupted. "That son of a bitch cost me millions of dollars! If I ever get ahold of Wu again, someone will need that money to bail me out!"

"Dad!" Delilah jumped in. "What is wrong with you?!"

"I'm sorry," he sighed. "It's been a bad couple of months."

"And deservingly, too," Cathie said. "After the stunts you and Ryan pulled trying to take over Klimmings Incorporated last year, I feel no pity for you."

Jeremy squinted his eyes as he stared at Cathie. "Yes, but that damn Peter . . ."

"On second thought," Vicki interrupted. "Why don't you go wait in the family room?"

Cathie's face lit up. "That sounds like a good idea! Come on, Jeremy, let's go."

He stood up, and Cathie drug him out of the living room, followed by Ryan. Vicki watched the three leave and proceed down the entry hall. Once they turned the corner, she turned around and caught Delilah looking over the family portrait in the living room.

"This is new," she said as she looked at the image. The new portrait featured Vicki alongside Ben, holding Katherine, and Miranda, leaving Peter entirely out of it.

"Yes," Vicki said. "We took that a few weeks ago, so it is fairly new."

"I can't lie, but it hurts to see me replaced up here. For so long, that's the image I've always seen over here."

"Don't think of it as a replacement, Delilah. It just was a much-needed update. After all, Katherine needed to be included."

Delilah nodded before turning away and taking a few steps toward the fireplace.

"If I can be honest with you," Vicki said. "I kind of regret having that image updated."

"Why?"

"I feel a little guilty about removing Peter from it. This is his house, still, but . . ."

She stopped before she went on any further. It hadn't occurred to Vicki that the Applegate family didn't know the actual reasoning behind the separation.

"I get it," Delilah said sympathetically. "Deep down, you still love Peter, but for some reason or another, you can't let him come back home yet. Is that right?"

Vicki looked Delilah in the eyes. "You're exactly right."

\* \* \*

"Amen."

Constance placed her napkin in her lap after her husband, James, wrapped up the Thanksgiving prayer. She took her fork and stabbed it into some of the turkey on her plate. Then, she brought the food to her mouth and savored the taste of the delicious Thanksgiving turkey.

"James," she let out. "This is amazing! It's so good."

"Thank you," her husband said in between bites. "I got the brine recipe from one of the wives who helps out in the church office." He took a sip of his white wine. "Says she serves it every Thanksgiving and Christmas."

"Well, she did a good job," Constance said before taking another bite. "We have so much to be thankful for this year."

"Exactly," James said. "We've had an amazing year at the church. Attendance is up, and our offering is well over what had been anticipated."

"Like I said," Constance repeated. "We sure are blessed this year!"

As the two enjoyed their meal, Constance's phone began ringing outside of the dining room.

"Oh no," she sighed as she dabbed her mouth with her napkin. "It's never good when they call on a holiday."

She stood from her seat and stepped out of the dining room, over to the front parlor where it was lying, vibrating against the wooden grain of the end table. She looked at the screen and didn't recognize the number. However, she took it, answered it, and put it to her ear.

"Hello?"

"Madame Vice President?" a familiar voice said over the phone. "This is House Speaker Rebecca White. I hope you are having a splendid day on this beautiful Thanksgiving."

Constance looked puzzled. "Speaker White, why are you calling me?"

"That is a good question, ma'am," Rebecca began. "I'm sorry to be interrupting your celebrations with your family. But I've been in discussions with some of my colleagues in the House, and these conversations have suddenly blossomed into something that needs your attention."

"Yes?"

"Well, our conversations have revolved around our confidence in the president's ability to lead and govern."

Constance remained quiet, allowing Rebecca to continue on.

"And I hate to come forward publicly right now, Madam Vice President. I felt it would be better to call you privately and talk to you about it."

"And what is that?" Constance still was confused about the point of this conversation. *What does she want? Doesn't she have something else better to do today?*

"Ma'am," Rebecca said. "I believe it is time to consider invoking the Twenty-Fifth Amendment and call together a meeting of the secretaries to hold a vote on the president's ability to remain in office."

Constance's jaw dropped. "I can't do that!"

"Think of it this way, Constance," Rebecca said. "If you decline to do anything about this, you will be betraying the country. You must uphold the Constitution of the United States and fulfill your duty to protect it. Sometimes that duty isn't easy."

The vice president began to feel anger growing. She wasn't appreciative of Rebecca calling on Thanksgiving to begin with. Add in that she was calling to try to oust the current president, and Constance was ready to end the call and return to her plate of food in the dining room.

"Rebecca," she said. "You've been trying to destroy the Klimmings Administration since its inception. How do I know that you're not saying all of this only to try and oust him from office?!"

"Think about how he's acted since his separation. Without even considering that whole ordeal with China, the president has become irrational. He's missing meetings and exploding on reporters." Rebecca paused. "I know you've seen the news, Constance. But, there's no denying that the president's behavior has become very erratic lately.

Constance remained silent, considering everything that the speaker had just said.

"One more thing," Rebecca said. "Out of the colleagues I've spoken with . . . they weren't all Republicans."

Before Constance could respond, she heard the phone call end. Stunned over what she had been told, Constance slowly moved the phone from her ear to the table.

"What's wrong?"

Constance turned around to see James standing in the parlor.

"That was Speaker White," Constance said. "She called regarding some conversations she's had with some members of the House."

"And what did she say about them?"

Constance swallowed hard. "She asked me to consider invoking the Twenty-Fifth Amendment."

\* \* \*

In the dining room of the Klimmings Mansion, everyone made their way to their seats while Vicki stood in the archway as they came in. While standing there, Jeremy approached her like a whipped puppy.

"I'm sorry for the way I acted earlier," he said. "That was not right of me."

Vicki smiled. "Thank you, Jeremy." She looked over his shoulder and saw Cathie standing by a chair, listening in to hear exactly what Jeremy was saying to her. Then, Vicki smiled as she realized that Jeremy hadn't come to apologize based on his own accord.

Before Vicki could turn to head to her seat, Charlotte turned the corner, looking as elaborate as she could.

"I'm so sorry I'm late," she said to Vicki as she hugged her. "The traffic was a nightmare."

"Sure it was," Vicki said, knowing that Charlotte was lying. "Your seat is right there."

Vicki identified the open seat between her spot at the end of the table to the left of Ryan.

"Oh, no no no no no!" Charlotte reacted. "I'm not sitting next to him!"

The Applegates, along with Miranda and Julie, looked confused as Charlotte refused to sit between her sister and Ryan.

"Charlotte," Vicki said. "What's wrong with that seat?"

"Don't you remember?!" Charlotte exclaimed. "The turkey incident from last year?!"

"Well, Ben isn't here this year," Jeremy added. "So I'm sure you don't have to worry about any turkeys sliding across the table at you."

Charlotte glared at Jeremy and then turned back to Vicki. "I must sit somewhere else, Vicki. It is imperative."

"Well, where would you like to sit?" Vicki asked her sister, gesturing to the table.

Charlotte turned around and examined the room. "How about that spot?" She went over to the seat opposite Vicki at the head of the table in front of the fireplace.

"Aunt Charlotte," Miranda said, sitting next to that seat. "That is Dad's seat."

Vicki rolled her eyes. "Miranda, just let her. It's not worth fighting over it."

She let out a deep sigh and took her seat as Charlotte sat in Peter's empty chair. Then, Vicki looked up at the table. Cathie, Jeremy, and Delilah sat to her left, and Ryan, Julie, and Miranda sat to her right. Looking forward, she looked at Charlotte. "Who would like to say the blessing?"

The people seated at the dining table remained quiet.

"Come on," Vicki said. "Someone's got to do it."

Jeremy let out a sigh. "I guess I could do it."

"No, honey," Cathie said, trying to prevent Jeremy from saying anything that would get him into any further trouble.

Julie leaned over to Miranda. "Is this awkward or what?" she asked her.

"This is pretty much normal," Miranda said to her. "Last year, Dad,

Ben, and Ryan got into it, and Ben pushed the turkey down the table, and it fell onto the floor next to Charlotte. Then, she got up, freaking out, and slipped and fell."

"Oh my God," Julie chuckled. "Seriously?!"

"I'm dead serious," Miranda said as she took her attention back to what was happening at the table. Because no one had volunteered to say the prayer, Charlotte had offered to do it. Even though Vicki was reluctant about it, she decided to let her sister go ahead.

"If everyone is ready," Charlotte said. "Bow your heads."

Everyone around the table bowed their heads except for Jeremy, who was having a hard time believing what was going on.

"I need a drink," he mumbled to himself before getting met with an elbow from his wife. "Ouch!"

"Our gracious God," Charlotte began. "Sixteen hundred years ago, you sent the Pilgrims to the Promised Land to found America . . ."

Julie raised her head, confused as to where this was going. She looked down the table and made eye contact with Vicki, who looked horrified.

". . . From that time on, you gave your sacred blessing to all who resided here, leaving us to create a nation so strong and mighty. You allowed us to take all the land from the rebels in the South, making us the greatest nation in the world."

Miranda raised her head, puzzled by what Charlotte was saying. As she looked down the table, everyone had raised their heads in bewilderment. Each person was confused with what Charlotte was saying in her prayer, yet she continued on.

"And then the depression hit, and our country struggled. But in your gracious goodness, you continued to provide and allowed us to channel all those hard times into anger and frustration during World War II. Lord, you were there for us then, and you will always be there for us when we need you. And for that, we thank you. Amen."

"Amen," Jeremy said before grabbing his fork. "Let's eat!"

* * *

Seated in the dining room of the residence of the White House, Ben ate his turkey in silence. Across from him sat Peter, who was also eating his meal quietly. Ben waited for him to look up to start some kind of a conversation with him, but Peter never did. Instead, he would take a bite of his food and then proceed to scroll through social media on his phone. Finally, after Ben had contemplated why he had chosen to spend his Thanksgiving with his father rather than spend it with the rest of his family, he decided to strike up a conversation.

"So, how has it been?" Ben began, placing his napkin on the table. "Living in the White House, I mean. How has it been here?"

Peter shrugged without looking up from his phone. "It's okay. It's definitely not home."

"You sure?" Ben asked. "We really miss you at home."

"Yeah," Peter said, continuing not to look up from his phone. "I miss you all too."

Ben took a deep breath as he became perturbed. "What are you going to do if Mom divorces you?"

Ben instantly realized that he shouldn't have asked that, but it caused Peter to lift his attention away from his phone. "Why the hell do you say that?"

"Because," Ben said. "It's possible, isn't it? She kicked you out in the middle of July, Dad. It's November now. What are the chances of her allowing you to move back into the house?"

"It's still possible," Peter said. "There have been many cases where people have reconciled after separating."

"Yes, but you and Mom haven't even spoken to each other since the separation began."

Peter nodded his head. "I know . . . and what worries me is what she may do if she decides she wants a divorce."

"What do you mean?"

"Ben," Peter said as he took his napkin from his lap, dabbed the corner of his mouth, and set it on the table. "Your mom is in control of my company right now. She has thirty-five percent of the voting shares . . ."

"Forty-five," Ben interrupted. "After Gabby's death and Miranda's transfer of ten of her own shares over to her, Mom ended up inheriting them after we finally came public about Gabby's death."

"*She* came public," Peter said. "I never wanted us to announce her death in that way."

"Then how did you want to announce it, Dad? Were you planning to tell the world that I found her dead in her bed, and then you panicked and had her buried in the family plot in the backyard?"

"I did not panic," Peter said. "I was concerned about what may happen if it came out that Gabby had killed herself."

"Well, everyone knows she shot herself now," Ben snapped back. "And because of you, Mom had to do it all on her own."

Ben took in a couple of breaths, trying to calm himself. "I'm sorry," he said. "It just worries me what may happen between you two."

Peter smiled slightly. "I understand, son. I get it. But I must ask you something."

"What is it?"

"Ben," he said. "In the unlikely event that your mom and I do not reconcile, I need you to promise me that you will do whatever you can to remove her from the presidency of Klimmings Incorporated."

Ben looked puzzled. "What?! Mom would never take the company away from you!"

"Really? I relinquished every bit of ownership whenever I began my campaign for the presidency. I own nothing in the company, Ben. Your mom controls all of my interest."

Ben had to refrain from letting his jaw drop. "Do you really think Mom would take the company away from you?"

"Well, let me just say this." Peter leaned forward. "I never expected her to kick me out of my own house."

Ben remained silent as Peter leaned back in his chair and resumed eating. Then, he turned to his left, where Katherine was seated in her high chair.

"I'm so glad you were able to bring her," he said as he tried to feed her a few small spoonfuls of mashed potatoes and gravy. "She's grown up so much."

As Peter successfully got Katherine to take a bite of the mashed potatoes, Ben watched, wondering whether he should consider what his father had told him or disregard it altogether.

\* \* \*

Charlotte slid open the back patio door, looking outside and seeing Vicki standing on the patio, overlooking the pool and the pool area. As she stepped out, Charlotte noticed a puff of smoke had drifted away from her sister.

"What a lovely Thanksgiving," Charlotte said as she closed the door and began to step over to Vicki. Her sister quickly tried to hide the cigarette she was smoking. "You don't need to hide that from me, Vicki. I already know."

"You do?" Vicki turned toward Charlotte with a cigarette in her hand.

"Yes," Charlotte said as she stood beside Vicki and looked out over the pool. "I stumbled across them one day at the office when you weren't there. I had some papers for you and went to put them on your desk, and there they were."

"So you were snooping then?"

"No," Charlotte lied. "I needed an expenditure report, and I ended up finding your cigarettes."

Vicki nodded as she took a draw from her cigarette. "I guess you're disappointed in me, then."

"No," Charlotte said. "I just want to know why. Why are you smoking again?"

Vicki let the air and smoke flow from her lungs. "It was a very rough summer. I needed something to help ease the stress."

"And then Gabby's death . . ."

"Then Gabriella died," Vicki said. "It's just been so hard with everything going on."

Charlotte nodded. "I bet so. I couldn't imagine what that phone call must've been like from St. Mary's."

Vicki fell quiet, struggling to come up with a response for Charlotte.

"It was bad," she lied. "I don't want to talk about it."

Charlotte turned to face Vicki. "But I do, Vicki."

Vicki's eyes widened.

"How did Gabby really die?" Charlotte asked.

"What do you mean?"

"I know she never attended St. Mary's. I traveled there and met with the school's headmistress. So when did she die, and how did she die?"

Vicki looked at Charlotte and took another hit off of her cigarette. "Let's sit down." She turned and made her way over to a patio table with chairs placed around it. Sitting near the table was an outdoor heater, which helped make the area around the table comfortable. Vicki sat in a chair, and Charlotte sat opposite her.

"It happened in February," Vicki began. "Benjamin had gone up to Gabriella's room to call her down for dinner, and when he got in there . . ." She stopped to wipe a tear from her eye. ". . . When he got in there, he found her."

"Did she kill herself?"

Vicki nodded as she wiped her eyes with her open hand. "I don't remember everything, but somewhere through it all, Peter decided that it was best that we go ahead and place Gabriella in the family plot. She was buried where she is now, next to Peter's father and mother."

"Oh my God, Vicki," Charlotte let out. "You've been holding that in since February?!"

She nodded. "After Miranda's miscarriage, I just couldn't hold it in any longer. I had to come out and announce that she had died, but I couldn't do so in any way that would get me placed in jail."

"Why would you be placed in jail?"

"Because I stood by and let Peter and his Secret Service people bury Gabriella in the family plot. I didn't try to stop them."

"How does Ben not know about this? Every time I seemed to bring up Gabby, he was always clueless about her."

"Poor Benjamin," Vicki said before taking another drag from her cigarette. "He started drinking heavily following Gabriella's death. Unfortunately, he drank so hard that he ended up forgetting the entire night altogether, leaving Peter and myself to carry the burden around."

"Damn," Charlotte sighed. She tried to process everything Vicki had just told her, making her wish she'd never been nosey in the first place. "I don't even know what to say."

"Charlotte, you can't say anything to anyone about this," Vicki stated. "It could continue to damage the family even further. I only told you because I feel you needed to know." Vicki took another puff from her cigarette. "And Gabriella was your favorite niece."

Charlotte let a friendly smile show to her sister. "I definitely understand, Vicki." She leaned forward and took Vicki's open hand in her own. "And if you ever need a friend to talk to, Vicki, you can always count on me."

# CHAPTER 13
## INVOKE THE TWENTY-FIFTH WITH ME

Constance sat in the vice president's office, running over the thoughts in her mind. Whether or not she should entertain the idea of pursuing the Twenty-Fifth Amendment continued to be the focal point of every thought of hers. It had invaded every aspect of her mind since speaking with Rebecca White yesterday.

"Madam Vice President?"

Constance looked toward the door and saw Janet standing in the doorway.

"Secretary Steele," Constance said. "What pleasure do I have to see you this morning?"

"I need to speak with you, ma'am," she said, closing the door behind her. She made her way over to Constance's desk and took a seat in one of the chairs in front of it. "I received a call from a Democratic representative who wishes to remain anonymous."

Constance's eyes widened. "I received a phone call from Speaker White yesterday," she said. "Just out of curiosity, did your conversation focus on a particular amendment to the Constitution?"

"Would the numbers be a two and a five?"

"They sure were," Constance said, leaning back in her chair. "I can't lie. I thought she was just full of it, Janet. But apparently, Speaker White was telling the truth."

"What did she say?" Janet asked.

"Well, she said that members of the House had spoken with her about enacting the Twenty-Fifth Amendment because of the president's irrational behaviors and such." Constance looked at Janet. "She mentioned that some Democrats were having the same discussions with her as well."

"That's what my source said too. Constance, do you think you are going to call together a meeting of Cabinet members?"

Constance remained quiet as she thought things over. "I don't know," she said. "This all came out of nowhere. How do you think the rest of the Cabinet would react?"

Janet sighed. "If I'm being honest," she said. "I don't know." Janet coughed before continuing. "But the president has been really off the rails lately. I can't think of any member who may be loyal enough to the president to tell him about the plan."

Constance nodded her head. "I have one in mind who might." She looked over Janet's shoulder toward the door. "Is the president here?"

"I think he's still eating his breakfast," Janet said. "I am supposed to meet with him soon, so he should be coming down soon."

Constance nodded. "I guess you should be on your way then. We don't need anyone to begin to suspect anything."

Janet nodded her head. "You've got a point." She stood from her chair. "I will be seeing you around then."

"I'll see you," Constance said as she stood. "And please keep all of this on the down-low. I don't need the president to find out about this."

Once again, Janet nodded before turning and heading out of Constance's office, leaving her sitting behind her desk. She let out a deep sigh and then picked up her phone lying on the top of the desk. She scrolled through her contacts and clicked on James' name. Then, she put the phone to her ear and waited until he answered.

"James," Constance said. "I need your advice on something."

"Yes, dear," James responded. "I'm about to have a meeting with the church board, so try to make it quick."

Constance sighed. "James, I just met with a Cabinet member about invoking the Twenty-Fifth Amendment. She told me that a Democrat reached out to her yesterday."

"So Rebecca White wasn't lying, then?" James asked for clarification.

"No," Constance said. "Apparently, she wasn't."

"May I ask who the Cabinet member was?" James asked, growing more curious.

"It was Steele."

"Damn. She's a good one."

"I know. I had a hard time processing everything as she spoke to me this morning. Do you think that the president's behavior has warranted it?"

James paused for a brief second. "Constance, I am going to be late . . ."

"James, answer the question. Do you think that I need to continue with this?"

"If you feel you should. Constance, what do you think? You've seen how he's acted recently."

"I'm definitely concerned," she said. "And so is Steele. Peter has never acted this way."

"Do you think that talking to him will help at all?"

"Hell no! You saw how he flew off the handle whenever the reporter spoke to him."

"Then you already have your answer then, don't you?"

Constance began to process the various scenarios that could transpire throughout this process. "James, if I start this, I will be the first vice president to do so."

"Honey," he said. "There has always got to be a first."

"Thank you!"

"Now, I need to get off the phone and head to this meeting. I'll talk to you whenever I get home tonight."

"I'll see you then."

Constance took the phone away from her ear and ended the call. She set the phone on the top of her desk and then leaned back in her chair, where she ran her hand through her hair and took a deep breath, considering all the repercussions that could come from pursuing such a drastic thing.

* * *

Ben took a bite of his scrambled eggs as Miranda entered the dining room.

"Good morning," she said as she made her way to the breakfast bar. "It looks like it's cold outside today."

"Yes," Ben said as he took his napkin and wiped the corners of his mouth. "Cold outside, just like it's cold in here."

Miranda turned around and headed to her seat with her plate of food. "You think it's cold in here?"

"No," Ben responded. "I'm not talking about the temperature, Miranda. I'm talking about the atmosphere."

Miranda took a bite of her eggs. "What do you mean?"

Ben took in a deep breath. "What do you think Mom plans to do with the company?"

"What do you mean by that?"

"Let's say Mom and Dad divorce. What do you think she will do with the company? Do you think she will step down as the president of it?"

"I would hope so," Miranda said. "Dad built that company from the ground up. It's his." She took another bite of her breakfast. "You don't think she will steal it from him?"

"I don't know," Ben said. "But Dad seems to think she will."

"Why?"

"He didn't really say. But now that Mom controls forty-five percent of the voting shares, she can almost take over complete control of the company."

"That's strange. After she told us about Gabby's death, Mom didn't bother to even ask if I wanted the shares that I had given to her back.

Instead, she just took them for herself."

"I know. That is why I am struggling with this. Dad may be right."

"What are you planning to do?" Miranda asked him as she took another bite of her scrambled eggs.

"Miranda," Ben began. "I feel that we need to call together a shareholder's meeting and hold a vote on company leadership."

"Are you out of your mind?!" Miranda exclaimed as she slapped her fork onto her plate, and an unnerving clanking sound emanated from them. "Mom has already been through so much, Ben! If we do this to her now, it's going to seem like we are turning against her."

"I know . . . I know . . ." Ben said as he wadded up his napkin. "But I don't know what to do about it all."

"You could talk to her."

"Can we, Miranda? You were in here whenever we tried to talk with her about Dad. You saw how she acted whenever we brought him up."

"Ben, you have to realize that Mom is still healing from the death of her youngest. The woman never got to properly cope and deal with her suicide because our father decided to play the role of God and bury her in the family plot out back."

Ben sighed. "You know, that really is some messed up shit, isn't it?"

"You think?!" Miranda stated. She picked up her fork and began pushing her eggs around her plate. "Ben, I know you love our father – and I do too – but I don't think that taking sides in our parents' fight is going to help right now."

"So that's it then? You're fine with Mom taking over the entire company, then?"

"No. That's not what I said. Should their marriage continue to deteriorate, and I see no path for the two of them to reconcile, then and only then will I entertain the idea of forming a coup against our mother in the board room."

\* \* \*

Martha opened the door to the Oval Office, causing Peter to stand up from where he had been sitting behind the *Resolute* desk. He looked toward the door to see Charlotte make her way in.

"Good morning, Charlotte," Peter said as he rounded the desk, greeting her with a hug. "What pleasure do I owe you today?"

"Well," Charlotte said as she followed Peter to the cream sofas to sit down. "I wasn't needed at the office today, so I decided that while I was in town, I would swing by and see if they would let me see you."

"Well, obviously they did," Peter said with a smile. "How are things?"

"I wondered how long it would take before you asked that," Charlotte said before laughing. "I would say that they are going just as smoothly as they could be."

"What do you mean by that?"

"Well . . . I feel that tensions are definitely beginning to brew in the Klimmings household. Not everyone is happy with the prolonged separation between you and my sister."

"Hey, the ball is completely in her court. She came in here with a packed bag and practically told me to stay the hell away from her. Since then, I have. Hell, I haven't even had the chance to speak with her."

"I understand," Charlotte continued. "But I could sense at Thanksgiving that your daughter wasn't thrilled with what was going on."

"*Miranda?*"

"Yes. She didn't mention the company very much, and after the meal, when Jeremy Applegate tried to mention it to her, she shut him down." Charlotte looked Peter in the eyes. "Peter, what is going on with that?"

"Your guess is as good as mine," Peter said as he got up and headed to the bar to make himself a drink. "I control no interest in the company right now. The plan when I ran for president was for Vicki to retain every bit of ownership in the company, and then whenever my two terms were up, she is supposed to give that back to me." He turned around and held out a glass toward Charlotte, offering a drink to her. She shook her head in declination.

"Anyways," Peter said as he turned back around and continued making himself a drink. "After Gabby's death, Vicki decided to take control of the ten voting shares Miranda had signed over to her, putting her closer to a majority than anyone else."

"Yes," Charlotte said as Peter returned to the sofa across from her. "I do find that peculiar. After all, she knew Gabby was dead whenever Miranda gave her the voting shares, so why didn't she just give them back to Miranda whenever she made that announcement?"

"Because she's power-hungry," he said before taking a sip of his drink. Then, he set the glass on the coffee table and paused. He ran through what Charlotte said and glanced up toward her. "What did you say?"

"Huh?" Charlotte responded. "What *did* I say?"

"Yes, you said that Vicki knew Gabby was dead when the voting shares were handed out. How did you know that?"

Charlotte took a deep breath, knowing that she would be in deep trouble with Vicki whenever she found out that Charlotte inadvertently told Peter that she knew about Gabby's death and cover-up.

"Well . . . after Thanksgiving," she started. "Vicki and I were talking in the garden, and she spoke about the night that you all found Gabby."

"What exactly did she tell you?"

"Everything."

Peter stood up from the sofa, snatched his drink, and walked toward the fireplace as he took a sip. "Dammit, Vicki!"

"Peter, I swear to you. I haven't told a soul about this."

He turned to her. "I'm not concerned about you. I know you'll keep it to yourself. It's your damn sister that pisses me off."

Charlotte fell silent, unsure of what to say.

"I just don't understand," Peter continued before taking another sip of his drink and then setting it on the desk. "She had all that time to talk to me, but she never did! I just don't understand."

He turned and looked out the side window toward the Rose Garden. At that moment, silence fell across the Oval Office. Peter continued to take in the sights from out the window. He watched as the cold wind rustled through the remaining leaves on the trees and looked at the clouds as they danced across the sky.

Charlotte slowly rose from the sofa and made her way over to him. She put her hand on his back and comforted him.

"It's going to be fine, Peter," she said. "She'll come around eventually."

"You think?"

"I am sure of it."

She took him in her arms and held him in an embrace. The two remained in each other's arms long enough for the door on the opposite side of the room to open without them knowing. Constance stood in the doorway, taking in the scene. Her mouth fell open before she took a deep breath and slowly closed the door. She turned and headed down the hall, turning right toward her office. When she got to it, she closed the door and locked it behind her.

She rushed over to her desk and opened her laptop. After signing in, she opened a new email and began typing. In this email, she started listing all of her concerns regarding the president and his behavior. Finally, when she had finished, she skimmed over what she had written and then attached each member of the Cabinet to it. Then, she took in a deep breath, said a silent prayer, and sighed before finally hitting the "send" button.

\* \* \*

At the turn of the calendar month, December came in with even colder weather than what was had at November's end. With the days becoming shorter and more gloomy, the Applegates began to have enough.

Jeremy and Ryan stood inside Jeremy's office at the Applegate Technology Headquarters Campus, just outside Belle Haven alongside the Potomac River. His office, which was mainly white with accents of red, was designed with a modern feel: red LEDs underlit crevasses and a few corners. Jeremy stood behind his desk, which was white and had glass legs on one side with white legs which curved to blend with the top on the other side.

Ryan sat in a red chair on the opposite side of the desk as Jeremy explained how things went as the company's president.

"Do you understand this?" Jeremy asked Ryan. "Because if you don't, now is the time to come forward and say something. I can have Delilah come in and manage the company if I need to."

"Dad," Ryan said, standing up from his seat. "I understand it all. Try not to worry about it. Everything here will be fine while you and Mom are away in the Bahamas."

"I just wanted to make sure. The company took a drastic hit when that damn President Wu resigned in China. It's been months, and we're *still* trying to sort things out from all that crap."

"Dad, like I said, it will be fine. I can manage the company for a month while you two are away."

"I know," Jeremy said as he sat in his chair. "I am just concerned about what will happen on the trip. Your mom and I have been a little rocky lately, and I just want to sort everything out while we're gone."

"If you don't mind me asking, why have things been rocky between you two?"

Jeremy looked at Ryan. "Peter Klimmings is the main reason. I did some things to try to undermine him, and your mom found out and wasn't happy about it all. You should know. You were there whenever Peter dropped the bomb that he knew that I was behind that China deal at Thanksgiving last year."

"I remember that," Ryan said, nodding his head. "That son of a bitch couldn't have done it discreetly. Instead, he had to go ahead and ruin the whole damn meal."

"No," Jeremy said. "I seem to remember Ben and you getting into it at Thanksgiving, and . . . didn't the turkey end up on the floor?"

Ryan laughed. "It did, and Charlotte ended up slipping on it and falling."

Jeremy let out a small laugh. "That was a good Thanksgiving."

"Yes, it was."

Jeremy patted Ryan on the shoulder as the two turned toward the back wall to look out the window facing the Potomac River. "So, you sure you got it all?"

"I am sure, Dad," Ryan said. "When you return from your vacation with Mom, the company will be in just as good shape as it is right now."

\* \* \*

Ben looked to his left at Delilah, lying in bed next to him. She turned her head back to him and smiled.

"Why is it that every time I come over to pick up Katherine, we always end up in bed?" Ben asked Delilah, who smiled back at him.

"I don't know," Delilah said as she rolled over so that it would be easier to look at him. "But it's good each time we do it."

Ben smiled. "I missed this." He leaned forward and kissed Delilah.

"Ben," she said. "We've been doing this since July. What are we?"

"Huh?"

"What are we? Like, are we dating or what?"

Ben looked toward the ceiling. "That's a good question. All this time, I hadn't really thought about it. I just assumed . . ."

Delilah sat up. "Assumed what?"

"I just assumed that we were Ben and Delilah."

"Ben and Delilah . . ."

"Yes," Ben said. "Ben and Delilah, just like we were a few years ago."

"Before our marriage caught fire and burned to the ground?"

Ben chuckled. "It wasn't your fault, Delilah. I was just as guilty in causing it to end."

She smiled at him. "That's sweet of you."

He smiled back at her. "So, did I answer your question at all?"

"Yes," she said before leaning forward to kiss him. "We're Ben and Delilah."

\* \* \*

Miranda rounded the corner of the bottom of the stairs, going through the archway into the living room, where Vicki was seated on the sofa watching the TV. As Miranda made her way closer to Vicki, she began to notice that she was watching the evening news, and as usual, the commentators were discussing the president. Immediately, Miranda could feel the air go cold as Vicki watched the TV and listened to them talking about Peter's last few months in office, pointing out how irrational he had become.

"Do you think that some of the things they're talking about are true?" Vicki asked her as she sat in the chair to Vicki's left.

"What?" Miranda said, intentionally trying to avoid the question.

"Miranda, I know you heard me."

She let out a sigh. "Mom, you've seen the footage. I've seen the footage. What do you think about it all?"

"I don't know," Vicki said, rolling her eyes. "I've been married to your father for thirty-five years. In all that time, he never acted like that."

"Why do you think that he's been acting like that?"

"I know where you're trying to go with this," Vicki said. "You're trying to get me to say it's my fault."

"No, I'm not," Miranda said. "I just want to know what you're thinking with all of this."

Vicki looked over at Miranda. She didn't say anything, but by the look on her face, Miranda could tell that Vicki didn't want to talk about it.

"Mom," Miranda continued. "It's almost been five months. What are you planning to do with Dad?"

Once again, Vicki remained silent.

"Mom, just give me an answer."

"I don't know."

"Come on, Mom," Miranda said, leaning forward in the chair. "You got to do better than that. You either still love Dad, or you don't. What is it?"

"I told you," Vicki said. "I don't know!"

"Well, so much time has gone by . . . we feel that things aren't even going to work out. What'll happen then?"

"Who do you mean by we?"

Miranda gulped. "Ben and me."

"What all have you and Benjamin been talking about?" Vicki said, becoming irritated. "Me? My mental state?"

"No, Mom. Not that."

"Then what the hell is it, Miranda?!"

Vicki stood from the sofa to look down at her daughter.

"We just talked about our concerns with the company," Miranda said. "We've been talking about the future in the event that you and Dad didn't reconcile."

"And what are you two planning to do? Oust me?!"

Miranda remained silent. She thought things over, trying to figure out how she should respond.

"I thought so," Vicki said before Miranda could provide any answer. She stormed past her and made her way through the archway.

"Mom, wait!" Miranda went after her, but by the time she had reached the bottom of the staircase, Vicki had already made it to the top, and she could hear her mom's bedroom door close.

* * *

James lifted the covers back and climbed into bed next to Constance. She was wearing her reading glasses, scrolling through her tablet, and looking over all of the day's news articles. As a surprise to her, she had found multiple stories of people criticizing her for her lack of leadership these last few months.

"Can you believe this?" Constance said, holding her phone closer to James so he could see the article. "They're railing against me because I haven't acted like a leader. They have no idea."

She pulled the tablet away before James could really look it over.

"Well," he said. "You *did* call together the Cabinet, didn't you?"

"Yes. We're meeting tomorrow night."

"Where at?"

"The White House. The president is supposed to be out of town, campaigning in Iowa, so I figured we could take advantage of it and meet in the Roosevelt Room."

"Why aren't you doing it in the Cabinet Room?"

"I thought about it, but I felt it would be too backstabbing.

Something like this shouldn't happen in the Cabinet room."

"Constance," James sighed. "You're literally organizing a group to remove Peter Klimmings from the role of president and grant that power to yourself."

"I had thought about that," Constance said. "I'd be the second female president."

"The fiftieth."

"I know. It's just so hard to wrap my head around." She ran her hands up her face, pressing on her temples before fluffing her hair. "I don't want to be president. Not this way."

"You think you'll convince them all?" James asked.

"I hope so," Constance sighed. "I have my doubts about Secretary Bird."

"The defense secretary?"

"Yes. He seems to be the most loyal to the president. If anyone prevents us from invoking the Twenty-Fifth, it will be him."

James nodded his head. "Constance," he said. "I want you to consider this."

"Yes," she said, taking off her reading glasses.

"If anything happens that causes this not to go through, you're going to have to announce a run for president."

Constance remained silent.

"Do you really think that he will ask you to be his vice president for a second term?" James asked. "Better yet, do you believe he even has a chance to be elected a second term after this?"

"I don't," Constance responded. "I really can't see him getting reelected."

"And you know that if you announce a run for president, you will have the full support of the Washington Pentecostal Church of God. We can try our best to pull over the support of the rest of the evangelicals."

"I figured that."

"Just think about it," James said. "This is a worst-case scenario thing anyways. I think you'll be fine, but it isn't going to hurt to always have options on the table."

"I hope so," Constance said as she laid back in bed. "This has never happened before, James. I'm scared about how people are going to see this."

"What do you mean?"

"Like . . . is it going to appear like a power grab?"

"No, honey," James said, comforting her. "It's not. People are already seeing how batshit crazy Peter has become."

"And that also concerns me, James," she said, looking up at her husband. "What is Peter going to do whenever he finds out?"

* * *

Michelle picked up her phone from her small bedside table, feeling it vibrate in her hand. She had just gotten out of the shower and only had a towel wrapped around herself. "Hello?" she said after answering the phone and placing it on speaker.

"Michelle, is that you?"

"Charlotte?"

"Yes, this is Charlotte," Charlotte replied. "Who is this?"

"Charlotte," Michelle said from the other side of the room as she dried herself off. "This is Michelle. You called me."

"I know that," Charlotte said. "But you sounded different. You don't have a cold, do you?"

"No."

"Good. I was afraid I was going to catch something from you."

Michelle stopped drying herself and turned toward her phone, running what Charlotte had said through her head.

"Charlotte," Michelle said. "It's almost eight o'clock, and I was getting ready to climb in bed and binge-watch some TV shows. What did you call me about?"

"I need to tell you something, Michelle," Charlotte said. "It's about Gabby."

Michelle sighed. "Charlotte, she died back in July. Don't you remember your sister's video?"

"Yes, but that wasn't the truth."

"Charlotte . . . are you drunk?"

"No, Michelle, I haven't been drinking," Charlotte said as she grew more irritated. "Just shut the hell up, and let me tell you what she told me!"

Michelle got quiet, and after a second, Charlotte finally began to tell her what she wanted to say. She described the evening of Thanksgiving when she went outside on the back patio with Vicki. She told Michelle how Vicki opened up about Gabby's suicide and the subsequent cover-up conducted by Peter and the Secret Service. Throughout the entire conversation, Michelle continued to dress in her pajamas, listening to what Charlotte was saying but consistently doubted whether or not she thought it was true.

\* \* \*

Denise opened the front door of the Klimmings Mansion and saw Julie standing on the other side.

"Miss Julie," she said. "Come inside." She stepped aside so Julie could enter the entry hall.

"Thank you, Denise," Julie said as she took her coat off and hung it on the rack. "Is Miranda here?"

"Miss Miranda is in the living room," Denise said before calling for Miranda. "Miss Miranda, Julie is here."

"Send her in," Miranda announced from the living room. Denise looked at Julie and extended her arm, inviting her to make her way into the living room. She proceeded and turned the corner, seeing Miranda on the sofa watching the evening news.

"Spending your Thursday night watching the news, are we?" Julie asked as she sat in the first chair upon entering the living room.

"Welcome to my life," Miranda said. "I don't get out much."

"I can see," Julie said as she looked up toward the portrait which hung above the bar. "Miranda, how about you and I go out tonight?"

"What?"

"You and me. Let's go out and hit up a few of the clubs in DC."

Miranda shifted slightly on the sofa. "Julie, I'm not ready to go out and pick up guys at the clubs yet. It's not even been a year since . . ."

She fell silent, not wanting to finish her sentence. However, she didn't need to. Julie knew precisely what Miranda was planning to say.

"It's coming up, isn't it, though?" Julie asked comfortingly.

"Yes. And the trial should be beginning within a month or so." Miranda adjusted herself on the sofa. "Julie, what if I am subpoenaed?"

"They're not going to subpoena you, Miranda. It will be fine, and before you know it, Jason will be locked away in jail for a very long time."

Miranda sighed. "I'll just be glad when all of this is over. I can't stand this feeling all the time."

Julie tried to crack a smile to show comfort and understanding toward Miranda.

"Hey!" she said. "What if we went to one of the gay clubs instead?"

Miranda cocked her head and unenthusiastically said, "Really?"

"Yes! It will be so much fun, Miranda. Have you ever been to one?"

"I have. And it wasn't fun."

"What?"

"It was a bunch of guys dancing around with each other, getting drunk, and I'm just not into all of that. Plus, what's it going to look like when two women in their late twenties show up to this gay club without a gay friend?"

"It's going to look like two grown women going to have a good time," Julie said before shifting to a serious tone. "But first of all, I am twenty-four. I am not in my late twenties."

Miranda smiled at her. "Okay," she said. "But that doesn't solve the gay friend thing. Won't they be upset if we just show up without someone who connects us to the club?"

"Honey," Julie said. "Clearly, you've not been to some of the clubs I've been to." She stood up from the chair and snatched the remote away from Miranda, turning off the TV. "So, let's go."

"Julie . . ."

"No. You already insulted me by calling me old, so you're going with me tonight."

Miranda rolled her eyes and took in a deep breath. "Fine. I'll go." She stood up from the sofa and entered the entry hall. "Let me go change and grab my bag. Then, we can go."

"Alright!" Julie said excitedly. "We're going to have such a good time."

\* \* \*

Inside the Roosevelt Room, Constance sat at the head of the long table. Her back was to the fireplace with the large painting of Teddy Roosevelt hanging above it. She looked down at her watch, which told her that there were two minutes until seven. She looked up at the opposing wall, glancing over the yellow wallpaper plastered onto the walls. As she waited, she continued to notice her right leg constantly moving.

*Calm down, Constance. It's all going to be okay.* Her mind raced with thoughts, and her heart rate intensified. Throughout her tenure as vice president, there hadn't been a moment in which she was more nervous than she was in this moment.

Finally, Constance heard the door open from behind her. She looked back at her watch, which read seven in the evening. Janet was supposed to be the first one meeting her, and by the looks of her watch, she had been right on time.

"Right at seven," Constance said as she rose from her seat.

"I assume you were expecting someone."

Constance's heart dropped into the pit of her stomach when she heard the familiar voice behind her. She froze, standing, looking over the table. Her back remained to the door as her heartbeat became more prominent.

"Tell me, Constance," she heard Peter say from behind her. Then, she heard the door close and remained still until he had moved into her line of sight. "Who were you expecting?"

"Mr. President," Constance nervously said. "I-I-I wasn't expecting you today."

"Curious how things transpire," he said as he took a seat in the chair directly to the left of Constance, facing her. "In fact, I had thought I would be on a plane to Iowa right now, but things change, you know." He glared at her. "Sit down."

She slowly fell into her seat at the head of the long table. The tension had grown tremendously inside the Roosevelt Room, and Constance felt as if the walls were beginning to close in on the two of them.

"This morning, I received an email that had been forwarded to me," Peter began. "And imagine my surprise whenever I found out what it contained."

Constance's eyes began to dart back and forth as she began to panic internally.

"Tell me, Constance," he continued. "What exactly does the Twenty-Fifth Amendment entail? I seem to have forgotten."

She remained quiet, trying to formulate a response to give to Peter without escalating things more.

"Tell me, Constance. What the hell were you planning to do?!"

"We . . . uh . . . we . . ."

"Spit it out."

"We . . . were going to di-discuss you."

"And what were you going to talk about in regards to me? Why couldn't you have just come to me, Constance?"

"Some members of the House had requested that we discuss invoking the Twenty-Fifth Amendment."

"And why the hell would you want to do that?" Peter asked as he stood from his chair and walked over to the fireplace behind Constance. "Constance, you hurt me right now. I took you in – a rising star in the Democratic Party – I elevated you even higher. You were set to run for office once I finished my second term." He intently looked deep into her brown eyes. "How could you do this?"

"Peter . . ."

"I want you to think about this," he said as he picked up the metal fireplace poker. "I built you up and made you what you are today, Constance. Don't think, for a moment, that you can turn on me and take over. Because in the flash of a second, I can destroy you."

He tossed the poker beside the fireplace, allowing for a loud clanking sound to erupt as it hit the stone. Constance jumped in her seat.

Peter moved back in front of her and took his seat again.

"I'm very disappointed, Constance," he said. "And unfortunately, there must be some consequences for your actions."

She looked up at him, not saying a word.

"I expect your resignation soon, Constance. I want you out of my White House. Do you understand?"

She remained quiet.

"Answer the damn question, Constance!"

"I-I understand."

"Good," he said as he stood from his seat. "I expect to have it before the sun rises tomorrow."

He turned and walked past Constance, opening the door and leaving. Constance remained in the room, where she began hyperventilating and crying. Within a few short minutes, it felt as if her entire political career had peaked and come crashing down.

# CHAPTER 14

## THE EX-HUSBAND

Prior to her marriage to Peter, Vicki Fitzgerald was married to the son of a wealthy corporate banker. She and Bill Davis married shortly after her eighteenth birthday and before she had even finished high school. The two moved into one of the houses Bill's father owned in Baltimore, where they began the first happy year of their marriage together.

However, following the conclusion of that year, things began to change. As Bill's father began to fall ill, his son needed to step in and help with his family more often. Rapidly ascending the corporate ladder in the same bank that employed his father, Bill began to find himself busier and busier, taking its toll on his time at home with his wife.

Finally, as the second year of marriage progressed, Vicki sat him down and told him about her intentions to divorce. It wasn't that she had fallen in love with someone else, but rather, she felt that the two had rushed into their marriage and still loved other things more than they loved each other. While Bill disagreed with her, he finally signed the divorce papers, granting Vicki Fitzgerald Davis the divorce she had wanted.

After Vicki moved back in with her family in Annapolis, Bill continued to focus on his family and career. Then, following the turn of the millennium, Vicki met a young entrepreneur who founded a company intending to streamline clean energy across America. He cared about the growing global warming and climate change concerns and made it his purpose in life to try to do whatever he could to protect the planet.

So, Vicki Fitzgerald Davis married Peter Klimmings in Norfolk in the fall of 2000. Nearly five years following, Bill had heard that the two moved to Silver Spring, Maryland, where they had constructed their new home. Controversy swirled over how they purchased multiple properties and demolished the housing to make way for their grand new home. Since then, Bill could not escape the Klimmings family in the news as Klimmings Incorporated continued to grow and flourish during the Obama Administration.

Finally, within the last couple of months, the news shifted from Peter's presidency to the turmoil that was ensuing within his marriage. Over the past thirty-six years, Bill regretted how he had dumped Vicki whenever his family needed him. He wished he had handled it all differently by including her in the process. He had thought about how she would have celebrated with his family whenever his father's illness had finally been cured. Unfortunately, none of that had ever happened. And instead, Bill lived most of his life in regret.

Finally, seeing the opportunity arise, he decided to do something about it. He took leave from his job and traveled to Washington. He rode in a taxi over to Klimmings Tower. As he stepped out of the car, he looked up at the tall building, admiring the reflective bluish-gray windows. Then, he proceeded inside, made it through the building security, and took the elevator to the thirtieth floor. He was nervous as he watched the floor numbers tick up, and he adjusted his yellow tie countless times before the elevator stopped and the door opened to the lobby of Klimmings Incorporated.

Bill took a deep breath and proceeded toward the brunette woman seated at the reception desk. When he stopped in front of the desk, she turned to him without looking at him and asked, "How can I help you?"

"Yes," Bill began, recognizing that it was Vicki's sister, Charlotte. "I am here to see Vicki Klimmings."

Charlotte looked up at Bill, and her eyes widened. "Bill?" she said. "What are you doing here?"

"To see Vicki," he said with a smile. "Is she in?"

"Yes," Charlotte said, returning a smile. She turned to the phone and pressed a button. "Vicki?"

"Yes, Charlotte," Vicki replied over the speaker. She had a tone about her voice that came off as irritated.

"I have someone here to see you."

"Who is it?"

Charlotte looked to Bill, who nodded for her to tell Vicki.

"Um," she began. "Your ex-husband."

There was a moment of quiet before Vicki responded. "Send him in."

Charlotte pointed to the door across from her desk. "She's in there."

Bill smiled and thanked her before he went to the door. He took in a deep breath and opened it. He looked into Vicki's office, looking at the lavender drapes that hung to the sides of the enormous window behind her desk. Bill could immediately see the Capitol Building and Washington Monument through the window. Then, he looked down at Vicki. Because the lights in the room were off, his eyes strained to adjust focus and make her appear less as a silhouette and more as a person seated at their desk.

"Good morning, Bill," Vicki said as she stood from her desk. She rounded it and made her way over to Bill.

He smiled as she turned on the lights.

"Sorry about it being dark," she said. "Sometimes I just can't stand the fluorescents in here."

"I get ya," he said. "Sometimes being in a room with them can give me a headache." He turned his attention back over to the window. "But with that view, why would you ever want to close the curtains and sit in here with just the lights on?"

"I know," Vicki said, turning back to the window. "It really is a nice view. Peter . . ."

She stopped speaking, realizing that she was about to begin talking about her current husband to her ex-husband. Bill turned back to Vicki.

"It's okay," he said. "You don't have to be careful not to talk about him. We were young, Vicki. Our marriage needed to end."

She nodded. "Yeah. I was just eighteen . . . you nineteen."

"We were kids."

Vicki continued to nod her head. Then, she looked over at the clock on the wall.

"It's eleven o'clock," she said. "How about we go ahead and go out for an early lunch?"

"That sounds good to me," he said. "I just arrived early this morning and checked into my hotel room. I haven't eaten anything yet today."

"I got the place then."

Vicki took her coat from the coat rack and opened her office door. "Charlotte," she said as she stepped out into the lobby, followed by Bill. "Bill and I are going to be at Finley's."

"Okay," Charlotte said. "What time will you be back?"

"I'm not sure," Vicki said before looking back at Bill. "We may not be back. We've got a lot of catching up to do."

Bill smiled back at Vicki.

"Okay, but you've got a meeting with the project manager for the West Virginia nuclear plant for later this evening," Charlotte said.

Vicki paused and considered her alternatives. "Cancel it," she said. "Or better yet, reschedule it for next week."

"You're building a nuclear power plant?" Bill asked in amazement.

"Yeah," Vicki said. "I figured it was about time this company diversified from solar and wind energy."

"Damn. You've really changed."

"For the better, I hope?"

"Definitely."

Charlotte looked at the two with a look of disgust on her face. "Alright," she said. "Why don't you two head off then? I'll keep things under control here."

"Alright," Vicki said. "We're off."

She led Bill to the elevator at the end of the lobby hall. As the two got on and the door closed, Charlotte realized how happy Vicki had seemed when Bill came in. In fact, it was the happiest she had seen Vicki in almost a year.

\* \* \*

Dana Gomez stood up from her apartment's couch and headed to the door. The doorbell rang again as she made her way over to it. "I'm coming!" she called out.

When she reached the door, she looked out the peephole and saw Michelle standing there.

"Michelle," she said as she opened the door. "What the hell are you doing here?"

"Dana," she said as she came in. "I have to share something with you."

"What is that?" Dana said as she closed the door.

"It's about Gabby."

"Gabby? Gabby's dead, Michelle."

"I know. I know. But I got a call from Charlotte last night that I wanted to talk to you about."

"What is it?" Dana asked as she sat back down on the couch. Michelle took a seat in the chair next to her.

"Dana, Gabby didn't die at St. Mary's like everyone assumes she did."

"What?!" Dana said as she jolted her head over to Michelle.

"Dana . . . Charlotte called me last night and told me that Gabby had killed herself back in the Klimmings Mansion in February."

Dana's eyes widened, and her heart sank. *Suicide? How could it have been a suicide if there was no gun in the house?*

"Dana, did you hear what I just said?"

"Yes . . . what makes you think that? Couldn't Charlotte have been drunk last night?"

"That's what I thought," Michelle explained. "But then I began to look into it all."

"Dammit, Michelle!" Dana scolded her. "I thought I told you not to screw around with that family. When you keep looking into things, you end up dead."

"Kinda like Gabby," Michelle said. "Dana . . . the point I am trying to make is that I went with her aunt, Charlotte, over to St. Mary's in Switzerland. We met the school's headmistress, and she told us that Gabby had never been enrolled in that school. And now with Charlotte's call last night . . . Dana, I think the Klimmings family covered up Gabby's death."

Dana nodded her head. "Even if they did, why would they have waited so many months before coming out and saying that she killed herself in some school in Switzerland?"

"I don't know, but something weird is going on."

Dana's heart began pounding as the thought of someone finding out about her killing Gabby became more and more of a possibility.

"Michelle, I know you feel guilty about how we treated Gabby in high school, but you got to let it go. She's dead now, and there is nothing we can do about it."

Michelle rolled her eyes. "You don't care, do you?"

"Of course I do, Michelle. I'm just not letting my guilt dominate my life."

Michelle stood from the chair. "You don't have to lie to me, Dana," she said as she made her way to the door. "You don't care that she's dead. You're just some spoiled rich girl who moves on and uses everyone she comes across."

Michelle opened the door and stormed out, slamming it behind her as Dana tried to chase after her.

"Michelle!" she called out after opening the door. "Michelle!"

As she looked down the hallway outside her apartment, she could not see Michelle. Then, she sighed and stepped back inside her apartment. Once again, the events of that night flooded her mind. She remembered how she had taken her father's gun just to intimidate Gabby, but because of how Gabby acted toward her and how she didn't show any sympathy about humiliating her in front of the entire school, she let her emotions control her. And, in just an instant, Dana knew her life would be changed forever.

She had managed to forget about that night, expunging it from her memory. But once Vicki Klimmings posted a video on Facebook announcing Gabby's death, all those memories finally flooded back into her mind. Since then, every single day, Dana had been haunted by her actions, growing more and more guilty with each day.

"Oh, Michelle," Dana sighed in her living room as she plopped onto her couch. She ran her hands through her hair and then pressed her fingertips to her temples. "If only you knew . . . If only you knew . . ."

* * *

"It's been forever since I have been here," Miranda said as she looked around the President's Bar and Grill restaurant. "But isn't this a little less formal than what we are accustomed to, Ben?"

Ben looked at her from across the booth. "Yeah, but it's good, so who cares how formal it is."

"True. I just wonder what the media will say if anyone recognizes us here."

"You kidding me? They don't care about us right now! They're all focused on Mom and Dad's separation."

"True," Miranda said before looking back at her menu. "I think I am going to get a burger. What are you going to get?"

"I don't know," Ben sighed. "I am going out tonight, so I think I may eat light for lunch."

"Really?" Miranda let out. "Who is she?"

Ben looked up at Miranda. "Why do you ask?"

"Oh, come on, Ben. With as much crap as we have gone through this year, I want to talk about something other than myself, Mom and Dad, or anything else political."

"Well," Ben began. "You know her . . ."

"Oh no, Ben," Miranda said. "It's not Julie, is it?'

"No," he replied. "It's not Julie."

"Good. I'd have had to have objected." She took a sip of her water. "Who is she, then?"

Ben took in a deep breath. "Delilah."

Miranda dropped her menu onto the table. "What?"

"You heard me.

"Ben! Why her? You two just got divorced in May! It's not even been a year!"

"I know . . . I know . . ." he said. "But we've been talking some whenever I have come to pick up Katherine for my weekends with her, and . . . I don't know . . . something just clicked between us."

Miranda glared at her brother. "You've slept with her, haven't you?"

"Multiple times."

"Ben!"

"It just happened," he confessed. "And dammit, it was good."

"I don't need to know about it all," Miranda said before taking another sip of her water. "How are you going to go about telling Mom? Dad?"

"I've thought about it," he said. "Dad is going to be so pissed whenever her finds out about our reconciliation."

"Uh-huh. And what about her family? Think about that crazy old man, Jeremy Applegate, for a second. He will flip!"

"I know . . . I know . . ."

Miranda shook her head slowly. "None of that worries you, though, does it?"

He looked his sister in the eyes. "I can't let what other people think of our relationship affect what Delilah and I have for each other."

"I understand," Miranda said. "During your marriage, many people were trying to offer their own opinions and thoughts on the entire thing. I think that's why it ultimately ended."

"I think you're right. It drove Delilah away and me to the bottle."

"Aren't you afraid that you may relapse?"

Ben looked at Miranda. He considered his feelings and concerns, reflecting on what had happened in the past. Then, he sighed and said, "No."

* * *

"This isn't up for debate," Ryan said on the phone in his father's office. "You have to make a decision. Either you tell Vicki Klimmings that your company cannot head up the construction with the plant, or else we are going to increase the cost of the cybersecurity plan with yours."

"But Mr. Applegate," said the man on the phone. "Your father has worked with us for years. How could you make these demands from my company now?"

"Think about what you just said," Ryan said. "My father has been loyal to you for years, so now it is your turn to be loyal to us. Think about your decision, and I look forward to hearing from you soon!"

Ryan placed the phone on the receiver and took a highlighter, crossing off the name of a company on the sheet of paper that lay on the desk. Above the company's name were other names of various companies, each with a yellow highlight over the top of them. As he placed the highlighter on the desk, he smiled, thinking about how proud his father would be whenever he returned from his trip. On his first day taking over the reins of Applegate Technology, Ryan had successfully contacted each organization that had ties with his father's company and Klimmings Incorporated. He then offered a demand that they drop the Klimmings family as a client or face the consequences with their dealings with Applegate Technology.

He looked forward and spotted Delilah approaching the glass door through Jeremy's one-way glass windows, allowing him to see who was coming to his office in the hall without them seeing whether he was inside. Quickly, Ryan quickly pulled some other documents over the sheet of paper indicating his plan and stood from his seat behind the desk. He ensured his jacket was still hung on the back of the chair before making his way over to the door, opening it before Delilah could even knock.

"God," Delilah cursed. "You scared the hell out of me, Ryan!"

"Sorry," he said, inviting her to come inside. "I saw you through the windows."

"Oh yeah," Delilah said as she looked at the windows. I have always hated those damn things. I don't understand why he feels the need to have to hide in his office."

Delilah stepped into the office, and Ryan closed the door behind her.

"It's not that he wants to hide," Ryan said. "It's that he doesn't want to be seen all the time."

"Well, what's he doing that makes him not want to be seen?" Delilah asked as she sat on the red sofa between the door and the window overlooking the Potomac River. "Is he cheating on Mom?"

"Delilah, you know as well as I do that Dad is too scared to cheat on Mom."

Delilah laughed. "True. She would kill him."

"You know she would," Ryan said as he pulled a chair over so he could sit next to the sofa. "So, what have you come here to talk about?"

"Well," she began. "I need to talk to you about something . . . and you're not going to like what I have to tell you."

\* \* \*

"Mr. President?"

Peter looked up from the *Resolute* desk to see Martha standing in the doorway of the Oval Office.

"Yes, Martha?"

"Charlotte Lee is here to see you."

Peter sat up in his chair. "Send her in."

He adjusted his jacket as he stood from the chair, rounded the desk, and made his way to the middle of the room. Then, the door opened, and Charlotte came in.

"Hello, Charlotte," Peter said as he approached her and hugged her. "How are you?"

"I am very concerned, Peter," she said after releasing from the hug. "I have some distressing news to share with you."

"What is it?" he said before offering Charlotte a seat on one of the cream sofas. The two moved over and sat on their own sofas.

"It's your wife," Charlotte began. "Yesterday at Klimmings Incorporated, she received a visitor."

"Okay . . ." Peter said, confused. "Shouldn't she be receiving

218

visitors pretty regularly? I mean . . . she *is* the president of the company."

"I know, but it's who it was that is disturbing."

Peter gave Charlotte a concerned look. "Charlotte, who was it?"

She took in a deep breath before telling him. "Peter, Bill Davis was the visitor."

"Bill . . ." Peter whispered, trying to remember who he was. "Bill Davis . . . Is that . . ."

"The ex-husband? Yes."

"That son of a bitch," Peter swore. "He saw how our marriage was strained on the news, and he's swooped in so he can try to steal her away from me!" Peter ran his hands across his face. "What did he say to her?"

"I don't know, Peter, but the two left shortly after for lunch." Charlotte caught the look on Peter's face but decided to continue. "They didn't come back."

"What?!"

"She was gone for the rest of the day. She even had me cancel a meeting with the project manager for the nuclear plant."

"Nuclear plant?! What the hell is going on in my company right now?"

"Peter, I didn't want to tell you this, but I know what it is like to have an unfaithful spouse."

"What do you mean?"

"When George was caught with that cheerleader," Charlotte confessed. "I didn't know how to process it all. Then, I found out how so many people knew about it, and none of them thought to tell me. I was so pissed."

Peter nodded his head. "I understand. Thank you for telling me."

Charlotte allowed a small smile to flash across her face, and Peter began to return the same whenever the door behind him opened and Henry Gates stormed into the Oval Office.

"Mr. President," he called out. "You *have* to watch the TV now!"

Henry ran over to the *Resolute* desk, where Peter kept the remote for the movable TV he had by the fireplace. As soon as Henry turned it on, it showed press coverage of Constance standing in front of a podium.

"Henry," Peter said, looking over the screen. "What the hell is going on?"

He looked over to the TV, trying to answer his own question, and then he saw it. The headline at the bottom of the screen read: "Zeemer announces Presidential Run."

"That Brutus!" Peter said just loud enough for Charlotte and Henry to hear. "The son of a bitch has done it now!"

"My God, Peter," Charlotte gasped.

"Mr. Gates," Peter said. "Clean out her office now!"

"Mr. President," Henry said, pointing toward the TV. "Listen."

Peter turned back to the TV just as a reporter finished asking a question. He didn't hear what the question was, but Peter certainly listened to the answer.

"That's a great question," Constance said as cameras flashed. "Right now, I do not plan to resign as vice president. I feel that it's important to continue to maintain my presence in the Klimmings White House through the end of his tumultuous term."

"WHAT THE HELL?!" Peter shouted. He jumped from the sofa and through his hands in the air. "What is that woman doing?!"

"Mr. President," Henry said, trying to calm him. "It'll be okay. I can speak with the campaign members and get you a shortlist of new potential vice president picks."

"She's got to go!" Peter shouted. "Throw her out! I don't care!"

"Mr. President, we cannot throw her out. Only Congress can . . ."

"SON OF A BITCH!" Peter yelled as he picked up the pot containing poinsettias on the coffee table between the two sofas, turned, and threw it across the room, crashing against the wall and busting. The flowers went all over the floor, and dirt littered the entire area.

"Damn," Charlotte let out. "Don't ever get on his bad side."

Henry glared over at Charlotte and then turned back to Peter. "Mr. President . . ."

"I can't!" he said. "I need a minute."

Peter stormed over to the door leading to the hallway that would take him to his private study. He opened it and continued out of the room, closing the door behind him.

Henry turned back to Charlotte, who had already stood from the sofa.

"Is he always like this?" she asked.

"No," Henry said. "This didn't start until after Vicki kicked him out of the mansion."

"Damn," Charlotte said. "She must be on his mind, isn't she?"

"I think so," Henry said. "And I'm afraid it's only going to get worse."

* * *

Rebecca White climbed into bed for the night, covering herself with the sheets and trying to make herself comfortable. Christmas was next week, so she had been busy trying to finalize her Christmas plans. She would be traveling home to Florida's 2nd District, where she would spend Christmas with her extended family. In fact, her husband had already traveled down there to prepare their home for their guests.

As Rebecca adjusted herself one final time, she noticed her phone on the bedside table vibrating. She snatched it and looked at the screen. The phone number was hidden.

Rebecca sighed and then decided to go ahead and answer the call. "Hello?"

"Is this Rebecca White I'm speaking with?"

The caller's voice was deepened and muffled. It was evident to Rebecca that this person wanted to keep their identity hidden, which intrigued her more.

"Yes," she replied. "This is her."

"Are you alone?"

"I am."

"I must be quick before someone catches on. I am a member of the Klimmings White House, and I must tell you some of the things that have been going on."

"And what would these things be?"

"Were you aware that President Klimmings was involved in the rebellion that occurred within mainland China over the summer?"

Rebecca's mouth dropped open. "What? No!"

"Yes," the caller said. "And in at least one instance, the president met with the rebels in the United States."

"Like *in* the United States?"

"Yes. There will be a package arriving at your office within the week. In it will be more information for you to look at."

Rebecca was completely shocked, not knowing what to say or even whether to believe the person who had called.

"I have to go," the person said. "Look for the package. It has every-thing you need to go about removing him from office."

Rebecca heard the click on the other end of the phone, signaling the end of the call. She took her phone away from her ear and tossed it beside her on the bed. Then, she let out a big sigh as she looked around her bedroom. There was no way she could sleep now, as her mind raced with all of the different possibilities that could come as a result from this news.

# CHAPTER 15

## HARK! THE HAROLD KLIMMINGSES SING

Jeremy Applegate opened the door to his office, seeing Ryan seated at his desk. He stopped and stared at him until his son realized he was standing in the office doorway.

"Dad! Ryan exclaimed, standing from his seat behind the desk. "You're back!"

"I am," Jeremy said as he swung the door closed. "We need to talk."

Ryan's eyes widened. "About what?"

Jeremy moved over to the red sofa. "Why don't you come sit with me over here . . ."

Ryan reluctantly made his way over to the sofa, sitting beside his father. He turned to his right and looked Jeremy in the eyes.

"Ryan," Jeremy began. "While your mother and I were on vacation, I received a phone call from someone within this company."

"Okay . . ." Ryan nervously said. "What did they say?"

Ryan felt like he already knew what his father was going to say, so he was most nervous about trying to explain his actions in such a way that he would understand it.

"Ryan," Jeremy said. "They told me that you had been contacting people with whom we've been doing business with and demanding that they do things or else we would cancel our contracts with them or increase prices." He paused for a second. "Ryan, what the hell are you doing?"

"Dad," Ryan began. "I have a good reason for all of this."

"Then what is it?"

"So, while you were gone," Ryan began. "I did a little digging and realized that a lot of companies do business with both Klimmings Incorporated and ourselves."

"Okay?"

"And so I decided to contact each of them and offer an ultimatum."

Jeremy's face lit up. "You decided to make them choose between our software and whatever jobs Klimmings had for them?"

"I did," Ryan said. "And for the most part, the majority of them agreed to my demands."

"And what about the ones who haven't?"

"They're still deciding."

"Do you think that if they received a call from me that it would help to give them a decision?"

Ryan looked surprised. "I think it definitely would help."

"Then I guess I'll be making some calls then," Jeremy said as he stood from the sofa and went over to the window overlooking the Potomac. "In the meantime, I think I will keep you in this temporary role. There's no reason why I need to return now." He made his way over to the door. "I think after Christmas would be a good time to return, don't you?"

Suddenly, Ryan remembered his conversation with Delilah a few days ago, and he realized that Jeremy didn't know about it. He knew it would not make his dad happy, just as it didn't make him happy when he learned it.

"Dad," Ryan said. "Speaking of Christmas, I have a good feeling we're going to be invited over to the Klimmingses' again this year."

"Why? Because we were invited over for Thanksgiving?"

"It's about Delilah," Ryan said. "You may want to sit down again,

224

Dad. I have something to tell you something about Ben and Delilah."

\* \* \*

Peter sat in his bedroom in the residence of the White House. He hadn't gone downstairs for the day, and it was already nearing eleven in the morning. As the Christmas holiday continued to near, he became increasingly depressed. This year, he would not be spending the day with his family, as he had for the previous thirty-four years he had been married to Vicki. He had hoped things between him and his wife would've resolved by now, but since he hadn't spoken to her in months, and she had recently been spotted out with her ex-husband, Bill, Peter had accepted the possibility that it may be a long time before he and Vicki even begin to sort things out.

On top of that, Peter felt like Julius Caesar, stabbed in the back by his own vice president. Since Constance's announcement, she has been mainly working from her home. However, people in the White House have been acting strange around Peter. In many ways, they've tried to stay away from him, distancing themselves when they can. Henry began seeing him less and less, and Martha reluctantly would call him whenever there would be someone there to see him or to inform him of a meeting.

As he sat there, his phone started ringing, startling him. He looked around, trying to find it before he spotted it sitting across the room on a table. So, he got up, picked it up, and looked at the screen before answering. "Charlotte! How are you?"

"I'm doing well," she replied. "I hope you are too."

"Eh, I'm managing. It's too damn depressing around here."

"I feel for you, Peter. You deserve so much more than what you're getting right now: an ungrateful vice president, a wife who doesn't appreciate you, and children who haven't contacted you in months . . . it's just not right."

"Well, Ben did have Thanksgiving with me last month, so I wouldn't say that they've *all* not spoken to me."

"True," Charlotte agreed. "Anyways, I called because I wanted to see what your plans were for Christmas next week."

"Christmas?" Peter said. "Right now, I have nothing. It's just going to be me, myself, and I."

"Well," Charlotte continued. "If you were up for it, I would love for you to come over to my house on Christmas Day, and we could celebrate the holiday together."

"Really? Aren't you going over and seeing Vicki?"

"No. She's got Bill to keep her company."

Peter fell quiet, causing Charlotte to feel guilty about what she had just said.

"I didn't mean for that to sound the way it did," she said. "I'm sorry."

"It's okay," Peter said. "How much have they been spending together lately?"

"Since he stopped by the office a couple weeks ago, they've seen each other almost every day."

"Dammit," Peter swore. "What the hell is going on?!"

Charlotte took in a deep breath. "Peter, come for Christmas. You can't be alone this year."

Peter sighed. "Let me think about it."

"You do that, honey."

Peter smiled for the first time in the past few days. "I'll talk to you later, Charlotte."

"You too."

He took the phone away from his ear and ended the call. Then, he placed the phone on his lap as he began to think about all the things that had gone on over the last few weeks and how spending Christmas with Charlotte may shine a light in a dark time.

* * *

Miranda sat admiring the Christmas tree in the living room of the Klimmings Mansion. She watched the twinkling lights shine off the glittery silver and gold ornaments on the tree. It was Christmas Day, and as she took in the sights of the tree, she thought of how this Christmas felt like everything but what Christmas Day should.

"Miranda?"

Miranda turned her attention to the left of the tree where Vicki was standing, wearing a silver gown. "Is there anything wrong?"

"No," Miranda lied, not wanting to burden her mother with her concerns on Christmas. "I was just looking at the tree."

"Yeah," Vicki said as she stepped closer to it. She touched the tree branches, feeling the tips in her hand. "I considered changing this tree's theme this year."

"Really?"

"Yeah. With Gabriella's death, I considered making the change." She let out a sigh. "But I didn't because she always loved this tree. It wouldn't be right to get rid of it."

"Mom," Miranda sighed. "Is that the real reason you wanted to change it?"

"What do you mean?"

"I mean, did you want to change it because Dad wouldn't be here today?"

Vicki huffed. "I don't want to talk about your father today, Miranda. I don't need him spoiling my Christmas."

Miranda opened her mouth to respond but was interrupted by the doorbell. She turned toward the entry hall as Vicki passed by her to go open the door.

"I got it, Denise," she called out before opening the front door. "Bill!" Miranda turned her head toward the entry hall to listen in. "I'm so glad you could make it today!"

Miranda was intrigued as to who this Bill character was. She knew he had been taking a lot of her mom's time away, but she still hadn't met him.

Miranda stood from the sofa as the two turned the corner through the archway.

"Miranda," Vicki began. "This is Bill Davis. He's a very good friend of mine, and I've asked that he spend Christmas with us today."

"It's nice to meet you, Bill," Miranda said as she approached him with her hand extended.

He did the same and shook her hand. "Thank you, Miranda," he said before turning to Vicki. "Good friend? We were married for two years. I would think that we would be something more than just good friends."

Miranda pulled her hand away from Bill's. "What?"

"Sorry, Miranda," Vicki said. "I must've left that part out. Bill was my first husband. We were both naïve and married right out of high school."

"Yeah," Bill said. "And some things happened that caused us to go our separate ways."

"But you're back now," Vicki said, looking to Bill, who turned his attention back to her.

Miranda stood in the living room, horrified. She could not believe what she was hearing and witnessing. "Excuse me," she said before turning away, going through the archway, and heading up the stairs. She reached the landing at the top and made her way across it to the door on the left. She quietly knocked and then opened the door. Ben was standing in front of his floor mirror with his dress pants on and no shirt.

"Miranda!" he exclaimed, quickly jolting around. "Couldn't you have knocked any louder?!"

"Shut up, Ben," she said as she closed the door. "Something horrible is happening downstairs."

\* \* \*

"Why is it nobody is ever here to greet us whenever we come over here for something?" Ryan asked as Denise held the door for the four members of the Applegate family to enter the Klimmings Mansion.

"I'm sorry, Mr. Applegate," Denise said, closing the door behind them. "I'm sure Mrs. Klimmings or someone else will be in shortly to greet you. Let me see if I can find one of them."

Denise scurried off down the entry hall, turning right. Ryan, Cathie, Jeremy, and Delilah remained there, where they began to shed and hang their coats on the coat rack.

"Must you be so rude to their maid?" Cathie asked Ryan. "She's just doing her job."

"I wasn't trying to be rude," Ryan replied. "I just wanted to ask because it's true."

"Guys," Delilah said. "Don't get into any arguments today. Ben and I have finally gotten back together, and all we want is for you all to just get along today."

"Well, that should be easy," Jeremy piped up. "Peter won't be here today, so we should actually have a civil celebration."

Cathie's eyes jolted over to her husband. "Must you always be an ass, Jeremy?"

"Not always," Jeremy said. "I wasn't on our vacation. What were some of the things you called me?"

"Oh my God," Delilah exclaimed. "Stop!"

She turned and headed into the living room just as Ben turned the corner from the bottom of the staircase through the archway at the other end of the room. He stopped and admired Delilah. "You look gorgeous."

"And you are the most handsome man here," she replied.

"Thanks a lot," Jeremy said from behind her. "Way to just put Ryan and me down."

"Go!" Delilah snapped, pointing for the Applegates to leave the living room. As they turned to head elsewhere, Denise rounded the corner, meeting them in the archway.

"Goodness!" she said, not realizing they were right there. "Mrs. Klimmings said to go ahead and get seated in the dining room. She and Mr. Davis will be down in a minute."

"Who the hell is Mr. Davis?" Jeremy asked, looking at the people in the living room.

Cathie once again gave her husband a look. Then, they proceeded to head out of the living room and to the dining room. As they were on their way, Ryan stopped and turned to Delilah.

"Delilah," he said. "May I speak with Ben for a moment?"

"Sure," she said, turning back to Ben and then back to her brother. "Just don't say anything stupid."

"I won't," he said, smiling at his sister. She returned a smile and then passed by him and made her way into the dining room. Once she was out of sight, Ryan turned back to Ben.

"What is it, Ryan?"

"Cut the crap, Klimmings," Ryan snapped at him. "You think that we are just going to accept you back into our family after you dumped my sister? You Klimmingses are all the same. You're selfish, arrogant, and trash."

"What the hell are you talking about?" Ben asked. "Delilah and I both ended our marriage together, and we both fell back in love with each other."

"Shut up. You know as well as I do that you are only with her so that you can see more of Katherine." Ryan looked around the room. "Where the hell is that child anyways?"

"She's upstairs, taking a nap."

"Shouldn't she be downstairs enjoying her first Christmas with her family?"

"Ryan, I'm not going to take parenting advice from you. You can barely take care of yourself."

Ben passed by Ryan and made his way into the dining room, where the Applegates had already been seated. He rounded the table and sat in his regular seat next to Delilah.

"What did he have to say?" she asked him.

"Nothing," Ben said as Ryan finally entered the room, and the two locked eye contact. "He was just being himself."

Delilah turned to her brother and glared at him. He pulled out his chair and sat across from his parents.

"I had hoped you would have listened to Delilah," Cathie quietly said across the table. "Don't start anything!"

As the two continued murmuring, Miranda entered the dining room and made her way over to her seat. She was wearing a sparkling green gown. Once she took her seat, she looked at Ben and Delilah before greeting her former sister-in-law.

Conversations broke out across the table as they waited for Vicki, who finally came into the room after many minutes had passed.

"Excuse me," she called out, trying to get everyone's attention. She turned to Bill, who was standing beside her. His arm was wrapped around her. "This is my ex-husband, Bill. He came by the office a couple of weeks ago and is in town for a bit, so I felt that it would be fine for him to spend Christmas with us."

Bill smiled at Vicki before turning back to the group. "I hope I'm not intruding. This is better than being locked up in some hotel room, eating Chinese takeout."

"Has anyone told you that that's always a possibility here too?" Jeremy quipped. "Last year, at Thanksgiving, the house servant had to order Chinese takeout for us because Ben over here flung the turkey across the table, and it landed on the floor by Vicki's sister, Charlotte."

Ben looked down the table at Jeremy. "Thanks, Jeremy, for reminding everyone about that."

"No problem," he replied. "Anyways, where is Charlotte today?"

"Not here," Vicki said. "She said she was going to be spending Christmas with someone special."

"Damn. I like her. She's funny."

As the table fell silent, Bill turned to Vicki and asked, "Honey, where do I sit?"

Miranda looked upward at Ben, who looked back at her. They both caught what he had called their mother, and they both became quite uncomfortable.

"Billy," Vicki said. "Why don't you sit over there?" She pointed to the empty seat at the head of the table in front of the fireplace, positioned between Ben and Miranda. The two once again looked at each other and then turned toward their mother.

"But that's Dad's chair," Miranda said.

"He's not here, Miranda," Vicki said. "If Bill needs a seat, he can sit there."

"No," Ben said, standing from his seat. "We are not replacing Dad today!"

Bill turned back to Vicki. "Honey, I can sit somewhere else if it's going to cause issues." He looked over to the empty seat between Miranda and Ryan. "I can sit there if that works."

"No," Vicki said. "That's where Miranda's friend, Julie, sits."

"But Mom," Miranda said. "She won't be here today. She's

traveled home to see her parents."

"Still, we aren't going to use her seat as the communal seat," Vicki said. "Bill, just go sit down."

"Dammit, Mom!" Ben exclaimed. "Dad built this house, and I will not allow him to be disrespected with you letting some stranger sit in his seat!"

Jeremy kept his attention between Ben and Vicki. Then he leaned over to Cathie and whispered, "I wish I had some popcorn. This is some good shit."

Cathie glanced at her husband and rolled her eyes.

"Benjamin!" Vicki stated. "I will not let you disrespect a guest in our house. As the head of the family . . ."

"Dad is the head of the family, Mom," Ben snapped back. "You just came in and threw him out. He *never* stopped being the head of this family." Ben turned to Delilah. "Come on, babe. Let's go."

"Ben," Delilah gasped. "Where are we going to go?"

"We can go pay Dad a visit," he said. "I'm sure he needs someone to visit him today. We can go upstairs, get Katherine, and leave."

"Ben," Miranda said, finally standing from her seat. "Please don't go."

"I must," he said. Then he turned to Vicki. "And Mom, I hate to do this, but if your actions continue . . . I see no way you can continue as president of Klimmings Incorporated."

Vicki gasped. "What the hell are you saying, Benjamin?! Are you going to oust me from my own company?!"

Jeremy's eyes widened as he was thoroughly entertained by the argument. Cathie took her napkin and dabbed her eye, trying not to show how upset this was making her.

"*Your* company?!" Ben replied, stepping closer to his mother. "It was Dad's company. And it always will be." Delilah finally rose from her seat and ran her hands down her gown, straightening it.

Vicki became angrier with her son. "So you and your fifteen percent of the voting shares are going to come together and remove me from the presidency?"

Delilah's eyes widened, and she turned to Vicki.

"Fifteen?!" Ben exclaimed. "Are you insane? I have thirty shares, Mom!"

"No, you don't," she said, pointing to Delilah. "Ask her about the fifteen shares she won following the divorce!"

Ben snapped his attention to Delilah, who was flabbergasted and couldn't form words. Jeremy perked up and made eye contact with Ryan while Delilah looked at the rest of the people seated around the table, trying to formulate some sort of response.

"Is that true, Delilah?" Miranda asked. "Are you a shareholder in the company?"

"Y-y-yes," Delilah stuttered before turning to Vicki. "How dare you! You promised me that you would keep it a secret!"

"You knew?" Ben asked her. "Why didn't you say anything?"

"I didn't want you to think I only wanted to get back together because of it!" Delilah said as tears welled in her eyes. "Excuse me."

She stormed out of the dining room, turning left and running out of the house. Jeremy jumped up and went after her, followed by Cathie.

"Go after her," Miranda said to Ben. "She's clearly upset by all of this."

Ben stood there, trying to think about what to do. Then, he stormed out of the room and turned right, making his way to the room with the staircase. As Vicki, Bill, Ryan, and Miranda remained silent in the dining room, Denise opened the side door, pushing in a cart full of the Christmas dinner meal.

"Merry Christmas!" she exclaimed and then looked at the people remaining in the dining room. "Where did everyone go?"

As silence engulfed the dining room, the sound of Ben's bedroom door slamming echoed in. Then, Miranda turned and stormed out of the dining room. She turned right, followed the entry hall to the sliding glass door, and turned right through the family room and down the back hall. She opened the door to Peter's office and locked herself inside. The lights were off in the room, but the drapes were still pulled back, allowing the light from the back patio and pool area to shine inside. She made her way over to the window and looked outside. Large, fluffy snowflakes were falling from the dark sky above. On the ground, the snow looked like little cotton balls as more and more accumulated.

A tear fell from her eye as she considered how different this Christmas was from Christmases past. It was nothing like it could have been, and her father's absence was beginning to really affect her.

She didn't have her phone on her, so she pulled the chair to the desk back and took a seat. She took a deep breath and then turned her attention to the phone placed on it. Miranda took the phone off the receiver and began pushing some buttons before putting the phone to her ear.

As the ringing sounded in her ear, she thought about what she would say and if it would be awkward.

"Hello?" she heard her father say from the other line.

"Dad?" Miranda replied as a tear streamed down her face.

"Miranda? Is that you?"

"Yes, it is, Dad."

"Oh, honey. It's so good to hear from you."

"Dad . . . Merry Christmas!"

* * *

Peter ended the call and turned back to Charlotte, who was seated on her velvet sofa in her living room. She had a glass of white wine in her hand.

"Was that Miranda?" she asked.

"Yes, it was," Peter said as he sat beside her. "That's the first time I've spoken to her since July."

"Wow," Charlotte said before taking a sip of her wine. "That's a long time."

Peter nodded. "But with what I did, I can understand why she needed time to process it all." He reached to his left, took his glass of white wine off the end table, and took a sip. "Charlotte, why are you being so nice to me?"

"Why wouldn't I?"

"You know about what happened with Gabby," Peter said. "Why are you continuing to be nice to me? Shouldn't you be mad? Pissed?

Something?"

Charlotte slowly shook her head. "No. I'm not mad at you."

"Don't you want to yell at me? Come on. Gabby was your favorite niece for crying out loud! Get your frustration out."

"No," Charlotte said. "I guess I'm so kind to you because I know what it is like to be shamed by family."

"Didn't Vicki not speak with you for a while?"

"After her divorce from Bill," Charlotte said. "I testified against them during their trial and said that I felt they were rushing the decision."

"Damn," Peter said. "I'm sure that pissed her off."

"It did! She didn't talk to me for about thirty years!"

Peter shook his head. "That sounds just like her, though. You know she won't acknowledge any calls I've made to her, and she won't respond to any texts or anything."

"Just like you said . . . it sounds just like her."

The two chuckled together before they took a sip of their glasses of wine. Then, they smiled and looked at each other.

"Thank you for inviting me over today," Peter said. "It's been nice to break from the dismal White House."

"It's no problem," said Charlotte. "No one deserves to be alone on Christmas."

Peter smiled back at Charlotte, who returned one. As the two looked into each other's eyes, they felt themselves pulling closer to each other until, finally, their lips latched together. Peter felt Charlotte's soft lips on his. He ran his hands up her back and neck as he kissed her. Then, she leaned backward, and he fell forward before reaching his hand to the lamp and flipping the switch, causing the room to go dark.

\* \* \*

Almost a week following Christmas and a few days before the new year, Rebecca White returned to the Capitol Building. Immediately, she put together a press conference, where she planned to make a dramatic announcement.

235

As she approached the podium wearing a navy blue business dress with American flags lining the background. She stopped as soon as she reached the platform and drew in a deep breath.

"Good morning," she said, smiling slightly at the cameras. "I hope that you all have a wonderful Christmas and that you all were able to spend valuable time with your families and friends. I, on the other hand, was faced with more troubling news over the Christmas holiday.

"Before the holiday break, I received a phone call from an anonymous source in the Klimmings White House. In this call, the whistleblower informed me of some disturbing actions taken by President Klimmings over the past summer. It appears that on at least one occasion, the president met with members of the Grand Rebellion, the rebel group out of China. These independent meetings by the president, not confirmed by Congress, come in clear violation of the Logan Act, established to prevent American citizens from negotiating with governments who have a dispute with the United States. Since this occurred during a time when tensions between the U.S. and China were high, and escalations toward nuclear war were ongoing, it gives me no other choice than to argue President Klimmings' actions were breaking the law.

"In addition, other actions taken by the president present extreme concern regarding the law and what he has the power to do. Because of this, I have no choice but to announce today that the House of Representatives will be moving forward with an official impeachment inquiry. I am directing all committees investigating the president and the president's personal and business dealings to operate in accordance with the impeachment inquiry." Rebecca paused to take in a deep breath. She looked into the camera directly in front of her and continued. "With this, we must remember that nobody is above the law."

# CHAPTER 16
## DANA'S DISCLOSURE

"With Congress returning for the new year, one question that remains on everyone's mind is what will come of Rebecca White's impeachment inquiry against President Klimmings, and how will this affect the president after dealing with an already tumultuous year both politically and personally."

Henry switched off the TV and turned around to Peter.

"Why'd you do that?" Peter asked him. He was seated in a chair in front of the bar and close to the *Resolute* desk. On his other side stood a doctor who was taking measurements and checking other vitals of Peter's.

"Mr. President," Henry said. "You are getting your annual physical. Why would you want any more stress from the news?"

"He has a point, sir," the doctor said as he took the stethoscope away from Peter's chest and hung it around the back of his neck. "Just from preliminary measurements, I can see that your heartbeat is slightly irregular, and whenever we performed your stress test, there were a few red flags."

"The hell do you mean by red flags?" Peter said, spinning around to the doctor. "I thought I was as healthy as a horse?!"

"It's that you need to take it easy, Mr. President," the doctor said. "You had a rough year last year. Your daughter passed away, you've had marital troubles, your vice president is challenging you for your party's nomination . . . I would be concerned if you hadn't been stressed."

Peter rolled his eyes. "I'll be fine. Us Klimmingses don't let anything keep us down."

"Sir, just be careful," the doctor said before looking at Henry.

"I'll make sure he doesn't do too much," Henry said.

"What the hell?" Peter exclaimed. "Am I some damn child?"

The doctor packed up his stuff and headed out of the Oval Office, leaving Peter and Henry alone.

"Mr. President," Henry said. "I've been going back and forth whether to tell you, but the vice president is here today."

"Here? Like in the White House?"

Henry nodded.

"Well, hell, Mr. Gates," Peter said, standing up and buttoning up his shirt. "Why didn't you tell me any sooner?"

Peter stormed through the door to the left of the fireplace. He proceeded down the hall and burst through the door just before the right turn. Inside, he caught Constance standing by her desk.

"How dare you?!" he shouted at her. "I brought you into this administration. I pulled you from Congress and elevated you, and how do you thank me?"

"I have no words for you, Peter," Constance replied. "Your actions warranted mine."

"You bitch," Peter cursed. "And yet you still haven't resigned." He stepped forward, pointing at her. "If I could fire you, your ass would be out on the street right now!"

"As I said, I have no words for you." Constance snatched some of the papers from her desk. "I'll see you on the campaign trail."

She quickly passed by Peter and tried to exit her office before he stopped her.

"Why are you here anyways?" he asked. "You have offices in many other locations, so why come back to the White House?"

"The impeachment committee is interviewing me and getting my testimony later this afternoon," Constance replied.

"So it was you, then?"

"What the hell are you talking about?"

"I confided in you over the summer, Constance. I told you that we knew about the rebel movement in China, and you took that as me meddling in the overthrowing of a foreign government."

"Peter," Constance rolled her eyes. "You're delusional. I didn't tell anyone about that because what you did wasn't against the law. You told me that you knew of the movement and sent military forces over there to distract China so that the rebels could pressure the Chinese president. Right?"

Peter thought over what Constance had told him and recalled the meeting between the two of them in the Klimmings Mansion, where he had lied to her about his involvement with the rebel movement in China.

"So obviously, you have someone telling lies about you," Constance said. "Unless there's something else?"

Peter remained silent and shook his head.

"Good. I'd hate to have my name tied to an even bigger scandal than your possible impeachment."

She passed Peter, who glared at her as she left, leaving him alone to stew in his own anger and confusion, wondering who it was that told Rebecca White about his plan with the Grand Rebellion.

* * *

Dana stood outside the White House. Protesters next to her chanted over and over regarding the impeachment inquiry. As she looked upon the White House, she began to think about how she had become consumed with guilt over what she had done to Gabby.

She took a deep breath before turning and walking through Lafayette Square, thinking about how she could secure an audience with the president.

* * *

Evening settled on the Klimmings Mansion, and Vicki stepped inside, closing the door behind her. She shivered as she took her coat off and hung it on the coat rack.

"Cold out?"

Vicki turned to see Denise, who had just come from the side hall.

"Yes, it is," Vicki replied. "A cold January evening. Makes me want some potato soup!"

"Will you be having dinner here, Mrs. Klimmings?"

"No, Denise," Vicki said as she passed her down the entry hall. "Bill and I will be dining in town again tonight."

"You've been seeing a lot of him lately," Miranda said as she turned the corner from the living room. "It must be getting serious between you two."

Vicki looked at her daughter and took a deep breath.

"Miranda," Vicki said, holding her finger out toward her daughter. "I don't need to hear it from you. What I do with Bill is my own business."

"I'm not trying to say anything," Miranda said. "I think that if you *are* seeing Bill a lot, Ben and I deserve some kind of explanation."

Vicki stepped in closer to Miranda. "I don't owe you two a damn thing."

She turned and stormed off, turning left to head upstairs, leaving Miranda alone in the entry hall with Denise.

"I'm sorry, Miss Miranda," Denise said from behind her. "If it makes you feel any better, she's been short with me too."

Miranda turned to Denise. "I'm concerned about her."

* * *

Delilah sat at the island in the kitchen of the Applegate Homestead, eating some yogurt with granola and scrolling through her phone. She had endlessly scrolled through her Instagram repeatedly, trying to keep her mind off things, but it wasn't working. Instead, her mind continued to think about how she and Ben hadn't spoken since Christmas.

*I should've told him about the shares.* She thought to herself. *Now he's gonna believe that I'm hiding things from him again.*

As her mind raced with these thoughts, her father, Jeremy, stepped into the kitchen, causing her to jerk around immediately.

"Sorry," her father said. "Didn't think anyone else would be down here right now."

Delilah looked down at her phone and noticed it was two in the morning.

"What are you doing up?" Jeremy asked as he went over to the fridge. "Couldn't sleep?"

"Yeah," she replied as she pushed the remaining yogurt in the bowl away from her. "Thought this would help, but it isn't."

"Got something on your mind?" Jeremy asked as he turned around with a glass of chocolate milk. He rounded the island and sat next to Delilah.

"Just thinking about things. That's all."

"Ben?"

Delilah nodded. "I know you hate the family, Dad, but I really do love him."

Jeremy sighed, reluctantly wanting to give advice regarding Ben Klimmings, but he saw how upset his daughter was. However, he knew that she loved him and that nothing would change no matter what he did.

"Listen here," Jeremy said, turning to her. "Just talk to him, Delilah."

"He hasn't texted me since Christmas, though."

"So? Text him. Maybe he's waiting for you to contact him." He took a drink from his chocolate milk. "That Klimmings family always did wait for things to be handed to them."

Delilah glared at her father, who took another sip from his chocolate milk.

"But here's what I will highly recommend to you, Delilah," Jeremy continued. "You must tell Ben that you plan to take control of your fifteen voting shares in Klimmings Incorporated. You earned that, and if you go further into a relationship with that hanging over you, it's likely to end in doom."

"Dad," Delilah said, confused about her father's motives. "Why are you giving me advice on him? You hate that family."

"I do," Jeremy said. "And one day, the Klimmings family will finally get what's coming to them. I mean, have you seen that impeachment shit going on right now?"

Delilah nodded.

"Anyways," Jeremy continued. "I know that you and Ben really do like each other, and whatever I do, you two are still going to like each other."

"Thanks, Dad," Delilah said, hugging him. "I think I'm going to go back to bed now."

"Goodnight, honey."

"Goodnight, Dad."

Delilah slid off the barstool and headed out of the kitchen, leaving Jeremy alone. He sighed, shook his head, and took another sip of his chocolate milk.

"Oh, Jeremy," he whispered to himself. "You know you're going to regret that conversation."

\* \* \*

"She left before breakfast again," Ben said to Miranda as the two got their breakfast from the breakfast bar. Miranda scooped some scrambled eggs on her plate first, followed by her brother.

"I just don't understand," Miranda said to Ben as they made their way over to the dining room table. "Why is she doing everything in her ability to avoid us?"

"I'm not sure," Ben said as he and Miranda sat down. "Maybe it's because of the way things happened at Christmas?"

"Surely she's still not upset over that?"

"You know our mother . . ." Ben took a sip of the coffee he already had poured before getting his breakfast. "Besides, I think she feels guilty about seeing this other man."

"Because she's still married to Dad?"

"Exactly."

"I just don't get it," Miranda said. "Why won't the two of them just get together and talk? They haven't even spoken to each other since July!"

"I know," Ben sighed. "Have you thought about the voting shares yet?"

"What do you mean?"

"Do you think that Mom is still suited for the job?"

"Ben, I don't know. Voting Mom out as president seems like a callous thing to do to her."

"Miranda, it's been six months. If they divorce, she is going to take a big chunk of that company with her."

"She still has the ten voting shares I gave Gabby. It frustrates me that she won't give those back to me."

"Ask her," Ben said. "She knew Gabby was dead when you put them in her name, and she didn't say anything."

"She tried to stop me, Ben," Miranda corrected him. "Besides, what are you going to do about the fifteen voting shares that Delilah apparently owns? I gotta be honest. I did *not* see that coming."

"Neither did I," Ben sighed. "It pisses me off that both she *and* Mom knew about that, and none of them thought to say anything to me."

"Yeah, Mom's been doing a lot of secret hiding lately."

Ben nodded, not saying anything, prompting Miranda to try to explain why Delilah didn't tell him.

"Hey," she said. "Think about this for a moment. Delilah probably didn't tell you because she didn't want you to think she was getting close to you for the shares. If she had really wanted them, then she would've already taken them from you."

"But that doesn't explain why she didn't tell me."

"Ben, think about her family for a second. Her dad is crazy, and her brother is becoming a little Jeremy. Can you blame her for wanting it to be a secret?"

Ben nodded his head slowly. "True." He took a bite of his scrambled eggs. As he chewed them, he looked up at Miranda and said,

"These are so good."

Miranda went to try hers but was stopped by the doorbell ringing. She looked up at Ben. "Who could that be?"

"I'm not sure," he said, standing up.

The two of them proceeded out of the dining room and into the entry hall, where they could see Denise with the door open. A man in a suit was standing in the doorway.

"Miss Miranda," Denise said, turning to her and Ben. "This man is here to see you."

Miranda walked closer to the door. "Yes?"

"Ma'am," the man said, offering a document to Miranda. "I represent the Superior Court of the District of Columbia. I came by this morning to serve you with a subpoena requiring you to appear in court next week."

Miranda took the paper and looked it over.

"What's it for, Miranda?" Ben asked her as she looked at it.

"Oh no," she sighed. A tear began to pool up in one of her eyes. "I've been summoned to testify in Jason's criminal court trial."

* * *

Peter sat on one of the Oval Office's cream sofas, watching the news. They were speaking to Rebecca White in the Capitol rotunda.

"I have no comment on the inquiry right now," Rebecca said. "But I do see some future discussions between many representatives and myself regarding the best method of action."

"Speaker White," a reporter said. "What comment do you have regarding the president's State of the Union address later this month?"

"As always, I invited the president at the beginning of the year to deliver the annual State of the Union address, to which he gladly accepted," Rebecca said. "I do feel that it will be quite tense with the vice president and myself seated behind him. After all, we both are trying to challenge him for the presidency."

Peter turned off the TV and ran his hands through his hair. "God, I just wish someone would take care of that bitch."

He stood up and stretched, feeling his back pop and crack. As he recovered, the door to the Oval Office opened, and Martha stepped in. From the way she entered, Peter knew she was frustrated.

"Mr. President," she began. "Do you have a moment?"

"Yes, Martha," he said, rolling his shoulders. "What's up?"

"A woman has been calling here over and over again, begging to speak with you. I told her there was no way she could come by and visit, but she won't let up."

"Okay."

"Sir, she claims to be a friend of your daughter."

"Miranda?"

"No, Gabby."

Peter sighed. "Who is it?"

"Dana Gomez."

"Dana . . ." he said, thinking about her. "I don't think I've met Dana . . ."

"Do you think she's making it up?"

"No, no, no," Peter said. "When Gabby was alive, she mentioned hanging out with someone named Dana. I just wonder what she wants."

"Sir," Martha said. "I have her on the phone right now."

"You do?" Peter said. "Go ahead and send her through to me."

"Okay."

Martha exited the Oval Office, closing the door behind her. Then, the phone started ringing on the *Resolute* desk. Peter made his way over to the desk and sat on it. He picked up the phone and put it up to his ear.

"This is the president."

"Sir?" the voice said on the other line. "This is Dana Gomez. I was your daughter's . . ." She paused. "Gabby's friend."

"Yes," Peter responded. "I remember hearing about you. What is it that you needed to talk to me that's so important that you need to call over and over again?"

"Mr. President," Dana began. "I need to talk to you about the night Gabby died."

Peter stood up. "Yes?"

"Sir, I know that Gabby didn't die at that school."

Peter dropped the handset. He was stunned by what Dana said. As he sat still, the cord caused the handset to swing back and crack against the *Resolute*.

"Hello?" Peter heard Dana say from the phone as it dangled in front of the desk. "Sir?"

He reached down and picked it up. "Why do you say that?"

"Because . . ." Dana began. She stopped and took a deep breath. "Because I was there when she died."

"You . . . y-you let my daughter kill herself?"

"No, sir . . ."

"Then how did she die then? She shot herself, Dana!"

"No, she didn't," Dana paused to take a deep breath. "I did."

Peter fell silent. Suddenly he recalled the night of Gabby's death. He remembered how Ben questioned the gun's whereabouts. Soon it started to make sense. Gabby had been shot in the chest rather than in the head, and her body showed no indication that she had shot herself.

*How did I miss all of this?* Peter thought. *Why didn't it make sense then?*

"You are a real son of a bitch," Peter said to her. "Why the hell did you do it?"

"It wasn't planned, sir. It was a spur-of-the-moment thing. I didn't know what to do, so I just ran."

"And here we are, almost a year later, and *now* you're coming clean about this?"

"I can ask the same of you."

"What?"

"Mr. President," Dana said. "What happened to Gabby? Why did you lie about her going to a school in Europe? Why didn't you just come forward about her death in the first place?"

Peter remained quiet.

"What did you do?" Dana asked.

"It's none of your goddamn business," Peter said to her.

Dana sighed. "Sir, I felt guilty about this for this past year. I think I'm going to come forward and tell the cops about my involvement in her death. I suggest you call me in the next few weeks to get your story straight."

Peter took the handset and slapped it back on the receiver. He took a couple of deep breaths before shoving the entire phone set off the desk and onto the floor.

\* \* \*

Charlotte watched as Vicki passed by her in the lobby of Klimmings Incorporated. She remained at her desk as the pleasantries were exchanged, and whenever Vicki entered her office, closing the door as she went in. Charlotte turned back to the computer and tried to do some work, but she couldn't. Her mind kept returning to what happened on Christmas night between her and Peter.

She took in a deep breath and stood up from her seat. Then, she rounded her desk and made her way over to the door to Vicki's office. She knocked on the door and opened it. Inside, Vicki lifted her head, acknowledging Charlotte.

"Yes, Charlotte?"

"Vicki," Charlotte said, closing the door behind her. "I need to talk to you about something."

"Charlotte, I got a lot of work to do," Vicki began. "The project manager for the nuclear plant sent me an email saying they can no longer take on the project."

"Well, I guess this can wait then."

Charlotte turned around and started to head out, but Vicki stopped her. "Hang on, Charlotte."

Charlotte turned around and faced her sister.

"Come over here," Vicki said, offering Charlotte a chair in front of her desk.

"Thank you," Charlotte said as she went over to sit down. "I need to tell you something. And you're not going to like it."

"Well, what is it? Might as well get it out in the open."

Charlotte took a deep breath before coming out and saying, "I slept with your husband."

Vicki froze in her seat. Her eyes widened some, and her mouth dropped open. "What did you just say?"

"It happened on Christmas," Charlotte said as she teared up. "I invited him over for the holiday because I didn't want him to be lonely. One thing led to another, and then, boom! Next thing I knew, I woke up next to him in bed."

Vicki licked her lips and adjusted herself in her desk chair. She tried her hardest to maintain her composure throughout this entire conversation. "Is that all?"

"Yes," Charlotte said as some tears streamed down her face. "I'm so sorry, Vicki."

Vicki nodded her head. "I understand, Charlotte," Vicki said as she stood from her seat and rounded the desk. She made her way over to the door and opened it. "Why don't you go ahead and take the rest of the day off?"

"Really?" Charlotte said. "I can go to the powder room and clean myself up some. I can still work today. I don't have to go right now."

"No, please," Vicki said. "I need you to be gone right now."

Charlotte acknowledged Vicki's request and left the office, refusing to look her sister in the face. She took her stuff and went down to the elevator when Vicki closed her office door.

Her vision became blurry from the tears that started to collect in her eyes, and she hesitantly made her way back over to her desk. She struggled to catch her breath between sobs and fell into her seat. After wiping her face and drying the tears, she flung open her desk drawer and pulled out the package of cigarettes that lay inside. As she flipped the box open and pulled out one, she thought about how her marriage was collapsing and falling apart.

*There's no coming back from this.* She thought as she lit her cigarette. *No coming back.*

# CHAPTER 17

## THE STATE OF THE UNION IS STRONG

Breathing slowly in and out, Miranda sat on the sofa in the living room of the Klimmings Mansion with her eyes closed. Next to her sat Julie, who watched her with care.

"How are you feeling now?" Julie asked her.

Miranda turned to her friend and smiled slightly. "Better," she said. "Thank you, Julie. You are such a good friend to me."

"It's going to be okay, Miranda," Julie said as she took Miranda's hand. "All you have to do is go to the courthouse and provide them with what happened."

"But just the thought of having to relive it . . ."

"I know, but I want you to consider this. If Jason was sick enough to do that to you, do you think he could do it to someone else?"

Miranda slowly nodded her head. "But Julie," she added. "You are the only one I've told about what he did to me."

Julie leaned back whenever she realized she was the only one who knew about the rape. "Not even your mom?"

Miranda scoffed. "Mom? No. It seems that as of lately, all she's focused on is Bill."

"Bill?"

"Have I not told you about him?"

"No," Julie said. "Who is he?"

"Mom's ex-husband," Miranda said, looking Julie in the eyes. "He showed up right before Christmas and had been taking all of Mom's time since."

"God," Julie let out. "This past year has been rough on your family. Is it always like this?"

Miranda shook her head. "Not really. I mean, we've always had our problems, but none like what this separation has brought."

* * *

Delilah stepped inside the George and Jefferson Coffee Shop. She looked ahead and saw Ben stand up from a seat at a table, indicating to her where he was. She smiled and made her way over to him.

"I'm so glad you agreed to see me," she said to him as she hugged him. "I was afraid you'd be mad."

Ben released from the hug before responding. "I gotta give it to you straight, Delilah. I was disappointed at first. You should have told me about the shares."

"I know," she sighed as she took a seat, followed by Ben. "I just didn't want you to think I was getting close to you for the wrong reasons."

"I thought that, but then Miranda talked to me about it all. She told me you had probably kept it a secret because of others."

"Like who?"

"Your father."

Delilah chuckled. "You're right. He definitely would be one to look out for."

"I bet he's jealous," Ben said. "He's wanted to get us Klimmingses for so long, and now, here you are with fifteen voting shares."

"Ben," Delilah said, taking his hand. "Despite what my father suggested, you should know that I am not going to take those shares from you, right?"

"You don't need to worry about that, Delilah."

"What?"

"Delilah," Ben continued. "I spoke with my attorney this morning, and I'm having your fifteen shares transferred to your name. Those were your shares, and you deserve them."

"Ben," Delilah sighed. "You didn't need to do that."

"I wanted to, Delilah. You are the love of my life, and I just can't see myself continuing on with this relationship if I am withholding something that is yours."

Delilah smiled at Ben, looking into his brown eyes. "I love you, Benjamin Peter."

"I love you too, Delilah."

Before she could lean in to kiss him, a barista approached the table and set two coffees down. As she walked away, Ben looked at Delilah and said, "Hope you don't mind, but I went ahead and ordered."

Delilah grinned and took a sip of her coffee, closing her eyes in enjoyment. Then, she said, "It's funny."

"What is?"

"Dad came downstairs last night and talked to me about the voting shares . . . and you."

"What did he say?"

"Well, like I said earlier, he suggested I take the shares," Delilah said before taking another sip of coffee. "But then, he gave me advice on you."

"Good or bad?"

"Good advice."

"Huh!"

"I know," Delilah said. "It's almost like he genuinely wanted what was best for me."

\* \* \*

Charlotte pulled into the parking garage under Klimmings Tower, driving around before finding a spot. Finally, she turned off her car, grabbed her bag, and got out of the vehicle. As she proceeded to make her way to the elevator that took her to the lobby, she passed by the spot for the president of Klimmings Incorporated. Vicki's car was already parked there.

"What the hell is she doing here so early?" Charlotte asked herself before continuing toward the elevator. She rode it up to the building lobby and then switched elevators, choosing another one to take her to the entrance of Klimmings Incorporated.

Once the elevator door opened, Charlotte made her way toward her desk. As soon as she reached the corner of her desk, Vicki turned the corner from her office, crossing her arms.

"God, Vicki!" Charlotte exclaimed. "You scared the hell out of me."

"Pack your stuff," Vicki said to her sister. "You're not welcome here any longer."

Charlotte looked at her sister, bewildered. "What?!"

"You heard me," Vicki said. "Pack it. I want you out."

Vicki turned and headed back into her office, leaving Charlotte standing by her desk, confused. She tossed her bag down and proceeded into Vicki's office. When she stepped inside, Vicki had just sat behind her desk and put on her readers.

"What, Charlotte?"

"Are you firing me?"

Vicki looked up from her glasses. "I mean, I'm not asking you to pack your things for the hell of it."

"Why?"

"Dammit, Charlotte!" Vicki cursed, standing from her seat. "You slept with my husband! Do you really think I want to see you right now, let alone have you continue working for me?"

Charlotte was flabbergasted. "But it was an accident. We didn't mean to."

"I don't care if you tripped and just fell onto him, Charlotte," Vicki said. "You slept with my husband."

Charlotte took a step backward, not knowing what to say.

"I need you to go, Charlotte," Vicki said as she sat back down in her chair. "Get out of my office."

She turned and left Vicki's office, heading over to her desk to collect her things. As she did so, she took her phone out and sent a quick text before packing up.

\* \* \*

Peter sat at the *Resolute* desk, fuming whenever Henry stepped inside the Oval Office. He stopped as soon as he realized Peter was not in a good mood.

"Mr. Gates!" Peter shouted. "Have you heard the news?"

"What news, sir?" Henry said as he took a step closer to the desk.

"Benedict Arnold received quite the endorsement today."

Henry looked confused, prompting Peter to offer clarification.

"Constance."

"Oh," Henry said. "Who endorsed her?"

Peter got up and turned toward the window. "She got the Obama endorsement."

"Oh no. But he endorsed you whenever you first ran."

"And apparently, now I am dangerous to our democracy, or so he says." Peter turned around to face Henry. "Mr. Gates, the whistleblower is not Constance. When I pressed her to see if it was her, she clearly indicated that she didn't know everything that happened between myself and the Grand Rebellion."

"Well, who do you think it is?" Henry asked, intrigued.

"Mr. Gates," Peter said, sitting back in his seat. "I've got it narrowed down to two people. It has to be either Eric or Janet."

"Why them?"

"Well, Eric was with me whenever I met with the Grand Rebellion, so he would be a clear guess. Janet is also suspect because Eric can't keep his damn mouth shut about anything."

"What about the Secret Service agents?" Henry suggested. "Couldn't any of them be the whistleblowers?"

"They could," Peter said. "But Don has them under such a tight leash that there's no way they could've told that bitch without him knowing."

"I hope he returns from his leave soon," Henry said. "I always felt better about your safety on the road when he was leading the detail."

"Don isn't intimidated by anything either. Nothing scares that man."

Henry slowly nodded his head. "Interesting."

"Anyways," Peter said, leaning back. "What did you need?"

"Mr. President," Henry said. "I have the first draft of your State of the Union address for the week after next."

"Good," Peter said, sitting back up. "Where might I find this draft?"

"I sent it to you," Henry answered. "Let me know what you think."

"I will," Peter said as he opened a drawer and pulled out his laptop. "I plan to read through it and add my own suggestions to it."

Henry nodded, then turned to head out but stopped before reaching the door. "By the way, sir, I saw your memoir released this week. How is it doing?"

"*Freedom Ain't Free* is already a best-seller!" Peter said with a smile. "I really think this book is going to help set the groundwork for reelection."

"So you think you can still win regardless of everything that's going on?"

"Henry," Peter sighed. "Read the book. You'll find it takes a lot more than a few inconveniences to take me down."

* * *

Vicki sat in her office, listening to the silence that consumed the room. It was much quieter in the office now that Charlotte was gone. *I can't believe Peter would cheat on me.* Vicki thought. Her mind was fixated on the idea of Peter and Charlotte hooking up on Christmas night. *I just can't believe him.*

She pulled open the desk drawer and opened the pack of cigarettes that sat inside. As she looked inside, there was one remaining. She sighed, took it out, put it in her mouth, and lit it. She groaned as she exhaled the smoke, exhibiting a slight cough.

Then, the phone on her desk rang. She had the calls forwarded from the receptionist desks to her office since no one was posted at them. She took the phone off the receiver and answered it.

"This is Vicki Klimmings."

"Vicki," the person on the other line said. "This is Ryan Applegate."

"Ryan?" Vicki let out. She was confused as to why he would be calling her. "What do you want?"

"No need to be rude," he said. "I just wanted to call about getting together sometime in the next week or so."

"What for?" Vicki asked as she took another puff of her cigarette.

"There are some things I want to talk to you about," Ryan said. "Would you be interested in getting lunch next week?"

Vicki thought it over. "Ryan, why do you want to get lunch with me?"

"Oh, Vicki . . . you'll want to have this meeting with me."

Vicki sighed. "Fine. Let's go for next Tuesday at one. There's a café I like to eat at on the tenth floor here at Klimmings Tower. Would that be good with you?"

"That's perfect!" Ryan said. "I'll see you then."

Vicki heard the phone click. She let out another sigh and placed the phone back on the receiver. Then, she took her cigarette back to her mouth, taking a long drag. She closed her eyes as she let the smoke flow endlessly from her lungs through her mouth.

* * *

A week had passed since Miranda had been called to testify at Jason's trial, and her anxiety grew more intense as the date came closer. Finally, the day had come, and she found herself sitting in the courtroom, taking in the wood paneling that coated the walls. As she took in the scenery of the room, the side door opened by the bench. Miranda jerked her attention in that direction and watched as two police officers walked her former boyfriend, Jason, into the room. As he got to the defendant's seat, he looked up, making eye contact with Miranda.

Chills ran down her body, and she shivered slightly. Sitting next to Miranda, Julie held her hand, offering some comfort. Miranda took a couple of deep breaths before the judge entered the room. Everyone stood up as the judge made his way to the bench, and after he took a seat, he signaled for everyone else to return to theirs.

He began the court by allowing the prosecutor and Jason's attorney to deliver opening statements to the jury. Miranda didn't pay attention to any of it and remained in her own world until she heard the prosecutor call out, "The prosecution calls Ms. Miranda Klimmings to the stand."

Immediately her heart sank deep into her chest. Her breathing increased in intensity, but she didn't stand up. She couldn't stand up. Instead, she remained seated, worrying about what she will be asked.

"The prosecution calls Miranda Klimmings to the stand," the prosecutor repeated.

Julie leaned close to Miranda. "They're going to force you to go up there," she said to her. "Or charge you with contempt of court."

Finally, Miranda took in a deep breath and stood up. She slowly made her way down the aisle toward the bench. During the long walk, she felt the eyes of everyone in the room gazing upon her. She felt her stomach tightening up as she got closer and closer. Finally, she reached the bench and approached the bailiff.

"Please raise your right hand," the bailiff said as Miranda raised her right hand. "Do you swear to tell the truth, the whole truth and nothing but the truth, so help you, God?"

"I do," Miranda said.

"You may take the stand."

Miranda rounded the bench and took a seat on the witness stand. She looked out at all of the people watching the court session. She saw Julie sitting amongst the other people. Julie held her thumb up, trying to offer Miranda encouragement and support. Then, Miranda turned her attention over to the jury. She looked over the twelve people sitting there, waiting to hear what she had to say. Finally, she looked over at Jason, who was looking back at her. She noticed his brown hair, smooth skin, and dreamy eyes. It took her back to what drew her to Jason in the first place.

"Ms. Klimmings?"

Miranda jerked her attention over to the prosecutor, who was speaking to her.

"Ms. Klimmings," the prosecutor said. "Would you mind telling the jury about your relationship with Mr. Dolmeir?"

Miranda drew in a deep breath. "Well," she began. "We started dating about two years ago. We broke up briefly during that time but got back together shortly after."

"Toward the end of your relationship," the prosecutor continued. "Did Mr. Dolmeir exhibit any behavior out of the ordinary?"

"Objection!"

Miranda looked over at Jason's attorney. "He's leading the witness."

"Sustained," the judge said. "Mr. Michaels, please reword your question."

"Sorry, your honor," the prosecutor said. "Ms. Klimmings, can you describe Mr. Dolmeir's behavior toward the end of your relationship?"

"It was different," Miranda said. "It just seemed that he had changed."

"Can you describe what about him made you believe he had changed?"

"Well, there was this instance where we were at his apartment, and he took me back to his bedroom . . ."

"Objection!" Jason's attorney exclaimed. "The witness is about to detail a romantic moment with Mr. Dolmeir. It has no bearing in this court."

"Overruled," the judge said before turning his attention to the attorney. "And sir, I'll decide what is and isn't appropriate for this courtroom." Then, he turned his attention back to Miranda. "You may proceed."

Miranda swallowed and cleared her throat. "When we returned to his bedroom, he showed me the wall next to his bed."

"And what was on this wall?" the prosecutor asked.

"It was coated," Miranda said before pausing. "It was coated with pictures of . . . of me."

The prosecutor approached the bailiff with a stack of images. "I would like to submit this as evidence to the jury," the prosecutor said. "These images show the wall in question in Mr. Dolmeir's room. As you can see, the wall is indeed covered with images of Ms. Klimmings."

The jury began conversing among themselves until the judge hit the gavel. "There will be order in my court."

Once the jury settled down, the prosecutor turned back to Miranda.

"Ms. Klimmings," he said. "There were plenty of reports in early February last year regarding you. Can you explain what those reports were?"

Miranda took a deep breath. *It's coming.* She thought to herself. *He's going to ask me about the kidnapping.*

"Well," she began. "The reports were about my disappearance."

"Disappearance? Did you disappear, Ms. Klimmings?"

"In a way."

"Ma'am," the prosecutor said. "That is a yes or no question. Did you disappear?"

"Y-yes."

"How?"

Miranda took a deep breath. "He chloroformed me in an alley and took me back to his apartment." She pointed to Jason.

"Your honor, please let it be known in the court records that the witness is physically identifying Mr. Dolmeir, seated in the defendant's chair."

"Do you have any other questions?" the judge asked the prosecutor.

"I do not," the prosecutor said as he returned to his seat. Soon after, Jason's attorney jumped up and headed toward Miranda.

"Ms. Klimmings," he said. "Could you describe your relationship with Mr. Dolmeir? What were some of the things you two did?"

"What?" Miranda asked.

"You heard the question," he said to her. "What were some of the things you two did?"

"We went on dates, went out to eat, went to each other's houses . . ." Miranda began.

"Did you two ever engage in any sexual activity?"

Miranda's eyes widened.

"Ma'am," the attorney said. "Let me remind you that lying under oath is perjury."

"Yes," Miranda said.

"So being in Mr. Dolmeir's bedroom wasn't uncommon then?"

"What?"

"If my client had images of you posted on his wall, why didn't you ever come forward and tell anyone about it?"

Miranda's heart began to beat faster. She didn't know how to respond to the question.

"I-I don't know."

"That's all I have," the attorney said before returning to his seat.

Miranda looked out toward Julie, who smiled in return. She mouthed the words, "You did great." In response, Miranda just stared. *Why did he ask about whether we had sex?*

"Ms. Klimmings," the judge said to her. "You may leave the stand now."

She looked at the judge, acknowledged him with a soft smile, and then stepped off the witness stand. She returned to Julie, who was still offering a supportive smile.

"Let's go," Miranda said to her. Her face slowly turned red as she continued down the aisle to the door.

Julie quickly jumped up from her seat and followed her out of the building. Once outside, she saw Miranda, who had started crying.

"Miranda," Julie said, approaching her and putting her arm around her. "What's wrong? You did great in there."

"They didn't even ask me about it, Julie. They didn't even allow me to tell them about how he raped me. He made me pregnant, and I lost his baby!"

She wrapped her arms around Julie, burying her face in her shoulder, sobbing. Julie held onto her friend tightly, comforting her.

"I'm so sorry, Miranda."

\* \* \*

The elevator door opened on the tenth floor, and Vicki stepped out. She turned to her left and approached the small café beside the elevator. She went to the host, who greeted her and informed him that she needed a table for two. Once seated, she ordered iced water and proceeded to look over the menu and the variety of sandwiches that it entailed.

While she sat there, numerous thoughts crossed her mind. Most of them focused on the curiosity of why Ryan had asked her to lunch. But then, she began to think about Peter and his affair with Charlotte. *How did it happen? Did he ask her beforehand? Did he even think about me when he was undressing her?*

As Vicki processed different scenarios in her mind, she caught Ryan turning the corner, and she signaled to him where she was at. He saw her and made his way over to the table.

"Thank you for meeting me today," he said as he pulled out the chair opposite Vicki and sat down. "Trust me; this will be worth your while."

"I hope so," Vicki said as the waiter approached the table and took Ryan's drink order. "Let's not beat around the bush, Ryan. Why did you call me here?"

"Vicki," he began. "I cannot lie to you, but I am very interested in Klimmings Incorporated right now. I've been following your plans to construct a nuclear power plant in West Virginia."

"Yes," Vicki said as she drank her water. "It's one of the first to be built since the seventies."

"I know," Ryan said as the waiter placed his drink on the table. "But that's not what intrigues me the most."

"What is then?"

"I want to invest in Klimmings Incorporated, Vicki. I want to have a role in helping to bring clean energy to the United States and restarting the country's nuclear program."

"Okay."

"But to do so, I have just one thing I ask."

"What is it?"

"Vicki, I want to purchase your forty-five voting shares from you."

"What?!" Vicki said, standing. "You're insane if you think I will sell out!"

"Vicki, Vicki, Vicki," Ryan said, urging her to sit back down. "Hear me out. With me on the voting share board, I can use some of my contacts from Applegate to help you. I can bring Klimmings Incorporated into so many new deals and cause you all to be able to build four or five new plants."

"But at the cost of the role of president?" Vicki said, sitting back down. "I can't do that to the company."

"Vicki," Ryan continued. "I'm not saying that you step down as president. I'm just proposing that you sell your shares to me. With me controlling forty-five percent of the votes and Delilah controlling fifteen, we can ensure that you remain on as president for as long as you like."

Vicki thought it over, looking back down at the menu.

"Think about it, Vicki," Ryan said as he stood up. "If I purchase your shares for the going rate plus, say . . . ten million . . . would it be worth it?" He stepped closer to Vicki. "After all, it's no secret right now that people have been pulling out of business with you. Nor is it a secret that your kids are planning to oust you."

Vicki snapped her attention back to Ryan. "They are not!"

"Really?" Ryan said. "How's the relationship with them right now?"

Vicki remained quiet as Ryan walked away from the table, leaving the café. As she sat there, she thought about the arguments between her and Ben. She thought about the strained relationship with Miranda. Then, she considered the future of Klimmings Incorporated. *What will happen if they try to vote me out and fail? What will happen if I sell out to Ryan? What will happen if I divorce Peter?*

\* \* \*

Martha opened the door to the Oval Office, seeing Peter seated at the *Resolute* desk. "Mr. President?"

He looked up, acknowledging her.

"Don is here to see you," she said, holding the door open.

"Send him in," Peter said, standing up from his seat. Martha stepped out of the room as Peter rounded the desk and made his way over to the door. When he was about halfway there, the door opened, and Don stepped in.

"Don!" Peter said, extending his hand to shake Don's. "It's so good to see you!"

"Same to you, sir!" Don said as he shook Peter's hand.

Peter released his hand from the handshake and offered Don a seat on one of the sofas. As the two sat down, Peter asked him how his time off had been.

"It's been nice," Don said. "After getting shot in London, the wife was concerned, so I think it was a good idea to take the past seven months off."

"Well, I wanted you to spend quality time at home. It was a little scary there in London."

"Was it? I thought I wasn't wounded too badly."

"You weren't," Peter said. "But the thought of losing my favorite man was scary."

The two laughed together. "Oh, I missed this," Don said. "I'm so glad to be back at work finally."

"You are?"

"Yes. It gets so boring at home sometimes."

Peter nodded his head. "I miss home."

"I heard about that," Don said. "It's a shame that your wife kicked you out of the house. Why would she do that?"

Peter glared at Don. "What do you think? I had you bury Gabby in the family cemetery the night she died."

"And then we covered it all up," Don continued.

"Exactly," Peter said as he made his way over to the bar. "You want something to drink."

"I'll take a Scotch," Don said from the sofa. While Peter was over by the bar, Don decided to change the subject. "So, what have you been up to lately?"

"Besides avoiding impeachment?" Peter said, returning to the sofa with Don's Scotch and bourbon for himself. "I've just been making final edits to my State of the Union address tonight."

"That's tonight?!"

"It is," Peter said as he took a sip of his bourbon. He swallowed the drink and thought about Gabby and the night she died. He had forgotten what Dana had told him about what had happened that evening. Suddenly, he remembered her plan to come forward about killing his daughter.

"Sir?" Don asked. "Did you hear what I asked?"

"Huh?" Peter let out, looking back at Don. "What did you say?"

"I asked you what you were planning to speak about during your address tonight."

"Oh, just the same ole shit," Peter said before taking another sip. "It's an election year, so I have to use this to make the case for four more years."

"True dat!" Don took a sip of his Scotch. Then, he looked over to Peter, whose gaze focused out the window behind the *Resolute* desk. "Sir, is there something wrong?"

Peter moved his attention back to Don. "Yes," he said. "There *is* something wrong." He drank the rest of his bourbon. "Don, I have a favor to ask of you."

* * *

Rebecca White stood behind the speaker's desk, looking out to the joint session of Congress. As she peered out into the crowd of senators and representatives, she looked at the Supreme Court justices and the members of the Cabinet. Then, she looked up toward the gallery and saw an empty seat.

"Hmm," she said to herself. "His wife didn't even bother to show up."

"Can you blame her?"

Rebecca turned to her right where Constance was standing.

"Goodness," Rebecca said. "I forgot you were there."

"Sure you did," Constance said as she pulled her hair back on the sides. "I see his children are here."

Rebecca looked back toward the gallery and noticed Miranda seated next to Ben. She recognized the other woman sitting next to Ben but could not remember her name.

"Who is that next to his son?"

"Her?" Constance asked. "That's his ex-wife, Delilah."

"What?! Why would he bring her here?"

"Rumor has it that the two of them are rekindling the fire in their relationship."

Rebecca's mouth dropped open. "No!"

"Yes," Constance said. "Makes you wonder why they divorced in the first place."

Rebecca shook her head and looked out toward the door. She saw the Sergeant at Arms come through the door and take a couple of steps into the chamber. "Here we go," she said before hitting the gavel.

"Madam Speaker," the Sergeant at Arms announced. "The president of the United States!"

Immediately, the chamber erupted in applause. Rebecca took in a deep breath and clapped a few times before stopping. Then, she turned to Constance, who had just stopped clapping.

"What do you think he's going to speak about?" Rebecca asked her.

"It's reelection year," Constance said. "He's going to use this as a campaign speech."

"Especially since the Iowa Caucus is next week."

"Exactly."

Rebecca looked back toward Peter, who was shaking hands with people as he made his way down the aisle in the chamber.

"Isn't it funny?" Rebecca said. "Tonight, on TV, all three people in the camera shot are vying for the presidency."

Constance let out a soft laugh. "You know," she said, turning to Rebecca. "I hadn't thought about that." She shook her head and continued clapping. "God, I love democracy."

Peter slowly made his way down the aisle before finally reaching the podium in front of the speaker's desk. Rebecca noticed his dark blue tie and the spotless black suit. He took the two copies of his address for the two women and turned around, handing Constance hers first. Then, he gave Rebecca hers. As she took it, he winked at her in an act of defiance. At this moment, he didn't care about the impeachment inquiry, nor did he care that the two were challenging him for the presidency.

Finally, he turned around, and Rebecca yanked up the mic on the speaker's desk. In one hard hit, she smacked the gavel down and announced, "Members of Congress, I have the high privilege and distinct honor to present to you, the president of the United States!"

Once again, the chamber erupted in applause, and Rebecca softly rolled her eyes. *The hypocrisy . . . just this past week, House Democrats were stunned by evidence in the impeachment inquiry. Now, here they are, clapping for the man that they want to get rid of.*

Rebecca smirked as Peter held his hands up to quiet the crowd. She sat down in her chair, followed by Constance, and opened the copy of the address that Peter had given her. She began to look it over as he began speaking.

"Madam Speaker," Peter began. "Madam Vice President . . . kids."

He turned toward the gallery, where he spotted Miranda and Ben. Applause broke out in the chamber again as Peter motioned for them to stand up. Miranda turned to Ben and slowly rose, followed by her brother. Peter joined in with the clapping, causing it to echo into the mic.

After a minute or so, the members of Congress began to retake their seats.

"Members of Congress, members of the Cabinet, Justices of the Supreme Court, and to the American people," Peter continued. "Tonight, we join here as one collective body. Tonight we encapsulate the soul of America. Tonight . . . we represent what America really is."

Once again, applause broke out. Behind Peter, Constance slowly rose from her seat. Rebecca took a deep breath and joined the vice president in applauding the statement.

Then, after everyone took their seats, Peter continued. "Three years ago, we embarked on a journey together to save our country from a deadlier fate than any we had faced before. Tonight, I want to share with you some of the accomplishments we have made throughout my time in office.

"After stifling off a debilitating recession – the worst since the COVID pandemic – I can proudly say that joblessness is down, wages are up, and our economy is booming!"

Democrats in the room began to clap, giving Peter a standing ovation. After a few seconds, they sat back down, allowing Peter to continue on.

"We demonstrated the strength of the American people when we were faced against a tyrannical Chinese government earlier this year. We remained steadfast and persistent, and as a result, President Wu's disastrous reign finally ended after facing pressure from a rebel movement in the country."

Once again, the Democrats stood up, applauding the president. Rebecca glanced to her right, seeing that Constance had risen and was clapping for the president's statements. She rolled her eyes and returned to the speech.

"Unfortunately," Peter continued. "Not all share the same sentiment. Recently those in leadership began to question the motives of the U.S. and our men and women in uniform. As most of you know, there has been an abundance of investigations brought up regarding my defense of our great nation in the House. Just before the end of last year, it was announced that an impeachment inquiry would be initiated in the House, and every investigation would be directed toward that inquiry."

Peter turned back, glancing at Rebecca White. As he did, a few boos were heard from some of the Democrats in the chamber. Rebecca scoffed at the president and rolled her eyes, causing the boos to intensify. By now, Constance was glaring at Peter, signaling her displeasure at how he was singling out the speaker of the House. Finally, Peter turned back toward the members of Congress.

"But we won't let that get us down! No, we won't!" Suddenly, the boos turned into an eruption of applause. "Hell no, we won't. We don't give a damn what they want us to do!"

The applause grew in strength as Peter raised his hands into the air. He smiled as he took in the cheers. Then, he dropped his arms and began to clap for himself.

Finally, Peter took back control of the room. He continued his speech, discussing many more things that he and his administration have accomplished over the past three years. However, instead of focusing on what happened to the American people, Peter hyped himself up, turning the State of the Union Address into what sounded more like a campaign speech than a traditional State of the Union.

He continued rambling about the great things he did, avoiding mentioning the absence of his wife, as well as other things that might portray him in a dark light. Not once did he note that he had resumed talks with Russia and the Russian president. Opinions regarding the country continued to be low. Even though Peter thought that bringing them in on conversations was necessary for the country, he also didn't want to say anything that would cost him votes.

Finally, after over an hour of continuing on and on about his accomplishments, Peter began to wrap up his speech.

"So, with that," he proclaimed. "It is my job to report to you the state of our union, and with that, I declare that the state of the union is not only strong, but it is thriving!

"And it will continue to thrive if I have the opportunity to continue to serve in this fantastic role as your president!

"Thank you! God bless you, and may God bless the United States of America!"

Only Democrats rose and clapped for the president. Rebecca and Constance remained seated, both horrified with the address Peter had just delivered. Then, Rebecca stood up and stepped away from the speaker's desk, leaving the chamber.

Peter made his way down the aisle, passing by members of the Cabinet. He stopped when he reached Eric and acknowledged him. "Eric."

"Mr. President," Eric said, shaking Peter's hand. "Great speech."

Peter could tell by Eric's reaction that he was uncomfortable around him. He just smiled and continued, proceeding up the aisle.

As he went on, he began to consider his request to Don earlier in the day. He thought about how across the city, Don would be visiting the apartment of Dana Gomez.

She opened the door, seeing Don standing on the other side. "Who are you?"

"Miss Gomez," Don said to her. "I am a representative of the president. May I come in?"

"S-sure," Dana said, reluctantly stepping back so that Don could enter the apartment. She noticed that he was carrying a small black bag with him

"Nice place," Don said as he looked around, setting the bag down.

"Thank you," Dana said, closing the door. "I assume the president sent you about my desire to come forward. I just started watching his State of the Union address."

"Yes. He sent me to settle that."

Dana nodded. "Could I get you a glass of water or something?"

"No, but thank you, though."

Dana looked down and noticed that Don was wearing black rubber gloves. Suddenly she became very uncomfortable. "Sir, could I request to speak with the president about this? I could stop by tomorrow . . ."

"No," Don interrupted as he looked into her eyes. "He wants this taken care of tonight."

Dana felt her stomach turn at his words. Immediately she sensed danger and began to think about how her phone was still in her bedroom, with the TV on. Quickly, she tried to dart back to get it, but her arm was caught by Don, who yanked her back to him.

Dana cried in pain as her arm was yanked out of the socket. Using her free hand, she tried to punch Don but missed his face. He then threw her against the wall, causing her to fall to the ground.

As she groaned in pain, Don fell on top of her. He put his hands around her neck, squeezing as hard as he could. She couldn't breathe, and her eyes began to bulge from their sockets while she kicked her legs, trying desperately to free herself. But it was no good.

Within a few minutes, Dana's body fell limp and lay lifeless on the floor. Don leaned back, trying to catch his breath. He pulled his shirt up to wipe the sweat from his forehead before heading to his bag.

He unzipped it and pulled out a thick manila rope. He proceeded to head back to Dana's bedroom, where he found a hook above her closet to wrap the rope around. Then, he went back into the living room, where

Dana's body lay, and drug her heavy dead body into her bedroom. Once inside, he took the rope and tied a noose around her neck. He took a deep breath before pulling the rope so that it appeared that Dana had hanged herself.

Once finished, Don pulled a chair into the bedroom, placed it underneath Dana, and kicked it over. He then went back into the living room and began straightening things up, removing the evidence of an altercation between him and the girl. As he completed the final chores of putting the apartment back the way it had been, he took his bag and made his way to the door. After opening it, he made sure to turn the lock on the doorknob so that it would lock as he closed it.

Dana's body continued to hang in the bedroom after Don left. The TV remained on, showing Peter walking up the aisle as he left the chamber. He continued to shake hands with members of Congress, smiling. Not because he felt his State of the Union address had been successful but because he knew the person who murdered his daughter had finally faced justice.

# CHAPTER 18
## THE IOWA CAUCUS

Vicki sat on the sofa in the living room of the Klimmings Mansion. She had just turned off the TV after watching the State of the Union address that Peter had delivered. She sighed and then turned to Bill, who was seated next to her.

"I should have gone," she said to him. "At least to support Miranda and Benjamin."

"Vicki," Bill said, putting his arm around her. "You told me that you had no desire to listen to him ramble on and on. Then you decided to watch it on TV."

"I know, I know," Vicki sighed. "I shouldn't have even watched it."

"It bothers you, doesn't it?"

Vicki looked at Bill, confused. "What?"

"That he slept with Charlotte?"

"Of course, it bothers me, Bill," she said, standing from the sofa. "I've been with that man for thirty-five years. He *never* cheated on me." She made her way over to the TV and fireplace. "Then, I tell him that I need him gone for a bit, and he just falls right into bed with my damn sister!"

"I'm sorry, Vicki," Bill said after getting off the sofa. He went over to her and hugged her. As he held her in his arms, the front door opened, and Miranda appeared in the archway to the living room. She stopped and looked disgusted as she saw the two hugging. Vicki spotted her and pulled away from Bill.

"Miranda," she said, shocked to see her home so soon. "I didn't think you would be home so early."

"Clearly," Miranda said before heading down the entry hall, heading to the staircase that way.

Vicki looked at Bill and said, "I gotta go talk to her."

"Go," he told her. "I'll text you tomorrow."

"Okay." Vicki watched as he left the house and then turned to go through the archway by the stairs. She quickly made her way up them and turned left at the landing. She knocked on Miranda's door. "Miranda, I know you're in there. Open up."

Vicki waited a moment before the door cracked open. "What do you want?"

"Let me in," Vicki said, pushing the door open. Miranda had already changed into her pajamas. "That was quick."

"I wanted to go to bed," Miranda said. "What do you want to talk about?"

Vicki sighed and sat down on Miranda's bed. "Come sit."

"No, Mom, I . . ."

"Sit!"

Miranda sat next to Vicki on the bed. She hung her head slightly as Vicki began talking.

"I know you and Benjamin aren't the biggest fans of Bill," she said. "But let me remind you that he is only a friend." She put her hand on Miranda's thigh. "Miranda, he is only a friend to me, nothing more!"

Miranda remained quiet, keeping her head low.

"Miranda," Vicki continued. "I'm sorry. I'm sorry for how I've treated you and Benjamin for the past couple of months. I'm sorry I won't acknowledge your father, and I'm sorry I didn't go to that damn

State of the Union address."

Miranda continued to stay quiet. A tear fell from her face, catching Vicki's attention.

"Miranda," she said. "What's wrong?"

Finally, Miranda looked up at Vicki. "Mom, you didn't even bother to come to Jason's trial last week. You didn't even bother to ask me how it went."

Vicki's eyes widened. She had forgotten about the trial, being completely consumed with thinking about the affair between her sister and husband. Vicki closed her eyes and took a deep breath. "Oh, Miranda. I'm so sorry."

"I could have used you there!" Miranda cried. "I needed you there!"

Vicki wrapped her arm around Miranda, pulling her in close.

"Miranda," she said. "I wish I had been there. I really did let you down, didn't I?"

Miranda wiped her face, but tears kept falling. She thought about whether she should finally tell her mom. Only Julie knew about it, and Vicki was her mother. If Miranda were to tell anyone else, she would be the one. But how would she take it?

Then, she made a definitive decision.

"He raped me, Mom."

Vicki let go of Miranda in shock. She looked at her daughter, seeing how distraught she was. "Oh my God," Vicki sighed, pulling Miranda in close. "Why didn't you say anything sooner?"

"I-I-I didn't know h-how," Miranda cried. "I-I felt like it w-was my fault."

"No, no, no," Vicki said. "That is not your fault, honey. You stop thinking that way. It was never your fault!"

Vicki continued holding Miranda close, letting her cry it out. As she sat there, Vicki thought about how she had neglected her family for the past year. She considered how they needed her more than they ever did before.

* * *

Six days had passed since Peter's polarizing State of the Union address. Since then, instead of focusing on the nation's issues, he turned all his attention to the upcoming Iowa caucus. He stepped off of Air Force One at the Des Moines International Airport, feeling the cold Iowan air hit his face. He proceeded down the stairs of the airplane toward the press. Behind him, Charlotte stepped out from inside Air Force One. She stood atop the steps watching Peter make his way down. As she took in the sights, she drew in a deep breath and let it out, smiling.

Peter stopped at the bottom of the stairs and turned back to Charlotte. He smiled at her before she started down, watching as the cold wind blew through her brown hair.

When she finally reached the bottom, Peter looked her in the eye. "Thank you for coming."

"It's no problem," Charlotte said as she took his hand. "Now, let's go win you an election."

* * *

Cathie opened the front door of the Applegate Homestead, seeing Ben on the other side.

"Ben!" she said, greeting him. "Come in! Come in!"

Ben stepped inside the house, looking to his right into the living room.

"What pleasure do I have to get a visit from you?" Cathie asked as she led him over to the sofa to sit down.

"Well, Mrs. Applegate," Ben started. "I felt that before I did this, I needed to speak with you first."

"Ben," Cathie said. "First of all, call me Cathie. You were married to my daughter for four years. We're way passed formalities."

Ben chuckled. "Sorry. I just felt that I should be formal for this moment."

Cathie leaned in. "What is it, Ben?"

"Well," he began. "I wanted to come to you and ask for your blessing in marrying your daughter."

"Again?"

Ben laughed. "Yeah, again."

Cathie joined him with a chuckle. "Ben," she said. "Why did you feel the need to ask about that?"

"It's a big decision," he said. "I just wanted to make sure you would be fine with it."

"Ben," she sighed before crossing her legs. "You need to do what's best in your heart. If marrying Delilah is that, then you need to ask her for her hand in marriage." She adjusted her posture on the sofa. "But I can't lie. I'm a little concerned."

He cocked his head. "Why?"

"Besides the obvious implications, Ben, the last time you were married to my daughter, you started drinking. Now, I know that you've since stopped and gotten a handle on things, but what if it happens again?"

Ben looked down at the floor. "Cathie," he said. "It is not my intention to even begin thinking about drinking again. To tell you the truth, I haven't even had an urge since the beginning of the summer last year."

"When the divorce happened?"

"It was after the divorce," he said. "Besides, I started initially drinking whenever I was a part of Klimmings Incorporated. Now, I am only a voting shareholder. So I have no part in the day-to-day business of the company. Plus, the alcohol is back on the bar at home now, so that temptation has pretty much gone away."

"And how does that make you feel?"

Ben sighed. "To tell you the truth, I thought I would miss it. But now, I am so happy that Mom gets to deal with all of that."

"Do you think she misses you at the company?"

"Yes and no."

"How so?"

"Well, lately, things have been tense between her and Miranda and myself. She's brushed us off and stuff . . . to the point where Miranda and I have discussed calling a shareholder meeting together to oust her as president."

"Goodness, Ben," Cathie let out. "That's horrible."

"I know," he sighed. "But Miranda told me that Mom finally spoke to her and apologized for how she's acted."

"So everything is fine between you all then?"

"I don't know," he continued. "Unfortunately, I don't see her being in company leadership very much longer."

\* \* \*

The elevator door opened, and Miranda stepped out into the lobby of Klimmings Incorporated, followed by Julie. Miranda began to make her way down to the empty receptionist desks while Julie took in the sights of the lobby. She looked over the pale yellow walls and oak doors each office had.

"So this is it, then?" Julie asked Miranda. "This is where Klimmings Incorporated is located."

"Just the offices," Miranda said, standing in front of the empty office that used to be her brother's. "Klimmings Incorporated contains many different individual plants across the country."

"Wow," Julie said as she approached Miranda. "Who's office is this?"

"This one?" Miranda asked, pointing at the empty office. "This used to be Ben's. Then, I used it some last year whenever Mom and I took over the board before we privatized the company again."

"And the other one?"

"That would be mine," Vicki said as she rounded the corner of the other office.

"Mom," Miranda said, taken aback by her mother's sudden appearance. "So I brought Julie by because I had a great idea."

"What would that be?" Vicki asked as she crossed her arms and leaned against the door's threshold.

"Well," Miranda continued. "I thought that since you needed a receptionist, you could possibly use Julie as one."

Julie looked up at Miranda. "Miranda, I could have asked her myself!"

Vicki smiled. "She's just being kind. That's Miranda's way." She looked toward her daughter and winked before turning back to Julie. "You have any secretary experience?"

"No," Julie said. "But I can pick up on things easily."

Vicki nodded her head. "Well, neither did Charlotte, and I hired her."

Miranda turned to her mother. "Why did you fire Aunt Charlotte anyway?"

Vicki let out a deep sigh. "I had my reasons," she said. "I don't want to talk about it right now."

"So," Julie said. "Do I need to fill out an application or anything?"

"Well," Vicki said. "No. I was thinking about contacting Doris, Ben's former receptionist, but I think she is at another job right now." Vicki led Julie over to where Charlotte's desk sat. "Even with Doris returning, we're going to need two receptionists again. If you want, I can walk you through some of the things the receptionist does, and if you're still up for it, then we can talk about the hiring process."

"Alright," Julie exclaimed. "Thank you!"

"I'm going to leave you two," Miranda said. "Julie, I'll be down in one of the malls on the lower levels. Call me, and I will let you know where I'm at."

"Okay," Julie said as Vicki started to show her where some things were and how things worked.

Miranda continued toward the elevator and turned back once again. She watched the two women working together and smiled. *Julie will be the perfect fit here.* She thought to herself. Then she nodded and turned, heading onto the elevator to go downstairs.

* * *

"You think you're going to come out with the win tonight?" Charlotte asked Peter, sitting next to him at his Iowa campaign headquarters.

"I better," he said. "The Iowa caucus is the most important primary of the election season."

"What happens if you don't win?" Charlotte asked as he turned on the TV.

"Then it's not going to be good," he said. "Polls are close between myself, Constance, and Governor Peck from California. It's really anyone's game, but whoever wins usually comes out with an advantage in the next primary."

"Oh." Charlotte nodded her head. "I've never caucused before, so I don't understand how it all works."

"Who does?" Peter confessed to her. "Iowa has to be a damn pain in the ass with this anyway. They have the first primary, and then whenever election year comes, they bitch and whine about all the ads and signs put up everywhere."

"Why don't they move it then?" Charlotte asked.

"Would you have heard of the state of Iowa if the Iowa caucus wasn't hyped up?"

Charlotte thought over the question. "Yeah. They have the potatoes, don't they?"

Peter chuckled. "Those are Idaho potatoes, Charlotte."

She laughed. "Same thing."

Peter shook his head before getting quiet. He looked up at Charlotte, admiring her eyes. "Thank you for all your support Charlotte. You don't know how much it means to me."

Charlotte let a soft smile show on her face. "You know it's no problem, Peter. You are special to me."

Peter smiled as he took her hand. He continued looking at her and smiled. Then, she laid her head on his shoulder and started watching the results from the Iowa caucus pour in.

\* \* \*

Bill turned the corner into Vicki's office. She was seated at her desk, flipping through papers. The TV in the far corner was on, and tuned in on the Iowa caucus results. He watched as Vicki was focused on her work. Then, he decided to knock on the door lightly. She jerked her head up, seeing Bill in the doorway.

"Billy," she gasped. "You scared me."

"Sorry," he said as he came in and sat in front of her desk. "I didn't mean to. Just wanted to let you know I was here, that's all."

She smiled at him and then looked back down at the papers. "I don't know what to do with all this."

Bill leaned forward, trying to get a look at what she was fumbling through. "What is it?"

Vicki sighed. "Ryan Applegate came to me last week," she said. "He offered to purchase my forty-five voting shares."

"Wow," Bill said. "Did he say how much?"

"The going rate, plus ten million," Vicki said. "But I don't know, Bill. This isn't my company after all."

"Wouldn't that make the decision easier then?"

"It should, but it doesn't." She stood up and stepped closer to the TV. "It's Peter's company, Bill. He gave me the shares whenever he ran for office. We maintained control of the company when it was public and then again whenever we privatized it early last year. The plan was for me to turn over control to him once his presidency ends. If I sell out, I'd almost be giving up on him."

"Maybe he shouldn't have cheated on you then?"

Vicki turned to Bill. "It's not that simple. If I sell out, then what will my children think?"

"Vicki," Bill said. "They're grown up, and they each own their portion of Klimmings shares. They'll be fine."

Vicki turned back to the TV, watching the results. She watched as Peter moved from first place in the Democratic caucus to second. "I can't sell him all forty-five shares."

"Why?"

She turned back to Bill. "Ten of those shares belong to Miranda," she said. "She gave ten shares to Gabby at the last shareholders meeting. When Gabby died, the shares moved to me. It's not fair that I sell those shares."

"So what about the other thirty-five? If those are yours, you're free to do whatever with them, right?"

"I don't know," Vicki said. "It just depends on what happens."

The TV cut to a shot at the Klimmings Headquarters. In the shot, Vicki saw Peter sitting with Charlotte on a couch, watching the results come in. She took in a deep breath and let it out, allowing her to finally come to a decision.

\* \* \*

Ben and Delilah took their seats at Finley's formal restaurant. They sat across from each other, allowing them to easily talk to one another. In the middle of their table sat a small candle.

"Isn't this weird?" Delilah asked Ben while she looked around at the restaurant's atmosphere. "The last time we were here, our marriage began to unravel."

"I thought about that," Ben said before taking a moment to look around the restaurant. "But that's why I felt it would be perfect to have dinner here tonight."

The waiter came to the table to take their drinks. Ben ordered his, and then the waiter turned to Delilah. She looked up at him and felt like she recognized the waiter as Clark. Delilah stared at him, trying to figure out what to say. But Clark stood there, looking at her.

"What would you like to drink?" he asked her.

Delilah continued to stare, not knowing what to say. Then, she turned to Ben, who looked concerned.

"Is everything alright?" he asked her.

Delilah looked back to the waiter, who looked different now. The waiter bore a similar resemblance to Clark, but it wasn't him. She let out a sigh of relief, knowing that her mind was playing tricks on her, and then finally ordered a glass of white wine.

When the waiter walked away, Ben leaned forward. "What was that all about?"

"I just thought he was someone I knew," Delilah said, taking a sip of the water that was already on the table. "But he wasn't. He just looked like him."

Ben looked at Delilah, admiring how she looked. "You look beautiful tonight."

"Aww," she said. "You're making me blush, Ben."

"I mean it! You are so beautiful, Delilah."

She smiled as he told her that. "I love you so much, Ben."

He grinned in return, reaching inside his jacket and pulling something out. "I was going to wait to give this to you later, but I just can't wait."

He handed Delilah a ring box, and she examined it. "Is this . . ."

"Just open it," Ben interrupted her. He had a big smile on his face.

Delilah looked up at him and then back at the ring box. She took in a deep breath and opened it. Inside sat a fourteen-karat black gold ring with a three-carat blue heart-shaped diamond in the middle. Lining the blue diamond and the black gold ring were small white diamonds wrapping around the entire band.

Delilah carefully took the ring out of the box and studied it. Her mouth dropped open as she took in the sight of the gorgeous ring. She looked across the table at Ben, who was fixated on her and the engagement ring she was holding.

"Delilah Applegate," he said to her. "Will you do me the honor of being my wife . . . again?"

She smiled as a tear welled up in her eye.

"Y-yes," Delilah said. "Yes, Ben. I would love to be your wife again!"

Ben moved from his seat onto his knee beside Delilah. He took the engagement ring from her hand and slipped it onto her ring finger. She immediately began to look at the ring and how it sparkled in the light.

"Oh, Ben," she said, looking him directly in the eyes. "It's perfect. I love you so much!"

He got up and kissed Delilah. As the two kissed, applause broke out in the restaurant causing the two to break apart and look around. The people in the restaurant were cheering for them, celebrating their engagement. Ben turned back to Delilah and smiled. She leaned in and kissed him again, looking forward to what their future would hold.

* * *

Peter and Charlotte watched as the final caucus results came in. It had been a long, close night that had drug on longer than anticipated, so

Peter sat up whenever the commentators said they had a big announcement.

"After a close night," one of the commentators began. "We can announce that Vice President Constance Zeemer is the projected winner of the Iowa caucus and will receive the most delegates in this contest."

Charlotte looked over at Peter, whose attention was attached to the TV. She put her hand on his shoulder and moved it up and down, trying to offer him some comfort.

"I'm so sorry, Peter," she said.

Peter continued watching the TV as they showed the results of the entire caucus. The TV cut to the campaign headquarters of Rebecca White, who had won the most delegates on the Republican side. She was delivering a victory speech, detailing what some of the next steps were. Then, the TV cut to Constance Zeemer, who was standing behind a podium waving to a small crowd. As the commentators spoke, Peter finally reacted to losing the Iowa caucus.

"Of course," Peter let out. He said nothing more, but Charlotte could see a fire in his eyes. This look was unlike any other she had seen before.

"It'll be alright," she said, trying to offer more comfort. "We'll come back in New Hampshire."

But Peter said nothing. He remained silent as he processed his loss and thought of ways to eliminate Constance Zeemer.

# CHAPTER 19
## "HELLO, GOD. IT'S ME, PETER KLIMMINGS."

Michelle Watson hadn't heard from her friend, Dana, since she last spoke to her before Christmas. After over a month of the two not talking to each other, Michelle finally texted her friend at the end of January. Typically, Dana would respond pretty quickly, but this time, Michelle received no response from her friend.

After waiting a few days, Michelle decided to pay Dana a visit and confront her face-to-face. She drove to the apartment complex that Dana lived in and made her way up to Dana's place. When she reached the door, she knocked loud enough that it echoed down the hallway.

"Dana," she called out. "It's Michelle. We need to talk."

She waited for a response but heard nothing, so she knocked again.

"Dana," she said as she beat on the door. "I know you're there. I saw your car outside!"

Once again, there was no response. Finally, Michelle had enough, so she took the door knob and tried to open the door. She groaned when she realized it was locked.

"Dammit," she called out. Then, she went back down the hall and continued downstairs to the lobby. She fabricated some story to the receptionist in the lobby about losing a key and successfully convinced them to let her borrow one.

Michelle then made her way back upstairs to Dana's room. She reached the door and announced, "Dana, I'm coming in!"

She put the key in the door and unlocked it, twisting the doorknob and opening it. As soon as the door swung open, she was hit with a rancid, rotten smell.

"God, Dana. What the hell did you let spoil?" Michelle stepped into the apartment and looked around. The living room lights were on, and everything looked as it usually did.

"Dana," she called out. "What is that horrid smell?"

She proceeded further into the apartment, turning left into Dana's room. Once inside, she looked around before turning to her right. That's when she found Dana's body hanging from a rope tied around a hook above the closet.

"Dana?" Michelle said in disbelief. "Oh my God, Dana!"

She promptly stepped over to Dana, realizing she had been hanging for a few days.

"Oh my God! Oh my God!" Michelle said, freaking out. "I gotta call the police."

She turned and ran out of the apartment and into the hallway. She pulled her phone out of the back pocket of her jeans and called the police.

"Hello?" Michelle said whenever she heard someone pick up. "It's an emergency. My friend . . . I-I think she hung herself."

\* \* \*

"All rise."

Miranda, Julie, and everyone else in the courtroom stood up as the judge proceeded to make his way back to the bench. During this time, Miranda turned her attention to Jason, eyeing the back of his head. *Why'd you have to do this, Jason? We had something good going, and you had to go and ruin it.*

"Please be seated," the judge said after he sat down. Once everyone took their seats, the judge turned to the jury. "Ladies and gentlemen of the jury, have you reached a verdict?"

The jury foreperson stood up and responded to the judge, saying, "Yes, we have, your honor." She held out a manila envelope for the bailiff to hand to the judge.

"Thank you," the judge said as he took the envelope from the bailiff. He opened it and pulled out a sheet of paper. He looked over it and then at the crowd. "I have here a document, signed by each of the twelve members of the jury, who were charged with reaching a verdict for this case."

The judge paused a moment, licked his lips, and then continued. "I will read the decision aloud. 'We, the jury, having duly deliberated over the evidence, and guided by the law that is contained in the charge of kidnapping in the first degree, do hereby find the defendant guilty."

A collective gasp was heard across the courtroom, and Miranda's heart dropped. Julie wrapped her arm around her and whispered in her ear, "They got him, Miranda. He's going to be put away for a while now."

The judge used his gavel to quiet the courtroom. "As for the sentencing of Mr. Dolmeir," the judge said. "I plan to do that next Monday, February eleventh. If there is no objection to that, then the court is adjourned."

The judge slapped the gavel down, stood up, and made his way out of the courtroom. Once gone, Miranda turned to Julie and wiped a slight tear from her eye.

"It's done," she said. "That's it, then."

"It's over," Julie said. "All that's left is the sentencing, and he should be getting quite the time in prison."

Miranda smiled and breathed out a deep sigh of relief. She turned toward the front of the courtroom, where she watched as officers of the court proceeded to take Jason out of the room. Then, she took another deep breath and considered what could have been had he not acted the way he did. She thought about how happy they were when they first started dating and how happy they would have been had they married.

She shook her head.

"What is wrong?" Julie asked her.

"Nothing," Miranda said as she watched the door close. "Just thinking about things."

\* \* \*

As the sun set and evening began to break on the Klimmings Mansion, Ben found himself sitting in the living room alone. He had received a text earlier in the day from his mother requesting the meeting of her, Miranda, Delilah, Charlotte, and himself. Obviously, he knew it was a shareholders' meeting, but he was curious about the reasoning. *Could she be resigning as president?*

While he sat there, he looked around the room. He watched the fire in the fireplace crackle and pop, and then he looked over to the portrait hanging above the bar. He stood up and stepped closer to it. Ben looked at the image of his mother with himself holding Katherine and Miranda and let out a deep sigh. Over the past year, so much had changed. He lost his baby sister, he divorced Delilah, he began attending meetings focused on his drinking problem, his mother kicked his father out of the house, and he is now planning to remarry Delilah.

He turned around just as he heard the doorbell ring.

"I got it, Denise," he called out, making his way over to the front door in the entry hall. He stopped in front of it and pulled the door open. "Delilah!"

Delilah quickly stepped inside, shedding her coat and placing it on the coat rack. "It's so cold out there!"

"I bet," Ben said as he wrapped his arm around her, trying to warm her. "The weatherman tonight called for wind chills in the negatives!"

"God, I'm ready for summer," Delilah said as Ben led her to the sofa, and she sat down. He made his way over to the bar.

"Can I get you something to drink?"

"I'd love a white wine if that's okay?"

"Yes," Ben said as he pulled out the bottle of white wine. "It's weird. I only ever get cravings for liquor whenever I'm stressed."

"And you're not stressed right now?" Delilah asked as he poured the glass.

"No," he said, turning and giving the glass to Delilah. He also had a glass of soda water in his hand. "I'm not right now."

"What if your mom resigns as president, and you have to step in?"

"Delilah, I'm not going to let things affect me like that again. When I started attending those meetings last May, I decided then that I was done." He took a sip of his soda water. "No more would I let alcohol dictate my life. I am free."

Delilah nodded as Miranda rounded the corner into the living room from the staircase. "Are you the only two here?"

"Yes," Ben said as he walked back over to the sofa. "Mom hasn't come down yet, and Aunt Charlotte hasn't arrived either."

"I'll be surprised if Charlotte shows up," Miranda said, going to the bar to pour herself a glass of white wine.

"Why do you say that?" Delilah asked.

"Because Mom fired her from being her receptionist."

"She what?!" Ben exclaimed. "Why the hell did she do that?"

"I don't know," Miranda said, heading to the chair next to Ben. "But she's hired my friend, Julie, to take her place."

Ben took a sip of his club soda just as Vicki finally came downstairs and entered the living room.

"There she is!" Ben announced.

"Are you all waiting on me?" she asked as she adjusted the long sleeves on her dress.

"Sort of," Miranda said. "Aunt Charlotte still hasn't arrived yet."

"Very classic of her," Vicki sighed. "Always late and destined to make an entrance."

Ben, Delilah, and Miranda all glanced around at one another, feeling the tension from Vicki when they mentioned her sister. Finally, she turned and stepped over to the bar, pouring herself a glass of white wine. When she went to put the cork back in, the doorbell to the front door rang. She stepped closer to the coffee table in front of the sofa and watched as Denise opened the door.

"Ugh," Vicki heard her sister let out. "You're still here?"

Vicki set her glass of wine on the coffee table and stormed into the entry hall. She took Charlotte by the arm and drug her down the hall, turning right to go down the side hallway. They passed by the kitchen and took the next door on the right into the sitting room.

Vicki flipped on the light after she pulled Charlotte into the room, letting go of her once she was inside.

"Vicki," Charlotte gasped. "What are you doing?"

Vick glared at her sister, took a few deep breaths, then slapped her across the face. Charlotte's head jerked to the side before she pulled it back, placing her hand on the spot where Vicki's hand hit her.

"What the hell was that for?!"

"That's for sleeping with my husband," Vicki whispered. "Maybe next time, you'll think twice about doing it."

Charlotte massaged her cheek. "Good God, Vicki," Charlotte reacted. "Have you ever considered anger management courses?"

"Shut up, Charlotte," Vicki said. "I love you, but sometimes you make it hard to like you."

"The same goes for you."

Vicki glared at her sister before opening the door again. "Get to the living room," she said. "We need to meet."

Charlotte passed by Vicki, continuing to massage her cheek. Vicki followed Charlotte to the living room. Once in, Charlotte took a seat in the remaining empty chair. Vicki proceeded to take her glass of wine and stand in front of the fireplace.

"I'm glad you all could make it here tonight," she began. "As shareholders of Klimmings Incorporated, I feel we have some things that we need to discuss."

"What are you planning to do, Mom?" Miranda asked her before taking a drink from her glass of white wine.

Vicki looked over at each person in the room as she drew a deep breath. "I need to discuss something with you all about the company's future."

As she began to form the words in her mouth, Charlotte interrupted her, saying, "What is that?!"

She pointed to the engagement ring Delilah was wearing on her hand. Delilah looked down at her ring and quickly hid it. Then, she turned to Ben, worried since they had not told anyone about their engagement. He smiled at Delilah and turned his attention to the people in the room.

"We have some news to share," he said, urging Delilah to hold out her left hand. "Last night, I asked Delilah to marry me, and she said, 'Yes!'"

Miranda's face lit up. "That's such good news!"

Charlotte hurried over to the sofa to get a better look at Delilah's ring. Soon, the entire room erupted in conversation. Even Denise came into the living room to look at the ring. The only one not entertained by the ordeal was Vicki, who remained standing in front of the fireplace, watching everyone gush over Ben and Delilah's engagement. Finally, Ben realized that she was still standing there, keeping quiet.

"Mom," he said to her. "What's wrong?"

Everyone slowly turned toward her, waiting to hear how she answered Ben's question.

"Nothing is wrong," she said quietly. "I just called you all in here to discuss the business, and we've all been wrapped up in other things instead."

"Mom," Miranda interrupted. "Ben and Delilah just got engaged. They deserve to share their news with everyone."

Vicki sighed. "I understand that, but I needed to talk with everyone tonight about something important regarding the company."

"Just spit it out, Vicki," Charlotte said. "Just tell us."

Vicki glared at Charlotte and then turned her attention back to the rest of the people in the room.

"I was approached by someone a few days ago," she began. "During our meeting, he offered to purchase my forty-five shares of Klimmings Incorporated voting stock."

"You surely couldn't have even given it a thought," Ben blurted out. "Mom, you have ten voting shares that Miranda gifted to Gabby. You *cannot* sell her shares!"

"If you would have let me finish, Benjamin," Vicki said, becoming irritated with her son. "Then I would have said that I am planning to sign over the ten shares to Miranda!"

"What?!" Charlotte exclaimed. "Why?!"

"Because, Charlotte," Vicki snapped. "They were Miranda's shares, and I didn't think it would be fair to sell her shares."

"So, you're selling out, then?" Ben asked, standing from the sofa.

"Yes," Vicki said, straightening her hair. "I debated it and debated it. Then, when I spoke with Bill about it, he made me realize that I needed to sell out." She took a deep breath and examined the looks on everyone's faces.

"You consulted with Bill before even asking our opinions?" Miranda asked Vicki.

She stuttered and stumbled over her words, trying to formulate a response. As she tried to figure out what to say, Ben turned to Delilah and said, "Come on, honey. Let's go."

"What?" Delilah said, confused. "Where?"

"I'm not sure yet," he said. "But anywhere is better than here right now." He looked at his mother and then took Delilah by the hand, and the two of them made their way out of the Klimmings Mansion.

Miranda turned her head toward her mother. "Mom," she calmly said to her. "I just hope you're making the right decision for you and not for what others want."

She approached her mother, embraced her in a hug, and headed upstairs.

* * *

"Today," Rebecca White said from the TV in the lobby of Klimmings Incorporated. "The House Judiciary Committee will vote on whether to forward its two articles of impeachment against the president to the House. When this passes, the House will begin debates over the articles before a final vote next Monday."

Julie leaned back in the chair behind the receptionist's desk. "This is so bad," she whispered to herself before running her hand through her hair.

She thought about what to say to Vicki whenever she came into the office. *Should I say anything at all?* She knew that Vicki and her husband hadn't spoken to each other for about half a year.

While she pondered what to do, the elevator door opened, and Ryan Applegate stepped out, making his way over to Julie's desk. He quickly caught her attention, and she turned to him, smiling.

"Good morning," she said. "How can I help you?"

"Yes," Ryan said, returning a smile to Julie. "Is Mrs. Klimmings here yet?"

"No," Julie said. "I don't know when she'll be in. Can I take a message for her?"

"That's fine. I'll just try to catch her some other time."

"Or feel free to drop by again," Julie spoke up. "I'm sure she'll be in some time." Julie found herself smiling as she looked Ryan over.

Ryan glanced back at her and winked. "Oh, I'm sure I'll be back."

He turned and went over to the elevator. After he pressed the button and the door opened, he turned around again to catch Julie admiring him. He smiled and chuckled as he stepped into the elevator and made his way back down to the lobby of Klimmings Tower.

When the door opened, Ryan was met face-to-face with Ben. He stopped in his tracks, making eye contact with him.

"What are you doing here?" Ben asked him.

"I can ask the same of you," Ryan stated as he stepped out of the elevator, allowing other people to board it. "You no longer work in this building."

"You're right, but I'm still a shareholder in the company, so why are you here?"

"I came here to speak with your mother," Ryan said. "Her and I have been in some business together."

"What kinda business?" Ben asked.

"None of yours. After all, you're no longer in this company."

"The hell if it is! My mom told us last night that she's planning to sell her voting shares, and I'm trying to figure out who it is that she's giving them to."

A smile grew across Ryan's face. "You're looking at him."

Ben took a step backward as his mouth dropped open. He couldn't believe it. "It's you?"

"Sure is!" he said. "I've been planning this for months."

"What the hell are you talking about?"

"Ben, you never learn, do you? I've spent the last couple of months contacting everyone with dealings between Klimmings and Applegate, and I issued an ultimatum to them. Either they drop Klimmings, or they lose us. It was simple, and since these other companies rely on the software we provide, they almost had no choice but to drop you all."

Ben suddenly became very angry with Ryan. "You bastard," he said to him. "So you've caused all these other added pressures on my mother?"

"I guess you can say that," Ryan said before leaning in close to him. "But maybe wait until the next shareholders meeting to do so."

Ryan stepped back and began walking away from Ben, laughing as he did so. Then, Ben took a deep breath and caught up with him. He grabbed him by the back of his jacket, causing him to turn around. Then, without thinking twice, Ben slugged him across the face causing a reaction from all the people in the lobby.

Before Ben could say anything, a security officer pulled him away from Ryan, who was holding his face and laughing.

"I'll let you have that one, Klimmings!" Ryan shouted to him as he was being pulled out of the lobby. "See you in the next meeting!"

* * *

Delilah sat on the sofa next to Cathie and Jeremy in the Applegate Homestead. She tried to hide the nervousness on her face but wasn't doing an excellent job at it.

"Delilah," Cathie said, leaning forward, slightly obstructing Jeremy's view of Delilah. He moved back and forth, trying to see over his wife as she continued. "What's wrong?"

Jeremy finally got to a place where he could see Delilah. He had a concerned look displayed on his face.

"Mom . . . Dad," Delilah began, looking both her parents in the eyes. "I have some news to share with you."

She took a deep breath and held out her left hand, revealing her engagement ring to them.

"Delilah!" Cathie exclaimed in glee. "This is so gorgeous!"

"Thank you," Delilah said, looking back at the ring. "Ben asked me a few days ago, and I accepted."

Cathie had a few tears of joy in her eyes that she wiped away. Then, she leaned in and hugged Delilah, celebrating this moment with her. As the two embraced, Jeremy watched from the side. He didn't like that his daughter would be marrying into the Klimmings family again, but he was taken back to his conversation with her in the kitchen last month.

*"I know that you and Ben really do like each other, and whatever I do, you two are still going to like each other."*

He drew in a deep sigh and finally said, "Congratulations, Delilah. I know how much you wanted this."

She released from the hug with her mother, looking up at Jeremy.

"Thanks, Dad," Delilah said with a few tears in her eyes. "I was so worried about what you would think."

Jeremy just smiled in return. He knew that whatever he said against the marriage between his daughter and the Klimmings' son would be met with retaliation from them and his wife. Yet, inside, Jeremy began planning ways to cause the engagement between the two to fall apart.

* * *

The following Monday approached, and the House began their vote on the two articles of impeachment against Peter. He sat behind the *Resolute* desk in the Oval Office, watching the live coverage of the vote, observing the numbers in favor rise each second. As he sat there, processing it all, the door to the Oval Office opened, and Martha stepped through the threshold.

"Mr. President," she said. "Your wife is here to see you."

Peter turned toward Martha in disbelief. He hadn't seen or even spoken to Vicki since last July, so it was a genuine surprise to him to hear that she was here to talk to him.

"Send her in," Peter said as he took the remote and muted the TV.

He stood from behind the *Resolute* desk and stepped around to the front, adjusting his tie and jacket in the process. Then, finally, the door opened, and Vicki entered the room. She was holding a manila file folder and was wearing a light pink business dress. Peter smiled when he saw her. "Vicki."

"Hello, Peter," she said, looking uncomfortable. She fumbled with the folder as she stood there, taking in the Oval Office. The navy-blue drapes and dark blue rug were the same as they had been since the last time she had been in the office.

"What do I owe this visit for?" Peter asked her. "It's been so long since I had seen you. I've missed you, Vicki."

She sighed. "I'm sure you have, Peter." She continued to mess with the folder, trying to control her nerves and deal with the uncomfortable feeling she had.

"Vicki, what is in the folder?"

She looked down at the folder and finally handed it to him. "Look at it yourself, Peter."

He reluctantly took the folder from Vicki, looking it over. Then, he opened it and began to look over the inside documents. He became stunned by what he saw, and his heart dropped to his stomach.

"Are these?" he asked Vicki, looking up at her.

"Yes," she replied. "I've filed for divorce, Peter." She turned away from him, stepping over to the fireplace to watch the fire crackle and pop as it burned the wood inside. "I can't continue to stay married to you after what you did to Gabby." She turned around to him. "Peter, I can't forgive you for what you did."

Peter watched the pain appear on his wife's face. He tossed the file folder onto the top of his desk and stepped closer to Vicki. "Honey, before you become set on the divorce . . . I have to tell you something important."

"What is it, Peter?" Vicki didn't even try to hide that she didn't care what her husband had to say.

He stepped over to the sofa to his right and sat down. Then he put his hand on the cushion next to him, inviting Vicki to sit next to him. She hesitated but finally came over and sat down.

"What is it, Peter?" she repeated herself.

Peter looked into Vicki's eyes, trying to make this an intimate moment. "Honey," he said. "Dana Gomez was found dead in her apartment last week."

"Oh my God," she sighed. "What happened?"

"The police think it was a suicide," Peter continued. "They found her hanging in her bedroom."

Vicki looked toward the floor, trying to process the news of Dana's death, but Peter continued speaking.

"Vicki, before this, Dana contacted me to tell me about what happened the night Gabby died."

Vicki jolted her head up to Peter. "What did she say?"

"She told me that Gabby didn't kill herself. Instead, Dana had come over to the house to talk with Gabby. One thing led to the next, and Dana pulled out a gun and shot our daughter."

Vicki's eyes widened in shock. She couldn't believe what Peter had just told her. For almost a year, Vicki believed her daughter had killed herself, and within an instant, her understanding of what happened went up in flames. Peter leaned forward and placed his hand on her thigh, trying to comfort her.

"Vicki," he said. "Our daughter was murdered the night she died. But, she didn't kill herself like we thought she had."

As she sat on the sofa, Vicki's mind raced with so many thoughts, trying to process the news that she was told. Finally, she stood up and turned back to the fireplace. "It still doesn't change things, Peter."

"Why not?" He stood from the sofa, looking at his wife. She continued looking toward the fireplace, not saying anything.

"Vicki," Peter said. "How the hell does this not change anything? You blamed me all last year for Gabby's death! You told me that it was my fault because of how I handled her coming out. And now . . . now that we know that she didn't kill herself, you tell me that it doesn't change anything?!"

Vicki spun around toward Peter. "Of course, it doesn't change anything, Peter. You didn't hesitate before you had your goons bury her in the family cemetery. You didn't consider any of the repercussions that could haunt your family. Instead, all you cared about was yourself!" She stepped in closer to Peter. "You focused on China and trying to save your presidency, and then whenever I finally took a stand for myself and moved you into the White House so that I could process everything that was going on, you went ahead and slept with my sister!"

Peter took a step backward. "I didn't sleep with Charlotte, Vicki."

"Don't you lie to me!" she shouted at him. "Charlotte came to me and told me exactly what you two did. She told me all about what you two did on Christmas night!"

Peter thought about what Vicki said to him, keeping quiet as Vicki stood stewing in front of him,

"Just what I thought," Vicki spat out. "You can't even think about how to get yourself out of this one." She went over to the door and turned around. "Just sign the damn papers and send them to my attorney, Peter. I don't want to drag this out longer than it needs to be."

She opened the door and left the Oval Office, slamming the door behind her. Peter stood alone in the room, processing what had happened between him and his wife. Then, he looked to the TV, where Rebecca White was announcing that the two articles of impeachment had passed the House.

He turned around and slowly made his way to the *Resolute* desk. In his mind, he saw his marriage ending and everything he had worked for going up in flames. His presidency was now in the hands of the Republican-controlled Senate, which would make it easier for them to reach the number of votes needed to remove him from office.

Then, he looked down at the desk, staring at the manila folder. He picked it up again, examining it. Memories began to flood his mind from his time married to Vicki. The fate of thirty-five years now rested on his signature on a piece of paper.

"Son of a bitch!" he shouted as he flung the folder across the room, causing the papers inside to fly across the room. He took his arm and swept the top of the *Resolute* desk clean. The phone, his laptop, and other classified documents cascaded to the floor. As Peter's breathing increased and his anger and frustration grew, he found himself by the bar cart, recklessly pouring himself a bourbon. A lot of liquid had missed the glass, spilling onto his hand and the floor. He took the decanter and chucked it across the room, hitting the coffee table between the two sofas and bursting. Bourbon had splashed all over it and onto the far sofa. Still holding the glass in hand, Peter tossed it toward the mantel, shattering it on impact. What little bourbon inside it caused the fire to grow in intensity.

Then, Peter moved back behind the desk to the table displaying many family photos. He took the corner of the table, flipped it over, and shouted, "Dammit!"

As the photos crashed to the floor, Peter took the American flag and flung it over. It collided with the President's flag before falling to the ground. Peter watched as the other flag slowly fell over to the table against the wall with the bust of Martin Luther King Jr. displayed atop it. The President's flag slammed against the table, causing it to bounce up and smack into the statue. It wobbled slightly before falling from the table and crashing onto the floor.

Finally, Peter began to catch his breath and return to his senses. He looked around at the disaster in the Oval Office. So many documents now littered the floor as the fire roared in the fireplace. He stepped over the shattered glass and the American flag lying on the floor, making his way over to the now-broken bust of Martin Luther King Jr. He knelt as he took the three main chunks of the figure and set them on top of the *Resolute* desk. Then, he fell to the floor, sitting there as he processed everything that had happened. He began to think about how a whistle-blower was the reason why he was impeached, and this whistleblower was still employed in the White House.

"It has to be him," Peter said, standing up. "It *has* to be him!"

He stormed over to the door to the left of the fireplace, flinging it open, and proceeded down the hallway to Henry's office. Fortunately, the door was ajar, so Peter went inside, startling Henry.

"Goodness, Mr. President," Henry exclaimed. "You scared me!"

"Sorry, Mr. Gates," he said. "I need you to get ahold of Secretary Bird."

"Why? Do you need to meet with him?"

"No," Peter said. "I need you to inform him that I'm firing him as defense secretary."

\* \* \*

"All rise."

Everyone in the courtroom rose as the judge came in and sat behind the bench.

"You may be seated," the judge said as he flipped through some papers, and everyone sat down. "We're here today for sentencing for Mr. Dolmeir." The judge looked up at Jason and his lawyer. "Mr. Dolmeir, would you please rise?"

Jason and his lawyer stood up from the table. Miranda turned to Julie, who was next to her just like she had been throughout the entire court proceedings. Then, Miranda turned back toward the judge, listening to his decision for the sentencing.

"Kidnapping is a serious offense," the judge began, addressing Jason. "And the law calls for a maximum of six-and-a-half years to be served for such a crime."

Miranda turned back to Julie. "Six-and-a-half years?!" she whispered to her. "That's it?!"

Julie took her hand. "It'll be okay," she responded. "It's going to be alright."

She looked back up at the judge, listening to what he said.

"So, after deliberating and considering the options, Mr. Dolmeir, I hereby sentence you to serve six-and-a-half years in a federal penitentiary, with the past year counting toward that sentence."

Again, Miranda turned back to Julie and buried her face in her shoulder. As she began crying, Julie listened to the judge as he finished carrying out Jason's sentence. He had no chance for parole and was required to serve his entire sentence. She placed her hand on Miranda's back, trying to comfort her friend, thinking about what may happen whenever Jason is eventually released from prison.

\* \* \*

Bill sat in the Klimmings Mansion with the TV on. The evening news was on, and he was watching the commentary on the president's impeachment. He allowed a slight smile to appear as he listened to the charges brought against him. Then, he heard a car pull up in the driveway, so he turned off the TV and made his way to the entry hall. As he heard the car door shut, he went to the door and opened it. Vicki had just ascended the steps and was preparing to open the door. Her face lit up when she saw him.

"I thought that was your car," Vicki said to him. "Who let you in?"

"The house servant," he said. "What is her name again?"

"Denise," Vicki said as she began to think things over. "Billy, why don't you move your stuff over here? Get out of that hotel room!"

"No! I can't move in here and impose on you all."

"I insist!"

"To be honest, I was actually about to leave soon anyways," Bill said, looking at his watch. "I have to be somewhere in a couple of hours."

"A couple of hours?" Vicki asked. "So we've got plenty of time, then."

She leaned in and kissed Bill, feeling his lips against hers. He pulled away after a second and looked her in the eyes. She looked back up at him, and the attraction between the two of them pulled them closer together.

"Shall we go upstairs?" she asked him.

Bill smiled and said, "Lead the way."

The two went through the living room, turning to go up the stairs through the archway. At the top of the landing, she led Bill to her bedroom, stopping on the threshold to kiss him again. She ran her hands up his shirt before pulling it apart by its buttons. As they continued to kiss, they moved into the bedroom. Just before Vicki pulled Bill onto the bed, he moved the door so that it slowly closed and latched, allowing the two of them all the privacy they needed.

\* \* \*

It had been a few hours since the sun had set, and Peter had remained seated in the study. He hadn't been back into the Oval Office since his episode earlier in the day, completing any work that needed to be done in his private study. He had always liked the room and its privacy, especially after the day he had. He had been considering everything that had happened: Vicki delivering the divorce papers, his impeachment, and firing Secretary Eric Bird after suspecting him of being the whistle-blower resulting in his subsequent impeachment. Peter had also forgotten that the New Hampshire primary was the following day, so he had paperwork with poll numbers and other campaign information on his desk in the study.

However, none of that was on his mind right now. Instead, he was more focused on Charlotte and her betrayal. He thought she was a friend to him, and with her telling Vicki about their affair, he knew she was far from being one. So finally, he took his cell phone out and scrolled through his contacts until landing on Charlotte's. He called her and put the phone to his ear. After it rang a few times, Charlotte finally answered.

"Peter!" she exclaimed. "How are you doing tonight?"

"Charlotte," he began. "Did you tell your sister about our little affair on Christmas night?"

She fell silent for a moment, trying to formulate some kind of response. "I didn't mean to, Peter," she said. "I felt so guilty about it and . . ."

"I don't give a shit, Charlotte," he interrupted. "You had no right to go ahead and do that without first consulting me!"

"She was my sister . . . and boss! What did you expect me to do?"

"I'd have hoped that you would have reached out to me and asked about telling her together!" Peter stood from his chair. "Dammit, Charlotte, you single-handedly destroyed my marriage to Vicki by doing this! Now, she thinks that I was trying to hide it from her and had no plans of ever saying anything!"

"Why didn't you tell me that you were feeling guilty about it?"

"You didn't give me a chance to, Charlotte! You went ahead and took care of it all yourself!"

She fell quiet over the phone, giving Peter time to consider what he would say next.

"Charlotte," he said. "I don't want to speak to you again. Do you understand?"

"Yes."

"Goodbye."

He took the phone away from his ear and ended the call. Then he looked at her contact information, studying the contact photo he had for her on his phone.

"Dammit!" he shouted before throwing his phone across the study. It bounced off the door, ricocheting into the wall and finally hitting the floor. He stood up, went out of the study, and turned right through the Oval Office. He looked at the mess that still filled the room. Then, he opened the door to Martha's office. She looked up at Peter as he stepped inside.

"Martha," Peter said. "I need you to get my motorcade prepared."

"Okay, sir," she said. "Where are you planning to go?"

"New Hampshire," he responded. He began to make his way out of the office but stopped and turned back around to Martha. "But I need to make a stop somewhere else first."

* * *

Charlotte set her phone down on the table and looked across the table at the empty chair. She took her glass of red wine and took a sip, looking at the restaurant's entrance just as Bill Davis came in. She motioned for him to come over, and after he noticed her sitting there, he made his way over.

"Hello, Charlotte," he said, sitting across from her. "Sorry, I'm late."

"You're fine," she said to him. "I just got off the phone with Peter right before you showed up."

"How did that go?"

"Well, Vicki delivered the divorce papers," she said. "But unfortunately, I screwed up bad. I told her about the affair as we had planned, and she went ahead and told him."

"What happened?"

"He said that he never wants to speak to me again." She took her glass of wine. "Bill, I think I really messed this one up. What if they get back together?"

"They won't."

Charlotte cocked her head. "What makes you say that?"

"Because Vicki and I pretty much sealed the deal tonight on that," Bill said, leaning back in his chair. "And after our meeting tonight, I'm stopping by my hotel room, grabbing my things, and moving into the Klimmings Mansion."

Charlotte lifted her glass into the air in agreement. "I'm so glad I thought to contact you when they separated. By the time this is over, we're both going to get what we want the most."

"I thought you wanted Peter?" Bill asked. "How are you going to do that if Peter doesn't want to speak to you anymore?"

"Oh, I want him, but having Peter isn't what I desire the most," Charlotte said before taking a sip of her red wine. "It's Klimmings Incorporated that I want more than anything. You see when George finally gets everything in order, and our divorce is finalized, my cash flow will not be the same as what I'm accustomed to. I cannot live without the fortune that is tied to the Klimmings Empire, Bill."

"You've always been focused on the money, Charlotte," Bill laughed. "You were whenever I was first married to Vicki and still are thirty-five years later."

Charlotte grinned in response. "What can I say? I'm an expensive bitch."

Bill laughed at her comment. "Before you know it, I'll have Vicki all to myself, and you'll have control of forty percent of the voting shares."

"Exactly," she said before taking a sip of her wine. "It's such a shame that Vicki had to give Miranda her ten shares back."

"I know," Bill said. "I get it, though. It wouldn't seem fair to sell something that wasn't yours."

"At least she has *some* morals. Of course, it has to come whenever we want something from her."

"That's why I love her."

"By the way," Charlotte continued. "Who is buying Vicki's thirty-five voting shares?"

"Ryan Applegate."

Charlotte almost dropped her glass of wine. "What?!" she exclaimed as she sat it on the table. "Why him?!"

"Well, he has a history of hating the Klimmings family, and right now, he was really the only person I could find who wanted to buy into the company." Bill looked at Charlotte and the upset look she had on her face. "Why? What's wrong with him?"

"Ryan and I dated over a year ago," Charlotte said. "He dumped me and moved on. Things haven't been good between the two of us since then. How do you know he will follow through with our plan?"

"Ask him for yourself," Bill said, motioning behind Charlotte. She turned and saw Ryan, who had just approached the table.

"Hello, Charlotte," he said as he sat at the table. "It's been a little bit since we've spoken."

"Ryan," she said grudgingly. "How are you?"

"Cut the pleasantries, Charlotte," he said. "I know you hate me, but if we are to finally screw over the Klimmings family, then we're going to have to work together."

Charlotte looked over at Bill. "This is between you two," he said. "I've got what I wanted."

She looked back to Ryan, who was smiling. "Come on, Charlotte," he said to her. "I want control of Klimmings Incorporated, and you want that Klimmings family fortune. Together, we can do that."

"But," Charlotte said. "If you only end up with thirty-five shares, and I have five shares, we're still ten shares away from having a majority."

"And that's where I got you, Charlotte," Ryan said. "You see, Delilah has fifteen voting shares. There's no way that she won't vote against her brother in competition for the presidency of the company. Given that, we basically will have fifty-five percent of the shares."

"You haven't heard then?" Charlotte asked him.

"Heard what?"

Ryan looked over to Bill and then back at Charlotte. "What haven't I heard?"

Charlotte leaned in closer to Ryan. "Ben Klimmings proposed to Delilah last week. They're remarrying."

Ryan sat back, stunned. He looked over to Bill, who nodded, confirming that what Charlotte had said was true. Then he took his hands and smacked them down onto the table.

"What . . ." he let out. "What the hell is wrong with her?!"

He quickly got up from the table and stormed out of the restaurant, leaving Bill and Charlotte alone at the table. They turned to each other and exchanged looks.

"What do you think he is going to do?" Bill asked Charlotte.

"I don't know," Charlotte responded as she sipped her red wine. "But if I had a guess, I would say that he plans to pay his sister a visit." She took another sip of her wine and set it back on the table. "And if I were a betting woman – which I'm not – I would bet that whatever he says to her will only push her and Ben closer together."

* * *

Peter stepped out of the Beast and adjusted his jacket. He looked up at the towering front façade of the Washington National Cathedral, taking in the Gothic architecture of the grand church. He heard the door to the Cadillac shut from behind, and Don stepped alongside him.

"Mr. President," he said quietly. "Would you like for me to go in with you?"

Peter remained quiet for a moment, looking at the two towers in front of the cathedral. "No," he finally said. "I need to speak with someone alone."

He began making his way up the steps to the front door of the building. When he put his hands on the doors to open it, he heard Don again.

"Are you sure, Mr. President?"

Peter turned to face him. "I am." He turned back and proceeded to step inside the cathedral, letting the doors close behind him, echoing throughout the interior, bouncing off the walls and vaulted ceilings. Peter made his way down the nave, looking toward the sculpture of Jesus Christ in the cathedral's sanctuary. In this moment, none of the cathedral's grandeur mattered to Peter. All he was focused on was the image of Christ located at the opposite end of the cathedral. It was just him and God.

"What am I?" Peter said aloud. His voice echoed throughout the interior of the cathedral. "Am I just a damn joke to you?"

As his voice echoed throughout the cathedral, there was no response. Peter continued down the nave, coming to the crossing, pausing for a moment.

"Have I not done all that I could have done? Was I not the one you wanted?"

Once again, there was no response.

"The second chapter of Colossians claims that *you* are the head over every power and authority."

Peter turned back toward the door to the cathedral, listening for a response, but once the echoes of his voice ceased, silence engulfed the building.

"Answer me, you son of a bitch!" Peter shouted after turning back toward the sculpture at the opposite end of the cathedral. "I spoke with you before running for president five years ago. You told me to run! You made me the president!"

He began his way up the steps toward the choir, continuing to shout.

"I brought this country out of a recession! I stopped a war with China! I rejuvenated relations with Russia! What the hell else do you want me to do?!"

Peter stopped as he got to the end of the choir, standing in front of the sanctuary, looking up at the sculpture of Jesus.

"Now they want to impeach me. My vice president is challenging me for the nomination. Polls keep showing that that bitch, Rebecca White, will outperform me in the general election. My family is falling apart . . . and now my wife wants to divorce me so that she can get back with her first husband!"

Peter paused, still waiting for a response. But none came.

"And then there was my daughter . . . Gabriella." He took a breath to compose himself before continuing. "She was my youngest. She was my favorite. And you took her away from me!" Tears were welling up in his eyes, but he persisted. "What the hell did I do to you? What the hell did *she* do to you?!"

Silence. There continued to be no answer.

"Why won't you answer me, you bastard?! Tell me why you took her from me!" Peter fell to his knees as the tears broke from the pools they had formed in his eyes. "Why couldn't you have taken me instead?"

He waited for a response, longing to hear something back, yet nothing came.

"The leader of the free world, my ass. The only thing that's come from this is pain . . . and misery . . . and heartbreak." Peter looked up at the sculpture again. "You've done all of this to my family."

He paused for an answer but continued to hear nothing in response.

"I don't even know why I even bothered with you," he said as he stood up from the floor. "I hate you . . . and I need nothing from you anymore."

Peter turned and began to make his way through the choir, wiping his face as he went. He took a few breaths, trying to compose himself. However, he began to notice how with each breath, his chest felt like it was tightening. He stopped halfway through the choir and adjusted his tie, trying to alleviate the discomfort. Unfortunately, nothing worked, and his chest only began to tighten.

"Don!" Peter called out, allowing his voice to echo throughout the cathedral.

Then, it hit him. His chest tightened considerably, feeling like a clenched fist was pressing down on him with as much force as possible. Peter cried out in pain and fell to the floor, holding onto his chest through his jacket. He rolled over onto his back and looked up at the cathedral's vaulted ceiling. *Ironic.* He thought as he shifted his gaze back toward the sculpture of Jesus, who looked so welcoming and accepting to all who entered the grand cathedral.

"Mr. President!" Don called out as he came running down to him.

"I need help!"

Peter looked toward Don, who had just made it next to him. He noticed Don's lips moving but couldn't understand anything coming from them. Then, the entire cathedral began to move out of focus, becoming very blurry.

More Secret Service agents made their way to the president, but Peter couldn't figure out anything that was going on. Instead, he closed his eyes and relaxed his head. The world around him ceased to matter, and silence filled the air.

**SAMUEL VOYLES** had dreamed of making his vision for the *Desperate Measures* series a reality since its inception during his first year of high school. Stemming from a mini-series consisting of fourteen install-ments, Voyles published the first book in the *Desperate Measures* series in the winter of 2022. Following that, Voyles obtained a master's degree from Indiana University and traveled abroad, using some of the locations he visited as inspiration for his stories.

Voyles lives in Southern Indiana, where he teaches middle and high school English full-time, using his experience in writing, editing, and publishing to help enhance his students' writing, making them better writers in and out of the classroom.

www.ingramcontent.com/pod-product-compliance
Lightning Source LLC
Chambersburg PA
CBHW032150190626
46814CB00005BA/1921